D0614996

RED WHITE AND THE BLUES

ALSO BY RYSA WALKER

CHRONOS Origins

Now, Then, and Everywhen

The CHRONOS Files

Novels

Timebound
Time's Edge
Time's Divide

Graphic Novel

Time Trial

Novellas

Time's Echo
Time's Mirror
Simon Says: Tips for the Intrepid Time Traveler

Short Stories

"The Gambit" In *The Time Travel Chronicles*
"Whack Job" In *Alt.History 102*
"2092" In *Dark Beyond the Stars*
"Splinter" In *CLONES: The Anthology*
"The Circle-That-Whines" In *Chronicle Worlds: Tails of Dystopia*
"Full Circle" In *OCEANS: The Anthology*

THE DELPHI TRILOGY

NOVELS
The Delphi Effect
The Delphi Resistance
The Delphi Revolution

NOVELLA
The Abandoned

ENTER HADDONWOOD

As the Crow Flies (with Caleb Amsel)
When the Cat's Away (with Caleb Amsel)

RED
WHITE
AND THE
BLUES

CHRONOS ORIGINS  BOOK TWO

RYSA WALKER

47N●RTH

This is a work of fiction. Names, characters, organizations, places, events, and incidents are either products of the author's imagination or are used fictitiously. Any resemblance to actual persons, living or dead, or actual events is purely coincidental.

Text copyright © 2021 by Rysa Walker
All rights reserved.

No part of this book may be reproduced, or stored in a retrieval system, or transmitted in any form or by any means, electronic, mechanical, photocopying, recording, or otherwise, without express written permission of the publisher.

Published by 47North, Seattle

www.apub.com

Amazon, the Amazon logo, and 47North are trademarks of Amazon.com, Inc., or its affiliates.

ISBN-13: 9781542019590
ISBN-10: 1542019591

Cover design by M. S. Corley

Printed in the United States of America

To my fellow travelers in this strange alternate timeline, in hopes of better days ahead.

PART ONE

GAMBIT

Gambit [from ancient Italian *gambetto*, meaning "to trip"]: A sacrificial offering (usually of a pawn) used to gain an early advantage in time or space during the opening moves of a game.

FROM *THE BOOK OF CYRUS* (NEW ENGLISH VERSION, 3RD ED) CHAPTER 4:7-8

[7]Do not attempt to conquer the world with force. Force yields only resistance. [8]True power comes from persuading the conquered that they have embraced The Way of their own free will.

∞ 1 ∞

"And that's *also* not food." RJ reaches into his daughter's mouth and fishes out a mangled leaf. There's no complaint from Yun Hee this time, so the leaf apparently wasn't as tasty as the yellow dandelion he'd extracted from her chubby cheeks a few minutes ago. She still looks a bit put out, though. RJ scoops the baby from the lawn and swings her up toward the bright autumn sky, earning himself a mostly toothless grin, followed by a string of leaf-flecked drool to decorate the front of his shirt.

He wipes the baby's chin with his sleeve. "June Bug and I are going inside to get some cheese puffs, since she seems to be in the mood to nibble. Do you guys want anything?"

Lorena and I both shake our heads. RJ's cousin, Alex, is too deep into whatever he's reading on his screen to even hear the question. It's a minor miracle that we were able to lure him outside for brunch on the patio and some fresh air. He's been holed up in the library, surrounded by his various computers and 3-D displays for at least twenty-four hours. The goal was to get food into him and then convince him to sleep. But I think the second half of that plan may be doomed, given that Alex just gulped down a large mug of black coffee and is now munching his way through the bag of caffeinated jelly beans he keeps at his desk.

He has good reason to be stressed. Even though we managed to restore the timeline, Jack is still stuck in 1966. It feels wrong, being here without him, and I suspect that it's at least as hard on Alex as it is on me. His best friend is stranded 170 years in the past, thanks to technology Alex himself invented—or rather, will invent at some point in the future, apparently with our help—so it has to be making him crazy that he can't bring Jack home. In my case, however, I can sort of be two places at once. I can spend the entire day and night in 1966 with Jack, pull out my CHRONOS key and drop in here for as long as I want, then blink back to Jack ten seconds after I left.

When I glance over at Lorena, there's a knowing look in her eyes. "When are you heading back to Memphis?"

"Not sure. I haven't had a swim in days, so I may head down to the basement for a bit. And Jarvis says I have messages waiting. I'm pretty sure at least one of them is from my thesis advisor, wanting to set a time for our meeting on Friday, and I haven't even thought about my research in over a week. So I need to spend a little time looking over my notes before—"

"Mm-hmm." Given Lorena Jeung's eerie knack for homing in on what I'm thinking, I'm not surprised she's unconvinced. "You should at least try what I suggested, Madi. If Jack is all comfy and cozy there and then, he's going to have a much harder time getting back to the here and now."

Last night, I'd promised to simply deliver Jack's suitcase and head back home. And I'd actually *planned* to do that when I left, but the more I thought about it, the less I liked him being there alone. Her theory that Jack needs to avoid getting too comfortable in the past is bunk anyway. He spent all day yesterday trying to jump home. Even after he said we were done for the day, that we'd try again this morning, he still reached for the CHRONOS key tucked inside his T-shirt at least a dozen times during the night, centering the medallion in his palm, no doubt praying that this time it would work. But it never did. He could lock in the location and could even see what was happening on the other end, but he couldn't jump—which is pretty much exactly what has happened on every other occasion Jack Merrick has tried to use the CHRONOS key.

Every occasion except one, that is. If Jack hadn't been able to make the key work that one time, I would be dead. John Lennon would have died, as well. Lennon was eventually murdered anyway, but his death would have been fourteen years early. Stopping that assassination—along with the premature deaths of Martin Luther King Jr., singer Mary Travers, and author James Baldwin—put our timeline back on its original track, averting a reality where the Vietnam War went on for six months longer and resulted in the deaths of nearly thirty-five thousand additional people, erasing millions of offspring they would have produced, including Lorena and Yun Hee.

Lorena is convinced that a chemical reaction is the only logical explanation for Jack's surge in time-traveling ability. She thinks watching someone kill me flooded his system with a mix of stress hormones and neurotransmitters that she can rattle off instantly and I can't remember at all, aside from adrenaline and testosterone. And she's probably right, but . . .

"I just don't think making Jack homesick is going to have the same effect as him seeing someone kill me. And I'm not sure how we could safely replicate those circumstances. I mean, one of you could hold a gun to my head, but I doubt Jack would believe it, so even that wouldn't trigger the same chemical response."

She doesn't say anything, which I'm beginning to realize is Lorena-speak for *You may have a point*.

"How long do you think it will be before you have a serum ready for him to test?" I ask.

Lorena shrugs. "A few days, at least, depending on whether Alex is confident about that field extender he's working on for the CHRONOS diary."

"It should be ready by tomorrow," he says without looking up from his screen. "I'm just running a few last tests to make sure the diary doesn't give off any signals that might be picked up by the security scanners in your building."

"Thanks," she says, flashing him a tiny, nervous smile. "I can't take any more days off. I'm in the hole as it is." Turning back to me, she adds, "I'm not scheduled for lab hours until Wednesday morning, though. Even then, my ability to work on this will be heavily dependent on who is in the lab at the same time. If it's anyone at Georgetown who's even remotely familiar with my current research, they're going to wonder why I'm dealing with blood samples, stress chemicals, and the like." She grabs the plates from the table and heads toward the kitchen. "I'll have to be extra careful. I can't afford to risk my job, especially with the future of this side venture currently up in the air."

The *side venture*, as she puts it, isn't really up in the air, although the set of her mouth tells me she and RJ may well decide to back out once we get Jack safely home from 1966. I can't blame her. Lorena, more than any of us, has a firm grasp of the dangers posed by the technology. Between the medallion that I uncovered, literally, in the garden and the one that my great-great-grandmother left hidden in the basement, we seem to have conveniently skipped the whole research-and-development phase of our newly formed company, AJG Research. Despite that, however, I'm still listed, along with Ian Alexander and Ryan Jefferson, a.k.a. Alex and RJ, as one of the three *inventors* of time travel in *A Brief History of CHRONOS*. I'm a historian—a literary historian—so I'm quite certain that the only thing I bring to the partnership is the genetic ability to use the device. Alex is the temporal physicist in the group. He'd heard rumors of a device like the medallion being tested by the government decades ago—rumors that Jack was able to confirm—but Alex said the research he's been working on in his postdoctoral program is still years away from human time travel, so he's almost as mystified by all of this as the rest of us.

RJ seems destined to be the sales-and-marketing side of our new partnership, but he's also here because of Lorena. Her job as a geneticist will be in danger if they find out she's working on a project like this, especially with someone like me. If she were adhering to the rules, Lorena would have already informed my graduate program at Georgetown that I'm genetically enhanced. Or, to be more precise, that I *inherited* multiple baseline enhancements, something I myself only discovered recently. I probably wouldn't have been admitted to the university, and I definitely wouldn't be on scholarship, if they'd known.

In a perfect world, I'd be more than happy to close the entire operation down and return to my studies. That was my plan once we repaired the rift. The past few days have convinced me that time travel is a very bad idea. History is fluid and visiting the past can wreak havoc on the future. But I'm no longer sure that terminating the research is an option. Even if we halt everything right now, there is no way to shove this genie back into the bottle. We might not know precisely how the medallions work, but they exist inside their own temporal field. The fact that we created the technology in some other timeline means that it exists in *this* timeline. And the folks who caused the rift are still out there, in some neighboring reality. They found a way into our universe once. Hopefully the fact that we're onto them will be enough to convince them to play their stupid game of Temporal Dilemma elsewhere, although I feel guilty even wishing that. These people traveled through time and space to purposefully alter our history, screwing with the lives of billions of people for their own amusement. As much as I never, ever want to deal with them again, I hate the idea that they might be doing the same thing in the reality next door.

That's why Alex is currently wound tighter than a magnet's coil. He was still struggling to figure out the basic parameters of this technology that he *should* have been more than a decade away from creating when we discovered it had been hijacked by interdimensional travelers. Now he needs to find a way to lock down something he barely understands if we're to have any hope of keeping them out.

"Alex?" When he doesn't respond, I tap on the picnic table between us. "Alex!"

He startles and looks up from his reading. "Sorry. Did you say something?"

"Jack is okay. He wanted me to tell you that he's *fine*. We'll eventually get him back here, assuming you don't kill yourself from stress." I reach across the table and squeeze his arm when he starts to protest. "I'm serious. Jack being stranded isn't your fault."

"Okay." Alex runs a hand through his blond hair, which is currently sticking up in jagged spikes, giving him a scarecrow vibe. "Maybe . . . maybe he should focus on short jumps first. Has he tried that? I was looking at the notes you made on Kate Pierce-Keller's diaries. The other guy, the one who was helping her . . ."

"Kiernan Dunne?"

"Yeah. He could use the key, but it was sporadic for him, too, like it is for Jack."

"Right. He had to wait between jumps. And longer jumps were harder for him."

Alex nods. "You, on the other hand, don't seem to be limited, or at least not in any significant way. I need to talk it through with Lorena, but it occurred to me just now that at least some of the traits that were altered may be stronger in females due to X-linked inheritance."

I raise a questioning eyebrow. "Which means . . . what?"

"Males inherit one X and one Y chromosome. Females inherit two X chromosomes. So if a genetic trait—or, in this case, a genetic enhancement—is linked to the X chromosome, it's more likely to be expressed in female offspring than male. It could also just be the luck of the genetic lottery, but it seems odd to me that you have less trouble using it when you inherited the ability from a great-great-grandmother while Jack inherited the ability from his grandfather."

That's true, although as he says the words, the face of my maternal grandmother, Thea Randall, flashes into my mind. Her resemblance to Great-Great-Grandma Kate, and even more so to Kate's aunt, known as Sister Prudence to members of the Cyrist religion, is absolutely uncanny. Although I don't think I can entirely discount the possibility that my genetic inheritance is coming from both sides of the family, I'm reluctant to add an extra layer of complexity to Alex's theory based on a mere suspicion. But it does remind me that I need to track Thea down and ask her some questions.

"Good idea," I say. "I'll get Jack to try some short jumps, both in terms of distance and time, when I go back. In the interim, though, would you please get some sleep? We need that brain of yours focused and at full capacity, not hopped up on espresso and buzz beans."

Alex makes a noncommittal sound. I sigh as I collect the last of the items on the table, and then head into the house. At least I can tell Jack that I tried.

The kitchen and living room are both empty, so RJ and Lorena must have taken the baby upstairs to their suite. I pour some more coffee into my mug, settle onto the couch, and ask Jarvis, my virtual assistant, to play my messages.

The first message is, as expected, from my thesis advisor. Another is from my Grandma Nora. She's the owner of this house, which originally belonged to her own great-great-grandmother Katherine Shaw, a CHRONOS historian I just met on my jump to 1966, although I kept our relationship a secret. I suppose there's a possibility that

Katherine would still allow her pregnant self and a bunch of her colleagues to get stranded in the past by her fiancé's sabotage, but that's the kind of thing most people would probably avoid if given a heads-up on the matter. If she did the logical thing and turned Saul in to CHRONOS security, however, I'm not at all sure what would happen to this timeline, to myself, or to Grandma Nora. It's the sort of conundrum that tangles up my synapses and gives me a headache.

The third call is from my maternal grandmother, Thea Randall, which isn't entirely a coincidence, since I left several messages for her with friends and also told my mom to have her call me if she checked in.

"Jarvis, return call to Thea."

"Yes, mistress. Voice only?"

"No. Put her on the wall screen if she answers."

Even though I really do need to talk to her, and actually came inside with the express intention of calling her, I find myself half hoping she doesn't pick up. Speaking with Thea is likely to give me a worse headache than thinking about temporal conundrums. The woman flits like a butterfly from topic to topic, giving cryptic answers to even the simplest questions. And the questions I need to ask her right now are far from simple.

Thea's smiling face pops onto the screen. Guess I won't be dodging the headache today.

"Madi, my angel! It's been *forever*. I got your messages, but it's been such a hectic week, you can't even imagine. In fact, you caught me just as I was heading out."

Thea is dressed, as usual, in one of her flowing caftans. This one is red and black and looks vaguely East Asian. It's cut to showcase metallic-gold tattoos on her shoulders. Her hair, which was dark and curly in her youth, is mostly silver these days, unless she dyes it, but her face still looks quite young. I'm sure my other grandmother, Nora, who is not at all fond of Thea, would say that this is the result of regular cellular-regeneration treatments and quite a bit of surgery. I think that's probably true, but it could also be genetic, thanks to the twisted branches of my family tree. I still haven't pieced together whether it's due to cloning or time travel, but it can't be simple coincidence that my maternal grandmother, Thea, looks almost identical to my *paternal* great-great-grandmother, Kate Pierce-Keller. I'm even more struck by that resemblance now, having watched an elderly Kate through the CHRONOS key for many hours during the past week, as I tried to decide whether to jump back and ask her advice before diving in to fix the time rift. And while Kate was at least fifteen years older than Thea is now, she looked very good for ninety.

"That's okay," I tell Thea. "I've been really busy, too. I won't keep you long. There are just a couple of questions I need to ask."

"Mila told me that you popped in, all stressed about inherited enhancements. You should have come straight to me. You know how easily agitated your mother can be. From what she said, I'm going to assume that you've found a medallion and you can use it, because there's no way your enhancements showed up on a genetics sweep—or at least not one approved by any major government. Far too much money has been spent to make certain that little secret *stays* secret."

I'd planned to broach the subject of enhancements with a bit more caution. I have no idea who might be listening. Jack said that the military-research unit his father was attached to came through the house before I moved in. They were picking up signals from chronotron particles, and even though they searched carefully, they never found the key that was hidden in a light in the basement swimming pool. For all I know, those people could be listening to every word. Which means they know I'm enhanced already, but Thea has just casually informed them that my mother was apparently in on it, or at least aware of it.

Might as well throw subtlety out the window at this point. Given Thea's personality, it never stood a chance in hell anyway. "So, you both knew I was enhanced?"

"Well, of course I knew. You're my granddaughter, after all."

"Did my father know?"

Thea shrugs. "You'll have to ask your mother. I don't know how much she told him. Or, for that matter, how much Nora told him. Mila would have been far better off if she hadn't gotten so involved. But your mother was always emotional. I think she actually loved the man."

I bite my lip firmly and take a deep breath. I'd hoped to keep Nora's name out of the conversation as much as possible. I've already spoken with her, and I'm convinced she didn't know about any of this. What really chafes me, however, is Thea's implication that my mother married beneath her station, as they said back in the era of the Brontë sisters. In truth, she'd married into a considerable fortune, which she managed to lose in just a few short months after my father's death, thanks to some truly abysmal investments. Pointing this out to Thea, however, would probably result in her pouting and ending the call. I've seen it happen numerous times when she's been talking to my mother. Thea never holds a grudge, though, and the next time they speak, all seems to be forgiven.

Or maybe all is simply *forgotten*?

Still, I can't let the comment pass entirely. "You think it would have been better for her to raise me alone?" I ask, repressing a shudder at that idea. I love my mother, but growing up, I ran to my dad if I skinned my knee or needed comfort after a nightmare. He was the steady one. Mila runs hot and cold, and I never know whether she'll overreact or dismiss me entirely.

"Oh, goodness, no, dear. Mila wouldn't have been *alone*. And you'd have had an entire community to surround you with love and give you a more . . . practical education than the one your father chose."

"He didn't choose my field of study."

She waves me off. "Well, of course he did. He comes from a nearly unbroken line of historians. And you chose to study history. The fact that you don't realize it wasn't your choice simply shows he did an excellent job indoctrinating you. Plus, he took you hiking on those awful mountains and gave Mila such nightmares by encouraging your swimming hobby. Although, to be fair, Mila's fear of water is completely neurotic. Swimming is almost as good as meditating."

I'm a little surprised to hear her echoing my thoughts on swimming, but her comments about my dad really aren't fair. "My father didn't *indoctrinate* me. He studied ancient Celtic culture. I'm a literary historian. They're really not the same field." I could argue the point further, but it doesn't matter. If she wants to believe my father was a master manipulator, fine. It's not going to change my opinion of the man. "Anyway, I think maybe I inherited an interest in history from both sides of my family. I've compared pictures, and . . . you're clearly related to Kate Pierce-Keller. Or more specifically, to her aunt, Prudence Rand. Is that why you didn't want my parents to marry? Because they're cousins?"

That's putting a rather dramatic spin on the situation—they're probably fourth or fifth cousins, and at least one generation removed, although the time-travel factor makes it hard to be certain. But I want to see Thea's response.

"Oh, sweetie, I guess Mila was right. You *are* wound up about this. Of *course* I'm related to Prudence, although my group gave up the name years ago and let the next batch of Sisters take it. Most of us are quite eager to move on. Too much pressure, and *far* too little sex, which you'd really think wouldn't be the case, since they used to consider her a fertility goddess. All those pictures of Sister Pru with her swollen belly, but there are so many guards around you when you go out in public that no man you'd be interested in could get within twenty yards. I could only take a few years of that."

There's a lot to unpack in that statement, but all I can come up with is a painfully obvious question that I already know the answer to. "So, you're a Cyrist?"

She laughs. "Oh, I'm a bit of everything. You know that. But in the end, as they say, all roads lead to Cyrus."

"I thought that was Rome . . ."

"Well, you could go back and check, couldn't you? I mean, to see if all roads really *do* lead to Rome?"

There's a teasing note in her voice. It's clear that she's trying to get me to admit I can use the key to travel. For some reason I can't quite put my finger on, however, I really don't want to do that. She and my mother seem to have been keeping secrets from me my entire life, and I'm not inclined toward sharing anything with them at the moment.

"I really have to run, Mads. Mila said you're at the house in Bethesda. I'm headed to DC very, very soon, and we'll have a nice, long chat. If you venture out of the house, though, please keep that medallion on you."

"Why?"

"Just a hunch. *The Book of Prophecy* says the next few days could be a teensy bit bumpy. But don't worry. I've taken care of everything, sweetie. Love you, bye!"

As she reaches forward to end the call, her sleeve slides back, revealing a bracelet on her right wrist. It's a fairly simple piece of jewelry for Thea, whose style tends toward the excessively ornate. Just a plain hammered-bronze cuff. The only ornamentation is the glowing amber stone in the middle, which is exactly the same shade that I see the CHRONOS keys.

FROM THE *NEW YORK*
DAILY INTREPID

CONGRESS NEARLY UNITED IN SUPPORT FOR WAR

(Washington, December 9, 1941) Congress has formally declared war against Japan in the wake of Sunday's bombing of Pearl Harbor. At twelve thirty p.m., President Roosevelt personally delivered his request before a joint session of the Senate and House, where it was approved with almost unanimous support.

In his brief address to Congress, the president proclaimed December 7, 1941, to be "a date which will live in infamy," as the nation was "suddenly and deliberately attacked by naval and air forces of the Empire of Japan." Current estimates of casualties from the attack are 1,500 dead and 1,500 wounded.

Additional reports indicate heavy losses from Japanese attacks in the Philippines, Guam, and Wake and

Midway Islands. Reinforcements are currently on their way to Hawaii, where repairs have already begun on damaged facilities, ships, and planes.

Following the president's speech, Congress debated for a mere thirty-two minutes. At 1:10 p.m., the House adopted the resolution, which had been passed ten minutes earlier by the Senate, thus formally entering the nation into a state of war. It was signed three hours later at the White House, in the presence of Vice President Wallace and leaders of both the House and the Senate.

Numerous isolationist groups, including the America First Committee, have pledged full support for the war effort. Charles A. Lindbergh, a leader of the movement, issued an official statement from the national headquarters of the organization in Chicago:

"We have been stepping closer to war for many months. Now it has come, and we must meet it as united Americans, regardless of our attitude in the past toward the policy our government has followed.

"Whether or not that policy has been wise, our country has been attacked by force of arms and by force of arms we must retaliate."

∞ 2 ∞

TYSON
CHRONOS HQ
WASHINGTON, EC
NOVEMBER 10, 2304

When I was seven years old, my great-grandfather died. He'd lived with us my entire life, so I was devastated. The very next day, my cat died. It felt like the universe had softened me up with the first punch, and just when I thought I couldn't possibly be more miserable, it had taken the challenge and come back in for that second blow. I told my mother it wasn't fair, and she agreed, pointing out that life was just that way sometimes. For weeks afterward, I followed her and my dad around, barely letting them out of my sight, terrified that they were the next targets of a universe that gets a sick pleasure from kicking kids when they're down.

The message on the display is definitely triggering my inner seven-year-old, because this feels much the same. Rich, Katherine, and I spent the last week getting the timeline back on track. Probably *more* than a week, if I tallied up the actual minutes, because I crammed at least forty-eight hours into a few of those days. I nearly got myself killed on two separate occasions. And we don't even get a few minutes to breathe before they hit us with this? I have a totally irrational urge to grab the console, which isn't much larger than my fist, and hurl it against the wall.

Not that I'd anticipated a parade or cheers from our colleagues. They aren't even aware that anything out of the ordinary happened, and if everything goes as planned, it'll stay that way. Angelo explained away the jolt that most of them felt during their trips as a temporary fluctuation, a bit of minor turbulence in the CHRONOS field. A few of the more seasoned historians seemed skeptical. I don't blame them. I've never heard of that kind of glitch in the field, and I doubt any of them have, either. I expect at least a few of them will pull Angelo aside later and question him more thoroughly, but no one pushed the matter at the time. With the notable exception of Saul Rand, who dropped his medallion off with the guard at the door and stormed out of the jump room, everyone followed standard protocol and headed off to the med pod for clearance. So, no. I hadn't expected applause or even a pat on the back. All I was hoping for was a stiff drink and at least ten hours of well-earned, peaceful sleep.

I'll still be having that drink. In fact, I may have several. But the words currently floating in front of the globe on the Temporal Dilemma display guarantee that any sleep I get will be far from peaceful.

SINCE YOU SEEM TO WANT TO PLAY . . .
OUR OBJECTIVE: PREVENT THE US FROM ENTERING WWII
LENGTH: THREE ROUNDS
RESTRICTIONS: FOUR-PLAYER TEAMS, CONTINENTAL US, NO PLAYER SUBSTITUTIONS, NO WEAPONS OF MASS DESTRUCTION, FIVE OBSERVERS PER TEAM

TEAM ONE: MORGEN CAMPBELL, SAUL RAND, ALISA CAMPBELL, ESTHER SOWAH

TEAM TWO: Tyson Reyes, Max Coleman, Katherine Shaw, Richard Vier

STAY TUNED FOR OUR OPENING GAMBIT!

Katherine laughs uneasily. "Good one, Angelo. Kind of *evil*, given everything we've been through over the past several days, but . . ." She trails off when she sees his face.

But she already knew it wasn't a joke. The laugh was just her way of releasing tension. Rich definitely knows, judging from the way he flinched and closed his eyes briefly before even reading the words on the screen.

"If this is a joke," Angelo says, "no one let me in on it. It's going to be hard enough explaining that last time shift without giving the government a whole new list of reasons to defund this entire project. Or maybe even erase it and everyone in this building in the process. Does that sound like something I'd joke about?"

"No," Katherine says. "You're right. Just wishful thinking on my part, because if this is real . . ."

She doesn't need to finish the rest of the statement. The last time shift could have radically changed our present reality. We managed to prevent the murder of seven people, four of whom—Martin Luther King Jr., John Lennon, James Baldwin, and Mary Travers—were historically significant to the point that their combined early deaths extended the war in Vietnam and caused ripples that radically altered the course of history. And we all know that the changes caused from extending the Vietnam conflict would be tiny drops in the bucket compared to the US never entering World War II.

Aside from a few unauthorized jumps from the isolation tank that Angelo will have to explain, and the aforementioned *turbulence* excuse given to historians who were in the field, there's nothing to suggest that the timeline was ever altered. Only the four of us in this room and the jump staff know what really happened, and I'm not even certain that they have the full story.

And the full story really, really needs to stay under wraps. The CHRONOS program has always been controversial. Even though we reversed the time shift, if too many people discover what happened, the government will almost certainly pull our funding. And, as Angelo just hinted, the odds are good that they will decide to take things a step further and retroactively erase the organization entirely or stick with remote surveillance instead of sending human agents. While that's an idea that seems quite logical to me after the past few days, it would effectively erase everyone at CHRONOS, thanks to the shopping list of genetic alterations we received before we were born. The package is referred to as "the CHRONOS gene" to maintain the fiction that we are given the single "chosen gift" that everyone else is granted, in keeping with the International Genetic Alterations Accords. But in addition to the genetic tweak that allows us to operate the equipment, they also adjust a multitude of other characteristics—mental, physical, and emotional—that they believe will make us more effective in the field and ensure that we're better suited for the specific eras and societies we'll be assigned to research. That's true for the many people who work at the agency in support positions, too, albeit to a lesser extent. If this organization is erased, some version of us might exist *somewhere*, but we'd be completely different people.

Katherine, Rich, and I understood that we were not on an official mission when we agreed to go back and try to fix the timeline. If we'd failed, Angelo wouldn't have been able to offer us much cover, but then it likely wouldn't have mattered because we'd all have been erased anyway. What truly grates is that we *didn't* fail and we're still facing the same consequences.

"How did they manage to send a message across timelines?" Rich asks.

"Apparently they didn't." Angelo rubs his face, probably trying to wake up. His eyes are puffy with exhaustion. "Security claims that the message came from *within* CHRONOS."

I glance toward the closed door that leads to the Temporal Monitoring Unit. "Do you think one of the time-chess players hitched a ride on our signal?"

"Seems unlikely. The message arrived about twenty minutes before you did—giving several of us a dual memory. Security isn't showing biometric data for any unauthorized personnel in the past twenty-four hours. No duplicates, either, aside from one fifth-year who did her splinter test yesterday afternoon, and that aberration resolved in eight minutes."

I wince, remembering my own experience with that test. Jumping back to hold a conversation with an earlier version of yourself isn't fun, to say the least. Nor is watching that earlier version, which we refer to as a splinter, blink out of existence. The headache that follows is brutal, as the brain tries to reconcile two conflicting sets of memories. I think that's one reason it's part of the curriculum—to make sure agents, who occasionally travel to the same event twice to experience different points of view, fully understand why you do *not* want to cross your own path in the field.

"Maybe they latched on to Max's signal," Katherine suggests.

"Who's Max?" Angelo asks.

"The *other historian* I told you about," I say, eyebrows raised slightly. "The one from the *future* cadre."

It takes a moment for that to process. Angelo is usually extremely quick on the uptake, but I doubt he's had much sleep over the past few days. His days haven't been a standard twenty-four hours any more than my own, and he gave himself several sets of double memories during our effort to correct the previous time shift.

"Oh," he says. "Her. Yeah. I remember now."

I cross over to push one of the buttons positioned along the right margin of the display, which would normally give me more details about the proposed game of Temporal Dilemma. The display just shimmers a bit and remains on the same screen. I press another button at random, with the same result.

"It's not part of the actual game," Angelo says. "Just a static message that popped up on every TD interface a couple of hours ago."

"*Every* interface?" Katherine asks.

"As far as we can tell. It's temporary, though. If you disconnect from the network, it resets to the usual game controls. We've passed it off so far as someone hacking into our system and using it to hack into the Temporal Dilemma network. But I'm not sure how long that explanation's going to hold. Sutter has already messaged me twice."

He gives us a grim smile, because we all know what that means. Sutter, who is head of CHRONOS security, can't tell exactly *what* you're hiding. He can, however, be fairly sure if you're hiding *something*, thanks to a prosthetic eye that gauges changes in body temperature, heart rate, and so forth, and he is tenacious about following each and every lead. There was a case, back when I was still in classroom training, where rumors began circulating that one of the historians was smuggling small samples of DNA and selling them on the side. A speck of Lincoln's dandruff, for example—the sort of thing that wouldn't show up on the standard Temporal Monitoring check we go through after a jump. Sutter figured out who had done it during the first interview, and the woman was out of the building by nightfall. But she told him she wasn't the only one engaged in that sort of activity, and apparently what she said registered as true on his scanner because it was like the Spanish Inquisition for the next few months. He questioned every active agent, every analyst, pretty much everyone in the building, aside from the students. We were quaking in our boots at the idea of that creepy eye scanning us, certain we were next. And we likely would have been, had the jump committee not told him to back off.

"He's probably getting calls from the security folks at Temporal Dilemma," Angelo adds. "Maybe even their lawyers. Their subscriber-assistance office has apparently been flooded with complaints because players had to shut down active games in order to get rid of the message."

"Which is very bad news for those of us whose names are on that message," Katherine says. "We're going to be targeted by the entire time-chess community."

I'm not sure who dubbed the game *time chess*. It's nothing like actual chess, aside from the fact that it emphasizes strategy and your moves are usually contingent on those made by your opponent. The level of complexity grows with the player, with the more advanced levels requiring a fairly nuanced understanding of not only history, but also economics, sociology, and government. You can play against the computer, one-on-one, or as part of a team, and there are time-chess leagues at every age level, from primary school through college, as well as recreational and professional leagues for adults. A few years back, a time-chess modification was added as a genetic alteration that parents could request as their child's one chosen gift, and it has proved to be popular. Fairly lucrative, too, since time-chess teams pay a decent salary and prize money at the professional level can be substantial if your team is highly ranked.

Within CHRONOS, time chess is known simply as The Game, and while it would be an excellent teaching tool for the classroom stage of our training, it's not part of the curriculum. I've heard rumors that it was used briefly when Temporal Dilemma released the original version, but the directors of the agency later decided that the principles of time chess were at odds with the core values we were being taught. While there are various game modes in time chess, most of them involve changing a historical event in a set number of moves.

That's one reason active historians rarely play. It just feels wrong to practice doing something that is essentially the cardinal sin of our profession. Our prime directive is to *avoid* changing history. We are simply there to observe and learn. But I suspect another reason most historians steer clear of The Game is those of us who have been in the field understand that time chess is a lousy substitute for actually being there. No matter how detailed a simulation may be, real life is always more complex.

Saul Rand is one of the few historians who *do* play. In fact, judging from the amount of time he spends at the Objectivist Club with Morgen Campbell, and also from the occasional snide comments Katherine makes, the man is a bit obsessed with it. He and Campbell are both highly competitive, and they've been known to spend weeks of their spare time on a single three-scenario tournament. Campbell at least has an excuse. The ability to time travel is the one thing his money hasn't been able to buy, at least in this timeline. Over on Earth Two or whatever, he seems to have found a way to get around those restrictions, both for himself and for his daughter, Alisa.

Katherine's eyes flick to one side in response to something on her retinal screen. She glances at the message on the TD display once more, then turns to Angelo. "I'm sorry. I have to go. It's urgent. I'll be back in fifteen minutes, tops."

Angelo gives her an exasperated look. "Fine. Fifteen minutes. But not here. Meet these two in isolation room one and they can fill you in. I've been awake for nearly forty-eight hours, I'm juggling three sets of memories, and I've still got phone calls to make before I can sleep. But before you go . . ." He nods toward the display. "This situation doesn't go beyond the people in this room. Not to *anyone*. Understand?"

A hurt look flashes across her face. "Completely. In case you've forgotten," she adds with a defiant tilt of her chin, "I'm quite capable of keeping a secret. Even from Saul."

Her last comment seems to have chastened Angelo, although I have no idea why. I exchange a look with Rich, who gives me a tiny shrug as Katherine hurries toward the door.

"Katherine?" Angelo waits for her to look back and then says, "When you see Saul, tell him to get his ass over to the TMU right now, *and* I want to see him in my office tomorrow at eight. Apparently, he skipped out-processing after today's jump. I get that he was annoyed with Grant about something, but that's unacceptable."

She gives him a curt nod and pushes the door open.

The three of us stand awkwardly for a moment, then Angelo says, "Anyway, this message was broadcast to a couple million Temporal Dilemma players before we were able to shut it down, so Kathy's right. Regardless of what else happens, expect to be grilled by the time-chess community. The TD folks said they were getting inundated with calls asking whether this was an announcement for an upcoming expansion module."

"Has anyone questioned the whole 'fluctuation in the CHRONOS field' excuse for the previous shift?" I ask. "And how many people know what actually happened?"

Angelo shrugs. "The four who were on duty know some of it. They'll have to wrestle with an hour's worth of conflicting memories. From everyone else's perspective, everyone who wasn't in ops at the time, there's no overlap. The timeline was fixed before it was ever broken from their point of view. There are records in the system of course. The jumps the three of you made from the tank are going to show up, and I haven't exactly decided how to deal with that. I thought we might be able to keep it inside the agency when it looked like it was just an isolated error on our part, but . . ."

What he means is an isolated error on *my* part. I was the one in the field at the time, at the speech in Ohio where Dr. King was shot, three years before his actual assassination in Memphis. I'd been too far away to alert him, but I'd tackled the girl next to me to the ground, almost certainly saving her life . . . and sticking her with a bunch of double memories in the process, since she'd been within the range of my CHRONOS key when the shift occurred. Historians and people on our support team understand the concept of a double memory, and it's tough even if you only have a few minutes of overlap. In the course of saving her life, I'd saddled Toni Robinson with several years' worth of memories that made no sense to anyone around her. Restoring the timeline also restored her sanity. The fact that I'm almost equally relieved by those two results tells me I need to steer clear of Memphis 1966.

"But," Angelo continues, "keeping all of this secret is a moot point, now. This message means we're under threat of attack. I briefed the White House immediately, and I have a face-to-face meeting tomorrow afternoon with the president, as well as the head of CHRONOS and the other members of the jump committee."

"What makes you think Morgen and his buddies will hold off that long?" I ask, nodding toward the message.

"I don't know that they will, but President Freidman is at some economic forum in Europe. And she wants to include the Solons and heads of the relevant departments, which means a lot of schedules to sync up. My preference was to meet today, but that would have meant talking with VP Graham, and he's in our corner even less than Freidman. If I could still use the key, I'd have jumped back a few days and given her advance warning. I even thought about having one of you go back and give me a heads-up so that I *could* do that, but . . . maybe it's for the best. Hopefully I can catch at least a few hours of sleep in the interim. And maybe then my mind will be clear enough to figure out how to pitch this disaster in a way that does the least damage to the agency."

"I think that's a lost cause," Rich says, slumping down into one of the chairs. "They're going to decide we're too big of a risk. And as much as I'd like to continue existing, they're probably correct."

"Hold on, though." I'd been thinking the same thing only a few minutes earlier, but as I heard the words from Rich, I realized there was a major flaw in our knee-jerk pessimism. "If this message is real, they *can't* erase CHRONOS. Think about it. You just need to make them see that we're their only hope of defense. Even if they find some way to block incursions from other timelines, there's no guarantee that solution will hold. I think the worst-case scenario is that they militarize us. Maybe they'll eventually change the nature of training for future cadres, but they're going to want to make sure we have people who can counter this sort of attack in the interim. I mean, unless they've found a way to insert the CHRONOS gene after birth, it will be a few decades before they have any other group to take our place. Erasing the agency would give the enemy carte blanche to use our timeline as their playground."

"That's an excellent point." Angelo's tone is somehow both relieved and apprehensive. "Even if they go all the way back and prevent the invention of time travel, it strains credulity to think that it would undo the development of the technology in all other timelines. Erasing CHRONOS would leave our timeline defenseless. Hell, once I make them aware of that, they might even *increase* our funding."

FROM THE *NEW YORK*
DAILY INTREPID

Aviatrix Laura Ingalls Invades White House Restricted Zone

(Washington, September 27, 1939) Famed pilot Laura Ingalls has been ordered by the Civil Aeronautics Authority to explain why her license should not be revoked after an incident yesterday near the White House. Ingalls, who recently came in second in the Bendix Transcontinental air race and is the only woman to have flown solo around South America, violated two separate civil air regulations today when she released hundreds of pamphlets from her Lockheed-Orion plane. The first regulation restricts aircraft from entering the zone surrounding the White House and the second prohibits the dropping of any material from an aircraft inside a municipality without permission of city officials and the CAA.

The pamphlets were the work of the Women's National Committee to Keep the United States Out of the War, an organization of isolationist women. Miss Ingalls claimed that while some of the papers might have drifted onto the White House grounds, the intended target was Congress. The flyers were, in fact, addressed "To All Members of Congress" and included the plea that Congress reject President Roosevelt's request to repeal arms embargo provisions of the Neutrality Act, claiming that "American women do not intend to again have their men sent to die on foreign soil."

Miss Ingalls continued her flight above the nation's capitol for several hours before landing at Washington Airport. Upon touchdown, she was met by officials of the CAA and taken in for questioning.

Correction: An earlier version of this article misidentified the pilot as Laura Ingalls Wilder, a children's author. Laura Houghtaling Ingalls is a distant cousin of Mrs. Wilder.

∞3∞

KATHERINE
CHRONOS HQ
WASHINGTON, EC
NOVEMBER 10, 2304

I've just finished noting that we're going to get reamed by the entire time-chess community when a green light flashes in the corner of my retinal screen, signaling an incoming message from Saul. I slide my eyes to the right automatically, intending to scan through the message quickly and send an automated reply telling him that I'm in a meeting.

As it turns out, there's not much to scan. The entire message is three short sentences. *Urgent. I need you. Bring first aid kit.* And then Saul's name goes dark, indicating that he's switched off his comm-link.

Great. In all the time we've been together, Saul has never once messaged me that *anything* was an emergency. Small details never seem to stress him out, and he has an uncanny knack for remaining unruffled even in the midst of chaos. I came home shortly after we moved in together to find that the zephyr in our new quarters had gone haywire. The eco-friendly shower's thermostat malfunctioned, melting a hole in one of the shower walls and the bath so the suite positively reeked of melted plastic and cologne—both his and mine. Saul, who was reading in the front room, apparently oblivious to the stench, calmly informed me that repairs were scheduled for the next day.

Why the hell does he need a first aid kit? Adhesive bandages and analgesic gel are standard equipment in all kitchens. Saul knows where they are, because he tossed me a bandage a few months back when I shattered a glass and nicked my palm. And for anything more serious than a small cut or burn, you simply hop into the lift and head down to the fifth floor, which houses our primary med unit. Or, in the case of a major emergency, you message the med unit, and they can have a team anywhere in the facility within a matter of minutes. If he were seriously injured, help would arrive in far less time than it will take me to find a first aid kit and get it up to our quarters.

Obviously, this is a test. Will I come when he needs me? Or will I ignore him the way his mother did? Saul Rand is thirty-one, nearly eight years older than I am, and yet sometimes it's like he's still a little kid.

Given the message that everyone else is looking at, the one flashing on the front of the SimMaster 8560 display, I really need to stay. I *would* stay, in fact, if I'd never peeked at Saul's journal entries about his mother. But I did read them, so I'm going to tell Angelo I need to go. Because in every way that matters, there's a ten-year-old boy on the seventh floor right now, waiting to see if anyone loves him enough to come when he cries for help.

Plus, I need to see him. That's where I was headed when the message came in from Angelo. If Rich hadn't been on the lift with me, I'd have ignored the order long enough to find Saul. Even though I know, logically, that he's not the same person I saw in the auditorium in Memphis 1966, I need to see his face, without that stupid scar snaking down his right cheek. I need to see his eyes, without that weird implant I spotted in the brief moment before Max-from-the-Future blasted him with her stun gun.

"I'm sorry. I have to go. It's urgent. I'll be back in fifteen minutes, tops."

Angelo is visibly annoyed, and he adds a totally unnecessary reminder that I am not to tell Saul about the message on the screen. I know the man is tired. I know he's under stress. But it still stings. Angelo Coletti knows better than anyone that I can keep a secret. *Even* from Saul.

I pause outside the jump room, trying to figure out where I might possibly find a first aid kit. The med unit is the obvious answer, but loyalty tests aside, if Saul wanted the med unit involved, he would have gone there in the first place. The prop room seems like the second most likely location. I'm almost certain Adrienne was carrying a medical kit of some sort when she did that series of battlefield-nursing jumps last year.

The wing that handles jump prep—costuming, props, makeup, and the like—is silent when I reach that section of the corridor, something that's fairly typical for this time of day. Earlier this morning, the hallway was bustling as the various technicians rushed about trying to get twelve historians ready for their jumps. It's barely noon now, but the wing is empty, and costuming is closed until tomorrow morning. The door isn't locked, however. I've gone in on a few occasions in the past if I needed something for an upcoming trip and wanted to avoid the prejump rush. It's not like there's anything in there you can steal, and you have to log in to the system to use the replicators.

My only hope of justifying this is to tie it to my current research agenda. The last place I remember seeing a med kit was at the Beatles concert, when Coliseum security and medical personnel tried to revive the people I'd stunned with the Timex gadget Angelo gave us prior to departure. If anyone asks, I can come up with some excuse for why I need to examine a kit from that era before the next jump on my schedule. Of course, if the message Angelo just showed us is real, that probably won't be my next jump, and explaining this print job will be the least of my worries. CHRONOS will be shut down before anyone has time to wonder why I'm printing out antique medical supplies.

Five minutes later, I'm in the elevator, carrying a white box with a red cross printed on the front. It contains several types of bandages, a tube of something called Acriflavine, scissors, gauze, aspirin, and half a dozen additional items.

As I'm about to open the door to our quarters, I remember the CHRONOS key still around my neck. If I'd arrived on the jump platform as usual, along with everyone else, I'd have handed my key to the jump coordinator, who would have filed it inside the cabinet until my next trip. There's no reason for anyone to carry a key. The entire building is inside a protective CHRONOS field, and the keys are normally in locked mode anyway, to prevent use except via the jump platform. Angelo unlocked three keys to enable us to travel back and forth from the isolation rooms while repairing the last time shift, and Rich and I returned to the isolation wing since, unlike Tyson, we hadn't been scheduled for an official jump today.

The key is tucked inside the dress I'm wearing, and it's inside the shield Angelo requested from the prop department before our jump to 1966, so Saul probably wouldn't even notice the light. But the circular outline of the key is still visible against the fabric of my dress, and Saul has seen me wearing it often enough in the field that he'd almost certainly realize what it is. Since I don't have pockets in this outfit, I tug the chain over my neck, wrap it around the key, and tuck the entire thing under the band of my bra, beneath my left arm. It's not exactly comfortable, but I'm not going to be in there long anyway.

Saul is seated at the table, dressed in black pants and a white shirt with one sleeve rolled up high above the elbow. The suit coat he'd worn for the morning's jump to 1911 Georgia is crumpled on the floor, and a mostly empty glass of what I'm pretty sure is scotch is in front of him.

"I brought the kit." It's an obvious point, given that I've just placed it on the table, but I want to stress that I *did* come, that I *did* bring what he asked before I have to add the part he won't like. "I can't stay, though. I was in a meeting, and I need to get back. What happened?"

He fumbles with the latch on the kit, using his left hand and keeping his right arm close to his body. "A stupid accident. Brushed my arm against the side of a woodstove before I jumped out. Hurts like hell."

The burn stretches halfway down his forearm. It's long, narrow, and a bright, angry red.

"I'll do it," I say, opening the kit. "You'd have a hard time wrapping it with one hand. But I need to clean it first."

"Just use the iodine."

"It's going to sting."

"Yes. I know what iodine is. Go back to your meeting. I'll take care of it myself."

I ignore him and open the bottle of iodine and a packet of gauze. "Hold your arm over the table." I dribble some of the liquid along the wound, then dab the edge with the gauze. He winces, and a tiny bead of sweat trickles from the edge of his dark hair down to the faint stubble along his jaw. "Why didn't you just go to the med unit? This is probably going to leave a scar."

"So? Maybe I want the scar. Maybe I *need* the scar to remind me not to do something so incredibly stupid again."

I always get the sense it's his mother talking when Saul is harsh with himself like this. Maybe his father, too, although his relationship with his dad is a bit murkier. Saul rarely mentions either of his parents. We've been together for several years, and I still haven't met them, although I've seen pictures. Saul is an almost perfect amalgam of the two, with his father's facial features and his mother's dark hair, although his is straight and hers falls in dark curls with streaks of silver. I did speak a few words to the two of them when they surprised

Saul with a video call two Christmases ago. It was cold and formal, so much so that I understood why he let the call go to voice mail the next year. I wasn't around when Saul went through training, but Delia once noted that he was the only student she knew who didn't perk up as the various holidays approached.

I'm fairly sure that his reluctance to talk about his family, to answer the inevitable questions any partner would have at the beginning of a relationship, is the main reason he left his old diaries unprotected. When I pointed out the fact that those files were open, just after we'd moved in together and set up a shared data system, he'd just smiled and said he wanted his past to be an open book.

That wasn't entirely true, however. The entries are edited. You don't grow up in the home of a data-systems administrator without picking up a few things. Although, come to think of it, I grew up as the daughter of a baker, too, and I couldn't create a decent cake to save my life. My father is a dear, sweet man, but I have never seen the value in his line of work. The food unit in our kitchen produces bread that is very close to loaves he bakes the old-fashioned way. High-end units can craft a cake that is far more elaborate and, at least to my unsophisticated palate, equally tasty.

But data is at the heart of everything. My mother's job frequently has an element of detective work. One of her occasional tasks when I was growing up was tracking missing content, especially things that had been purposefully deleted. I always enjoyed watching her try to piece together the puzzle.

That's how I knew Saul had edited his private journal entries. They weren't extensive edits. Just a sentence here and there. At first, I was annoyed he hadn't been honest, but then it occurred to me that it had taken quite a bit of effort to tweak those files. He apparently *wanted* to be completely open but was afraid to show me everything. And I could hardly object, since I hadn't even kept a private journal before I began field training. Did I really expect him to reveal his deepest, darkest when I was unable—and if I'm being perfectly honest, *unwilling*—to do the same?

The one thing the entries I read made abundantly clear was that Saul's family was dysfunctional, maybe even abusive. That fit pretty well with other things he'd told me, including the fact that he'd actually gotten two chosen gifts—the CHRONOS gene and a black-market intelligence boost that his father's family had been getting for generations, even during the era when genetic enhancements were entirely outlawed. An add-on genetic tweak is always risky, but even more so when the first alteration is something as complex as the CHRONOS package. Anytime he makes a mistake or does something the slightest bit wrong, he jokes that his parents should ask for a refund. And I've learned that there is one phrase you never, ever say to Saul Rand during an argument. You do not ask, even rhetorically, if he's crazy. At first, I couldn't understand why he was overreacting to the phrase, but then I realized that losing his mind is his greatest fear.

I suspect the unedited versions of his journal paint an even bleaker picture of his childhood, and it would be very easy to dredge up the missing data to confirm that. With a tiny bit of effort, I could probably even hack into his current journals. I'll admit I've been tempted on a few occasions, but that would be an invasion of Saul's privacy. And despite the edits, the older journals give me at least a partial window into his soul. Sometimes I wish Rich, Tyson, and others at CHRONOS could read them. They might not be so quick to judge, so quick to assume that Saul Rand is a pompous jerk. He's a different person when we're alone.

That brings to mind another *very* different Saul, and the thought sends a cold shiver through me. Did that other Saul, the one I saw in 1966 Memphis, choose to keep the scar on his face as a reminder of some error? Did he also have an emotionally abusive parent inside his head, judging his every move?

Saul must notice the shiver, because he places one hand over mine. "Thank you. I'm sorry for pulling you out of your meeting and for being an ass, okay? It's not as bad as it looks. I doubt it will even scar. The whole thing just ticked me off," he says as I finish dressing the wound. "Grant wasn't at the stable point when it was time to leave. The official story is that he had food poisoning, but the truth is I found him trashed in the back of a bar. I was trying to drag the drunk gox out of there, and I wasn't paying close attention to our surroundings. This was my reward for being careless. If I'd gone to the med unit, I'd have had to explain it, and they're probably already suspicious about the whole food-poisoning story. So . . . I draped my jacket over my arm and came straight home. This is why I hate dealing with trainees. They're always trouble."

I loop the edge of the gauze under one of the other layers and tie it off. "Except now you're the one in trouble. You can't just skip TMU."

"Yeah. I know. They already messaged me. Twice. So did Angelo. That's why I turned off my comm-link."

"Angelo says you need to get over there ASAP, and he also wants to see you in his office in the morning. Maybe you should just let Grant take the heat for what he did?"

Saul gives me a wry smile and leans forward to press a kiss against the side of my mouth. "Perhaps. But where would *you* be if I'd done that five years ago?"

It's an excellent point. Now I feel a little guilty—and more than a little hypocritical—for suggesting that he hang Grant out to dry. Had Saul done that on our first jump together, when we were studying a small Rhode Island village in 1780, it's quite possible that I would have been at the center of an official inquiry. There's even a slight chance I would have been booted from the program. We were in the village to study reactions to New England's "Dark Day" in 1780, when the sky was so dark at noon that people had to light candles. I was a bit nervous, both because it was my first nontraining jump, and also because I'd had a raging crush on Saul Rand from the moment I laid eyes on him during my second year of training. Angelo had reluctantly teamed us up because the retiring historian whose place I was taking had been a specialist in woman-centered religions. A minister from the town, formerly known as Jemima Wilkinson, who billed herself as the Publick Universal Friend, had actually predicted the "Dark Day," claiming it was a harbinger of the end times.

There was a scientific reason, of course. A combination of smoke from massive forest fires up in Canada and a dense fog resulted in not only the Dark Day but also a bloodred moon the night before. One of my clearest memories of that jump is Saul standing at the window, holding his key up to compare it to the moon and saying it was the same shade of red as he sees the CHRONOS medallion.

The most vivid memory, however, is the fear that my career was about to grind to a halt before it could even really begin. A woman who was gravely ill was supposed to die while we were there, and for some reason, she didn't. I'm still not sure what action of mine could possibly have saved her life. It must have been something I did, however, because Saul didn't go anywhere near her. She died in childbirth a few years later anyway, and the minor alterations to the timeline made only the tiniest blip on the TMU report when we returned. I'd had to dig deep into the archives to uncover any changes at all. But Saul had been ready and willing to vouch for me if there *had* been an inquiry, and shared worry over that prospect brought us closer.

"You're right," I tell him. "I'm just concerned about you not getting this taken care of properly."

"Tell you what. We'll compromise. It's a Game night, anyway. I'll head to the OC now and get Campbell's doctor to look at it. You can tell Angelo you just missed me."

I struggle to keep my smile in place. With all of the chaos and doubling up on days, I'd actually forgotten that tonight is one of his Game nights. He's up to three per week now. He always says that

I'm welcome to come along, and occasionally I do. But I've never enjoyed Morgen's sense of humor, and I always feel like a third wheel. When Saul is playing, he barely notices I'm there. And while there are plenty of things I can do at the OC aside from watching Saul and Campbell screw around with virtual history, including an excellent spa and a world-class VR deck, I always find myself wondering what's happening in Campbell's private gaming suite. Has his daughter decided to drop by? Thanks to Saul's policy of making his past an open book, I'm unfortunately aware that Alisa Campbell and Saul have a history. It's clear that they don't like each other, but Saul apparently never let that get in the way of a good sexual encounter when he was younger, and Alisa is always on the prowl. So, rather than lurking in the background in Morgen's suite, I generally opt for a quiet dinner at home, followed by a glass of wine and a book. My jealous imagination is no less active when I'm here on the sofa, but at least I can avoid Campbell's snide innuendos, his leering glances, and his foul-smelling dog, a fat Doberman who skulks around as if he's plotting the perfect moment to sink his teeth into your thigh.

"But, Saul . . . Angelo said you needed to check in with TMU immediately."

"Which is why you'll tell him you *just* missed me. And they'll be closed long before I get back. Maybe Morgen and I will have time to finish this final scenario, if he picks up the pace a bit. I swear the old guy is getting senile." He tilts his head to the side, concern in his eyes. "And you should really get some rest. You look exhausted."

My smile stays in place. But it's even more forced now, since I find myself wondering if Alisa will be around as Saul and Morgen play, looking well rested, gorgeous as always, and undoubtedly ready for action.

Oh, come on, Katherine. You do look exhausted. You are exhausted. Maybe, just maybe, the man is concerned about your well-being.

"I am a bit tired," I admit. "I think I'll turn in early."

"Good. We can sleep late tomorrow. I'll bring back chocolate croissants. Breakfast in bed. Then maybe a little . . . exercise." He follows this with a slow, suggestive lift of his eyebrows. "And after, we can do some research for the Memphis jump. Is that what you're wearing?"

He means the jump to the Beatles concert, which was originally scheduled for next week. I open my mouth to say that jump has been canceled. But I'm still not sure what official reason we're giving for that. And I can't believe that I thought to hide the key and realized I didn't have pockets and *still* didn't consider that he might wonder why I'm in costume on a day when I'm not on the jump schedule. Maybe he's right about me being exhausted.

"Yeah. I was at costuming when Angelo called me. Because I was late for a meeting with him." The answer is so lame that I cringe inwardly. We never have meetings with the costuming team. But Saul is now reading something on his retinal screen. I'm not even sure he heard me. Which is good, but it also pisses me off.

"Get chocolate *and* almond croissants," I say. "And grab a couple of those fresh mangoes if they have them." To be honest, I can't tell much difference between the fruit grown in the OC greenhouse and the fruit our food unit creates, but I don't want Saul to feel like he's getting off too easily.

"Deal. Now go. Can't have Angelo mad at both of us." He swats me playfully on the rear as he says the last words, and I stare down at his hand, remembering an almost identical version resting possessively on one cheek of Alisa Campbell's ass, just before that other Saul tumbled to the ground. Saul gives me a questioning look, and for a brief second, his right eye seems to pulse and darken. It's a trick of the light, of course. Or maybe just my overactive imagination combined with the lack of decent sleep. I blink, and both of his eyes are again their normal blue.

I turn quickly toward the door, eager to get out before I give something away. "Love you. Don't forget the mangoes."

Once I'm in the hallway, I lean back against the wall and take several deep breaths. I need to stop letting my imagination run wild. The man in Memphis looked like Saul. But he *wasn't* Saul. There were physical differences, so it stands to reason that there would be at least as many differences in personality, right?

And maybe even differences in personal history. That other Saul definitely saw me during the concert. His eyes even lingered on my face before taking the inevitable stroll downward. On that count, at least, he was very much like my own Saul. But there had been no recognition in his eyes. The same was true for Alisa Campbell. She had looked right past me, and I've been up in her face on several occasions, so she sure as hell knows who I am. Either there's no Katherine Shaw in their timeline or our paths haven't crossed. And given that I was genetically engineered for the sole purpose of being a CHRONOS historian, if there's no me at CHRONOS, that's basically the same thing as there being no me at all.

I don't think my presence in his life is the only difference between the two versions of Saul Rand. It is, however, one difference that seems fairly certain and—scars and bionic eyes aside—one of only three that I can state with certainty. The other two differences of which I'm certain are that my Saul would not murder anyone in cold blood and that he would not upend history on a whim. Yes, he likes time chess. It probably isn't an exaggeration to say that he's addicted to it. But no matter how much he enjoys his marathon Game nights with Morgen, it's just that—a game.

A game that he's very good at. Perhaps not *quite* as good as he believes himself to be, but we are apparently up against some alternate version of Saul Rand. If the fate of the timeline rests on figuring out his team's strategy, I can't help but think it would be an advantage to have *this* version of Saul on our side.

Now I just need to find a way to convince everyone else.

FROM THE *NEW YORK DAILY INTREPID*

COUGHLIN SUPPORTERS PROTEST RADIO BAN

(July 10, 1939) Supporters of Father Charles E. Coughlin continue their weekly protests outside radio station WMCA, located at 1657 Broadway. In January, this station was among several who barred Father Coughlin from delivering his weekly radio address because he refused to submit it in advance to WMCA officials, who were concerned about the radio priest's ongoing inclusion of propaganda, bigotry, and racial and religious prejudice in his sermons. In particular, the station was concerned with a program in November of last year in which Father Coughlin alleged that officers of Kuhn, Loeb, and Co., a local investment firm, were instrumental in financing the Russian revolution. His source for this, he claimed, was a classified Secret Service report on Jewish efforts to support the communist-led revolution.

Lewis L. Strauss, a partner in the firm, stated that "the charges and the inferences he makes as to support of Communism by my firm are absolutely untrue." In his defense of his statements, the priest repeated a claim that nearly all members of the USSR's Communist Central Committee are Jews.

In his remarks Father Coughlin also said: "There is no Jewish question in America. Please God, may there never be one. However, there is a question of Communism in America. Please God, we will solve it. If Jews persist in supporting Communism, directly or indirectly, that will be regrettable. By their failure to use the press, the radio and the banking house, where they stand so prominently, to fight Communism as vigorously as they fight Nazism, the Jews invite the charges of being supporters of Communism. As Christ said, 'You are either with me or against me.'"

Statements such as these have attracted the attention and support of the Fascist press in Europe. The editor of the Italian newspaper, *Regime Fascista*, praised Father Coughlin for his efforts to show "the peril to humanity and especially to Christianity of the demagogic and provocative words of President Roosevelt."

While Father Coughlin stands by his assertion that Nazism is a reaction against communist influence, Father Coughlin denied that the speech was anti-Semitic or un-American and said he would let the public be the judge.

∞4∞

MADI
PEABODY HOTEL
MEMPHIS, TENNESSEE
AUGUST 21, 1966

Five ducks waddle out of the elevator, moving quickly down the center of the red carpet, as they do every morning at the Peabody Hotel. A small crowd gathered on either side of the procession applauds as the quintet scurries up the steps to the fountain in the center of the lobby. It's mostly little kids, but there are also quite a few teens and tweens in the bunch.

Most of the postconcert crowd cleared out yesterday, but there seem to be several stragglers, including two sisters on the other side of the fountain from where Jack and I are standing. They're in their early teens, wearing Beatles T-shirts they no doubt purchased at the Mid-South Coliseum Friday night—a drum with the band's logo and a banner beneath proclaiming *1966 World Tour*. They were wearing those same shirts when I saw them in the elevator with their mom yesterday, looking happy but also a bit spent after a night of excruciatingly loud music that was still somehow barely audible over the screams of the crowd.

For a brief moment, I'm hit with the thought of how different things would be for them, for the other twelve thousand or so attendees, and for millions of people around the globe if we hadn't managed to stop the assassination. And Lennon's assassination was just one of the tipping points. The real changes wouldn't have begun to accrue for several years, and none of the hundreds of people in this hotel would have even known that their lives had been altered, that they'd been shoved into a different reality simply for the sake of a stupid game.

Thinking about that is beginning to rattle my nerves again, so I drag my mind forcefully back to the present. One of the ducks sails through the stream of water cascading down from the top basin, shaking its wings in the spray. I need to be more like the ducks. They are fully in *this* moment, seemingly oblivious to their audience, to the oddity of the fact that they are ducks who live in a hotel. They pay almost no attention to anything around them unless it's duck or water.

I lace my fingers through Jack's. He squeezes my hand, and his hazel eyes remain on the ducks in the fountain, but I have the distinct feeling he's merely humoring me.

After I arrived, we spent several hours working with the medallion. I set a stable point in the hotel room, and Jack tried to jump forward a few hours. Then we set our sights a bit lower—a few minutes. And then a minute. On the second try, he managed to blink forward a single minute. I was ecstatic. He'd actually used the key again.

Jack, on the other hand, wasn't impressed. He tossed the key onto the bed in disgust, noting that it would take an entire lifetime for him to get back to 2136 at that rate.

He's right, and I completely get why he's discouraged. Normally, Jack isn't a glass-half-empty kind of guy, and I hate seeing him like this. So, when I realized that it was nearly eleven o'clock, I suggested that we come down here to the lobby. I hadn't mentioned the ducks, and I hoped the silliness of the whole procession might cheer him up a bit. But it doesn't seem to be working.

I dig a gentle elbow into his ribs. "Come on! If ducks getting the literal red-carpet treatment doesn't cheer you up, I'm not sure what will."

He puts one arm around me, but my bag is between us, and his kiss lands more on my cheek than my mouth.

I move the backpack to my other arm. "Maybe we could have another go?"

It's an in-joke, given our rather disastrous first kiss. He smiles, as I'd hoped he would, and hits the target this time.

"Much better. Practice makes perfect."

"I hope so," he says, clearly thinking about the CHRONOS key again. "Maybe we should get some food while we're down here. Richard said the pancakes are good. We can grab a table while the crowd is still watching the duckies."

As it turns out, we're a bit too late to be seated immediately. It's Sunday morning, right at checkout time, and when we get to the restaurant on the other side of the lobby, there's already a line at the hostess station. We put our names on the list and wander around the lobby for a while until a table opens up. Jack selects a few tourist brochures from the stand, and the two of us sit on a love seat near the front desk while he thumbs through them. I'm not sure whether he's doing it for cover or simply scouting out the entertainment options in case he's stuck here.

In that moment, I realize Lorena is right, at least in one respect. Every minute I spend here with Jack, while she's waiting for a chance to work on a serum or Alex is trying to figure out some other solution, is really just prolonging his agony.

"I'm going to head back after breakfast," I tell him. "Once they have something concrete that we can test, I'll come right back."

"But you said it could be a week or more before she has anything."

"A week for me, yeah. But not for you. Even if it's months, from your perspective, I'll only be gone a second. Every minute I hang out with you here is a minute where you're on edge and worried.

I'm being selfish, just because I'll miss you while I'm stuck in 2136 without you."

"Then that's no good. I don't want you to be lonely, either."

We stare at each other for a moment, and then I shake my head. "Oh my God, we're *that* couple. The one who stays up half the night because they can't decide who ends the call first."

He puts the brochures on the bench next to us and slides his arm around my shoulders. "Compromise. You come back for a few minutes each day. Even at the outside limit, that's just an hour or so for me here. And you can spend the rest of the time working on your thesis." I wrinkle my nose, and he laughs. "So that's your real reason for being here. You're procrastinating. Fine, then. Go visit Nora. Or track Thea down—"

"Oh, wow. I forgot to tell you." I fill him in on my call with Thea.

"Can she use the CHRONOS key?" he asks when I finish. "Because if she can, maybe she actually *is* Prudence."

"I don't know. That's one of the questions I was going to ask, but she said she had to go. She's apparently going to be in DC soon. I suppose I can ask her then. Or see if my mom will actually give me some straight answers now that Thea has confirmed the main thing I was wondering. Both of them knew about the enhancements, and neither of them told me. I'm pretty sure they never told my dad, either. So I'm more than a little miffed at both of them."

The suggested ten minutes is up, so we head back over to the restaurant. The hostess tilts her bouffant-blond head to one side as she examines the chart on her clipboard. "Table or booth?" she asks in a high, chirpy voice. "One of each just opened up, so y'all can take your pick."

Jack tells her that we'd like the booth. We follow her as she leads us through the restaurant, stepping around a middle-aged black man who's busing one of the tables. We're a few steps away from the lone empty booth, which I'm glad to see is out of the glare of the morning sun, when everything around us shifts.

FROM *A BRIEF HISTORY OF*
CHRONOS, 4TH ED (2302)

Strong pressure from advocates of government transparency and accountability, both within the United States and abroad, resulted in the creation of an international society known as the Chrono-Historical Research Organization (CHRO) in 2231. CHRO was initially tasked with the challenge of creating a code of ethics for historical researchers, including strict prohibitions against any sort of timeline manipulation. In an effort to ensure that the timeline was not altered, the first academic research did not involve human interaction of any sort but relied instead on input from small transmitters that recorded activity at various locations and historical junctures.

While CHRO recordings provided historians with a great deal of raw data, they left many questions unanswered. The Natural Observation Society (NOS) lobbied for greater freedom of research, stating that it was very difficult to put historical events into their proper context when forced to rely solely on recorded information. Analysts often misinterpreted events because they were viewing them through the lens of their own time and culture. The only way to fully understand history, they argued, was to become immersed in the language, customs, and technology of that era. In 2242, NOS devised a series of protocols that aimed to minimize, if not entirely negate, corruption of the timeline by genetically encoding historical researchers. Time travel would thus be restricted to a very small number of carefully trained historians who would travel to a set destination and return directly to their point of origin.

The two organizations merged in 2247 to form the Chrono-Historical Research Organization and Natural Observation Society (CHRONOS), and they moved quickly to develop a system that would ensure optimal safety for both the timeline and the historians involved.

As with any scientific endeavor, those who participated in the earliest efforts were a rare breed, willing to risk their lives in search of greater knowledge. Seven researchers were killed within the first five years, and three others were institutionalized due to complications with the genetic encoding. These pioneers paved the way for future generations of researchers, however, whose historical trips were safe and hazard-free.

∞5∞

I smooth the last wrinkle from the custom label and hand the bottle of sambuca to Rich. "What do you think?"

He squints slightly and reads the words printed on the gladiator's shield. "'*Ave Imperator, morituri te salutant.*' Hmph. A little morbid, don't you think?"

"Gallows humor. I'm trying to lighten the mood a little. The man studied ancient Rome, and he's about to go into battle for the future of CHRONOS."

"Yeah, but . . . 'We who are about to die salute you'?"

"If he fails to convince them, we're all literally history. We can print a different label, though, if you have a better idea."

"No. You're right. He'll laugh. I'm just . . ." Richard shakes his head. "It's like we're waiting for the other shoe to drop. And we don't know whether the stomp will be courtesy of our opponents from the other dimension or handed down by our own government. Angelo might be able to sway the president and her cabinet, but the Solons . . . they won't hesitate to wipe out CHRONOS if they think it's in the public interest. They're going to analyze the situation strictly from the perspective of the common good, without any sort of emotion."

I'm tempted to correct his very narrow and all-too-common view of how the Solons operate. I'd probably think the same thing if my father didn't teach political science. The Solons have been the primary decision makers in the United States for nearly a century. Some variant has been adopted by most advanced democracies. In the US version, one hundred men and women are chosen at random. During their two-year term of service, the Solons operate under a sort of chemically induced stasis, with partial amnesia. Having no knowledge of their own race, gender, economic status, or any other information that might incline them to produce biased legislation helps to ensure that laws are created for the common good.

Solons members aren't robots, though. They're still people, even if they have—temporarily—given up all specific memories of their private lives in order to govern more equitably. And they have specific, complex rules that balance individual rights against the common welfare.

But I doubt Rich is in the mood for an esoteric discussion about our legislature, and we're already running a few minutes late, so I focus on the concrete. "Like Angelo said, they'll probably *increase* our funding. Assuming this isn't a practical joke by our friendly assholes from the dimension next door, we're the only line of defense. That fact is emphasized in pretty much every page of the report Angelo sent over. There's no way any rational person could look at that report and not realize that the continued existence of CHRONOS is in the public interest now more than ever."

"Well, any rational person connected to *our* government would agree," Rich says. "But you know we can't be the only ones with the technology. The Southern Alliance might say they decided not to pursue time travel, but our sensors have picked up chronotron signals from numerous locations that aren't connected to CHRONOS."

"Hey, you know what they say about a common enemy bringing people together. We need all the help we can get, so maybe the president should send the report to their leaders, too."

Rich rolls his eyes, because we know that's not likely to happen. The Northern Alliance, which isn't strictly within the northern hemisphere but also includes Australia and a few other far-flung states, hasn't been at war with the Southern Alliance in nearly seventy years, although there's occasional violence in some areas where our allies share borders or resources with theirs. Conflict between the two sides is more economic than anything else, but there are still two distinct sides. No way in hell would either side ask for help in a matter like this, and they'd each bend over backward to point the finger at the other one, so it's safe to assume that the incident report we prepared won't be traveling south anytime soon.

That report also includes a summary of twenty scenarios of three moves each that we've determined are most likely to prevent the US from entering World War II and how we might be able to combat them. Rich, Katherine, and I made a jump back to the last week of October, the most recent time either of the isolation tanks was empty, and fed the scenarios into the SimMaster to generate that section of the report. For a while, we all stayed in the tank together, watching the thing work, until we realized that didn't make much sense. After that, we took turns jumping back to see if it was still coming up with options that seemed remotely plausible, although it was mostly me and Katherine, since Rich was scheduled for Q&A duty last night with a group of music students who might have questions he actually could answer, so he was reluctant to cancel it. Most historians dread public Q&A sessions, which are a relatively new requirement, intended to emphasize our value to the community. It wouldn't be so bad if the tour groups would actually stick to your area of expertise. Any historian will talk your ear off if it's a topic they know in depth. But in these sessions you always get at least one person who is determined to ask questions on something you know nothing about. And even with questions that *are* in your wheelhouse, most are the basic sort that could just as easily be answered by a digital assistant.

I was the last one to jump back to October 30th and check the computer, just before I printed out the label for Angelo's gift of liquid courage. It was, and in fact still is, churning away, but the probabilities attached to the scenarios are steadily approaching zero, and I'm not sure how much extra value we're getting at this point. There are *so* many potential combinations, and there's not much else we can do until the other side makes the "opening gambit," as they called it, even though that phrase seems kind of redundant to me.

So far, the machine has run nearly a hundred scenarios, but we picked the top twenty because Angelo didn't want to overwhelm the officials with too much data. The goal is to show the value of CHRONOS in combating a threat that is currently beyond control using any means aside from time travel. The three of us are planning to go back this afternoon and shift the simulation to a second task that will take far longer—figuring out how much is likely to be altered if the US never enters the war.

"I do hope you're right that they'll actually listen to reason, though." Rich drops the bottle of sambuca into his backpack. "And maybe once everything is out in the open, this won't be resting entirely on our shoulders. You and Katherine both have some relevant experience, but we have at least a dozen historians who are better suited to handle this than I am. Seriously, can you imagine a single scenario where changing some bit of music history is what kept us out of the war? And that reminds me. Katherine asked yesterday whether I know *Max's* research specialty. I told her I thought it was early twenty-second century."

I snort. "That's pretty accurate. She's been studying that era since birth."

"Yeah, that was my thought," he says. "But it was actually a bad choice, because it got Katherine to wondering why Max was in 1966 if she was a modernist. I said maybe she's a subject specialist like me."

"She is, actually. Madi's working on a thesis in literary history."

"Really? How the hell did she end up developing time travel?"

"No clue," I say, chugging back the rest of my coffee, which has gone cold. "But I need to talk to Angelo about going back to at least give her a heads-up. I don't think we can just assume that they sent their invitation to Madi in 2136, given that they called her by the false name she gave Katherine. They don't seem to know that she's Madison Grace."

"Which doesn't make sense. They hitchhiked on her signal, right? Yours and hers."

"Yeah. I don't know. Maybe they're just . . . sticking out their thumbs to anyone passing by? I mean, if you're concerned with getting to a particular destination, maybe you're not tracking the origin of the traveler. Either way, that's probably information that we don't want them to have. Madi's identity, I mean. Otherwise, their next gambit might be to just undo time travel in this sector of the multiverse by taking her and her partners out of the equation."

"That would leave them with a wide-open game board. Good point."

We take the lift down to the lower level. Katherine and Angelo are supposed to meet us in the courtyard. It's a Saturday, so the first floor is teeming with tourists, including a line in front of Tate Poulsen, our Viking specialist, who must be the unlucky guy stuck with Q&A duty today.

Rich pulls me toward a corridor that leads to a side exit, rather than the door directly in front of us.

"What?" I ask.

"That's supposed to be my Q&A shift. Angelo said he'd get someone to cover for me, since we were working on the scenarios. Tate's probably already pissed enough without seeing me strolling across the lobby."

"But you did Q&A last night . . ."

"I did," Richard says. "So there's a decent chance it's *you* he's pissed at, not me, because this was one of *your* sessions I promised to cover—"

"When you lost the bet with me in Memphis."

"Exactly. And I have no clue whether it's my name or yours on the list."

I groan and pick up the pace. Poulsen is fairly easygoing, but I have no desire to get on the bad side of the guy whose genetic-design team used Thor from Marvel Comics as a template when they set out to craft a Viking historian.

A clear floor-to-ceiling barrier in both the lobby and the corridor provides an unobstructed view of the small courtyard that sits at the center of CHRONOS HQ. The courtyard was once the front lawn of a library and the historical center for the city of Washington, DC. A holo-statue of Andrew Carnegie, the donor for the original building, stands at the center, along with two curved benches retained from the original construction that span most of the courtyard. *A University* is carved into the stone of the left bench and *For the People* is carved on the right. Pictures from the late 2000s show a wide staircase between the benches, leading up to the building that was eventually replaced by the current complex. The training wing is on the other side of the courtyard, so this is where students always congregated to get a bit of fresh air and sunlight at lunchtime back when we were in classroom training. It still tends to be occupied mostly by students and teaching staff, even on the weekends, and there's a small cluster of third- or fourth-year students currently playing hoverball in one corner of the yard.

Katherine and Angelo are seated on the right bench. She's clearly trying to convince him of something, although we're still too far away to hear what she's saying.

"Damn," Rich mutters. "I knew we should have gotten here earlier."

"Why?"

"She's trying to talk him into having Saul work with us on this."

"Did she tell you—"

"No," he says. "She didn't have to."

I don't question him. He's known Katherine far longer than I have, and probably knows her better than anyone, even Saul, who seems far too focused on himself to really bother understanding anyone else, even the woman he's engaged to. There's a decent chance that all of CHRONOS will eventually be focused on reversing this time shift, but Angelo isn't going to rush to pull Saul into the fold. He doesn't trust the guy any more than I do.

Just as I'm opening my mouth to make that point, I feel an odd twinge in the pit of my stomach. The coffee. I must have chugged it too fast. Before that thought can fully form, however, everything around us shifts. The students playing hoverball vanish, along with the holostatue of Carnegie. The classroom wing behind them disappears as well, replaced by the older building I remember seeing in photographs. Arched windows and three words etched on the panel below the flat roof—*Science, Poetry, History.* There are a few people on the steps in front of the library, including an elderly man who is staring rather pointedly at the two of us.

Above us, the sky is now a brownish gray. Some of the trees on the edges of the courtyard look similar, but they seem less vivid, almost anemic. The only things that look the same are the curved benches on either side of the stairs.

And Katherine. She's still on the bench, her eyes fixed on the spot where Angelo was only a second ago.

Rich's step falters for a moment, so I'm guessing he was hit by the same fleeting nausea. Then he takes off running toward Katherine. I follow at a slower pace, still conscious of the old guy watching us. He has a mask of some sort over the lower half of his face, and he peers over the top of it toward us with narrowed eyes. If everything around us seemed to blink out, it stands to reason that from his perspective, we blinked in. He appears to be the only one paying attention to us, and I'm really hoping he'll decide he might need to get his vision checked. That will be far less likely, however, if we do anything else that attracts his attention.

I sink onto the bench on the other side of Katherine. "We need to keep things low-key, all right? I think someone spotted us."

They both nod. We sit in silence for a moment, and then Rich says, "So, what the hell happened? Did the government zap CHRONOS without even seeing the evidence? I'm thinking that's gotta be it, because the building would be here, at the very least, unless someone disabled the CHRONOS field protecting it. Or is this the end result of the other side's opening move? Either way, if the agency is gone, then how . . ." He trails off as Katherine's hand moves up to the pendant beneath her blouse, which is identical to the ones that Rich and I are wearing.

"How are there still CHRONOS *keys*? If the agency was erased . . ." Katherine stops, steadying her voice. "I know the keys are inside a CHRONOS field . . . by definition, I guess. But if there's no CHRONOS, then no one created the keys and we should be gone, too. Right?"

She's looking at Rich, expecting him to have the answer. Normally, I would be, as well, since he's always been more adept at sorting out the various conundrums attached to time travel that make most people's heads throb. But I'm the one with the answer this time. I just need to figure out a way to explain it that doesn't spill the beans about Madi.

"I'm pretty sure that as long as the CHRONOS field is active, the keys exist even if the timeline changes. They're a constant. Even if the agency was never created in this reality, it was in the next reality over, and unless you crack open the key and destroy the field, you can't get rid of them. And if you did try to disable them, you'd need to make damn sure none of them were left in the past because then there's a risk that someone reverse engineers it and the whole thing starts again."

One skeptical eyebrow arcs above the rim of Rich's glasses. "And you know this . . . how?"

"Just an educated guess. That's how it should work, right?"

He sighs. "Hell if I know."

Katherine stands abruptly and starts to scan the buildings around us. "I have to go. I have to find Saul."

Richard winces. "Katherine, no. He's not . . . I mean, we'll find a way to fix the timeline and bring him back, but regardless of what caused this, Saul wasn't under a key. He's not going to be—"

"Saul is at the OC." She turns on Rich, eyes blazing, and points toward a building a few blocks away. "The Club is still there. See?"

Morgen Campbell's building is indeed there, in the same location as always, just across from Franklin Square. It looks as if it *might* be a few floors shorter, but it could just be that buildings nearby are taller now. A number of those buildings seem different, although I'm not sure I could pinpoint exactly how. I'm certain, however, that there was an office building across the street instead of the park that's there currently. And there's now a pub of some sort on the corner, *Sim and Stim*. I'm certain I've never seen that before. The top half of the building has been rented out as a billboard. First it displays an ad for some sort of exercise system, then three different campaign ads. One is for someone running for the DC-2 congressional seat, another is for an alderman, and the last one is for a judicial position. I don't know about the second one—I've never even heard of an alderman—but elections for the first and third were replaced by the Solons lottery nearly a century ago.

The other odd thing I notice is an increase in air traffic, mostly delivery drones, which are supposed to use the old subway tunnels this time of day and stick to a low flight path for the last hop of their route. Dozens of them fill the air above us now, some traveling much higher than usual. Maybe that's part of the reason the sky is thick with smog. The clothing seems different, too, and not just the face masks, which about half of the people are wearing. Their clothes seem more formal, I guess, and there's not much skin in sight. Rich and I seem to be the only ones in short sleeves. There aren't many women out as I look around, and Katherine seems to be the only one in pants. The others are in skirts that hang to mid knee, and it occurs to me that the old guy on the steps might have been reacting to our unusual dress rather than—or in addition to—the fact that we popped in out of nowhere.

Katherine is already halfway down the path toward the sidewalk. Rich is clearly dreading arguing with her about this, so I take the lead. She's not likely to listen to either of us anyway. But someone needs to at least caution her there's not a chance in hell that her version of Saul is still around, so I head after her. To be fair, I'd have a lot more sympathy for what she's going through if it was pretty much anyone else on the planet other than Saul.

"Come on, Katherine. Yes, that's Campbell's building. And Campbell might be fine in this timeline. He might be the same asinine gox as always. But he doesn't have the CHRONOS gene. Or . . . at least he didn't in our timeline. Anyway, my point is, if Saul exists at all, he's not going to be the same person. He won't be at the OC. If by some miracle he *is* there, he probably won't look the same. And he won't recognize you."

"You don't *know* that," she says. "Not for certain."

"He wasn't wearing a key. I saw him drop it off with the guard when he stormed out of the jump room yesterday. We wouldn't have keys, either, if we hadn't been jumping back and forth to oversee the simulation in the isolation tank. But you're right," I admit. "I don't know for certain. There's only one thing I'm certain about right now. Regardless of whether this is the result of our government cutting its perceived losses on the whole time-travel question, or the result of a stupid interdimensional game, the problem we have to address is *in the past*. We can't do a damn thing to fix it from here." I view the restoration of Saul as one of the unfortunate side effects of fixing the timeline, but I decide to leave that bit out.

Katherine doesn't slow her pace. "We don't even know if the keys still work, Tyson. Yes, they protected us during the shift, but does that necessarily mean they're still functional in a reality where they were never invented?"

I don't have an answer for that. The keys *should* still function, but I can't exactly check to be sure while we're out here in the open. My uncertainty on that point seems to have buoyed Katherine's spirits a bit, probably because it means my view that her version of Saul isn't around could be wrong.

"I'll ask at the concierge desk," she says. "If the Objectivist Club doesn't have Saul Rand listed as a member, then you're right. Whatever version of him that exists here isn't the same person." There's just a hint of sarcasm in those last few words. "Then I'll know, and we can move on to whatever steps we need to take to fix this. Okay?"

"I'll go with her," Richard says as we round the corner onto the sidewalk. "She's right. We have to check. Why don't you try to find Max? Assuming, of course, that the keys still work."

I expect a barrage of questions from Katherine as to why we're assuming Madi still exists when we're assuming the exact opposite about Saul. But she doesn't seem to be listening anymore. In fact, she's several paces behind us, staring at the skyline. I wouldn't have thought it possible for her to go any paler than she did after Angelo vanished, but it's as if all the blood has drained from her face.

Following her gaze, I see a Cyrist symbol, tall and stark white against the sky, standing atop a massive temple. It's at least a mile away, but still visible due to its perch on a slight hill. Something about it seems a bit off, but I can't quite place it.

"That's new," Rich says. "I thought that cult fizzled in the 2000s."

"Apparently not," I say. "At least it answers the question about whether this is simply CHRONOS being erased. I mean, even without the benefit of the SimMaster's analysis, I think we can agree there's not much chance that erasing a time-travel agency would resuscitate a religion that died out over a hundred years before time-travel research really took off."

Katherine pulls her eyes away from the temple and continues toward the Club, or what she's assuming is the Club. It could easily be something else entirely. I have no clue whether Morgen's ancestors had the building designed specially or simply bought one that suited their needs.

I also have no clue why the Cyrist symbol elicited such a strong reaction from her. But I'd bet this CHRONOS key that it has something to do with Saul.

FROM THE *NEW YORK DAILY INTREPID*

CONGRESS REJECTS ROOSEVELT'S CALL TO WAR

(Washington, December 13, 1941) Late last night, the House of Representatives voted 242–185 to reject President Roosevelt's recommendation that the United States join Great Britain and the Netherlands in declaring war on Japan, after a narrow win in the Senate. Roosevelt's resolution was prompted by the December 7 attack by Japanese forces on two military installations in the Dutch East Indies.

Representative John D. Dingell, Democrat, of Michigan, told his colleagues, "It could have been us! This attack could easily have been on our base at Pearl Harbor, and indeed, the next attack will be upon us if we allow this travesty to stand without defending our allies. Why are we fiddling and fuddling over legislation when all hell's fire has broken loose around the world, first in Europe and now in the Pacific? I will never be satisfied until Adolf Hitler's mangy, worthless hide is tanned and nailed to a barn door, and I'd be happy to add Emperor Hirohito to the wall as well, after this cowardly attack."

An opponent of the resolution, Representative Carl T. Curtis, Republican, of Nebraska, argued that the administration has been too ambiguous about its ultimate goal. "They cannot seem to decide whether we are going east or west. If we enter the conflict against Japan, we will inevitably be pulled into war in Europe. And no military expert can claim there is any wisdom in spreading our forces thin in a vain attempt to fight around the globe at the same time."

Representative Hamilton Fish, Republican, of New York, a member of the America First Committee, read from a recent speech by Mr. Charles Lindbergh, spokesperson for the isolationist group, which advocates a policy of strict neutrality in the current conflicts. "A declaration of war against Japan is merely a pretext. The true goal of this resolution, a goal driven by shortsighted Jewish groups and their allies, is to ensure that we enter the war against Germany. As I have said in the past, the greatest danger to this country lies in their large ownership and influence in our motion pictures, our press, our radio, and our government."

President Roosevelt anticipated the loss but stated that it was important for members of Congress to be on record, so that the American people could know where their elected officials stand on this vital issue.

A Gallup poll taken in mid-November showed 68% of the American public in favor of increased aid to Allies in their struggle against the Axis powers, even at the risk of being drawn into the conflict. Roosevelt will be advocating legislation for increased aid to the Allied powers when Congress returns from break in January.

∞6∞

KATHERINE
WASHINGTON, DC
NOVEMBER 12, 2304

Saul isn't at the OC. Saul isn't *anywhere*. I knew this even before Tyson launched into his condescending mini lecture. I knew it as soon as I saw Angelo disappear while sitting less than a foot away from me.

I'd just finished explaining to Angelo why we needed to pull in Saul to help formulate our strategy. He responded with a few vague excuses that really boiled down to the fact that he doesn't like Saul, even though he'd never admit it. I saved my strongest argument for last, noting that if there were any similarities at all between the Saul we're opposing and my Saul, that would make him ideally suited to predict his counterpart's moves in The Game. Angelo didn't have a rebuttal prepared for that point, and I could see him trying to think of some plausible reason to say no. Instead, he evaded the question, noting that Rich and Tyson had just come through the door.

"Good," I told him. "This affects them, too. Let's get their opinion." That was a bit risky, as strategies go, because Rich and Tyson aren't exactly charter members of the Saul Rand Fan Club. But they're both practical enough to recognize the truth, especially when we're in a situation where we need all the help we can get.

Angelo shook his head and laughed. "Gods above, Kathy, you are te—"

Was he going to say I'm terrible? Tenacious? Testing his patience? And is it weird that the questions of what that last word might have been were what ran through my mind first, before anything else could register?

By the time Richard reached me, the shock of seeing Angelo, a man I've known almost my entire life, simply vanish had started to kick in. I remember asking Rich how the CHRONOS keys could still exist if the agency didn't, but I can't remember what he said. My mind had already moved on to the realization that if Angelo was gone and the agency was gone, then Saul was gone, too. I tried to text him on my retinal screen, but it wasn't working. Not a huge surprise, given that it's CHRONOS issue and CHRONOS is now missing. And if the agency didn't exist, then my mom never worked there. She met my father after she started work at HQ. They probably never met. They could both be . . . anywhere. Or nowhere at all.

My mother has enough seniority that she gets longer weekends now, and they were supposed to be in West Virginia at the cabin they share with a few other couples. Without my comm-link, though, I have no immediate way to check on either of them.

But Saul had left for the Club just before I came down to meet with Angelo. The OC is in easy walking distance. I was terrified that the building wouldn't even be there, but I forced myself to glance over my shoulder toward K Street.

The skyline looked very different. So, for that matter, did the sky. But the building was there. I hate the OC on general principle, but I've never been happier to see anything in my life because the existence of that building meant there was something I could check. Something concrete I could focus on. And I desperately needed to focus. I knew that if I didn't get up from that bench, I was going to start screaming.

I was still pretty close to the screaming point when Tyson began lecturing me. The last thing I need is someone explaining the obvious and trying to talk me down. I already know the truth. All I want is to get to the OC and confirm it so that I can move on to finding a way to fix this mess.

But as I turn onto the sidewalk, a building on the left side of K Street comes into view, and the sight literally stops me in my tracks. The curved white symbol atop the temple is nearly identical to one that I sketched for Saul and Tate in the OC's Redwing Hall. The arms are wrong, though. I'm quite certain of that, because I designed the stupid thing.

It was one of the rare evenings at the OC that wasn't completely miserable, probably because Saul's former roommate, Tate Poulsen, was there. Saul holds the mistaken opinion that I'm attracted to tall, blond Vikings. I suspect it's *Saul* who's attracted to tall, blond Vikings, and therefore assumes that everyone else must be. Personally, I've always been more inclined toward brains than brawn, which is probably a good thing for Saul, because even though he is exceptionally handsome, his build is long and lean, while Tate is a solid wall of muscle. Tate's a nice guy, and I enjoy his company, but the main reason I was glad he was with us at the Club that night was because Saul's jealousy of his former roommate meant he resisted the temptation to wander off upstairs for a bit of time chess or one of his verbal jousting matches with Morgen Campbell.

Even in his absence, however, Campbell had dominated the conversation that night. The time-chess scenario he and Saul had been working on back then was one of the longer varieties where you tweak societal variables, like the form of government, economic system, and so forth, at an early stage, with the goal of effecting a specific long-term change. As a religious historian, Saul tended to play to his strengths, and the fact that Campbell is a fervent atheist gave him added incentive to change the religious landscape. He had been following a strategy he'd employed in earlier games, where he'd changed the timeline by inserting a hybrid religion. Instead of starting from scratch, he built on this odd little group that had a few brief surges in popularity in the 20th and 21st centuries. Small cults like the Cyrists were a dime a dozen back then, and the only reason I can think of that this one stood out to him was that the name of their main prophet was the same as Morgen Campbell's dog.

I remember wishing Saul and Tate would move on to talking about something else, because some part of my mind was (and is) *offended* by the Cyrists. That's really the only word I can think of that comes close to describing it. It's not their belief system that bothers me. I don't even know that much about their faith, aside from the fact that most people considered the group a bit odd and then, briefly, they moved into the mainstream. The feeling is really more of a niggling sense that they shouldn't *be*.

Tate and Saul had been joking about verses to include in *The Book of Cyrus*, a gag gift that Saul was planning to give Morgen once the simulation was done and Saul was declared the victor. Tate said they should come up with a symbol for the cover, something that reflected several of the different faiths Saul had cannibalized to create his Franken-religion. More out of boredom than anything else, I pulled out my device and made a few rough sketches. Saul had said the symbol needed elements of a cross, obviously, for Christianity. We added the ankh mostly because it was such a tiny tweak to draw that loop at the top. The lotus flower was for several different Asian religions. I was about to show the final sketch to Saul when I had the idea to turn the horizontal arms into an infinity symbol as a droll little nod to CHRONOS. Saul had declared it perfect, saying that was exactly the extra touch it needed.

I don't think he won that particular time-chess match, although he'd clearly expected to, since he went to the trouble of creating and printing out the book. Instead of giving it to Campbell, he'd simply stashed the thin volume, with its much smaller gold-foil version of the Cyrist symbol, on top of his dresser. Did that copy have the infinity symbol? I'm almost certain that it did. I've seen it dozens of times since then, sitting on top of the dresser, collecting dust.

Or rather, it *was* sitting there. That dresser doesn't exist anymore. Our apartment doesn't exist. I force myself to look away from the temple on the hill, with its almost-Cyrist symbol. The only thing that's important right now is to keep moving toward the OC and get this over with.

"Katherine," Tyson says, matching his pace to mine. "Marching straight into the OC without any idea what this timeline is like and without knowing for certain what caused the shift . . . does that *really* sound like a good idea to you? We need to slow down. Find a place to get some information. My comm-link isn't working. Is yours? All I've got showing up are two local contacts—you and Rich. My retinal screen isn't connecting at all."

Even though I want to keep walking, I know he's right. So I stop and turn back toward the two of them. "Fine. What do you suggest?"

We briefly discuss our options, which are limited, to say the least. The lack of a comm-link means we don't have credits, so whatever we do will have to be free. That rules out the sim café across the street. But maybe . . . I glance back at the building that stands where CHRONOS used to be.

"Good idea," Richard says, following both my gaze and my train of thought. "That building was a library. Or a history center. Those are usually free."

I think I'd been blocking out our surroundings and the people on the street while I was focused solely on getting to the OC. As we backtrack to the main entrance, however, I realize we don't exactly blend in. Our clothes are wrong. The colors are too vivid, and the designs far too casual. There are only a few women on the sidewalk, and a few more at the park watching a group of kids at the play area.

Only one of them is in pants, and hers are far more formal than what I'm wearing. Richard, Tyson, and I are dressed more like the children in the park. I feel conspicuous, and hurry toward the shadows near the entrance.

An engraving above the door reads *PVBLIC LIBRARY*, but the sign on the door indicates that the building is currently the *DC History Center*. That's a major change in and of itself, since this area has been part of the East Coast administrative bloc (or EC) for well over a century. Tyson pulls out his key, sets a local point, then rolls the time back several minutes. I'm about to ask why, and then I realize he's setting up an escape hatch. If we go in and something goes wrong, we can get out. Assuming the keys work.

He transfers the new stable point to our medallions. "It would be nice to test whether these are fully functional, but I think that would draw a bit more attention than we'd like. And if they don't work," he adds with a grim smile, "we're pretty much screwed anyway."

When Rich pushes the door open, I see several holostatues, including one that looks a lot like the Carnegie statue that was in the CHRONOS courtyard. Beyond the displays in the center of the room is a line of kiosks that stretches along the back wall. Either technology is a bit behind in this timeline or these are historical exhibits. If it's the latter, I hope they're functional. They remind me a bit of the computers in the preschool center I attended when I was small.

Luckily, the room is not crowded. A young man is at one of the kiosks with a small child, and an elderly woman is seated at another. There's no librarian on duty, which is a bit strange. I've never been in a library that didn't have a specialist at the desk to help locate data that's cross-referenced or archived.

There is definitely a security system, though. As we step into the room, I feel the faint tingle of a body scan. It could be a simple sweep for weapons or other contraband, but it's probably also biometric. Which is not unusual. We're scanned each time we enter the nonpublic areas at CHRONOS, partly to make sure there are no unauthorized people in the complex, but also to ensure that no one is using the time-travel technology in unapproved ways. But this scan seems wrong. Like the kiosks, it triggers a feeling almost like nostalgia, because the tingle was a lot like the cheaper security scans I remember from ten to fifteen years ago, coupled with a second, milder dose of the sick feeling that hit me when Angelo blinked out. Rich and Tyson must notice something is off as well. They exchange a look, and then Rich nods toward one of the empty kiosks.

An animated display pops up when we're a few steps into the room. It's an eagle—I *think*—in a bright-red sports jersey. It appears to be speaking, but I can't hear anything. I tap the comm-disk behind my ear automatically, but it doesn't help, so they must have their audio on a different frequency. The eagle seems to be waiting for a response, and even though I have no idea what the thing asked us, I take a stab in the dark. "Twentieth century, please."

I'd like to have asked for a more current era, but the fact that the door said *DC History* rather than *EC* worries me. It could simply mean the center only covers the period when the region was known by that name, before it was broadened to include most of the Eastern Seaboard in the late 2100s. Or maybe that didn't happen in this reality, and asking for that information would raise suspicions. Better to settle for confirming that this is indeed the result of the game, and maybe we can gradually work our way over to another kiosk when we're not being watched by an animated eagle.

There's a brief pause and then the avatar begins moving toward the second kiosk from the left. The screen inside the kiosk blinks on, then the bird extends a wing in an *after-you* gesture. Its face shifts from the cheery grin to something more somber, and then the bird disappears.

"Wonder what that was about?" Tyson says.

Rich shrugs and steps up to the display. "No clue. If it was a human avatar, I might have been able to at least partially read its lips, but it's kind of hard to read a beak." He taps the right side of the screen, which is labeled *20th* in a bold, black font. The display shifts to reveal buttons for each decade, with an additional button at the top labeled *Overview*. "Here goes nothing."

He presses the button labeled *1940s* and then *1941*. The screen shifts to moving images. Newsreels. With no sound.

"Great," Tyson mutters.

But the visual is enough. We roll through highlights of 1941, right into 1942, without any sign of the Pearl Harbor bombing and the declaration of war. The rest of the decade continues with occasional glimpses of battles in Europe and the Pacific, but no evidence of US forces being engaged. A negotiated surrender by the European Allies, although it's impossible to tell the terms. No iconic images of Rosie the Riveter. No D-Day. No Manhattan Project. No United Nations.

He then goes back to 1940, since he skipped that one in the rush to check on Pearl Harbor. One of the first clips in 1940 shows a tall, blond man speaking to an auditorium, with the caption *Lindbergh and Others Wounded at NYC Rally; Ends Senate Race to Protect Family*. A row of seated individuals, mostly men, are behind him on the stage, and farther back, there's a massive mural with George Washington flanked by American flags. The man staggers backward a step and then slumps forward over the podium. He seems familiar, but I can't quite place him. One of the seated men is hit, too. Another guy, wearing wire-rimmed glasses and clerical robes, looks like he's going to aid the speaker, but then he ducks behind the podium. The preacher seems vaguely familiar, too. I think he's one of the odd evangelists that Saul studies.

When the clip ends, Richard is about to tap the next decade, but Tyson and I both stop him. "Go back and pause on the speech," Tyson says.

Richard does.

Tyson stares at the image, and then shakes his head. "I thought at first this was Madison Square Garden. It was one of the places we considered going when I was doing my training with Glen." He winces, no doubt remembering that Glen, who was one of his primary mentors, no longer exists. "We were looking at the connections between the American Nazi movement and the Klan. In the end, we did a couple of jumps to the Hitler Youth camps the Bund was running in rural New Jersey instead, but I read several accounts of this big rally for Washington's birthday in 1939 when we were writing the research proposal. This is the next year, but . . . I'm almost positive that's the same backdrop painting of Washington. They even had a video. There was a huge protest against the rally because, I mean, who wants their tax dollars going to pay for the police presence needed to protect an assembly of more than twenty thousand Nazis, right? One Jewish protestor stormed the stage, but no one was hurt. Lindbergh didn't even take part in the 1939 event that I remember. It was strictly a German-American Bund rally. The other guy who was shot in the shoulder, that's their leader. Fritz Kuhn, or maybe it's Franz. And the tall, dark guy behind Lindbergh is Lawrence Dennis. Fascist writer. He also wasn't there. I'd remember if he had been, because he's on my long-term research agenda. Coughlin wasn't there either."

"*That's* his name!" I say. "I thought I recognized him." I step forward and tap the screen to zoom in on the preacher's face, but the display goes blank, followed by the message *Unregistered User*.

I yank my hand away. Rich quickly taps the display and the home screen pops up again.

"Whoa," he says in a low voice. "I guess that means there's another me around here somewhere. Or at least someone who's a close enough match that it fools the sensors. Not you, though."

"Not a big surprise, really. The odds of my parents meeting if there's no CHRONOS are very, very slim. Want to check and see if you have a doppelgänger, Tyce?"

"I'll pass," Tyson tells me, glancing toward the other side of the room. I don't see anyone except the family who was at one of the kiosks when we came in. Tyson seems on edge, although I can't pinpoint anything specific that should have his hackles up. Well, aside from the fact that we're in a brand-new timeline where pretty much everyone we know seems to have been erased.

Richard starts the clip again. "Lindbergh is the only one of these guys I'd ever heard of before all of this. Mostly because of his son getting kidnapped. And there was a dance craze named after him in the late twenties, when everybody was going crazy over pilots. I didn't know he was shot, though. Didn't even know he was a politician."

"He wasn't in our timeline," Tyson says. "Pretty sure he never ran for office. But he was a huge isolationist. Made a bunch of anti-Jewish statements, too. His name is mentioned in two of the scenarios we included in the report, but I don't think either of them had him getting shot."

Richard groans. "The report we gave to *Angelo*. The report that we all have in our files that we can't access without a functioning comm-link. How the hell are we supposed to counter their moves without that data?"

Tyson says that he has a few notes and images on the CHRONOS diary in his bag, but not the report.

"Lindbergh was in one of the scenarios that Saul and Morgen played," I tell them. "They based it on some book, or maybe it was a movie. An alt-history thing where Lindbergh was elected in 1940 instead of FDR. Someone was shot in that scenario, but I don't think it was Lindbergh. Zoom in on the preacher."

Even though I hadn't immediately remembered the preacher's name, his face was instantly recognizable. The snarl seems a bit more subdued, but he still shakes his fist and screams into the mic, just like he did in the clips I watched with Saul.

Two things, however, are different. The man's trademark raised fist now has a lotus tattoo. And beneath his clerical collar, stark white against his dark cassock, is a Cyrist symbol.

"The Cyrists converted Father Coughlin." I peer more closely at the photo and see that he's wearing the version with the infinity sign for the arms. Maybe that part of the symbol was just dropped over the centuries since 1938 in this timeline?

"Father . . . who?" Richard asks.

"Coughlin. Radio priest from—" Tyson stops abruptly, then says, "We need to go, okay? The tall guy keeps looking over here, and I'd prefer not to have to blink out if we can avoid it."

He's right. Two people—real, live humans, not weird bird avatars—are now standing on the far side of what I assume was once an information or circulation desk. They glance away when I look in that direction, but they're definitely checking us out. And since we may need to come back to this time at some point, it's probably best to keep our faces off their version of a most-wanted list.

Rich swipes the display to end our session, and we head for the exit at a casual pace. Tyson makes idle conversation with Rich as we walk past the desk, something generic about the score of a game. I glance at the two men in the reflection of the door. Neither of them follows, but their eyes are definitely tracking us, and one is now talking on an ancient-looking handheld communicator.

We pick up our pace as soon as we hit the courtyard. When we turn the corner, I force myself to look at the skyline. The OC is still there, and so is the temple. But now, the symbol has the curved arms of the infinity sign.

"It changed," I say. "While we were in there, the Cyrist symbol changed."

They both stare at it, and then Tyson says, "It looks the same as always to me."

"Yes. *Now* it does. But before, the arms were straight."

Richard shrugs. "Maybe a trick of the light?"

I shake my head, but don't push the issue. In order to clarify why I'm absolutely certain on this point, I'd need to explain my own connection to the symbol, which would open up a huge can of worms. Saul shouldn't be held responsible for something that's very clearly the work of his double from the other timeline.

"Could also be a hologram that changes," Tyson suggests. "Although it looks more like a physical structure to me."

Rich says, "What were you saying about this Copeland guy?"

"Coughlin. Saul did a series of jumps studying radio evangelists, and the man also worked with a conservative women's group that I have scheduled for the last year of my field research. I think his first name was Charles. He was a Catholic priest located in Detroit, but he had a massive radio following."

"Was he an antiwar activist?" Tyson asks.

"I don't think so. He was just against intervention in that particular war. Saul played some of his radio sermons during his research for the trip, and his rhetoric wasn't pacifist at all. But he was anti-Jew. Virulently so. The Catholic Church began reining him in a bit. And it eventually came to light that he'd taken money from the German government to use his platform to spread Nazi propaganda."

"Wonder what caused him to convert?" Rich says. "I mean, those religions aren't all that much alike, are they?"

"No. Some surface similarities, but . . ." I shake my head, trying to clear it of that vague tickling sensation again. "Catholicism had a long history even before Coughlin's time. And Cyrisism was just one of those odd religions that had a brief heyday."

"Or not so brief," Tyson says, looking at the temple. "So do you still want to go to the OC, or . . ."

I'm about to say yes, but Richard saves me the trouble. "Of course. Like I said before, we have to check. Let's split up. Wherever and whenever Max is, the shift should hit her key at the same interval that it did ours—so about thirty-six hours after we left Memphis."

The two of them continue discussing logistics, and I wait, although my patience is wearing thin. It's partly that I want to get to the OC. But I also want to get away from a skyline that includes that weird shifting Cyrist symbol attached to a massive temple that makes it very clear the group didn't fade into obscurity at all. It also makes me suspect that the Cyrists' change of fortune is connected, in some fashion, to the alternate version of Saul.

FROM THE *NEW YORK DAILY INTREPID*

ON THE RECORD BY DOROTHY THOMPSON

(February 23, 1939) To the Intolerant!

I wish to address myself today to the intolerant, to those Americans determined, even though it may cost their lives, their livelihoods, and their very existence, to preserve the core principles of our government—that all men are equal before the law and accountable to those laws and to society for their conduct.

There are, of course, those who give mere lip service to this view, but there are many who believe it with great passion, who will not tolerate any other view. These people, these intolerant people, are the patriots that our nation needs most desperately in this hour. They are the men and women whose principles may save our nation from its enemies both outside and within our borders.

For an alliance has been formed between followers of Charles Coughlin (under whatever religious title he may be using today) and those who follow Fritz Kuhn. Their goal, simply put, is to abolish American democracy as we know it. This alliance, heretofore unofficial, with the two groups simply offering casual support and publicity to the venture of the other, has now become apparent and quite official in regard to the recent rally at Madison Square Garden, called by the German-American Bund under their slogan "Free America!"

The Bund and the Christian/Universal Front are led by exceptionally capable, ambitious men, and their reach extends to millions through Coughlin's radio broadcasts, combining as he does his sparse bits of religion with his odious political views. Together, these two men intend to twist the instruments of democracy and free speech in order to bring about a Fascist regime.

They will not, of course, use the actual word Fascism. As Sinclair Lewis noted in *It Can't Happen Here*, American Fascism will surely wrap itself in the Stars and Stripes and present all those who oppose it as anti-American. Indeed, Lewis's book, dismissed by many as sheer fiction, provided an uncanny description of the meeting I witnessed in Madison Square Garden on Monday night, with its storm troopers willing to manhandle anyone daring to voice opposition.

Well, my fellow Americans, the storm troopers are here and more than ready to deal with "unruly elements." I was just such an unruly element when I rose to call them out, to laugh at those who speak of the Golden Rule in the same breath that they argue for racial purity and an Aryan code of ethics. They responded by employing our own New York City police as auxiliary storm troopers to escort me from the building as chaos erupted and protestors swarmed the stage.

Once outside the building, I learned that three people—a mother and her two daughters—were killed as panicked Bund members rushed for the exits. Like many of those in attendance, I believed that I heard an explosion from the upper level of the auditorium at almost the same instant that the demonstrators broke through the barriers to show their disapproval of the gathering. As one activist noted, the free spread of ideas is a noble thing. But when the idea being spread is that people of another race or religion are undeserving of political and economic rights, when the speakers are in fact espousing intolerance, then there is a great danger to allowing those views to go unchallenged. At some point, our tolerance for their intolerance becomes dangerous to the very notion of democratic government.

The deaths last night were tragic, but they were not surprising in an environment that foments hate and distrust. Those outside the building were right to be angry that their tax dollars were being used to pay for 1,700 police officers to patrol the area.

Police officials are investigating both the purported explosion and the cause of the three deaths. We have seen this charade before. They will call in members of every leftist group in the city. If there is sufficient outcry and the actual culprit cannot be found, some convenient scapegoat—or perhaps, several—will be prosecuted.

There will, however, be little attention to the others who are responsible for last night's tragedy, for they are the same people who will be seeking "justice." But the truth remains . . . three people would still be alive today if our leaders had possessed the courage to say no when propagators of hatred and intolerance sought permission to use the resources of our great city to spread and celebrate their poisonous ideology.

∞ 7 ∞

TYSON
PEABODY HOTEL
MEMPHIS, TENNESSEE
AUGUST 21, 1966

A fat phone book in a blue fabric-covered binding hangs from a silver cord just below the telephone, taunting me. This is an exercise in futility. I know this beyond any doubt, even after only a brief glimpse at the history of this timeline. There will be no listing for Lowell Robinson in Memphis in 1966.

When I left Rich and Katherine in 2304, I initially set the key for the day after the Beatles concert, planning to jump in and intercept them immediately after the time shift hits. At the last second, however, I realized that it didn't make much sense to go in unprepared. So, I've spent the last twelve hours or so trying to scrounge up cash and information about the new and definitely-not-improved USA circa 1966. If Jack is stuck here, he'll need money and some sense of the history of this new reality without WWII. Given the US's decision to remain neutral, that conflict is generally called the Second European War, even though it obviously stretched well beyond Europe. I guess it was hard to justify calling something a *world* war when the preeminent military power of the era chose to sit it out.

The time shift will hit Madi's and Jack's keys in about ten minutes, and I need to get to my booth in the restaurant soon so that I'll be in place to explain everything afterward. But the phone book caught my eye and I have to know. Knowing won't make it any easier, but it's like a mosquito bite. It hurts worse after you scratch it, but that unscratched itch will drive you crazy.

I enter the booth and thumb through the white pages. Lonnie Robinson, Lorenz Robinson. Two Louis Robinsons followed by a Lucius. No Lowell. If the man exists, he's not in Memphis. There's no guarantee he ever met Antoinette's mom. In fact, the mathematical odds would suggest that they ended up in separate camps and maybe even in separate countries when the 1946 Great Diaspora to Canada and West America began. Fewer than 10 percent of the African American population stayed in what remained of the United States, and the percentages were even lower in the South.

Even if Antoinette Robinson exists, she's not the same person. She never stood outside a drugstore in downtown Memphis with her friends and her sister, waiting for a ride to the concert. She's never even heard of the Ronettes or the Beatles, because neither group exists.

The fact that she doesn't exist shouldn't bother me nearly as much as it does. Looking at things from my usual vantage point in 2304, there are millions of people who don't exist as a result of this timeline shift, and millions of others exist who never would have in our reality. But Toni Robinson has become a touchstone for me, for reasons that aren't entirely rational. With everything shifting around us, my memory keeps pulling up that fleeting point in time and space when I first saw her leaning against the wall of the pharmacy, the sleeveless orange dress vivid against her dark skin. That image is the one true thing for me. That is what I will work to get back to, even if I never speak to her again. Any universe in which that event never happens will be a compromise too far.

"Looking for someone, Tyson?"

I shove the phone book back onto the shelf and turn to find a tall woman in a tailored skirt and jacket leaning against the wall next to the water fountain, her arms crossed in front of her. She's standing in almost the same position that Toni is in my flash of memory, but in almost every other way, this woman is the polar opposite. Her blond head, capped off with one of those boxy hats that are apparently still popular in this version of the mid-1960s, is tilted to the side as she examines me. She's clearly modeled herself on the icy blondes in Hitchcock's movies—although I have no clue if those films even exist in this timeline. I probably wouldn't have recognized her, because conservative chic isn't Alisa Campbell's usual style, but her voice gave away her identity instantly, husky with a slightly teasing note.

Of course, this isn't the Alisa Campbell I know. That Alisa can't time travel. But the woman's expression as she walks toward me answers one of my questions about this alternate reality. Yes, there's a version of me in that world. And apparently, it's a version who has made at least some of the same mistakes that I have. *Enjoyable* mistakes, but mistakes nonetheless.

"I was going to order a pizza," I tell her, "but nowhere seems to have New York style."

Alisa shakes her head indulgently. "You'll spoil your breakfast, Tyce. Or maybe not. It always *has* taken at least two trips to the buffet to satisfy your appetite."

Her tone makes it abundantly clear she's no longer talking about food, and I have to laugh. This version is every bit as blunt and transparent as the one I know. "What do you want, Alisa?"

Her pale-green eyes scan me from head to toe, which she probably intends as at least a partial answer to my question. But then she heaves a dramatic little sigh. "Bad girl, Alisa. No consorting with the enemy. It's a shame we're not on the same team, though. We could have so much fun." She reaches into her bag and pulls out one of the little fingertip drives time-chess players use to back up completed games. "We had to make a few adjustments to the rules as we went along, because we've never actually played against a local team before. As we were mapping out our strategy, we realized you will have a far stronger than average incentive to cheat, so we needed to add a few safeguards. No major changes, of course. Just a few tweaks to make sure the match runs smoothly."

"Rule changes are the sort of thing you're supposed to negotiate before play begins. What's to stop you from changing them again midstream?"

Alisa gives me a tiny shrug. "It's not as if you have any choice. We're still well within typical game parameters. But if the judge decides to dock us a few points, it's not going to change the outcome."

"Exactly who will be judging this?"

"That's good news for your team, actually," she says. "After careful consideration, we decided to grant you home-field advantage. Our TD rules are slightly different, so we used yours as the starting point. There were some minor alterations, but for the most part, we'll be playing by your rules."

"So, are you saying we recruit a couple of time-chess judges?" As I say the words, I realize I'm not at all sure where I'd recruit them from. Does Temporal Dilemma even exist in our current timeline? I'd always gotten the impression that The Game was created as a sort of substitute for those who didn't have the CHRONOS gene. But maybe not.

Alisa laughs. "Hardly. Human judges couldn't be unbiased in something like this. How could you expect them to rule strictly on the merits of the game when their own timeline is at stake? Even your Solons would have trouble being impartial. Hell, even *our* Solons would probably have a hard time with this one. They have a tough enough time with intergenerational justice. I'm pretty sure interdimensional justice would completely break them."

There's an even better reason that we'll never know the Solons' thoughts on interdimensional justice or this godforsaken game. Based on the election signs I saw across the street from the DC History Center, the Solons don't exist in the new timeline that's been spun off. Alisa apparently doesn't know that, but then I doubt the changes to the timeline a few hundred years down the pike are particularly relevant from their point of view.

"The SimMaster 8560 will be the judge," she says. "Just as it is with your more mundane time-chess tournaments. This drive contains our moves and an accurate tally of consequences, both intended and a few wonderful little bits of serendipity that came our way. It was almost as if your universe *wanted* us to win." She hands me the drive. "We've calibrated this to work *only* with that specific SimMaster model, which I believe your technicians will find to be networked to a rather . . . distant location."

"Except our technicians won't be finding anything. Your little stunt erased them."

Alisa stares at me for a moment, mouth open. Then she begins to laugh. "Oh, my. How unbelievably inept. Why would they let that happen?" Her expression sobers. "You still have your full contingent, I hope? Because I can't imagine my brother okaying substitutions, especially since we're apparently going to have to provide you with a second SimMaster."

I file the fact that she said *brother* and not *father* away to discuss with the others. While it's certainly possible that the guy I saw arranging the 1965 shooting during the march from Selma to Montgomery is Morgen Campbell's son, I'm now guessing it's far more likely that he's a clone.

Alisa flips her right hand over, revealing an onyx cuff around her wrist. The cuff, which seems to operate like a spring-loaded holster, spits her CHRONOS medallion directly into her palm. Such a simple gadget, but it would have saved several generations of historians a whole lot of time if someone had thought to equip us with it.

She glances up from the interface and catches me staring. "Do you like it? I designed it myself."

There's no point in lying, so I say, "Yeah. Cool idea."

"Why, thank you. Be right back." She blinks away without even looking to see if people are watching. They aren't—the hall is thankfully empty—but the habit of checking carefully before using the key is so ingrained that her brazenness makes me uneasy.

A few seconds later, Alisa pops back in. She abandoned the tailored look while she was away in favor of a skintight, translucent silver jumpsuit that leaves absolutely nothing to the imagination. I gulp, partly because the sight is dredging up some interesting, albeit rather uncomfortable, memories.

Alisa reaches forward and slips a small black SimMaster console into the front pocket of my pants. "Morgen says to tell you to be more careful with the equipment this time." She runs one finger along the outer edge of my thigh and then steps back, her face all business now. "A few things to keep in mind. First, the system is locked for judging, so you can't run your scenarios through the machine to test them."

"You're kidding? We make our changes in real time, without any sort of test?"

"Of course," she says. "That's what we did. It's really not much of a game if you let the computer determine your moves."

It takes a moment for that to fully process. Time chess is hard enough when you use the system to test the potential outcomes of your moves. The prospect of playing without that is staggering. "And we're supposed to just accept on faith that your side adhered to that rule as well?"

"Why would we cheat, Tyson? Like I said, it's not much fun if you just take the moves the computer advises. Now, where was I? Oh. Second, if the system is connected to real-time data, it should pick up your countermoves independently, assuming they're successful. But as a formality, all moves made on the playing field must be officially entered into the system within one hour by a team member."

"So, one hour as determined by the chronometer on that person's medallion?"

"Yes," she says, her tone clearly indicating that this was a stupid question on my part. "Third, the fingertip drive I just gave you must be inserted into the SimMaster within . . ." She pauses and checks the display on her key. "Four hours and eighteen minutes from now. So you might want to set an alarm. Fourth, the timer for the game itself begins as soon as you insert the file. From the moment you insert that drive, you will have the same amount of time that we did, exactly two days, forty-eight hours to the second, in which to reverse our changes. Which means you need to be ready to enter your initial predictions before the drive is inserted. And finally, all four players on your team and your five observers must be within a ten-meter radius when play begins. Otherwise, they are in violation of the rules and will be removed from the roster."

"What do you mean by *observers*?"

She frowns. "Observers. The people who pay to go into the field with you. To assist you. Do you call them something else? Minor leaguers? Time tourists? You killed *two* of ours last round, so don't expect that we're going to let you off easy. And just so you know, the observer you have staying at this hotel had better watch his back. Saul knew Crocker for more than a decade. As soon as the clock starts ticking, he'll be looking for revenge. If not before. Morgen might shrug off you killing Bailey, but Saul is territorial about his people."

The name Bailey isn't ringing any bells, but he must have been the sniper Madi shot in the attic in Montgomery as he was about to begin firing on Dr. King and the other marchers at the City of St. Jude. I definitely remember the other guy. He was the one posing as a member of a nearby branch of the KKK, trying to convince a bunch of teens to shoot John Lennon. We have a version of him on the crew at CHRONOS, or rather we *had* a version before the crew was erased.

"I think we're going to need a copy of your rule book, because there are some major differences. We don't take time tourists into the field. And since you've erased CHRONOS, that means assistants are pretty much out of the question."

She shrugs. "Your choice. We'll still limit ours to five, as promised, although Morgen isn't exactly happy about how this is cutting into his profit margin, especially now that he's required to reserve two slots for educational purposes." It's clear from her tone she's not a fan of that requirement, either. "As for the rule book," she says, "we included a copy in the file. Two quick words of caution, however. First, you might want to be careful with peripheral moves. Obviously, the system only measures the moves each team enters. If you go screwing around and make changes in a scattershot fashion, you might technically win and still not recognize the timeline you wind up with. And second, while I'm sure you would *never* try to cheat, Tyson, please be aware that any attempt to hack the data or the machine will result in immediate forfeiture."

"Forfeiture of the entire game?"

Alisa gives me a disdainful look. "Of the game. And also of this timeline. If you tamper with the simulation, I can promise you that my father will make this one of our permanent simulation grounds."

"What if we win?"

"Then we'll move on to the universe next door. But . . . I wouldn't get my hopes up if I were you. Even if you do somehow manage to reverse our little historical renovation, the contest will then be decided on points. And your team is seriously outmatched. Saul is the only person who has ever beaten Morgen and vice versa . . . and they're playing on the same team this time. I'm no amateur, either. I started time chess back when I still had to be put down for an afternoon nap. And Esther . . . well, Esther is just plain ruthless. When you take a look at the tally, you're going to discover that our style points are through the fucking stratosphere. We actually maxed out both chron and geo, with bonuses in each . . . although I guess I probably shouldn't have told you that." Her smile morphs into something that looks a lot like pity. "You're *not* going to win, Tyson-From-Another-World. It's simply not possible."

And then she's gone.

FROM *THE BOOK OF CYRUS* (NEW ENGLISH VERSION, 3RD ED) CHAPTER 6:1–12

[1]Do not seek the blessing; seek The Way and the blessing will find you. [2]Those who believe and remain faithful to The Way will defy all odds and exceed all expectations. [3]Envision your blessings and your journey to prosperity will begin.

[4]The price of prosperity is loyalty and adherence. [5]Do not simply defend The Way. Vigilantly search for untruths that disparage The Way—and once found, attack the untruth. [6]Those who oppose The Way are enemies of Earth and of all life upon it. Their lies cannot be tolerated by the faithful.

[7]Neither should you be yoked with unbelievers. What do strength and weakness have in common? What fellowship can light have with darkness? [8]Choose The Way of the light, and surround yourself with only those willing to sacrifice all in order that all may be given unto them.

⁹Choosing The Way and shunning all enemies requires strength and courage. ¹⁰If you have courage, then you can change anything. If you are your own master, those lacking courage will follow you.

¹¹Always remember that the strong are the masterwork of all creation. Lead others to the light by your example, but if they do not see, they cannot be Chosen. ¹²Turn your back to those who will not follow, lest their weakness poison you.

∞ 8 ∞

MADI
PEABODY HOTEL
MEMPHIS, TENNESSEE
AUGUST 21, 1966

Jack and I are looking directly at the hostess when she vanishes. People at nearby tables who had been minding their own business before, focused on their food or their conversation, now have their eyes fixed on us. Are they thinking that it's far too early for anyone to be as drunk as we no doubt appear? Or did we just pop in out of nowhere from their perspective?

I clutch Jack's arm, struggling to stay on my feet as my stomach lurches again. He grabs me, but I think it may be as much for his own support as for mine. Judging from his expression and his sharp intake of breath, he's feeling the same thing I am.

And while I couldn't swear to it, I believe most of the faces looking toward us are different. The man who was busing the table is gone. Another guy, who looks to be in his early twenties, with pale skin and freckles, has taken his place. Or rather, taken his role, because he's now clearing a table one row over.

The walls are a different color, too, and there are now tiny vases on the tables, each holding a single yellow flower.

My nausea and dizziness gradually lessen. "Damn it," I whisper to Jack. "What happened this time?"

"No clue. But I think we're about to find out."

He nods toward the booth, which is no longer empty. Tyson Reyes is seated, facing us. I can see the orange glow of his CHRONOS key through the fabric of his dress shirt. He's wearing a blazer, but no tie. Aside from Jack, he's still the most informally dressed person in the restaurant. He gives me a grim smile when our eyes meet, and my stomach sinks again.

Someone clears her throat behind us, and I turn to see a young woman. Her hairdo is less poufy than the earlier hostess, but she's holding an identical clipboard and two menus. "I'm afraid our tables are full. I can put y'all on the list, if you'd like, but it'll be a long wait. Maybe y'all should try the diner down the street?"

There is definitely a hint of judgment in her last words. And she's lying. The restaurant is barely half-full. I see at least half a dozen empty tables and booths, far more than there were before the time shift.

Jack's arm stiffens slightly under my grasp. "My wife is a bit dizzy," he says coolly. "We're . . . expecting."

My first thought is *expecting what?* But then I realize he means I'm pregnant. Not the first excuse I'd have picked, but I roll with it, placing a protective hand on my abdomen.

"And we already have a table," I tell her, nodding toward Tyson. "We're meeting a friend."

"Oh." Her voice is still cool, but there's a hint of sympathy in her eyes. "Y'all have a seat, then, I guess. Get her off her feet."

The hostess plops the two menus onto the table as we slide into the booth. She says she'll be back with another menu for Tyson, but he gives her a broad smile and says it won't be necessary because he's been planning his order since he woke up. He uses the same folksy tone I've heard him adopt before when talking to locals.

It usually works rather well. Tyson is a good-looking guy, and he can slip effortlessly into a Deep South drawl. His charm offensive doesn't seem quite as effective on this waitress, however. There's a hint of wariness in her answering smile as she sizes him up. His hair is cropped close, just as it was the last time I saw him, but his eyes are brown today. He apparently decided to ditch the blue contacts that CHRONOS generally outfits him with when he's in time periods where race might limit his mobility. Tyson hadn't gone into much detail about that issue, simply stating that his genetic-design team decided to leave him "racially ambiguous" so he could research both sides of the civil rights movement, unlike the vast majority of historians whose race, along with quite a few other characteristics, is modified before birth so that they'll be a better fit for the research agenda they're eventually assigned. I'd gotten the distinct impression, though, that Tyson was tired of shifting race depending on which side of the movement he was currently tasked with researching.

I don't blame him. The whole thing feels offensive to me, even though he explained that racial norms are a bit different in his time. That seems reasonable. There are huge differences, after all, between my own time and this one. The Civil Rights Act of 1964 was passed only two years ago, and prior to that restaurants and hotels like this could legally refuse to serve customers based on skin color. Looking around, I can see there still seems to be quite a bit of bias, since Tyson is the darkest person in the dining room aside from the man clearing tables.

Correction. The man who *was* clearing tables before the time shift, who has now been replaced by a younger white guy. Which has me wondering about the status of civil rights in this timeline.

"How did you know we were in the restaurant?" Jack asks once the waitress is gone.

"I checked the room first. When I didn't find you there, I assumed you were down here."

It probably should have occurred to me earlier that Tyson, and most likely Richard and Katherine as well, has stable points set *inside* the hotel room Jack and I are using, since they were the previous occupants. Which means they could have viewed anything and everything that happened in the room over the past day and a half, including several occasions when Jack and I were engaged in . . . well, let's just call it mutual stress reduction. Hopefully, none of them has voyeuristic tendencies.

"And I'm starving," Tyson continues. "I've had to make five different jumps in order to get enough money to cover our breakfast and your room."

"But we have money. And Richard already . . . ," I begin and then realize what he means. "Oh."

"Yeah. Not in this reality. Have you had any luck using the CHRONOS key?"

I say yes at the same instant that Jack says no.

"He's had *limited* success," I amend. "And Lorena is going to work on a serum as soon as she gets some time at the lab."

"You probably shouldn't count on that," Tyson says, dropping his voice to a barely audible whisper. "I haven't been to 2136. None of us had a *Log of Stable Points* with us when the shift happened, so we're limited to what's on our keys. There are only two points on my key that were listed as stable for any year after 2100, and they're both inoperable now. The changes to the timeline are fairly massive that far out, and the odds of your friend still having that job are slim. You're sure they were under a CHRONOS field when the shift happened?"

I nod. "Lorena took the day off."

"But how can we know when it hits them?" Jack asks. "For that matter, how did you know when it would hit *us*?"

"The chronometer in the keys," Tyson says. "Apparently, the timing is linked to the connection between one of the clock genes in the CHRONOS alteration and the field that surrounds the key. Richard could probably explain it better—he's always had a more solid grasp of the whole temporal quantum-entanglement thing. But the gist of it is the medallions have an internal clock that is synced to all of the others. We felt it hit about thirty-six hours later . . . although it wasn't nearly as big of a physical jolt for us as it was for you just now, since 2304 is a lot further away from 1941. But the medallion has to be in contact with someone who has the gene to trigger the internal clock, and none of the people currently at your house have the CHRONOS gene, right?"

"Right," I say. "So . . . I calculate a day and a half out from the first time I went back to the house after we saved Lennon."

"Wasn't saving Lennon supposed to reset everything?" Jack asks Tyson.

"It did. Until our friends in the timeline next door decided it would be fun to break something else."

"I need to go home and check on them," I say. "Make sure they're okay."

Tyson nods. "Definitely. And then we need to get ourselves to a point in time where we can fix this."

"You mean that's what *you* need to do," Jack says. "Right? You and the other *trained* historians. Madi's not . . ." He trails off, shaking his head, because it's clear from Tyson's expression that I'm included in whatever plans he's making.

"Jack's right," I say. "Whatever just happened, I am *not* trained for this. We got lucky the other night. I'd be a liability, not an asset."

"I disagree strongly on that point," Tyson says. "I watched you in that attic in Montgomery. You have good instincts. I'm pretty sure I'd be dead if that wasn't true. But either way, I'm afraid the decision isn't mine. You're on the roster." He reaches down to the bench next to him and picks up a small diary that's sitting on top of a flat brown paper bag. The diary is virtually identical to the one currently in my backpack.

He opens it to a page near the back, then slides it across the table toward us, pointing to a link near the bottom. When I tap the link, a holographic display of a globe appears above the surface of the book. I glance around to the other tables nervously, even though I know the image is only visible to someone with the CHRONOS gene. Anyone else watching will just see me staring at an old book. Or, more accurately, they'll see me staring at a point a few inches *above* an old book. Odd perhaps, but not something that would set off alarm bells. And the others in the restaurant are completely oblivious to the fact that reality just shifted around them. Although it might be more accurate to say that reality shifted around *us*.

Based on the image hovering above the diary, I'm guessing the shift was caused by the United States opting out of World War II in this timeline. And the people who caused that temporal rift are cordially inviting me to help fix the damn thing.

I tilt the display toward Jack. He squints at it, almost like he needs reading glasses. I'm about to ask if he wants me to read it aloud when he pushes the diary back a few inches and says, "So, the US is a Nazi outpost now?"

"Technically, no."

I arch an eyebrow at Tyson. "I can't say I'm particularly liking the *technically* bit."

He slides the brown paper bag across the table. "A little reading for later. Don't let anyone see you with it. Although I'm pretty sure anyone who did see you with it would assume it was a joke, since the publication date is 2022."

I peek inside and find a paperback book with a yellow-and-black cover. On the bottom half of the cover is an oddly truncated outline of the United States, minus California and four other western states. Across the top is a title that begs the question why anyone would *want* to be seen with the book, even if it wasn't time-travel contraband— *The Complete Dummy's Guide to US History Since 1950.*

"Keep in mind," Tyson continues, "that the book is as much propaganda as it is history. But to give you the brief version, Hitler's forces stopped at the Atlantic Ocean. The Stars and Stripes are still flying outside, not the swastika. There aren't quite as many stars, because the country divided into socioeconomic zones. Germany kind of . . . mellowed, I guess, after Hitler died in 1952. And the US went in the other direction. Ideologically speaking, at this point, you'd be hard pressed to tell the difference between the US and the Third Reich, although our system has more odd religious quirks. Most people of color saw which way the tide was going and got the hell out while they still could. As for the long-term effects of the time shift, they're major and global. There's still a cold war of sorts, but what remains of the US is allied with Europe against China, Japan, and Russia. Sometimes, the cold war heats up, and we end up fighting in wars along the periphery of our territories."

Jack looks back at the display, squinting again. "I don't recognize some of the names on the other side, but Madi's not listed in either column."

"Morgen Campbell and his daughter, although I'm thinking this version of him is a clone for reasons I'll get to in a moment. Saul, obviously. I didn't see Esther Sowah in Memphis, but she's one of our historians," Tyson says. "And she's friendly with Saul in our timeline, so I'm not too surprised to see her in the mix on the opposing team. And then our team."

"I'm under the fake name I gave Katherine," I explain. "Thanks to *A Brief History of CHRONOS*, I couldn't use my real name, and we decided it might make more sense to tell Katherine I was from a future class of historians. God—what year did I even tell her? I can't remember."

"Pretty sure you told her 2318," Tyson says. "But I don't think we're going to be able to keep up that fiction. Katherine has already gotten a bit of false confidence from it, saying that we must win this round, too, otherwise there wouldn't be historians fourteen years into the future. She *knows* that's not how it works, but I think she's just grasping at any available straw right now."

"I can't really blame her for that. But I never spoke to *any* of the people from the other timeline. Katherine is the only person I gave that name to. How did it end up in their message?"

"That's a very good question," he says. "I'll add it to the list."

Tyson looks wiped out, and I kind of feel bad about bombarding him with even more questions. But he's the only source of information I have. "Could your computer system pinpoint exactly what was changed?"

"Oh, it probably could have, but it's gone missing. Along with the rest of CHRONOS."

My mouth falls open. I have the feeling that this shouldn't be possible, but it takes me a moment to pinpoint *why* it doesn't make sense. "All of it?"

"Everything," he says. "Building, people . . . if Rich, Katherine, and I hadn't been carrying keys, we'd be gone, too."

"But I thought the headquarters building was protected under a CHRONOS field," Jack says. "Same as Madi's house. How could it just vanish?"

Tyson goes on to explain the political situation in 2304, which Katherine's diaries had painted in a somewhat more idyllic light. "We think the government just . . . switched off the field around the agency. Angelo had already sent them our report and was headed over at that very moment to explain to them why doing something like that would be exceptionally stupid, since we're their only line of defense. But he didn't get a chance to make that argument."

"Without that report, you'll be flying blind," Jack says.

"Not exactly. We're fairly certain that two of the pivot points are that the Japanese never attack Pearl Harbor, and someone tries to kill

Charles Lindbergh. There's also something with a priest who's now a Cyrist, but that may be peripheral . . ."

I don't really hear much of what he says after the word *Cyrist*. Thea's caution during our call earlier is now echoing in my mind.

Just a hunch. The Book of Prophecy *says the next few days could be a teensy bit bumpy.*

FROM *THE BOOK OF CYRUS*
(NEW ENGLISH VERSION, 3RD ED)
CHAPTER 7:18–19

[18]To suckle the weak equally with the strong is folly. [19]There can be no true progress until we reject the foolish idea that the strong have a moral obligation to the weak.

∞9∞

A small line of people has already gathered outside the Objectivist Club when Richard and I finally get there. The Club doesn't open for nonresident members until noon in our timeline, and apparently, it's the same in this reality. That's never been an issue for Saul. Due in part to the fact that several members of his family are residents and in part to his friendly rivalry with Campbell, Saul comes and goes as he pleases.

I'm actually glad to see the line. Hopefully at least a few of them will be chatty, and we'll be able to gather some information about anything that might be different in this reality. That's the first thing they teach you as a historian. Your initial task is to listen and observe until you're comfortable and reasonably certain your interactions with the individuals from that era will seem natural and not in any way out of the ordinary. We already have one strike against us. While most sections of the OC in our timeline allow casual clothing, and the spa and pool are clothing optional, the Redwing Room and other exclusive areas have a more formal dress code. Judging from the people in front of us, I'm guessing that code extends to the entire club now. The outfit I'm wearing—narrow purple pants with a matching multicolored tunic—didn't seem at all outrageous when I selected it this morning, but it's horribly out of place here. Richard's attire isn't much better—he's in denim pants and a brown T-shirt that shows a bushy-haired man playing a flute bracketed by the words *Jethro Tull* at the top and *Living in the Past* at the bottom. The shirt is actually kind of amusing for a time traveler, especially one who studies music history, but it's a questionable choice when every other man in the line is wearing a coat and tie.

On the walk over, Rich and I agreed to play it by ear. If by some fluke we manage to get in, we'll use their resources to find more information and then inquire about Saul. I think it's far more likely we'll be stopped at the door, at which point I'll ask for Morgen, dropping a few bits of information that I hope are still true of this version of the OC's owner.

There are three groups of people in front of us. One is a cluster of men who are chatting about something I'm not following at all, mostly because their speech is peppered by a slew of acronyms and abbreviations. Behind them is a middle-aged couple in attire that reminds me a lot of the 1850s in terms of the drab color scheme, although the cut is more functional and modern. Something strikes me as odd about the woman's face, but I can't quite place what's bothering me. She's one of the few who's not wearing a mask—she has tiny nose filters inside her nostrils—but that's not what's sticking in my mind.

Directly in front of us is a younger couple, and judging from their conversation I'm going to guess that they're only planning to be a couple for a few hours. The clothing worn by the girl—and I'm using the word advisedly because she can't be much over eighteen—makes my outfit look modest. Her skirt is short enough that we're treated to a glimpse of her butt cheeks each time she takes a step. They're nice butt cheeks and I'm not easily offended, but I don't think the same can be said for the woman in front of them.

"I've been here a couple of times before," the girl tells her escort. "The last time was utterly lish. My friend took me on a shopping spree at one of the exclusive shops on the promenade before we went to our booth. The shops can print out an entire outfit, including jewelry, in under a minute. You have to see it."

The older woman glances back over her shoulder and gives the couple a poisonous look, but the girl continues talking, either oblivious to the woman's censure or simply not caring. Her companion notices, however, and flushes a deep red. "Sure," he says in a low voice. "Maybe we can stop by . . . after."

At exactly noon, the oldest member of the group of men at the front taps at the door with his cane. I'd thought the walking stick was just an affectation, but he stumbles slightly, and one of his companions grabs the old man's elbow to steady him. A few seconds later the door opens, and we file inside. The display on the right wall as we enter shows a static listing of locations inside the Club on one side and a slideshow of images showcasing the Club's features, many of which remain the same in this timeline. Most of the shops, the spa, and other recreational facilities take up the basement level, below the main restaurant and lobby. Redwing Hall, private booths, and the primary gaming complex are still on the second floor. Above that are several levels of offices, and the top twenty floors are member residences.

I expect to see the standard sentry system at the door. Usually, when you step inside, you simply stand there for a moment until the body scan is complete and then enter when the interior door opens. Or, in some cases, you leave because Morgen Campbell is no longer extending you credit. But today there's an impeccably dressed guy in his twenties standing just inside the doorway. His hair is parted in the middle and slicked down on either side in a fashion that was popular in the 1920s and had a brief, unfortunate resurgence a few years back. The group of men and the older couple in front of us must be regulars, because the doorman nods and waves them in without ceremony. He holds out a print reader to the younger man, who presses his thumb to the screen, looking a bit nervous. After a few seconds, the door opens. "Enjoy your evening, Mr. Walters." The young guy nods, placing his left hand on the girl's waist as they go through the door. A blue flower is tattooed on the back of his hand.

Richard looks every bit as nervous as the previous guy as he presses his thumb to the pad. When the door opens, the doorman says, "Ah, Mr. Vier. This appears to be your first visit?"

"Uh . . . yes." Rich seems to be trying to think of something else to say, but the doorman saves him the trouble.

"We have full reciprocity with the OCNYC, of course. Your charges will be posted to the account on file." His eyes then turn toward me, and he runs one hand across his well-oiled head as he takes in my outfit. "Will you be needing a private booth, or . . ."

"Oh, no," Richard says. "No. My wife and I were hoping to have lunch in the Redwing Room. We were at a costume event to raise money for . . . a friend who's running in the local alderman's race."

I smile at the doorman. "Yes. Silly me. I packed a second set of clothes but forgot to bring it with us. So we're going to need to visit the promenade first."

He nods. "By all means. The layout of the Club is very similar to that of our NYC facility, but feel free to stop at the information kiosk if you have trouble finding the services that you require, Mrs. Vier. Shall I reserve a table for two at twelve thirty, or will you need more time on the promenade?"

Richard tells him that twelve thirty will be fine. We step into the main lobby, a massive room that is even more opulent than the OC I'm used to. The place seems less crowded, too. Usually the main floor is bustling, since it's open to the public. But the crowds on the main level today are closer to what you normally see in the more exclusive upper rooms.

A lift tube carries us down to the basement, which doesn't look like a basement at all. The pool and faux beach that take up the left side of this level are similar to what I've seen in the past, but the ceiling in this reality has had a major upgrade. It now displays a clear summer sky with wispy clouds that float above the swimmers. Several small spa kiosks are arranged on the far side of the pool. The right half of the basement level contains an array of small specialty shops, including a bakery with a logo that looks a bit like the one on the box when Saul brings home pastries, but I'm pretty sure that one was called Foster's and this is Fason's. There's an ice-cream shop next to that, where a woman and two young girls are seated, each with an empty container of gelato in front of her, and each engaged with her own handheld device.

In our timeline, people run these kiosks, but none of the shops here are manned. I'm sure there are at least a few real live humans monitoring the cameras and making sure you only leave with what you've paid for, but to the casual observer, it looks like the honor system is alive and well at the Objectivist Club.

I rarely frequent the promenade shops at the OC. One advantage of being with CHRONOS is that we have fairly decent clothing printers at our disposal. When we're at HQ, we generally only wear the jumpsuits we refer to as scrubs, and it doesn't take a very complex printer to spit those out. Anything I can't put together in my quarters can be obtained in costuming for a few credits.

It takes only a couple of minutes, however, to locate the custom boutique our cheeky friend in the line outside the Club mentioned to her date. After thumbing through the menu, however, we realize it will take considerably more than a few credits to clothe the two of us. Richard shakes his head as he presses his thumb to the paypad. "Sure hope my *alternate* self has more credits in his account than I do. Or did."

The printer here is even larger than the one in costuming, and the girl was right about the speed. In less than five minutes, we're headed for the dressing rooms, new clothes in hand. We leave the shop in outfits that are close enough to the ones we saw on the sidewalk and in the lobby, but should also work for the late 1930s or early 1940s. A suit for Rich, and a tailored dress with a narrow, calf-length skirt for me. We make it to the Redwing Room with ten minutes to spare.

"Some things haven't changed." Richard nods toward the collection of animal trophies and portraits that decorates the walls. Most of the portraits are of stuffy old men, but there are a few stuffy old women in the mix, including a distant relative of Saul's family. At the very end is a portrait of Morgen Campbell when he was in his early thirties, looking virtually identical to the younger version that Tyson showed me through his CHRONOS key—stocky, but not yet fat, with dark hair, a slightly crooked nose, and a ruby signet ring on his pinky finger. The layout of the room is the same in this timeline—a three-story atrium surrounded by tall trees and other greenery that partially obscures the offices that surround the room on the upper floors.

The hostess, a stunning young woman with auburn hair, tells us that our table will be ready soon and asks whether we'd prefer to wait in the bar or stroll around the game room. We choose the latter, because if Saul is here, he'll either be there, showing off his skills to other time-chess players, or else in Morgen's quarters, engaged in one of their mano-a-mano showdowns.

But he's not here, I remind myself. *He's not with Campbell, either. You know that he can't be. This is just so you can tell yourself that you looked. That you didn't leave without at least attempting to find him.*

It only takes a couple of minutes to loop around the game room, which isn't crowded, and I'm able to confirm that Saul isn't at any of the consoles. And the odds of him being with Campbell this early in the day are really slim, since Campbell is a night owl. The guy is rarely even awake this time of day, and he doesn't like to play until he's eaten and taken his stimulants.

Rich is quiet as we walk through the game room. He knows me well enough to understand why I have to do this, even though we both know this is almost certainly a complete waste of time. When we return to the Redwing Room, the hostess leads us toward one of the small tables on the periphery, near what most of us at CHRONOS call Morgen's throne, the slightly raised platform upon which the fat gox holds court at the various social gatherings he hosts, usually with that ancient Doberman at his feet. The throne is empty today, and it may be the first time I've ever had mixed feelings on that point. At least once a year, he holds exclusive gatherings for CHRONOS historians in this room. Most of us don't like the man, but the food is good, he serves real alcohol, and we know everyone else will be here. So we tolerate his questions and, in the case of female historians, his leering glances and the occasional bit of innuendo.

"You okay?" Richard asks. His brows are knitted in concern, his gray eyes slightly magnified by the lenses of his horn-rimmed glasses.

That's when I realize what was odd about the older woman's face in the line outside. She was wearing glasses, like Rich. Hers had silver rims, but they made her eyes look kind of small, so I don't think they were cosmetic. Now that I think about it, I've seen several other people in glasses, too. In our timeline, Rich's glasses are an oddity. One of the things he hates about Q&A sessions is that kids want him to take them off so they can look through them. The design team purposefully left him with substandard vision to add a touch of realism to his character when he travels, something that annoys him to no end. But the sort of defect that they added in his case is one that would be resolved with a modification before birth or, in rare cases, with a series of simple surgeries. Mods like that are freebies, so routine that they don't count as the chosen gift each child is granted automatically. The old man's cane was a bit odd, too, thinking back.

Age-related mobility problems are generally handled by shoes that project a force field designed to steady the wearer.

"Richard, have you seen anyone with obvious genetic modifications? Or tech implants? I haven't even seen a tat communicator, just people with watchbands or handheld units."

"You're right," he says. "In fact, the only tattoos I've seen at all are those small lotus tattoos. About a third of the people I saw in the game room were wearing them. I'm trying to think if there's ever been a time I was in Redwing Hall and didn't see at least a few people flaunting their cosmetic chosen gifts."

The entire purpose of the chosen-gift system is to prepare a child for his or her career. Absent a bribe or political connections, the chosen gift is determined by the government in order to fill specific job quotas. In most cases, families save up to pay that bribe, because investing wisely in a chosen gift is one way to break out of your economic class. About once a generation, the Solons pass laws that require strict adherence to the rules of the International Genetic Alterations Accords. The bribe taking stops for a year or two, and then gradually ratchets upward again.

Wealthy families, however, often select a chosen gift that isn't related to any field of work, or even the arts. It's fashionable to pick a gift that people can see, a gift that is ostentatious and strictly for show, simply to point out that you have so much money your offspring don't need a practical chosen gift. There's a whole shopping list of modifications to choose from. Saul said he knew a guy growing up who could change colors to match his surroundings. A woman who lives at the OC in our timeline has wings. They're not functional, merely for show—golden, glittery things that she flutters during conversations the same way many people talk with their hands. I've always wondered if she's happy with the choice her parents made for her, but that's not the kind of thing you ask.

We take a minute to look at the menu. I really can't imagine eating anything, so soup might be the safest option. As I tap the display to close the menu, however, I get the feeling that someone is watching me. No. It's more like they're scanning me. Richard must feel it, too, because he glances at something over my shoulder.

"Fuck," he says. "Sutter. And he still has the eye."

I can't bring myself to turn and look, but it's a moot point. Sutter is at our table a few seconds later, along with two guys who are nearly as well muscled as Tate Poulsen. And Richard was right about Sutter's prosthetic eye. It looks slightly different to me, but I've never spent much time looking directly at Sutter—no one does if they're smart. Sutter points something that looks like an old-fashioned ink pen at Richard. One of his two muscle-bound bookends steps forward to grab Richard's arm, and the other grabs mine. "Not sure what game you two are playing," Sutter says as he reaches for Rich's backpack, "but it's over."

I'm tempted to pull out my CHRONOS key right now, but I'm pretty sure that would be a major mistake, since there's a decent chance that Sutter and his lackeys will assume we're going for weapons. Plus, it takes a couple of seconds to lock in a stable point, so I guess we'll have to wait for an opportunity to blink out.

Sutter motions for the guards to follow him. Every eye in the place is on us as we're hauled out of the restaurant toward the lift. We exit on the third floor and are marched down the corridor that overlooks the Redwing Room. As I glance down to see if the other diners are still watching us, I spot a man emerging from the game room. Tall and thin, with short dark hair and a pale complexion. It *could* be Saul, but I can't see his face through the branches of the trees, and the security guard keeps dragging me forward.

"My legs aren't as long as yours! Could you stop for a second?" To my surprise, the guard listens. I take a step backward and can now see the doorway.

The man who might have been Saul is gone. So is the guard's patience. "Move it," he says.

Sutter stops at an office a few yards ahead of us. He presses his thumb against the pad, and the door opens, revealing a small cubicle with a desk and three chairs. We're pushed into the two chairs in front of the desk, and Sutter takes the third, facing us so that we get the full effect of that freaky, pulsating eye. Right after his butt hits the seat, his head jerks up and he taps the comm-disk behind his ear.

He listens for a moment, then looks over at the guards who are standing near the door. "Go up and check on Campbell. He was due in Redwing a half hour ago. We may have a . . . situation." The slight disapproving twist of his mouth tells me that there's another similarity in this timeline. Morgen Campbell has a deep and abiding love of stimulants, which necessitates other drugs to help him sleep. Saul has, on numerous occasions, arrived at Campbell's quarters for a scheduled game, only to find the man barely conscious.

"You want both of us to go?" the guard on the left asks, giving the two of us a brief glance.

Sutter chuckles once and taps the pen thing he's holding against the desk. "I think I can handle this."

When the guards are gone, Sutter clips the pen gadget to his shirt pocket and begins rummaging through Rich's backpack. I hold my breath, expecting him to pull out Rich's CHRONOS diary and start inspecting it. He does, briefly, but it doesn't work for him, and his attention seems to be on something else in the bag. He extracts a bottle with Latin words on the label and holds it up to the light. "Can't say I recognize the brand. But since there are no outside beverages allowed in the OC, I'll just be keeping this." There doesn't appear to be anything else in the bag that interests him, so he tosses it aside and pushes a button on the desk. A display appears on the wall behind him. It's a picture of a young guy. He's very handsome. In fact, he reminds me quite a bit of an actor I stumbled upon while researching a jump to the 1930s. I can't remember the man's name, but he played Heathcliff in *Wuthering Heights*.

"Richard Vier . . . meet Richard Vier. Do you want to explain to me how your fingerprints are a match for his? Because you're sure as hell not identical twins, and I don't think Mr. Vier is going to be especially happy when our New York branch informs him about the tab you're running up on his account. And you . . ." He turns the eye toward me. Well, both eyes, but they move slightly out of sync, and I'm not particularly worried about the ordinary one. "You're not in the system at all. Either you're not a citizen or someone paid to scramble your data. Which is it?"

I open my mouth, not entirely sure what I'm going to say, but Sutter holds up one hand. "I've got a feeling your story is going to be the more interesting of the two, so why don't you let him go first, sweetheart?"

"She's not your sweetheart," Rich says calmly, both hands clasped in his lap. "And we're not telling you a damn thing."

I shoot him a look, trying to figure out why he's trying to rile Sutter up. True, he'll almost certainly know that anything we tell him is a lie, but I thought we were playing for time, waiting for a few seconds unobserved so that we could use the key. But then Rich's forefinger reaches up to a tiny button on the Timex watch Angelo gave each of us before we left for Memphis. An instant later, Sutter's head thuds against the desk.

"I forgot all about the watches. Wish I'd had the forethought to wear mine."

Rich grins. "It wasn't exactly forethought. I just forgot to take it off last night." He stuffs the diary and bottle back into his backpack, then tugs on the chain inside his shirt to pull out his CHRONOS key. "Shall we?"

"Yes, but . . . hold on." I take a few steps toward Sutter and unclip the tiny pen gadget he was aiming at us when he told the guards to take us away. I have no idea what it is or how to use it, but it's almost certainly a weapon.

"Good idea," Richard says. "We can figure out how to use it later."

I take one final look at the doorway before pulling up the stable point in Memphis. There are plenty of tall, dark-haired men in any reality. The guy I saw out there couldn't have been Saul. All of the keys, with the exception of the three Tyson, Rich, and I were wearing, were locked in the operations suite, so there's no way he could have survived the time shift. There's still a tiny, niggling doubt, which I'm pretty sure is going to echo in my head, however, and I consider setting a local stable point for this office so I can come back and silence it. But I push the temptation aside. It would be a distraction, and I need to focus. My best hope of getting Saul back—of getting my parents, Angelo, and everyone I know back—is to reverse this damned time shift. And as Tyson said earlier, we can only do that in the past.

FROM *THE TEMPORAL DILEMMA USER'S GUIDE*, 2ND ED (2293)

Appendix B: Style Points

As most TD players are aware, games often end without a temporal change. In such cases, victory is determined by game points, which are awarded for the achievement of concrete, stated objectives and subobjectives. (See appendix A for details.)

With the release of Temporal Dilemma 1.6, a new component was added to the scoring rubric: style points. Without that twist, TD would be far less challenging and, we would argue, far less exciting!

There are five major categories of style points:

1. **Character Assist:** Pull major historical characters into your simulation. Bored with simple assassination plots? Convince someone else to do the dirty work, and rack up the style points!

2. **Chronological:** Give your simulation an extra layer of complexity by restricting your moves to a small

window of time. Bonus: Make your moves in reverse chronological order.

3. **Geographic:** Limit your moves to a specific continent, country, or state. Bonus options: All moves in one city and/or within a 1- or 5-kilometer radius.

4. **Social Movement:** Utilize existing political, religious, and social organizations. Bonus: Create your own political party, religion, or social movement to change the timeline.

5. **Government:** Unseat a major political leader at the ballot box. Bonus: Achieve your objective through legislation and litigation alone. (Expert mode only.)

6. **Probability:** TD runs millions of background calculations, assigning a probability that any given move will affect the timeline. Receive up to fifty bonus points for each move played by a winning player or team that has a probability of less than 10 percent effectiveness if taken alone. Combine tried-and-true methods with something totally off-the-wall, and watch those probability points rack up!

The examples here are just a few of the ways you can achieve style points. See the full catalog for additional options. When playing in Assist mode, the computer will recommend actions that could help you accumulate style points, or you can browse the index on your own (alphabetized, by category, with numerical values). Play with style and watch your win ratio soar!

∞10∞

I blink. We'd been keeping our voices low since Madi and Jack sat down at the booth, but apparently, we weren't keeping them low enough. Two women at the table across the aisle are now staring directly at me. I take a bite of my pecan pancakes and then continue in a slightly louder voice, "And then in act two, it will look like Tony, the James Darren character, is actually the one who shot Lindbergh. My friend seems to think we can sell it, assuming *Time Tunnel* is green-lighted for a second season. He came really close with his script for *The Green Hornet* a few months back. Actually got it into the hands of a janitor at the studio who's convinced the producers to buy scripts in the past. And the janitor only charged Lewis fifty bucks because he really liked the story, but the studio passed on it. It'll probably cost more this time, but split between the four of us, it shouldn't be too bad."

Neither Madi nor Jack has the slightest idea what I'm talking about. There's a very real possibility that the eavesdroppers don't, either. In our timeline, the ads for the upcoming series *Time Tunnel* have been running for several weeks. I saw one plastered to the inside of a bus stop near Mid-South Coliseum. Given the magnitude of the changes, I doubt the TV schedule for 1966 is exactly the same, but hapless writers must still be trying to sell screenplays in this reality because one of the women chuckles, and when I risk a glance back at their table, they've both returned to focusing on their breakfast.

For the next few minutes, we do the same. I make random comments about the fictional script between bites. Madi and Jack mostly just move stuff around on their plates and nod at appropriate intervals. By the time I finish my pancakes and move on to the scrambled eggs, our eavesdroppers are gone.

"I don't know how you can eat," Madi says.

Jack agrees. "It still feels like someone punched me in the stomach."

"I've had a bit of time to adjust to the news."

"No," Madi says. "I meant *physically*. You didn't feel the shift?"

"Felt it back in the courtyard at HQ—well, what used to be HQ, but not just now. You only get the jolt once, and we were further removed from the triggering event, so it was a fairly mild one. I don't think it would matter either way, though. There's only so long the body can go without fuel. All I've had is a candy bar since breakfast and that was . . ." I stop to tally up the hours since Rich and I had breakfast. "About thirteen hours ago. Like I said, I've had to be creative. If we get stranded, we're supposed to head to the nearest CHRONOS safety-deposit box. There's one in most major cities, usually at the oldest major bank. Not that anyone has ever *been* stranded before this, but that's the stated protocol we learn in training. You're supposed to pick a new identity packet from the collection, along with some starter cash, and then you assimilate as best you can. But when I got there, I discovered there are subtle differences in the currency and—"

"Wait." Jack looks confused. "If the agency was erased, if it never existed, then those safety-deposit boxes shouldn't exist. Right?"

Madi shakes her head. "They should still be there. The diaries—"

She falls silent as the waitress approaches the table to see if we need anything else. We tell her no, and she heads off to get our check. I could actually do with another stack of pancakes, but cash flow is going to be an issue for us at any point after 1941.

"Are you planning to finish that?" I ask Madi, nodding toward her mostly untouched waffle.

"No. Help yourself." Then she looks back at Jack. "As I was saying, though, the diaries have a CHRONOS field, and they leave a diary in the box."

I'm about to ask how she knows that, when she turns to me and adds, "But what if the bank was never built? I mean, that has to have happened in at least a few cases, right? What happens to the box?"

"Good question. Probably the box continued to be in that same location when the shift occurred. Which means a number of people back in the early 1800s or whenever found a curious box they couldn't open. But that's just a guess. Anyway, I had to go back to a point before the rift caused all of these changes and get cash there, then find a place after the rift that was willing to trade in old bills, at a massive markup, of course. I was hoping to get up enough so that you could rent a place outside of town, somewhere you won't encounter so many people, but . . . maybe we can find a smaller hotel. We need to get you out of here, though. Hope you didn't have anything of value in the other room, because unless it was under a CHRONOS field, it's gone. And . . . both of you, don't take those medallions off. Sleep with them. Shower with them."

Color drains from their faces as they get my point.

"Are you sure?" Madi says. "I mean, did you check our birth records?"

"In your case, I think it's obvious. I haven't checked Jack's status yet. But we have to go on that assumption, at least until we can get somewhere advanced enough to check that sort of data. I was thinking maybe your place could be the new CHRONOS HQ. We're going to need a base of operations."

"If it's just you," Madi says, "then sure. But Katherine is the original owner of the house I live in. She'll be in her seventies when she purchases it, and there have been some renovations since then, but having her see the place seems like a very bad idea. And she can't know who I am. That could really screw up the timeline."

"Madi, I think you're going to find that the timeline is already pretty screwed up, both now and in 2136."

"But not *permanently*," Jack says. "The goal is to fix this. And you could unravel the whole chain of events that leads to CHRONOS being founded if Katherine changes course and Madi's ancestors aren't born. She wouldn't even exist outside of a key."

"True. But that's the case for all of us right now. And our options are limited, both in terms of time and money."

Jack looks like he's about to protest further, but Madi holds up her hands. "Fine. You're right. I'll try to keep things vague with Katherine, but . . . CHRONOS being erased probably changes everything anyway. As a heads-up, though, I don't think you're going to be impressed with our tech. The Anomalies Machine seems ancient even to me."

I pull the SimMaster from my jacket pocket. "We'll have to make do. The bigger issue is going to be patching this into your existing network and coming up with three initial predictions in a matter of hours. They apparently racked up the style points. She said they maxed out chronological and geographic, with bonuses."

Jack shakes his head. "What does that even mean?"

"I'm not entirely sure," I admit. "I don't have the full list of style categories, but I do know that to max out geographic, you have to confine your moves to a single city. And based on some of the changes we saw in those videos in 2304, I think we can safely guess that the city is New York. When we get to your place, I'll see if I can nail it down further. But first, we need to find a place for Jack."

"I'll be fine," he says. "As Madi pointed out a few minutes ago, she can just come to this moment and tell me how things went. Not like I can be of much use." There's a hint of bitterness in his voice, and Madi gives him a hurt look.

"That's not what I meant, Jack."

He sighs. "I'm sorry. That came out wrong. I'm just—"

"You're frustrated," I say. "You want to help. That's good. We're going to need all the help we can get. Even if you can't jump, you can assist with research and monitor the stable points. And . . . you can't stay here. Once the game officially starts, you'll have a target on your back. According to Campbell's daughter, Saul didn't take too kindly to you . . . ," I stop, lowering my voice even further. "To you *removing* one of his observers from the last match."

"But . . . I did the same thing," Madi says.

I shrug. "Morgen is apparently less put out about losing pawns. Because that's how they look at these observers. Alisa is hard to pin down on anything, but I got the sense that professional players use them as a revenue stream, since they pay for the privilege of tagging along, and/or use them in dangerous situations where they don't want to put their own necks on the line. I'm guessing they each had at least five in the field, probably more, because Alisa kept emphasizing that they were limiting the upcoming game to just five, like that was some sort of huge restriction. And it's a totally moot point, since we don't have five other people who can use the key. To be honest, though, Jack, even without this complication, I'd have suggested getting you out of here. You're likely to attract attention if you're here for more than a day or so. Your accent, mostly." I nod toward the table where the nosy women had been sitting. "That's probably what attracted their attention as much as what we were talking about."

Madi looks at Jack and then back at me. "*His* accent? You're kidding. He barely has one. You'd think mine would be more of a problem."

"He sounds Californian, and the West Coast states seceded to join Canada when the US signed the nonaggression pact with Germany in 1944. The California border is one of the spots where there are still fairly frequent skirmishes. Your accent may be more pronounced, but they won't be able to place it. It's more New York or maybe British, and the Brits are allies."

"I've never even lived in New . . . York . . ." Madi's eyes widen and she reaches into her bag to pull out a familiar-looking diary. "Do you have enough cash for a train or bus ticket to upstate New York? Jack won't even have to hide what he's doing," she says as she begins scanning through the diary's pages. "In fact, they might be able to help."

"You *know* someone?" Jack says. "In 1966?"

"Family. Sort of. I haven't actually met them yet. The place where they live has a weird name . . . hold on a sec."

I'm glad to hear it's not someone she's close to, because she's not thinking this through. "Madi, anyone connected to CHRONOS is gone. They never even existed. So if these people are descended from historians, I don't think you're going to find them."

"They're under CHRONOS keys."

"Oh. You're sure?"

She hesitates for a moment and shrugs. "As sure as I can be of anything right now, which is admittedly far from certain. The diary written by my great-great-grandmother Kate Pierce-Keller said that Kiernan and Kate Dunne took three keys back to 1912. Kate Dunne is the one that I mentioned to you before, Tyson, when I said that I knew of someone who was sort of a . . . duplicate, I guess, from another version of our timeline. Anyway, there's a photo album of their family back in my grandfather's library in Bethesda. They were under a CHRONOS field until they died, at which point the keys were returned to Kate—that is, to the version of Kate who is my ancestor. You, Rich, and Katherine were under keys and you still exist, so it seems more than likely that they do as well." A few seconds more of searching in the diary and then she says, "Skane—Skaneateles, although I may be mangling that pronunciation. There's a stable point in Seneca Falls, which is fairly close by. I'll head there after I check on Alex and the others."

"You should probably contact them *prior* to 1941," Tyson says. "Otherwise, logistics could be a bit difficult."

Jack frowns, clearly trying to puzzle something out. "But . . . will they have felt the shift yet? I mean, if she goes back to before it happens."

I have to think about that one for a moment. "I honestly have no idea. If I had to guess, I'd say no. Maybe they'll feel it about thirty-six hours before the critical event that flips the timeline? But again, I'm just guessing."

"Too bad," Jack says. "It will probably be easier for Madi to make her case if they know there's been a major timeline alteration. Do you really think these people will be willing to take on a houseguest they don't even know?"

Madi shrugs. "Only one way to find out."

I pay the check, and we head toward the exit. The hostess who gave all of us the stink eye earlier is at the door. She tells us to enjoy the rest of our day in a bored, flat tone, but she's still watching me in a way that *almost* makes me regret not wearing the blue contact lenses. I'm glad I won't be staying long. The original 1966 was unfriendly enough to someone of mixed race, but this new version is several orders of magnitude worse.

Once we're in the corridor leading out to the lobby, I pull a bundle of papers and a hotel key from my jacket pocket and hand them to Jack. "These are your IDs and a marriage license. Stop by the front desk and present the license to the clerk, otherwise the purity police aren't going to let the two of you into the elevator together. Don't wave the papers about too much. We're lucky it's the mid-sixties instead of a few years later when they shift to photo identification, but these still won't hold up to much scrutiny. Oh, one more thing . . ." I reach into my pocket and give Madi a handful of temporary tattoos. "Each one of these lasts a few days, although you can remove them sooner with alcohol. They'll save you a lot of hassle."

Madi stares at the tiny pink and blue lotus flowers in her palm. "You've got to be kidding me."

"Nope. And there will almost certainly be a *Book of Cyrus* in the nightstand, right next to the Bible. If you guys aren't up to speed on your early twenty-first-century cults, you might want to give it a quick skim."

I check the time. "Rich and Katherine are going to be at the stable point in less than a minute. I need to get up there and fill them in. We'll meet you at your place, Madi."

She nods and they leave, taking a right toward the front desk. I turn left, heading for the steps that lead up to the stable point on the mezzanine. I'm directly in front of the fountain when two shots ring out in rapid succession. Something whizzes past my head, and the ducks, who were swimming happily only a moment before, issue a chorus of loud squawks. Their reaction time is only slightly faster than that of the humans in the lobby, who scream and scurry to take cover behind the sofas and chairs clustered around the room.

If I'd been walking just a bit faster, I'd probably have seen the sniper. Instead, the upper section of the fountain blocks my view— although not as much as it would have a few seconds earlier. A chunk is now missing from the top basin. That's probably what zipped past my head, not a bullet.

Jack and Madi were not close enough to any large pieces of furniture to take cover, but they're crouched in front of the registration desk. Neither of them seems to have been hit, but the guy just to Jack's left wasn't as lucky. He's still conscious, but sprawled flat on the marble floor, with a rapidly widening bloodstain on the right shoulder of his shirt. I motion toward the back exit and mouth the word *go*, hoping Madi takes my meaning. The papers in Jack's pocket would probably get them past hotel security, but they are not going to hold up under the full scrutiny of the national police, and the clerk is already dialing.

Madi grabs Jack's arm, and they sprint toward the hallway near the elevator. I go in the opposite direction toward the stairs. Richard and Katherine are already there, standing at the railing. Through the balusters, I spot something that looks very much like a body on the floor in front of them. I glance over my shoulder to the lobby, where the two security guards are now huddled next to the injured man.

I take the stairs two at a time. When I reach the top, Richard is pulling Katherine toward the alcove that hides the stable point. She's holding something about the size of a ballpoint pen. Her eyes are fixed on the shape next to the railing, which is indeed a body, sprawled on top of a rifle. A smoking hole at the center of the man's shirt exposes a bloody crater with blackened edges beneath it. An odor that can only be burning flesh fills the air. I can see the purple glow of a CHRONOS medallion shining through the fabric of the dead man's back pocket. So much for Alisa's assumption that Saul would wait until the timer started.

My CHRONOS key is already out when I reach Katherine and Rich. "Give me your keys!" I press the back of my medallion to Richard's and load the stable point Madi gave me. "Transfer it to Katherine. I have to get rid of the body."

"You don't have time!" Katherine says, nodding toward the lobby below. One of the two security officers is now heading this way, gun drawn.

"Just go! I'll be right behind you."

I crouch down, hoping the railing obscures my movement and gives me a bit of cover. The officer begins yelling for me to halt as my hand slips inside the man's pocket and closes around the medallion. I roll away from the body, which vanishes the instant it's outside the

CHRONOS field. The rifle, however, doesn't. The cop is now pounding up the stairs. So I do the only thing I can and pull up the location on my key. I can see Katherine and Rich standing inside a living room. Rich is still inside the stable point.

The officer is at the top of the stairs now, raising his gun, his finger on the trigger. If Richard doesn't move, any jump I attempt to that time and place will fail. But I don't have the second it would take to check.

Time for a leap of faith.

FROM *A BRIEF HISTORY OF TIME TRAVEL*, 4TH ED (2302)

The proposal for the merger of the Chrono-Historical Research Organization (CHRO) and the Natural Observation Society (NOS) received approval from the International Temporal Security Council (ITSC) in 2247, following several years of negotiations and despite numerous objections from several member states. A member of the council from the African Union, who asked for anonymity, stated there was a strong sense that the United States would remove itself from the treaty if some accommodations were not made to allow for human historical research, and the council eventually determined it was better to keep the United States within a weakened treaty rather than have it operating entirely outside the guidelines, which could easily result in increased global interest in acquiring and possibly exploiting the technology. The Natural Observation Society was gradually gaining strength within the US and had a cadre of human subjects ready to begin research as soon as the merger was green-lit. The conditions set by the ITSC were that the safeguards proposed by the NOS, including posttravel temporal monitoring, be strictly enforced, and that the number of historians authorized to travel in any given era be limited to thirty-six, less than half of the number originally proposed.

Initially, historians were restricted to the study of US history only, but this was waived after a decade with no apparent incidents. Historians were pulled into CHRONOS from allied countries, and the research gradually expanded to include all parts of the globe, although there is still a rather distinct North American bias to the research.

Despite approval of the merger and research program, several member states lodged objections in writing, noting that a number of the supposed safeguards were flawed. For example, one provision was that a council member of the ITSC be provided with a CHRONOS key so that they could monitor whether there were changes to the timeline. Some critics noted that having a single person or even a small number of individuals as monitors would leave the system susceptible to bribery. Others pointed out that while the medallion issued to the temporal-security monitor clearly does emit *a* temporal field, there is no guarantee that it is the *same* temporal field being used by CHRONOS.

∞11∞

MADI
MEMPHIS, TENNESSEE
AUGUST 21, 1966

The air is thick with the smell of diesel smoke, which billows from the exhaust of the long silver bus idling at the curb of the terminal. It looks old, and I doubt the inside smells any better, but I'll be glad once Jack is inside and on the road. While I'm fairly certain we weren't followed, standing out here in the open is making me nervous. I keep hearing the echo of that rifle in the lobby.

We got really lucky with the bus schedule. The first leg of Jack's trip ends in Nashville, and that bus was due to depart just fifteen minutes after we arrived at the station. If we'd missed it, he'd have been hanging out here until late afternoon.

"I wish I could come with you," I say. It's true, even though I know thirty-four hours on a bus will be miserable, even without the eleven hours of layovers he's stuck with due to scheduling gaps at his transfer points.

"Me, too," he says. "But we barely had enough for a single ticket."

He's right. Between the cab fare to the bus station and the ticket to Geneva, New York, that we just purchased, we're down to only six dollars and a handful of change from the money Tyson gave us at the hotel.

I sigh. "It's probably for the best. I've got work to do. I need to polish up my powers of persuasion, otherwise this bus ride is going to be kind of pointless."

"At least it's getting me out of Memphis. I don't know what happened up on the mezzanine, but I'm guessing it wasn't good."

That's probably an understatement, based on Katherine's expression a few seconds after she arrived at the stable point in my living room in 2136 Bethesda. I watched through the key to see if they made it, and Katherine seemed to be in shock. Rich looked stunned, as well, and Tyson arrived flat on his back a split second after Rich cleared the stable point. I was tempted to jump forward to find out exactly what happened, because I know Jack is curious. But he'll have to stay that way until tomorrow evening. We have no clue how many times I'll have to use this key over the next two days. Adding in jumps just to satisfy our curiosity seems like a bad idea when I don't really know what my limits are.

"I'll meet you at the station in Geneva tomorrow. That's the closest station to Seneca Falls. If the Dunnes can't or won't take you in, we'll find someplace else."

The bus driver is about to close the door. I give Jack one last kiss, earning a look of stern disapproval from the driver. Apparently public displays of affection aren't acceptable conduct in this timeline. Jack hurries up the stairs and makes his way to the middle of the bus, but there aren't any window seats open, so I don't know if he sees me waving as the smoke-belching beast pulls onto the street.

When the bus is out of sight, I go around the corner, set my key for twenty minutes prior to the time Tyson and the others will arrive, and blink. When I open my eyes, I'm back in the house in Bethesda. I pull in a deep breath of blessedly smoke-free air. The foyer is empty, so I go upstairs to the library, the one room where I can usually count on finding at least one person, since Alex rarely leaves his computers. And sure enough, he's still there, despite his earlier assurance that he'd try to get some sleep.

"Jarvis," I say as I enter the room, "set a timer for nineteen minutes. Then page Lorena and RJ and ask them to join me in the library."

"Yes, mistress."

Alex looks up. "A group meeting. Not good news, I'm guessing, since you don't have Jack with you."

"Jack's okay, but no. It's not good news." I cross over to my great-grandfather's desk on the far side of the library. The mere sight of the desk, piled high with books and notes from my research, triggers a twinge of you-should-be-working-on-your-thesis guilt. Which is stupid, given everything that's currently going on, but then guilt generally isn't rational. For all I know, my thesis advisor might not even exist in this new reality. Hell, Georgetown might not exist.

"Jarvis, how many people lived in Skaneateles, New York, in the 1930s? And how far is it from Seneca Falls?"

He corrects my pronunciation—it's apparently *skan-ee-AT-ah-less*, rather than *ska-NEAT-a-less*. "The population in 1930 was 4,725. The town is approximately twenty miles from Seneca Falls."

I yank open the top drawer of the desk. An envelope of 1930s-era cash is stashed inside. I grab a few of the bills and put the money in my bag, along with the *Log of Stable Points*.

"Is public transportation between those two cities easily accessible in 1930?"

There's a short delay, and then Jarvis says, "I'm sorry. Public-transportation data for that time period is unavailable."

"I'm going to take that as a no, then." I'm not really confident enough in my knowledge of that era to risk wandering around asking for directions, so I start scanning the shelves, looking for the photo album I spotted a week or so back.

When I first saw this library seven months ago, I'd thought that the soft amber glow inside the bookshelves that line these walls was designed to protect the hundreds of old books in the collection from harsh lighting. That was before I found the CHRONOS key and realized that the glow from the shelves is the same shade as the medallion is for me. The temporal shield that surrounds the house and most of the yard emanates from this room. Alex says that he's pretty sure the library was once the only protected area, and whoever created the field around the house just expanded on what was here.

I locate the photo album two sections over and flip through. Sure enough, there's an article from 1923 a few pages in, with a picture of Kate Dunne taking part in a Seneca Falls pageant celebrating the seventy-fifth anniversary of the first women's rights convention. The article says that the women marched from the tiny church where the Seneca Falls Declaration was signed to the larger Trinity Episcopal Church on the banks of Van Cleef Lake for the rest of the ceremony.

That was definitely the article I remembered seeing, but I was hoping it would be a bit closer to the date of the time shift, so I keep flipping through the pages. The next image is dated 5/18/29 and shows a pretty, dark-haired girl in a cap and gown in front of a sign that reads *Skaneateles Central High School*. Two pages over, there's one of Kiernan Dunne and his two sons, all three drenched to the bone, stacking sandbags along the shore of that same church twelve years after the suffrage pageant. *Preparing for Floods. Trinity Church. 6/6/35.*

Bingo.

RJ clears his throat at the doorway. "Is something wrong? Lorena's trying to get Yun Hee down for a nap."

"It's okay. Might be better to have you break the news to her anyway."

"That doesn't sound good in the slightest," he says genially, sinking down onto the couch. "Jack's okay, isn't he?"

"Last I saw him, yes. Someone fired at us in the lobby of the hotel, but they missed. We were able to slip out the back, and Jack is now on a bus from Memphis to upstate New York. I need to head to that area circa 1935 so that I can convince Kate and Kiernan Dunne to take him in thirty-one years later. Three historians from CHRONOS are going to arrive in our living room in about fifteen minutes, and the Anomalies Machine is going to start going crazy at some point between now and then."

I launch into a more detailed explanation, and about halfway through, both Alex and RJ wince. A second later, the display connected to the ancient computer in the corner blinks on. I don't feel the jolt again, so apparently Tyson is correct about it only hitting you once.

Alex curses, shoving the virtual displays aside. We join him at the Anomalies Machine, watching as lines of data scroll upward so quickly that it's hard to even tell they're composed of words.

"Can that computer handle this much data?" RJ asks. "It's even older than the one Grandma had in her attic."

Alex nods. "I made some adjustments. It's feeding into the main system now. I was going to disconnect the old display, but I didn't have time. Were they able to figure out what was changed before CHRONOS was erased?"

"Some of it. You can ask them yourself. They'll be here shortly."

"Not Katherine, though . . . right?"

I'm in complete sympathy with the look of alarm in his eyes. The idea of Katherine being here, in a house she purchased 130-some years ago, when she was about five decades older than the woman who will land in my living room in a few minutes, feels inherently wrong to me, as well. I'm quite certain we're setting ourselves up for a whole new batch of problems.

"Katherine, too," I say. "I don't like it, either, but we're short on options. Time is limited, and we need a base of operations with modern technology. Well, not modern from their perspective, but still far better than anything we'll find in 1940. And speaking of technology, can you extend the CHRONOS field on one of the diaries on the shelves the way you were planning to do for Lorena? You won't have to worry about whether it can get through security scans, since I'll be taking it back to well before those were even a thing."

"No promises," Alex says, "but I'll see what's in the cabinets to work with."

After he retreats back into his den of digital displays, RJ heads off to fill Lorena in on what's happened, and I go up to my room to put on the one and only dress I own that isn't several centuries ahead of the fashion curve for my jump to Seneca Falls. I ask Jarvis to set the filtration system on high in the four remaining bedrooms in the house so that they can air out a bit and check the closet next to the laundry room for extra linens. Then I head to the kitchen and start a carafe of coffee. As it begins to brew, Jarvis informs me that my nineteen-minute timer is up. Katherine blinks into the living room as I watch through the kitchen door. She's dressed in a robin's-egg blue suit and heels. A matching blue hat, which looks a bit like a folded dinner napkin, is attached to the right side of her head. She staggers forward and collapses into a nearby chair. Something roughly the size and shape of a pencil is clasped in her right hand. Richard arrives a second later and stands there, staring at her.

He seems to be frozen in place, and when it's clear that he's not moving of his own volition, I call out from the doorway, "Rich! Get out of the stable point. Tyson's coming."

Richard takes a step forward just as Tyson appears. Tyson's shoulder clips the back of his ankle, and he stumbles, nearly falling over the coffee table. In addition to the CHRONOS key in Tyson's hand, I spot a second key hanging from his wrist by a black cord.

"What the hell *is* that thing?" Tyson asks, nodding to the object Katherine is holding. "And where did you get it?"

The question seems to snap Katherine out of her stupor. She looks around the room, first at Tyson, then at Rich, and finally at me. "It . . . belonged to Sutter. We ran into some trouble at the OC. He's still in the security business, but he's apparently working for Campbell in this reality. Same creepy eye, though. Richard tapped the Timex gadget Angelo gave us and knocked him out so we could escape, and I decided to grab this in case we needed a weapon."

"Yeah, well, I think we'd have been better off if Rich had tapped the Timex gadget again and just knocked out that guy on the mezzanine. That thing fried a hole the size of a pizza in his back, and it would have led to a whole lot of questions. Although that's still an issue, since the officer saw both of us blink out—he was a split second away from shooting me. If you hadn't stepped out of the way when you did, Rich, I'm pretty sure our team would have been down one player."

Richard pales and looks over at me. Would he have moved out of the stable point if I hadn't reminded him? I don't know, and I get the sense he's wondering the very same thing. It's one of those chicken-or-egg time-travel questions that make my head hurt.

"Sorry," he says to Tyson. "I was just kind of . . . stunned from seeing Katherine shoot the guy. And I tried to use the watch gadget again, but Angelo was apparently right when he said it would require a while to recharge after use."

Katherine nods. "I saw Rich tapping the watch, but it wasn't working. And the guy was firing the rifle down into the lobby, so I decided to try this thing. There's just the one button, right here on the side." Tyson and Richard both flinch when she holds the pen out toward them. She stops and gingerly places it on the table next to the chair, being careful to point it away from us. "And you're certain the man was dead?"

"Oh, yeah. No question at all about that." Tyson holds up the second key. "Dead and also erased, so there's no way they can go back and intervene to save him. That means we've taken out three of their observers, so they're probably not going to be pleased. Alisa implied Saul might be seeking revenge on Jack for killing that guy at the concert. He was apparently one of their observers. But she said that would be after the timer started, so I don't think we can count on them playing by the rules."

"When did you see Alisa?" Rich asks.

Tyson brings them up to speed, and when he finishes, I nod toward the three piles of linens on the sofa. "I've no idea how long those have been in the closet, but if you each grab a stack, I'll take you upstairs so we can figure out who sleeps where. There are plenty of rooms, but most of them haven't been used in years, maybe even decades. I've set the ventilation system to air them out a bit. Hopefully it won't be too bad."

"We'll be *fine*," Katherine says. "I spent two weeks in the sixteenth century during training, and even though I drenched myself in bug repellent, I still came back with bedbug bites. This isn't roughing it. I'm sure you've had far worse assignments, too. Although . . . do you think they might have an extra blanket? I sleep better in a cool room under a mound of blankets."

"Sure." I go back to the linen closet and return with the heaviest of the two remaining blankets. As I hand it to her, she scans my dress with a skeptical eye. "Is that what your costume department put together for 1940? The hem seems much too long."

Her tone is casual, despite a slight hint of judgment. I haven't been able to talk to Tyson privately and have no clue how much he's told her about my actual identity, although the fact she thinks I have a costume department suggests that he hasn't told her much, if anything. I shoot him a look that makes it clear he needs to be the one fielding her questions.

"She needs to get her friend to a safe location first," Tyson says. "The guy who's stranded in Memphis? He's the person the sniper was aiming at."

"Oh. The accidental traveler." Katherine frowns. "That actually makes the fashion situation worse. It's definitely wrong for 1966."

"But it should be fine for the 1930s," I say with a touch of annoyance. "From what Tyson says, the cash we have on hand will be worthless after the timeline diverges. And I won't know what to expect after that point. The time period *before* the rift is a known quantity."

Katherine starts to ask another question, which is perfectly reasonable, since what I just said makes no sense at all without the additional information about Kate and Kiernan Dunne. But I cut her off, pointing to the staircase closest to the front door. "All of those bedrooms are empty. They each have a bathroom, if you need to freshen up. Pick a suite, then let's meet in the library, at the other end of the hallway, so that I can introduce you to the other people in the household before I go."

Inside the library, the computer is still whirring merrily away, compiling its list of people who will never exist and events that will never happen, along with a separate list of those that *shouldn't* exist and happen but nevertheless will in this twisted reality. I sigh and ask the question I've been putting off. "Jarvis, scan public records for Nora Grace."

A few seconds later, he says, "I'm sorry, mistress. There are no public records for your grandmother."

I knew he'd say that, but it's still hard to hear. "How about the other members of my family?"

After a short pause, he says, "There are no records for your mother, but Thea Randall is currently living near Miami, Florida. The number you have for her is still active."

Alex pushes away from his display and turns to look at me. "That raises two major questions. First, who owns this house? I mean, nothing inside the house changed, since it was under a CHRONOS field, but it also exists in the world out there."

"True. It's almost as if this place is a building in the Harry Potter stories that is invisible to Muggles."

He gives me a confused look, so I guess he hasn't read those books. "Anyway, the house should still be subject to tax obligations, utility bills, and so forth. If Nora Grace doesn't exist, who's keeping that current? In addition, I've been looking through the changes since 1941, and they're staggering. We're currently at war with something called the Eurasian Union, which isn't going particularly well for our side. Maryland isn't even a state anymore. The Cyrists seem to have had a major resurgence and are the fourth most popular religion worldwide. So my second question is . . . with all that going on, doesn't it seem peculiar that your other grandmother would have the same contact info?"

"Good questions," I say. "Jarvis, who owns and pays taxes on this house?"

"The title for this building has been held by Cyrist International since 1992. It has, however, been exempt from taxes since 2017, when it was registered as a Cyrist shrine."

The three historians are now at the library door. "A Cyrist shrine?" Katherine says. "Why?"

"I'm not entirely sure," I say, even though I have a strong suspicion this is connected to Thea's final comment when we last spoke and that amber stone on the bracelet she was wearing. I can't deal with it now, but I'm going to need to call her mysteriously still-active number fairly soon.

After I make introductions, Tyson hands Alex a black rectangle not much larger than his hand. "Do you think you can patch your system into this?"

Alex gives it a dubious look. "That depends very much on how backward compatible it is. And how intuitive. I'm a physicist, not a computer scientist."

Katherine steps closer to examine Alex's network of displays. "I *might* be able to help. Not with the antique over there," she adds, nodding toward the Anomalies Machine, "but with porting the data from your main system over to the SimMaster."

"Well, whatever we're going to do," Tyson says, "we need to move fairly quickly. We've got a little less than three hours before we have to plug in the files Alisa gave me. We all need to be present when that happens in order for it to sync up with our keys, and we need to have our three initial predictions ready to enter by then."

"Is the time limit determined by the simulation machine, or will it be reading each of our keys to make sure no more time than that has elapsed?" I ask.

Tyson isn't sure, so I tell him I'll be back within two and a half hours, just to be on the safe side. I'm about to pull up the stable point for Seneca Falls, when I remember the photo album on the desk. I pull out two photos—the one of Kate in the suffrage parade and one of the entire family at Christmas that's dated 1970—and stick them inside one of the CHRONOS diaries, which I then shove into my bag, along with Jack's change of clothes.

When I turn around, Katherine is running her finger along the edge of one of the shelves a few feet away. "Odd that these books are under a CHRONOS field. Apparently, the entire house is as well, or else your friend's memory would have been wiped," she says, nodding toward Alex, "and you wouldn't have a computer that tallies up the anomalies. What exactly *is* this place?"

"It's the original research site for CHRONOS technology," Tyson says.

Katherine frowns. "But we're not allowed to jump to that era. Why would Max have been researching—"

"It's Madi, actually. Madison Grace."

Katherine's eyebrows shoot up at my statement, as I expected they would. She seems to be trying to figure out whether I'm joking, but I don't have time to walk her through the entire chain of events.

"Go ahead and tell her what she needs to know," I say to Tyson. "She'll find out most of it eventually. And at this point, the odds seem pretty solid that I'm going to end up having to spend the rest of my life under a CHRONOS field either way."

FROM *THE PEOPLE'S GUIDE TO US HISTORY SINCE 2000*, 15TH ED (2136)

At the conclusion of the First Genetics War in 2097, members of the United Nations entered into a unanimous international accord banning all genetically targeted bioweapons. The issue of genetic enhancement and modification, however, continued to be a source of disagreement between nations. While there were some regional accords on the issue, they were limited in scope and difficult to implement in the absence of international norms. The failure to place meaningful restrictions on the type and number of alterations made for a fragile peace.

By 2110, small conflicts began erupting between member states over the failure of some nations to adequately track their citizens with significant genetic alterations. Human rights concerns loomed large as well, given the widening gap in wealth between those who could afford alterations and those who could not. Refugees from the United States poured into the Western Alliance, claiming that their status as unenhanced kept them from obtaining decent jobs that would support their families. As they could not afford to purchase enhancements for their offspring, this created a permanent underclass.

∞12∞

The bank of computers that the physicist, Alex, is using as the core of his system is much older than anything I've worked with in the past, but the data structure is fairly similar to the one used in simulation machines. Some version of Temporal Dilemma has been in play for over sixty years, and customers pushed for backward compatibility so that classic simulations could be replayed by each new generation with the same limitations as in the original. This was partly due to requests from professional players engaged in tournament play, but many casual TD aficionados also like the fact that they can beat their uncle's score on his War of the Roses scenario or whatever and not have him claim they only won because he was playing on a much slower system.

It only takes about twenty minutes for us to find a work-around, or at least what we *hope* is a work-around. We won't know for certain whether it actually works, however, until we plug in the disk to initiate the system and begin the game, and we can't do that until Max—or rather Madi—gets back from 1935.

In one sense, I wish it had taken longer to sync up the computers. That was something that required me to focus intensely on each concrete step of the task. Now I'm stuck thinking about the overarching problem, and it's not just Angelo vanishing that keeps popping into my mind unbidden, or that brief glimpse of a man who might have been Saul at the OC, but also a tiny pinprick of light streaming out of the ink pen from hell and blowing a crater the size of a dinner plate into the back of that man in Memphis. I believed the device would do *something*, or I wouldn't have tried it. But I never imagined it would do *that*.

I don't regret killing the man. He was shooting into the lobby. There were families with children down there. If I were in the same situation, knowing what the device could do, I would use it again. But that doesn't stop the scene from replaying in my mind every time it's unoccupied for more than a few seconds.

Alex is an odd duck. He may not be a computer scientist by training, but I suspect he would have been a very good one. I get the feeling he's more comfortable working on his own than as part of a team. Or maybe I just make him uneasy. Based on what Tyson and Madi have just revealed, my being here could cause an entirely different rift in the timeline. It's a bit mind-boggling to realize that at some level, in some reality, the responsibility for all of this—the time shifts, CHRONOS, my very existence—lies with the young man staring fixedly at a 3-D model of something I'm quite certain would make my head pound mercilessly if I asked him to explain it.

I can't say that I see any of myself in this Madison Grace. Or any of Saul, for that matter, and I assume he's somewhere in her gene pool as well. Nor do I fully understand how I could be Madi's ancestor when she was born more than a century and a half before I was. Okay, yes, I get how it's possible in the technical sense. But how do I end up in a situation where I willingly stay behind in the past? Is it as a result of this time shift? Do we fail? Am I pregnant right now?

My head is swimming with those questions and a host of others, but I suspect that the most I'll get from anyone here are vague answers. I understand their reluctance to tell me more than the bare minimum. The more I know, the more likely it is that some action I take will keep a necessary chain of events from unfolding. That doesn't stop me from wanting to know more, however.

Tyson, Richard, and the guy they call RJ are working on mapping out our strategy for opening moves. I need to be over there. Tyson and Rich rarely play The Game, and RJ had almost certainly never heard of it before this fiasco began. But I have to clear my head first. Maybe get some of the coffee I smelled when we first arrived.

"I'm going down to the kitchen," I tell Alex. "Can I bring you anything?"

He shakes his head and taps a thermos on his desk. "What color is the key for you?"

The question takes me a bit by surprise. Not because I've never heard it. On the contrary, it's all historians can talk about for the first few weeks after we begin practical training. It's more hearing this man ask it, when he may well be the person who decided to color-code our response to the key in the first place. Even Angelo didn't seem to fully understand the logic behind it.

"I see the key as a pale orange."

Alex sighs. "Well, that's going to complicate things a bit. It's orange for Madi, too. Hopefully, I'll be able to tell them apart." His forefinger flicks at the display hovering in front of him, sending a cluster of colored bubbles flying toward me. "Can you spot yours?"

I stare at the bubbles for a moment. There are purple bubbles and amber bubbles, some of which have clear bubbles tacked onto the side. There are also two teal bubbles and two that are the pale-orange color I see when I look at a CHRONOS key. I always had a difficult time explaining the shade to anyone until I took a jump to the mid-1970s for a women's rights march in Chicago. It was a hot day and I purchased something called an Orange Creamsicle from an ice-cream vendor. When I opened the wrapper, I began laughing, which was probably rather confusing to the other marchers in line. The ice-cream pop was the exact same color as the medallion. Once I was back home, I managed to get our food unit to spit out a fairly decent replica so that I could show Saul.

"Those," I say, tapping the pale-orange bubbles. "The others are darker, and a bit more yellowy. What are the clear bubbles?"

"Our hitchhikers from the other timeline," he says. "If I could figure out where they're coming from, what specific reality, I might be able to block them, but we don't have a lot of data points. So far, they've only latched on to Tyson and Madi, as far as I can tell. I hadn't analyzed all of them yet, however, and now most of the colors that were on the display are gone."

I ask him why they'd be gone given that this house is under a CHRONOS field, and he begins explaining that this is a historical display of chronotron pulses writ large, not something he's measuring inside the house. There's something about Einstein-Rosen bridges and finding the negative energy of the exotic matter that keeps a wormhole stable, but by the time he reaches that bit, I'm not really listening. It's partly because the science is over my head, but more that I'm distracted by a single red bubble at the bottom of the screen, like a bloodred moon. It's gone before I can even point it out. Alex must have seen it, too, however, because he's staring at that section of the screen.

"Where did it go?" I ask. "You saw it, didn't you? Right there. What color was it?"

Alex frowns. "Red. But . . . it's gone now. And that shouldn't happen without another time shift. Which we would have felt, and we didn't. Maybe it was just a reflection." He nods toward the tall windows across the room. "There's a helipad on the office building across the street."

I stare at the spot where the bubble was, willing it to come back, if only for a second, just to confirm that it wasn't a reflection. But that sector of the display remains blank.

"I'm . . . going to go get that coffee now." I back away from the display, angry at the tears hovering just below the surface. Tyson motions for me to join them, but I ignore him and hurry toward the door.

Unfortunately, the kitchen isn't empty when I get downstairs. The woman I haven't met yet, the geneticist, is there with her daughter, both of them on the floor in front of the patio door, looking out into the backyard. It's a nice yard, with trees and a small shed beyond the brick patio. It was probably even prettier when the place was first built, but it's more of a large courtyard now, hemmed in by tall buildings on all sides.

A row of juice glasses is lined up on the countertop.

"Don't use those," the woman says. "They're being requisitioned as lab equipment. The mugs are in the cabinet next to the fridge. And the food unit is crap. It can handle pasta and makes a decent rice or oatmeal, but don't try for anything fancy. Makes okay coffee, though."

"Thanks. Good thing I'm not hungry, I guess." I fill a mug and take a deep breath before turning around. "I assume you're Lorena?" When she nods, I say, "Katherine Shaw. How old is your little girl?"

"Almost eleven months."

"She's adorable." Both the child and her mother didn't exist in the previous timeline. Do they exist in this one? I don't know, and it's not really the sort of question you want to ask someone, especially on short acquaintance. I'm about to make a polite excuse and head back up to the library, when she asks if I enjoy my job.

The question catches me off guard, partly because it doesn't really make sense. I can't imagine not enjoying my job, since I was quite literally *made* to enjoy it, and I don't know anyone who doesn't enjoy his or her job. That's the beauty of the whole chosen-gift system, at least in the cases where parents choose wisely. There may be other things you could imagine doing, which you think might be fun or interesting, but none of them would suit you better than the job you have.

Although, as I think about it, Morgen Campbell might be one exception to that rule. I'm not sure what chosen gift his parents selected for him. It probably wasn't related to a job. He inherited the Objectivist Club, along with numerous other properties, so they probably weren't too concerned about him entering any sort of profession. But I'm quite certain he'd rather be a historian or maybe a professional time-chess player than run the OC.

"I do enjoy my job," I tell her. "I'm not sure how much you know about the system in my time—"

"Oh, I know about the chosen-gift system. I read *A Brief History of CHRONOS*. Maybe I should phrase it as a hypothetical. Do you think you'd choose your job if you had to train for it the old-fashioned way? If there was a chance that you'd work really hard and still suck at it?"

"I'm not really sure how to answer that. I *think* so. On the one occasion where I thought a mistake might result in me being forced to do something else . . ." I shake away the thought, both because it's still scary to think about and because it reminds me again of Saul and that bloodred moon. "It was awful even contemplating it. I know that historians miss it once they stop doing fieldwork, although if they spent their time well, they've collected enough data to give them plenty to write about for the decade or so until they retire. So yes, I enjoy it. Although I'll admit I prefer the days *without* time shifts that completely upend the historical record. Do you like being a geneticist?"

She nods, staring down into her cup. "Very much. It's horrible to admit it, but I went a little stir-crazy during the months when I was home after Yun Hee was born. I loved spending time with her, loved having that time as a family, but I missed my lab. Missed my research. Even so, I didn't realize how much I defined myself by that job until it was gone. RJ . . . he's moved from one job to the next. Doesn't really matter to him. In fact, he'd be happy to stay home with Yun Hee if my salary was a bit higher. I've been at that lab for seven years, though, and I checked just now. The building doesn't even exist anymore. I couldn't bring myself to see what else has changed, because I know it's going to be massive. All I had to do was look out this door—we've got skyscrapers on all sides now. Used to be smaller apartment buildings, mostly. There used to be a willow tree, but it's gone. It's a wonder any of the trees survived with so little sunlight. Between the buildings and the smog, very little seems to be getting through."

Dark day. Bloodred moon.

I pull in a deep breath. "Hopefully, we'll be able to fix it. And on that note, I should head back up. It was nice meeting you."

Lorena doesn't respond. It's possible she didn't hear me or that she's preoccupied with her own thoughts. But I suspect it's also because meeting me, meeting any of us, hasn't been at all nice for her.

As I leave the kitchen, she says, "Could you ask RJ to come down? And tell the others that they might want to get food or whatever in the next few minutes. I'm going to play around with the replicator to see if I can get it to spit out some basic chemicals to work on that serum for Jack. I doubt I'll have much success, but it gives me something to do."

When I get back to the library, RJ is talking with Alex. I pass along Lorena's message and he heads downstairs. Tyson has taken over one of the computer terminals. Rich is on a couch near the window, scanning through the index of what I'm guessing is a history book that was under the CHRONOS field. A small stack of books is on the coffee table in front of him. I pick up the one on top, running my finger along the heavily creased spine. *The Unfinished Nation: A Concise History of the American People, Volume 2 Since 1865.* It's old, and the cover is worn at the edges, but it's solid. Sturdy. But in another way, it's remarkably fragile. If not for the CHRONOS field in this house, the book wouldn't exist anywhere in this reality. Or, at least, it wouldn't exist in this form. There might be another version by the same author, maybe even with the same title, but the history inside would take a sharp turn in the early 1940s.

"I wouldn't bother with those," Alex says, glancing at the books we're holding. "It takes too long to search, and we have a much larger collection in digital format. Hold on a sec." He enters a few commands, waits a moment, and then calls up the house's virtual assistant. Richard and Tyson seem to find it amusing that Madi named the assistant Jarvis, apparently in reference to some comic book. Alex asks it to compare the list of speeches given by Charles Lindbergh between 1938 and 1942 in both the files on the household's internal system and publicly available external information sources.

About thirty seconds later, two lists of speeches appear side by side on the wall screen. Both timelines are in sync up until early February 1939. In our timeline, Lindbergh's speaking schedule continued, albeit at a slower pace, until December 1941, when his isolationism was pushed aside due to the attack on Pearl Harbor. In the new timeline, Lindbergh begins giving more speeches, both in person and via radio. In mid-March, he embarks on a series of rallies with several other isolationists, which increase after he announces his run for the Senate and culminate in an event at Madison Square Garden on February 22 of the following year, which is a commemoration of Washington's birthday and in memory of a woman and her two small children who were killed at the Pro-America Rally in 1939 by Jewish protestors. A gunman fires three times at the stage, hitting Lindbergh and Kuhn, yelling something about death to Nazis, then kills himself before the police can capture him. Lindbergh drops out of the Senate race a few days later, citing concerns for the welfare of his pregnant wife and two small children.

"Whoa," Tyson says. "The 1939 event is the Madison Square Garden rally I told you about earlier. The German-American Bund event. Glen and I were there, and no one was killed. Some guy went after Fritz Kuhn, the Bund's leader, but he wasn't even armed. Police grabbed him. The worst thing that happened was that the guy got roughed up and literally lost his pants in the struggle before they carted him off to jail. So, I think both of these are solid initial predictions for the other side's first moves—they must have arranged for the death of the woman and kids, and then the attempted assassination of Lindbergh the next year at the memorial."

I glance back at the description for the rally where Lindbergh was shot. Most of the other speakers were men, but there are four women, two of whose names I recognize from my own research.

"Elizabeth Dilling and Laura Ingalls. They were active in the mothers' movement, protesting any US involvement in European wars. Opposed to offering any sort of aid. Ingalls was a pilot. Dilling was notorious for seeing communist and Jewish conspiracies behind absolutely everything. She was toxic."

"You've studied them?" Tyson asks.

"Not in person. Their movement is on my research plan, but I was waiting a few years so that I'd be at least a tiny bit closer to their demographic, which is solidly middle-aged. But I did the usual background study while writing up my research agenda during the last year of classroom training. I'm almost certain the America First Committee isn't supposed to be organized until the war actually begins in Europe . . . in the early autumn. The group started in September of 1940, I think. The isolationist movement itself was already rolling along full speed, but they wouldn't have billed it as an America First rally."

We spend several minutes debating whether the America First Committee getting a head start is a big enough change that it might be one of the specific moves the other side made, or whether it is something that emerged organically. None of us really has a clue one way or the other at this point.

"What about Coughlin?" Rich says. "They're calling him *brother* now, rather than *father*, and that's definitely a Cyrist cross he's wearing."

Tyson seems skeptical. "Even though that's a difference, do you think it's large enough that it could actually have an impact? It seems more like something they might have changed inadvertently, as a result of another move, rather than a move itself."

I take a deep breath, trying to decide whether I should tell them about Saul's use of the Cyrists in his games with Morgen and my role in designing the Cyrist cross. Even thinking about the symbol bothers me right now. I keep seeing that giant outline against the murky sky, and the way it changed over a matter of minutes. But is the design really all that original? Aside from the infinity sign, it's just a synthesis of a bunch of other religious icons.

"Plus," Rich continues, "I can't see how a radio preacher in Detroit—even a really influential one like Coughlin—converting from one religion to another could possibly play a role in keeping Japan from attacking Pearl Harbor. To be perfectly honest, I can't see how *any* of the things we've found could do that."

"We may be overthinking this," I tell them. "The initial predictions you enter at the start of The Game are little more than a crapshoot in a complex scenario. If we use Coughlin, for example, we'll need a bit more detail in order to get any appreciable credit for the answer. Why he switched religions, who talked him into it, and how it helped flip the timeline, for example. You don't need all of those, but just tossing out an event without any supporting data will cost us. Likewise, if we go with something broad, like America First launching six months or so early, we need to figure out where the change happened. When? How? And I'm not even sure that there *are* definitive answers to those questions. The initial predictions just give you a place to start, assuming that you get something correct."

"She's right," Richard says. "I mean, we should definitely *make* initial predictions, but we need to be aware that the odds of any one of them being completely right are really, really tiny. Lindbergh would be a safer guess. We know where and when he's shot, and we know the method, and who did it. We can scrape enough information together to make an educated guess on why it helped tip the timeline. Might be enough to give us a few extra points in reserve."

"True," Tyson says. "Getting back to Coughlin, though. Cyrists aren't pacifists, are they? Leaving Japan out of it for now, how would that guy switching religions help keep the US out of the war?"

"The mothers' movement I mentioned worked closely with Coughlin," I say. "And he's still basically the same person, even if he's changed his affiliation. The real question is *when* the change occurred, and how. We're not going to get many points if we only lay out a single piece of the puzzle. But hopefully their style-point total will be low."

Tyson shakes his head. "Nope. Alisa said their style points are— and I quote—'through the fucking stratosphere.' She said they maxed out two categories with bonuses. And while she's not exactly the world's most reliable source, I didn't get the sense that this was a lie."

I pull in a sharp breath. "Maxed out *two*? Damn. That's almost unheard of. Morgen maxed out a single category a year or so back, mostly in a stroke of luck. Saul says he hasn't stopped bragging about it since."

Alex says, "Could one of you explain this style-points thing to me? It sounds like you're saying that even if our side wins, even if we manage to reverse the timeline shift, they might still win because they did it with style?"

Tyson, Rich, and I exchange a look.

"That pretty much sums it up," Rich admits. "Although, it's more that you earn extra points for not taking the easiest path. Getting actors from the timeline to help you is better than doing something yourself. Convincing them is better than paying them, although I suspect that's going to be a bit hard to police in a real-life game. And there are other factors the system considers, like limiting the geographic area, the time frame, using average people on the street as opposed to major historical actors—all of those things add up. Which means once we figure out their specific changes, we have to think creatively about *how* we reverse them."

"Seems the playing field is tilted considerably in the other side's favor," Alex says.

Tyson responds with a bitter laugh. "Not to hear them tell it. Alisa says we've been given home-field advantage."

"Seems only fair," I say. "It's our timeline, so we are literally playing on our home field. They have almost nothing at stake."

"True," Tyson says. "As best I can tell, the only benefit is that the rules are derived mostly from our version of Temporal Dilemma. The only exception was the whole issue of observers. They're not a factor in computer simulations, but apparently Morgen wasn't willing to give up the cash he earns from selling those slots."

"Fleece the gamers," I say. "That's how Morgen's family amassed their wealth, and I suspect it's his default move in any reality. Did Alisa happen to mention which categories they maxed out?"

"Yeah," Tyson says. "Chron and geo."

"And they're using our rules on style points. Hmm. I don't guess either of you has a copy of those in your backpack?"

"Nope," Rich says. "I have a custom bottle of sambuca that was supposed to be a gift for Angelo, a spare pair of glasses, and a CHRONOS diary that mostly contains information about the 1960s and connections to musical history from other eras."

Tyson shakes his head. "Alisa said there's a copy on the drive, but we can't access that. As soon as we plug in the drive, we have to be ready to start the game."

"Okay, then, we'll have to rely on what we remember," I say. Judging from their expressions, however, we'll apparently be relying on what *I* remember. "Oh, come on. You guys played at least a few times, right?"

Rich shrugs. "When I play, I'm just trying to flip the timeline and avoid looking like too much of an idiot. Style points are considerably beyond my level of expertise."

"I played as a kid," Tyson says. "A couple of times at the OC since then. The only thing I remember about style points is the geographic category. To max out, you have to make all your moves in a single city. Most of the time that's the nation's capital, but in this case, judging from the vids we saw, I'd say New York seems more likely."

"Right. The bonus for the geo category is making your moves only in locations not directly connected to the main objective, so yeah . . . New York is a safer bet than Washington." I add *NYC* to the notes on the screen. "There are a few different ways to max out chronological, but the bonus is for moving in reverse order, which is risky because it means you can't consider any follow-on effects. So if whatever you change in move three alters the impact of your first two moves, or even reverses them, you're screwed. The bad news here is that if we want to negate those style points, we'll have to work backward as well. The most popular way to get full points for the chronological category is to limit your moves to a two-year period, although there are some kitschy things added to later iterations, where you make every move on a specific day of the week, a specific time of day, or only on even-numbered days. Serious players usually avoid those because they're a pain to engineer, and they can also screw with style points in the other categories because they limit your flexibility. So it seems like a safe bet that they went with the two-year window."

"The earliest date we have for any of these is the event at Madison Square Garden on February 20, 1939," Rich says. "The last that we know for certain is Lindbergh being shot roughly a year later on February 22, 1940. Assuming those predictions are both accurate, the other event—which I think we'll all agree must have something to do more directly with Japan—would need to happen between February 1938 and February 1941 in order to maintain that two-year window.

Although . . . do we know when Coughlin switched from Catholic to Cyrist?"

We find that Coughlin's official announcement was on February 13, 1939, but there are slight deviations in the historical record several months before that. The first occurred exactly a week after Coughlin stated that the Nazi persecution of Jews during Kristallnacht, a few weeks prior, was a justified response to Jewish persecution of Christians. These comments were made during his regular Sunday radio sermon, which was syndicated nationwide and reached a weekly audience of as many as thirty million listeners. Leaders in the Catholic hierarchy were highly critical of Coughlin's comments, but they had been critical for quite some time and hadn't managed to fully rein him in. His latest remarks were a bridge too far for some of his advertisers, however, and several stations that carried his show, most notably WMCA in New York City, demanded that he submit his scripts in advance for their clearance, since the broadcasts were live. Coughlin refused.

All of that tracks with the previous historical record. At this point, however, things start to diverge. In the current timeline, Coughlin supporters began picketing WMCA the very next day. Several days later, it was announced that the station was under new ownership and would again be carrying Coughlin's sermons. Things seemed to die down a bit over the holidays, and then on February 12th, the Bund started running new advertisements for its Pro-America Rally at Madison Square Garden. The two posters for the Pro-America Rally are virtually identical, except that the new poster includes the names of several additional speakers, including Lawrence Dennis, Elizabeth Dilling, and *Brother* (rather than Father) Charles Coughlin. It was apparently a clerical error, but there must have been other stuff going on in the background that the church hierarchy learned about, because the next day, Coughlin held a press conference, declaring that the Catholic Church had failed to recognize the threat of communism and the role of the Jewish people in its spread. While he would still remain a Catholic in his heart, and continue to pray that God would put the church back on track, he would be continuing his ministry under the wide umbrella of Cyrisism, where people of all faiths could find a home . . . although there was a clear inference that this didn't include Jews. He would now be known as Brother Coughlin, in keeping with Cyrist custom, but he would still view his vast audience of listeners as his children.

Alex calls up Jarvis again. "Save list on the screen as *Lindbergh speeches*. Then compare internal and external sources, and highlight differences in the historical record that involve Japan between February 1938 and February 1940, inclusive."

The list isn't long, and most of the differences seem too superficial to be what we're looking for. There's a mention of additional economic sanctions against Japan, but that would probably have increased tensions. The reported mugging of two Japanese tourists. A one-day difference in the date of a diplomatic meeting. One item stands out immediately, however. According to an article from the archives of the *Daily Intrepid* (which is apparently the *Daily Intrepid-Herald* after January 1941 in this timeline), a security officer at the New York World's Fair was killed while trying to prevent an attack on Kensuke Horinouchi, Japanese ambassador to the US. Horinouchi was preparing to give an address on Japan Day at the New York World's Fair. He suffered a minor injury when he was tackled to the ground. The attack was not, however, mentioned in an exhaustive four-hundred-page dissertation, *A Sociopolitical History of the 1939–40 World's Fair*, that was protected by the CHRONOS field. It almost certainly would have been mentioned, since the attacker was supposedly a nephew of Earl Browder, head of the Communist Party USA. It's definitely the sort of item the dissertation would have covered, given that the author devoted an entire chapter to an unsolved terrorist attempt to bomb the British Pavilion at the Fair the following summer, on the Fourth of July, which was thwarted at the cost of two police officers' lives.

I ask Jarvis to pull up all the differences in the historical record for the World's Fair. He coolly informs me that my voice isn't recognized, and so I punt to Alex. Again, the list isn't long and most of the changes are minor. A few events with different or additional speakers. A few additional protests, including one by members of the local America First chapter. A protest speech by Coughlin, who is now listed as head Templar for the Cyrists' midwestern region, outside the gates of the Fair on opening day, claiming that the event was funded by international communist sympathizers. Ongoing protests by Coughlin's organization the Christian Front, which seems to have become the Universal Front in this timeline, urged both Cyrist and Christian men "to crusade against the anti-American forces of the Red Revolution."

The last four articles in the list, however, all deal with a single event—the aforementioned bombing on the Fourth of July. This time, however, the bomb was not removed by the officers, both of whom survived to patrol another day. The small case was instead placed under a cluster of bushes near the Court of Peace at the fairground, where it exploded during a parade by members of the US Navy and Marines. When the bomb exploded just after five p.m., seventeen people—eight military and nine civilians—were killed. Another thirty-two were hospitalized. At the command of Mayor La Guardia, the New York City police rounded up nearly a hundred likely suspects for questioning, including members of the German-American Bund, assorted fascists, and members of Coughlin's Universal Front, who had been protesting the internationalist theme of the Fair since it opened the year before. A British spy was arrested as he boarded a flight for London the following week. He eventually confessed to planting the bomb but swore that he'd planted it in the British Pavilion, not the Court of Peace, with the charge set to go off overnight. The goal had been to frame the German-American Bund for the attack, and they'd planned it carefully to ensure there was no loss of life and the only damage was to British property inside the pavilion.

"Okay," Rich says, after we add this latest change to the board. "That complicates matters. Which three events did they cause, and which ones are spin-offs? They can only do three, right?"

"Right," Tyson says. "Although I can't help but wonder how the system is going to handle incidental events. I mean, when you're playing as a simulation, you enter your moves directly. But with this, you could have major unintended consequences that are never officially entered. Alisa actually said they'd had several bits of serendipity when things went their way, and I can imagine scenarios where those might be the changes that flipped the timeline. Take that bombing. If you're playing on a sim-system, you just enter in that you were placing a bomb in that location with X number of casualties, including the maharaja of East Bhutan or whatever. But someone actually placing a bomb—or in this case, moving it—can't guarantee that they'll take out their target, can't guarantee the number of casualties, and can't really even guarantee that the bomb will work. They might trip on something on the way to the location and end up killing themselves, although come to think of it, they'd probably outsource risky work like that to one of their lackeys. The system really needs to take that into account, especially if these people aren't clued in to the fact that they're changing the futures of real live humans. That observer Katherine shot at the hotel and the two Jack and Madi erased all took on far greater risks than the actual historians."

That comment, of course, makes me think yet again of the man in Memphis, who was almost certainly an observer. A man who paid God only knows how much money to travel through time and across dimensions to help radically alter history and who was perfectly willing to pick up a rifle and fire it into a crowded lobby. But did he know they were real people? Or did he believe they were the humanoid equivalents of the eagle avatar we saw at the history center? He certainly didn't have any qualms about shooting at them, and that's one reason I didn't hesitate to fire on him in turn. One second, he was leaning against the railing, pointing the rifle down at the lobby below, and the next he was on the ground with a dark-red hole in his back.

Rich huffs angrily. He doesn't often get irritated at Tyson, so the stress and lack of decent sleep must be getting to him. "Those guys volunteered. Probably even paid for the privilege of coming over here and screwing up our timeline. They knew what they were getting into."

Tyson is quiet for a moment and then gives Rich a nod of admission. "Sure. I'm not saying it's the same as killing innocent bystanders. But . . . we don't know how much information they have. They might well believe that this is some sort of hyped-up VR experience. Do they know it has real consequences for us, or do they view us as we might view nonplayer characters in a game? I'm just thinking that if I were judging the contest, or programming the simulation, I'd probably deduct points for being overly careless with pawns . . . on either side." He holds up a hand at Rich, who looks like he's about to object. "We may not have any choice, but I'm just saying that I think any damage to the observers could hurt our score. Plus, they're people who may not have full information on this competition. Maybe we should try to avoid harming them. I'm not blaming Katherine. Nor am I blaming Madi or Jack. In their places, I'd have done the exact same things. In fact, if I hadn't been seeing double at the time, I'd have been the one to take that shot in Montgomery."

"So why even bring it up?" Rich asks. "Because it sure sounds like you're assessing blame."

I put my hand on Richard's arm. "It's okay. He's right. Obviously, we should avoid killing if at all possible. Maybe it's a good thing that we don't have observers in the field. At least we're not putting anyone else at risk."

We narrow down our initial guesses to five, all of which seem speculative and probably dead wrong, but that's the norm in time chess. I've only seen a handful of initial predictions pan out, even in professional-level play. We're holding off on deciding which three of the five to select until Madi returns. I very nearly ask why Madi didn't simply return an hour ago, but then realize she's probably trying to limit her time around me, due to fears of screwing up the long, tortuous path that leads to her eventual conception. I'm guessing she'll cut it close to the wire and show up just before we enter the fingertip drive into the console at a little after four p.m. That gives me about forty-five minutes.

"I'm going to go get a shower," I say. "Once the clock is ticking on the game, we'll barely have time to brush our teeth."

Rich follows me into the hallway, and when we're about halfway down the corridor, he pulls me aside. "Are you okay?"

I nod, but the concern in his voice brings tears to my eyes in an instant, and he pulls me into a hug.

"It's okay," he says as I bury my face into his shoulder. "If you need to cry, then cry. You lost more today than any of us. I barely see my family. Same goes for Tyson. But you see your parents all the time. Angelo, too. Your bond with him is different than ours. And then . . ." He sighs. "Oh hell, I might as well just say it."

I take a step back, drying my eyes on my sleeve. "Might as well say what?"

"I saw Saul back at the OC. Or at least I think it was him. I didn't get a close look, obviously, and it could also be the Saul from our current timeline, not the . . . um . . . original. Or maybe even the one playing for the other team. I should have told you earlier, but I was worried that you'd want to go back and check, and right that minute, we really needed to get out of there. We can go now, though. I set a stable point in Sutter's office."

A laugh rises up through the tears. I managed to resist temptation, and here Richard is, putting it right back in my path again. "I saw him, too, Rich. If it was Saul, it pretty much has to be either the version from this timeline or his alt-reality doppelgänger. For now, we have to focus on fixing the timeline, and chasing down someone who simply can't be my Saul isn't the best use of our time. But thank you." I tiptoe up and place a kiss on his cheek. "You're a good friend."

When I pull back, I realize he's blushing, and I'm reminded once again of Saul's jokes about how he needs to watch his back around Richard, that Rich would off him in a heartbeat if he thought it would give him a chance with me. Now I wonder if maybe Saul isn't right on that count. Well, not in thinking that Rich would kill him. That's just silly. But I think he's right that Richard's feelings go beyond friendship.

Hell, who am I kidding? I've suspected that for a long time. I just didn't want to admit it, because it makes things awkward.

I tell Rich that I'll see him back in the library shortly and head to my room. The stack of linens is on the bed where I placed it earlier. I push it aside, toss my hat on the nightstand, and sprawl out on the bed.

If Saul had never become my research partner, would my attraction to him have remained a schoolgirl crush? I'll never know, but I think it's possible. And if the girl in that 18th-century Quaker village had died as she was supposed to on our first trip, Saul and I might never have bonded. And maybe then I'd have realized before now that my best friend since age ten is quite good looking these days, with wide gray eyes behind his glasses. They're the same gray as the ones that looked back from the image in Sutter's office, although those eyes didn't have the same warmth.

While it's not the kind of thing that should be running through my head mere hours after learning that Saul and CHRONOS no longer exist, it is just a passing thought. There's no reason I should feel at all guilty for having it. But I still kind of do.

FROM *THE TD OFF-WORLD PLAYER'S GUIDE*

DEFENSIVE GAME (MODIFIED FOR OFF-WORLD TEAM PLAY)

1. Once team one (Viper) has entered its moves, it may not enter the timeline again until team two (Hyena) has responded.

2. Team members may not actively engage during play, nor may physical force be used against an opposing player to prevent them from making a move. (This is waived if the opposing team has substantially breached the rules.)

3. All participants may be recorded anytime they are within range of an observation point or an official observer from the opposite team. These recordings will be broadcast to viewers of *TD Off-World*. This is a requirement of our sponsors, and there are no exceptions to this rule.

4. All four players and all observers must be within a ten-meter radius of the SimMaster when play begins. Any individual with the CHRO-NOS gene (permanent, inherited, or temporary) who is within range of the SimMaster when play begins will be counted as an observer and subject to the rules of play.
5. Initial predictions: Enter the location, the date within one week, and the precise action for full points.
6. Final entry: Include the location, exact date, and precise action taken, along with any style-point considerations. Must be entered within one hour of move being taken.
7. The system can only measure the moves that are entered based on the information given by each team. Team Viper is not responsible for unintended alterations to the timeline that occur due to incidental encounters by its team members or observers.

∞13∞

MADI
SENECA FALLS, NEW YORK
JULY 6, 1935

The stable point is hidden at the back of what used to be the Seneca Falls Wesleyan Church, a plain, boxy building a few blocks from the canal and Van Cleef Lake. When I first pull it up on the key, rain is coming down in steady sheets. The only thing in my house is an airbrella, which they definitely didn't have in the pre-WWII era, so there really isn't much I can do other than scroll forward to a moment when the downpour slacks off a tiny bit and blink in.

When I round the corner of the building, I'm surprised to see that the building is no longer a church in 1935. Its red bricks have been painted over, and a large sign reading *Ford Garage* hangs above the door. Above me, the sky is a solid blanket of dark gray. On the plus side, it's the middle of summer, so the rain is just wet, not cold. But it will be hard enough to make my case to Kate Dunne without looking like a drowned rat when I introduce myself. I duck into a small market on Fall Street and purchase an umbrella, then begin the short walk to Trinity Church.

No one is on the church grounds when I arrive. I find a dry spot in an alcove near the front of the building, set a local stable point, and start scanning forward. People begin arriving around three, some on foot and others by car. I scan forward to a few minutes after four, pan around to make sure the coast is clear, and jump in.

My plan is to get a moment alone with Kate, but there only appear to be a few women around, all of them inside the church, and none of them under sixty. I walk around the side of the building to the back, where a group of about a dozen men has gathered on the strip of land between the building and the lake—which is really just a wide place in the canal—and wait, pressing my back to the wall to keep out of the windblown rain. It's a futile effort, and I'm just about to retreat inside and try to find a window to watch through, when the door a few yards away from me opens and two teenage boys step through. The one in front is pushing a wheelbarrow.

"Pretty sure it's blasphemy to take a shortcut through a house of God with a wheelbarrow," the shorter one says as a middle-aged man follows them into the yard.

"Your brother is right, Harry. If we end up in hell, it's on your conscience." There's a lingering hint of an Irish accent in the man's voice. He's dressed in jeans, work boots, and a white shirt with the sleeves rolled up to the elbows, and his hair is dark, just a tad longer than the prevailing fashion, with a touch of gray at the temples. When he turns toward me, I'm certain it's the man in the photo album. Any doubts I might have had are erased when I see the scar on the inside of his left arm. One of Kate's diary entries said he gave himself that scar clawing out a CHRONOS key that Prudence Rand had hired a doctor to embed in his arm.

It's no surprise then that the color drains from his face when he catches sight of the medallion around my neck. "Who sent you?" he demands. "Simon? Or Prudence?"

"No one sent me. I know their names from Kate's diaries, but I've never met either of them."

That may only be a partial truth in the case of Prudence, and a bit of hesitation must show on my face, because Kiernan leans in toward me, jaw clenched. "Fine. I don't really care who sent you, when you're from, or where you got that medallion. But I want nothing to do with it. And if you're smart, you'll toss it into the lake and forget you ever saw the bloody thing." He steps out into the rain, striding purposefully toward a pickup parked at the very edge of the lot, where two men standing in the back of the truck are handing out sandbags.

I follow him, my shoes squelching in the mud. "No one *sent* me. I found the key in the garden of my Great-Great-Grandmother Kate's house, buried next to a dog toy. And I'd love nothing more than to toss the cursed thing to the bottom of the ocean, Kiernan Dunne, but if I do that, everything you and she worked for will come unraveled."

His legs are much longer than mine, and he's several steps ahead when he whirls around, eyes blazing. "I fought my battle already, miss. Whatever's happening in your time, Kate—*my* Kate—and I can't help you. That's your future. You fix it."

"Except it's your future, too. Their future." I nod toward the truck, where his sons are waiting for the man in the back to hand them a couple of sandbags. "Six years. That's all you have left before everything goes to hell."

Several of the other men in the yard are giving us odd looks. Kiernan lets out an audible huff and then stalks off toward the front of the church. Again, I follow. Halfway to the parking lot, he ducks into an alcove.

"Listen," he says when I join him. "I *know* there's a war right around the corner. I've got two sons, one of whom will be itchin' to enlist on day one and the other who'll probably get sucked in because he's prime draft age. Kate and I knew that was on the horizon from the day they were born. We decided that whatever happens, happens and we'd face it like everyone else. And then . . ." He sighs, and a smile lifts one corner of his mouth. "And then I'm pretty sure she jumped ahead and checked anyway, even though she'd never admit it. She stopped worrying quite so much, and I'm guessing it's because she knows they make it through. But even if she's wrong, the war on our horizon is one that has to be fought. Same as when we took down the Cyrists. Good people don't just stand aside and let evil win."

"You're *wrong*," I say. "Sometimes they do stand aside. Sometimes people, people who are normally good, are only willing to fight back if evil lands the first punch. And it's not enough if evil hits someone else. They have to feel the weight of the punch. Then, only then, do they wake up enough to fight. You *know* that's true. If it wasn't, Hitler wouldn't be steadily gaining power in Europe."

His eyes soften slightly, but he shakes his head. "Doesn't matter. Neither of us can use the key any longer. I'm sorry, but—"

"I'm not asking you to get involved directly. All I'm asking you to do is take in a refugee . . . in 1966. Only for a week or so. And even if you say no, I wanted to tell you that you might want to keep your entire family inside a CHRONOS field . . . I don't know the exact date and time the shift happens, but I suspect it's right around December 7, 1941."

Kiernan's eyebrows go up when I say the date. "Sweet bloody hell." He stares down at the mud for several seconds, then sighs and rubs his temples. "Listen, I've got work to do warding off this flood. Meet me tonight at eight at Vacca's. Cross the bridge, take a right, and it's maybe two blocks down. You can make your case to Kate, although I can tell you already that she's gonna be in a foul mood about this."

"Fair enough. I'm not exactly overjoyed about it, either."

He gives me a nod and heads back to join the sandbagging crew. Given that a flood is coming, the odds seem good that the rain will get worse, not better, between now and eight. Might as well make the walk while it's still daylight. So, I hoist the umbrella, which very nearly turns inside out in the wind, and head off toward the bridge.

Vacca's is on the corner, a redbrick building that appears to be half grocery and half restaurant. When I find a narrow drive between two neat Victorian houses, I step inside, set a local point, and then jump forward to seven fifty-five. I tell the waitress at Vacca's that two people will be joining me, and she seats me at a table near the back.

"You're lucky the weather's so awful," she says as she fills my water glass. "Usually we're packed on Saturdays, but I guess nobody wants to venture out in this. Can't really blame 'em."

By eight fifteen, I'm pretty sure that Kiernan Dunne is a dirty, rotten liar who simply said he'd meet me here in order to get rid of me. I order a glass of wine and a salad, mostly to have something to do while I wait, but as soon as the food is in front of me, I realize I'm actually pretty hungry. I'm debating whether to go ahead and order pasta, too, when the door opens and two women step inside, followed by Kiernan. One of them is definitely Kate. Her hair is pulled back into a bun, unlike the vids I've seen of my great-great-grandmother, where it was long and loose even into her eighties, but her eyes are the same vivid green. It's the same green as the younger girl with her now, in fact, who is almost certainly their daughter. She's around my age, pretty, with dark shoulder-length curls and her father's olive skin.

It's instantly clear that Kiernan's prediction about his wife's mood is dead on. Kate's eyes narrow when she spots my CHRONOS key, and when I extend my hand, she ignores it. Her daughter rolls her eyes and steps forward. "Cliona Dunne," she says, shaking my hand. "I believe you've met my father already. And the woman with the antisocial personality disorder is my mother, Kate."

The comment gets a grudging smile from Kate as she takes one of the two chairs across the table from me. "One psychology class, and Clio thinks she's Sigmund Freud."

"I'm Madison Grace. Most people call me Madi." I hand her the two photographs from the volume. "You'll want to keep those inside a CHRONOS field. These were part of an album you sent to Kate Pierce-Keller, who was my paternal grandmother's grandmother. I don't know how much your husband has told you, but . . ."

I trail off as the waitress approaches with a breadbasket and a bottle of Chianti. They must come here often enough that she knows what they like, since she was occupied with another table when they walked in. She chats with them for a moment about the rain and then asks if it's coming down as hard over in Skaneateles. When the pleasantries are over, she tells them the special is lasagna Bolognese, which they all choose. I'm not entirely sure what's in a Bolognese sauce, so I opt for linguine with pesto, and the waitress heads to the kitchen with our order.

"Madison Grace," Kate says, once she's gone. "You're one of the three who invented the damn keys, aren't you?"

"I guess? I mean, that's what the *Brief History* says, so that must be what happened in some iteration of this timeline. All I know is that I decided to plant a garden in the backyard in Bethesda and I pulled out a plastic bone and a CHRONOS key. And that discovery apparently sped everything up by a few decades."

"Daphne," Kiernan says.

Kate's eyes soften. "I'm amazed that she got close enough to a CHRONOS key to bury it. Daphne hated those things." She turns to Clio and says, "Daphne was my grandmother's Irish setter."

"How can you be certain this will happen?" Kiernan asks, which answers our question about whether they would have felt the time shift this far into the past.

"Because it's already happened. And it's not the first time. There was a rift in the 1960s. Several key figures were assassinated—or rather, assassinated early, in the cases of Dr. King and John Lennon. US involvement in the war in Vietnam stretched out a bit as a result. We fixed that problem, and then almost immediately—"

"Let me get this straight," Kate says. "You find the key in Katherine's garden, figure out how to use it, and suddenly we have two time shifts. Have you considered that maybe you should stop using the key?"

I take a deep breath before answering, reminding myself that her tone is at least somewhat warranted. Some version of me apparently helped create the device, which led to its misuse by Saul Rand, her kidnapping, and her very near death. In addition, for the past two decades, she's had to deal with the fact that if she steps outside of a CHRONOS field, she will simply cease to exist. "I'd be delighted to stop using it, but as I told your husband, my use of the medallion isn't what triggered the shift. Or . . . at least, not directly. Are you familiar with Temporal Dilemma?"

The three of them nod and exchange a confused look.

"Of course," Kiernan says. "Time chess. Saul's bloody game. But surely you aren't saying a computer game caused the time shifts?"

I explain what we've learned so far as we eat dinner. The fact that I can't answer at least half of their questions reminds me we are still flying blind in so many ways. I've been honest with them up to this point, and even though I suspect it's not going to help my case, I press ahead with the one thing I'd really prefer not to tell them.

"We killed two of their people—their observers, as they call them—in our last confrontation. The man I killed had a sniper rifle aimed at a concert across the street and was planning to assassinate several civil rights activists, including Dr. King. The man Jack shot was about to kill me. This Morgen Campbell guy doesn't seem to be holding my actions against me, or maybe he doesn't know I'm the one who took out his sniper. But Saul Rand is apparently not happy with Jack. And Jack is stranded—that jump to Memphis was the first time he ever managed to use the key, and I don't know if he's just tapped out or what, but we can't get him back to 2136. The geneticist on our team is working on a solution, but the time shift means she doesn't have a lab anymore. I need a safe house for Jack in 1966, somewhere he can help us with research. If either of you can still pull up a stable point, we'd welcome your help, too. We're authorized five observers, but with CHRONOS no longer existing, there's really no one for us to pull in."

Kate's arms are crossed, her back pressed against her chair. "Can't say I'm exactly broken up about CHRONOS not existing. And you're asking us to take in someone Saul Rand would like to see dead."

"Well . . . not the Saul Rand you're thinking of," I say. "He's from another timeline."

"He's still Saul Rand." There's an edge to her voice, and it occurs to me that she's also from another timeline, so this might be a personal peeve of hers. "And that's asking us to take a rather major risk."

"She's right," Kiernan says. "Giving sanctuary to someone with a bounty on his head effectively puts a bounty on ours. But . . ." He turns toward Kate. "I'll be over eighty by then. You won't be far behind. We can make sure the kids—who will be grown, probably with children of their own by then—are safe. Someone once gave me and the other Kate refuge from the bloody Cyrists, and I'd likely have been dead if she hadn't. I told you this decision would be yours, and I'll stand by that. But I'm willing to take a little risk to pay that debt forward, if you are."

Clio has been mostly quiet, almost to the point that I wondered if she was paying attention. Now, however, she puts her fork on the edge of her plate. "If the two of you don't want to or can't take this guy in, I will. I'll be in my fifties by then, so hopefully I'll be doing well enough to have a spare room or at least a sofa. But I think everyone is overlooking a really big issue. We're about to live through twenty-five years under a very different government and society. Even if they manage to repair the rift, we're under CHRONOS keys. Our dual memories are going to be massive."

There's a really long silence at the table, and then Kate says, "No. *Our* dual memories are going to be massive."

Clio arches an eyebrow. "Isn't that what I just said?"

"What she means is that you have another option," Kiernan says. "It's been nearly ten years since either of us could lock in a stable point. We're stuck moving through time in single-day increments, so we'll have at least vague memories of two different chains of events. But if you stay in the period *before* the time shift, you can avoid that entirely."

"We'll find a spot where you can lie low and wait this thing out. If they manage to fix it," Kate adds, "our new memories will mostly overwrite the old. And if they don't, then you join us in 1941, and we find a way to fight within the system. Or we head north. The Canadian border is only a few hours' drive."

Kiernan's eyes catch Clio's. It's a fleeting look, but they're clearly communicating something. Kate catches it, too, and says, "Oh, no. You are not getting involved in this, Cliona Dunne. These people have trained for years. Using the key to travel home from Chicago more quickly is one thing, but using it to actually time travel . . ." She stops, probably realizing that she'd just advocated Clio using the key to remain in the past and avoid the double memories. "They're trained for this. You're not."

"I know better than to get involved, Mom. Dad and I were just a little surprised that you were suggesting I use the key at all. Of course, if I'm stashed in the past, you'll have to be the one who takes in Madi's friend."

There's a slight pause and then Kate says, "Fine. I'll make a note to expect a houseguest in . . . thirty-one years."

Clio then turns to me. "When and where are you meeting your friend?"

"The bus station in Geneva. August 23, 1966. His bus is scheduled to arrive a little after three."

"So four, if he's lucky," Kate says. Clio and Kiernan nod knowingly, so I assume that station has a reputation for delays.

"We'll have someone there to pick him up," Clio says. "Were you planning to jump directly home, or do you need a ride to the station?"

I glance at the time. Between the walk to the church, the twenty minutes or so I spent there talking with Kiernan, the walk over here, and dinner, it's been a little over an hour and a half.

"I'd *like* to meet him there so that I can catch him up on our progress," I tell her. "But I'm on a tight schedule. How far is it?"

Clio tells me it's about twenty minutes in good weather, but a half hour on a rainy night like this one.

"Why don't I drop the two of you off at the Strand and drive Madi to the station?" she says to her parents. "Then I'll circle back to pick you up."

"But you'll miss the movie," Kate protests. "And you love Bette Davis."

"I've already seen it, Mom. We got that one nearly a month ago in Chicago. And I'm dying to learn about the fashions two hundred years from now."

We drop Kate and Kiernan off at the theater on Fall Street, just a few doors down from the stable point where I'd jumped in earlier. The marquee reads *The Girl from 10th Avenue* and *Coming Soon—The Glass Key.* Clio pulls the car, a boxy-looking thing that I think might be a Model A, into the small lot next to the theater to turn around. I brace for the fashion questions she mentioned earlier, thinking that she's going to be woefully disappointed given my preference for casual over trendy. But instead she pushes a button on the control panel of the car. It squishes in, then she reaches into her bag and fishes around for something. After a moment, she pulls out a battered pack of cigarettes. A piece of card stock—a ticket, maybe?—is stuck between the package and the cellophane wrapper. She taps one out of the pack and then offers one to me.

"No, thanks," I say. "You know those things are really, really bad for you, right?"

Clio grins and drops the pack onto the bench seat between us. Then she yanks the button thing out of the dashboard. It's now glowing bright red, and I realize it's a cigarette lighter. "Not as bad for me as you'd think," she says as she lights up. "These are from 2170. Smokeless smokes. The only thing burning is paper, and I'll get just a tiny hit of nicotine. Still not entirely safe, but believe me, there are worse habits I could have picked up over the past five years. And I'm celebrating."

It's an odd choice of words given what I've just told her. "Celebrating what?"

"A personal victory."

I'm not really in the mood for twenty questions, so I ignore her cryptic comment. She'll tell me if she wants me to know. As we reach the edge of town, she yanks on the metal stick that protrudes upward from the floor of the car and the engine revs a bit louder. Blades flip across the windshield in a mesmerizing rhythm, diverting the rain. Clio guides the car along the highway almost effortlessly, tapping her cigarette against the wheel, and I find myself wondering what it's like to drive something this large. I've never operated a vehicle bigger than a scooter, and that was only when I was a kid. I don't think my mother has, either. My dad flew a small craft that a friend of his owned a few times, but it had an override for pilot error. Nora said that she drove when she was younger, but even back then there were safety features in the event that an animal rushed onto the road or your tires hit a patch of water. She said the cars her parents owned had balloons that inflated if you were in an accident and restraints to hold you in place. This vehicle has none of those things, and while Clio seems like a competent driver, I'm kind of wishing I'd refused the offer of a ride, especially when she takes her eyes from the road to glance in my direction.

"You can only have four historians as leads, but you said there were observers, right? People who could serve as assistants?"

"Yes, but—"

"I couldn't say anything in the restaurant because my mom would have had a conniption. But I have a lot more experience using the key than she believes. I'll fill her in on all of that later tonight, and I think she'll eventually come around, but either way, I'm in."

"I appreciate the offer, Clio. But I'm a little worried that you'd have a target on your back. Like I said earlier, we killed two of their observers during the last round. Katherine killed another one today who was shooting at me and Jack, and the game hasn't even officially begun yet. Or maybe they were just aiming at Jack. It seems like there's a certain degree of immunity for the main players, but they treat observers as pawns, and I'm not comfortable with putting anyone else in that position."

Her mouth twists wryly. "That's a wonderful sentiment, and I appreciate your concern for my well-being, but can you really afford to be so noble? I'm volunteering, and you need help. I've been in more dangerous situations. Plus, you said earlier that your best guess for time and place is 1939 to 1940 New York. I've spent a lot of time then and there. The Yankees' winning streak ended in 1940 and . . ." She shrugs.

That feels a bit like a non sequitur. "Baseball, right? Are you a fan?"

"Dear God, no. I mean, I kind of was as a kid. My dad loves the game, and we used to go into New York City once or twice a season to watch the Yankees. But that was before I was forced to sit through the 1939 World Series and the 1940 regular season, over and over, because Simon Rand kept getting these damned epiphanies for how he could continue the Yankees' streak for one more year. Only he made it worse. They were second in their division, but whatever he did put them one game behind the Indians, and he had to go back and stop himself from paying the bribe or whatever."

I understand very little of that, aside from the name. "Simon Rand. He was with the Cyrists. Saul's grandson, right?"

"Yeah. I've been stuck babysitting him for the past few years, trying to keep him from clueing in to the fact that the Cyrists lost their battle in 2015, or whenever."

"But he could just jump forward and find out, couldn't he?"

"Sure. If he'd really wanted to know. If he'd really wanted to grow up and face the consequences of aiding and abetting a genocidal maniac. But he preferred the freedom of playing time tourist." She takes another long drag of the cigarette, which really doesn't seem to be emitting much smoke, and then says, "My dad once said he thought maybe Simon *did* know what happened. Maybe he saw how things ended up for him and just wanted to prolong the inevitable. Play around for as long as he could in his personal historical sandbox. Mostly before the 1960s. He said history got boring by the time we got involved in Vietnam, but I think he just didn't like being around after Marilyn Monroe died. And he was definitely obsessed with her. He sent roses to her suite at the Lexington the entire time she was married to DiMaggio. It caused a bit of a problem between the couple. DiMaggio had the doorman refuse all flower deliveries, but they still kept showing up, because Simon had rented the room the year before they moved in and set a stable point. I think DiMaggio felt guilty about the whole thing, because legend has it that he sent a dozen roses to her crypt three times a week after she committed suicide, right up until he died in the 1990s. Only, that's not entirely true. DiMaggio sent roses once a week. Simon, determined to outdo him, set up a standing order with the same florist. I don't think he ever managed to screw up the nerve to even speak to Monroe before she died, but he had an active imagination, a CHRONOS key, and he was a bit of a voyeur."

"Ick."

"And no," she says, "since I suspect you're wondering. He tried with me exactly once, when he'd had too much to drink and struck out with the singer he was fixating on at some nightclub. But in addition to smokes from the future, I picked up a little gadget that gave Simon Rand a nasty jolt of electricity. I think the real thing that kept him from pushing it further was that while he was recovering from the shock, I told him if he ever touched me that way again, I'd go back to when my father *could* still use the medallion and he'd have to explain himself. There may also have been something in there to suggest that he'd be dining on his own testicles, because I was mad as hell. But I think it was less the physical threat and more that he needed a reminder that I'm Kiernan Dunne's daughter. Simon is, as my mom would say, one sick puppy, but he loves my dad."

She cranks the window slightly to flick out a bit of ash. "Sorry. I'm rattling on. But I haven't had anyone I could discuss this with since . . . well, since the relationship that Simon managed to end by constantly popping in with demands on my time. And, yeah, I could talk to my dad about it, but any time I mentioned it, I could tell he just felt guilty that he couldn't be the one keeping Simon occupied. That it was wrecking my life. Because it *was* wrecking my life."

"But, eventually, Simon *did* jump forward and do his part to start the Culling like Saul asked, right?"

"Yes. I jumped ahead to when they were building the Sixteenth Street Temple in DC and set a stable point in what would eventually be Patrick Conwell's office. And every time Simon popped in with some great new trip we needed to go on, the first thing I'd do was check that stable point. He was always there, exactly where my dad said he was at the end. And because he was still there, I followed him to another Yankees game. Another bar. Another Broadway show. Because I was scared that if I didn't, I'd check that stable point and he wouldn't be there. That he would *undo* it. That he'd change something and wreck everything my mom and dad worked for, and then we'd end up with God only knows how many millions of people dead in the distant future, when I'll either be getting ready to blow out the candles on my one-hundred-and-third birthday cake or be dead myself. Probably the latter, since I've managed to squeeze about seven years into the past five, between my actual life and time-tourist duty."

Clio takes another drag on the cigarette and smiles, although there's something a little crazed about her expression. "And *that* is why I'm celebrating. It's all over now, and I can move on. Dealing with Simon Rand cost me a hell of a lot, and I don't just mean my time." She pushes the pack of smokes toward me and taps the paper stuck inside the wrapper. "Check that out."

I reach inside and extract what is indeed a ticket. *New York Yankees, Inc. Yankee Stadium. Grandstand Admission: $1.10.*

"That's for game 115 of the 1940 season, against the Indians. I was supposed to meet Simon outside the stadium a half hour prior to the game. He didn't show. Which has never happened before. I thought maybe he'd finally decided to get it over with, finish Saul's task and take whatever consequences followed. But then I get back to my boardinghouse in Chicago and find a message from Dad to call home. After he explained about the meeting with you tonight and asked if I could jump over and join them, I got to wondering again about Simon's absence. So I checked the stable point for some of the other dates we've been at Yankee Stadium. I checked the box seats he bought. I checked the standard stable point on Broadway where I meet him when he wants to take in a show. And I didn't find him *there*, either. I'm missing, too, which is weird and makes my head hurt, because I have excruciatingly clear memories of those trips. But I also sort of remember *not* making them."

"Simon must have been outside a CHRONOS field when the shift happened."

"Yeah. I have a hard time imagining him without the key, though. And I don't know how this affects the timeline. Simon played a role in the Culling, and everything my mom and dad did, and . . . God, I still have to tell Dad." Clio's smile is gone now. "They grew up together on the Cyrist Farm, and they were like brothers at one point. I don't know if he'll be happy or sad. Probably a bit of both." She stops and shudders. "If this had happened three weeks ago, Dad wouldn't have been under a key, either. Mom was so freaked out about me living in Chicago that he gave me the spare key, the one he'd been wearing just as a precaution since Aunt June died."

"June? Was she at the Cyrist Farm, too?"

She nods. "At various times, yes."

"I met her when I accidentally figured out how to use the key. She was your aunt?"

"No. That's just what we kids called her. She lived with us until she died about nine years ago. I think she missed being a doctor, but her credentials were from something like 2025, so I doubt they'd have been much use in 1912. She was the doctor for all of the Pru babies on the Farm. Did you know about that?"

"Some," I say. "I've read your mom's diaries. Well, a *few* of them were her diary entries. Most of them were from Kate . . . I mean, Kate Pierce-Keller."

She reduces her speed a bit as the lights of a small town come into view up ahead. "Oh. You mean Other-Kate."

I have to chuckle. "Funny. That's what *she* calls your mom."

"And that's what my mom calls her. Which shouldn't be a surprise, really, given that they're basically carbon copies."

It hits me then that Kate Dunne is almost certainly the only version of Kate in this reality. The fact that the Dunnes were under a key *prior* to 1941 is the only thing that protected them. I haven't checked to be certain, but Jarvis said that Nora doesn't exist. Katherine never owned the house, and I'm pretty sure if I scroll back in time on the stable point in my bedroom, I'll see it empty throughout. All that's left of Kate are the items protected inside the house, the books her son tried to save from the previous timeline, and her diary entries. Even if we win this game, the odds of restoring the exact set of circumstances that will allow me to see Nora or my mother again seem very slim. I feel a rush of grief, not just for them, but also for Kate. After listening to her rants about the Cyrists and CHRONOS, and spending hours watching her as she sat on the couch in my room just days before her death, it feels like I knew her.

"I only gave Dad back the spare medallion because Simon found . . . this . . ." She pulls up the edge of her skirt to reveal a garter. The medallion attached to it is inside a leather pouch, but I can still see faint dots of amber light along the seams.

When she releases the hem of her skirt, her hand is shaking. "Oh, damn it. He knew. He *knew*."

She yanks the wheel sharply to the right and pulls onto the shoulder. Tears are streaming down her cheeks, and I can't help but marvel at her rapid reversal of mood. For several minutes, her body shakes with sobs. I have no idea what to say to comfort her, so I just pat her arm and wait for it to end. I'm not even sure why she's so distraught. From her comments a few minutes ago, it was pretty clear that she hated the guy.

When she finally pulls herself together, she yanks her CHRONOS key out of her sweater and begins scanning through stable points. I can't see what she's looking at, and for once, I'm kind of glad, because it feels like I'd be invading her privacy. I just stare at the rain drizzling down the window and try not to think about the fact that I really need to get back to my own time.

After a moment, she puts the key away. "He's not there. But he wasn't at any of the other places I know he went, either. I can't prove it or disprove it, but I think the son of a bitch actually . . ." She bites her lower lip. "I think this was Simon's spare key. The only thing that saved him from being erased in Conwell's office was the fact that he was wearing a spare."

There's a very long silence, and then she puts the car back into gear and pulls back onto the road. "When we left Seneca Falls, my plan was to tell you that there was one condition on my offer to be one of these observers. I know the time period, almost certainly better than anyone on your team. I *want* to help. And if you have only two days, you're going to *need* my help. But . . . my folks unfortunately raised me to be honest, so I was going to tell you up front that I had an additional motive. My first priority would be to win this stupid game and restore the timeline. But if there was any way at all to accomplish it, I also planned to make sure Simon Rand bloody well *stayed* erased. And *now* I find out he's probably the only reason my dad still exists."

∞

GENEVA, NEW YORK
AUGUST 23, 1966

Kate was right. The bus is late.

When Clio dropped me off around nine thirty back in 1935, the bus station, which is really more of a bus *stop*, was closed for the evening. I scrolled through to three o'clock today, and then continued viewing the spot in one-minute increments until it finally pulled in just outside the gas station, around a quarter of four. I set a local point behind the ice machine on the side of the building. Clio then transferred the stable point at her parents' house to my key, and I pulled up the point in the foyer at the house in Bethesda, but she said that it was already on her key. I seriously doubt any of them have been idly surveilling my house nearly two hundred years in the future. But I will definitely not be going down to the kitchen clad only in my undies the next time I get a craving for a midnight snack.

I blink into a bright, warm, and breezy morning. It occurs to me as I open my eyes that I should really have waited not simply for the bus but to see Jack get off the bus. The sound of the shots fired at the

Peabody come rushing back, the memory of my heart pounding as we ran for the back door. Jack would have had to change buses twice, first in Nashville. Had another sniper been waiting? For that matter, is a sniper waiting here? The bastards piggybacked on my jumps once. What's to stop them from doing it again?

Those thoughts had barely surfaced yesterday. I walked down the rain-soaked streets of 1935 Seneca Falls without thinking once about snipers lying in wait, following me in their scope from some hidden perch. True, I was focused on my task, but I've still got plenty on my plate. No, the main reason I'm thinking these things right now is that I'm more afraid of someone killing Jack than I am of someone killing me. I lost my father six months ago. Now Nora and my mom are gone. Jack is all I have. Well, I have Thea, too, I guess. But given her connection to the Cyrists, I'm not entirely sure whether that belongs in the positive or negative column.

The flag flying at the bank across the street isn't doing much to calm me down, either. It's the first one I've seen in this altered version of the country. Tyson told us at the restaurant yesterday that the US had been divided into economic zones, but he didn't say how many. Twenty, apparently, given the number of stars on the flag, arranged in five even rows of four.

Then the door opens. Jack steps out, squinting against the afternoon sun, and I hurry toward him. Given the dark direction my thoughts traveled a moment ago, it makes me nervous to see him standing out in the open, nervous to *be* standing out in the open. I try to relax when Jack pulls me into his arms, to breathe him in and be content that we've made it this far. But I'm still bracing for the crack of a rifle.

"They said no?" he asks.

"What? No. I'm just . . ." I pull in a steadying breath and nod toward a small convenience store across the road. "Kate will be here shortly. I'll just feel better when we're not standing out here in the open."

Of course, I'm *not* entirely certain that Kate will be here. We're three decades and a time shift away from the point where she made that agreement. She could have changed her mind. She could have followed through on her idea of spiriting her family away to Canada.

We cross the road and enter a small store across the street with hand-lettered signs in the windows. Jack ducks inside while I stand at the doorway watching for Kate. After a minute, he comes back with two sodas. "I was looking for something without sugar or unsafe chemicals, but that's apparently not an option. The cashier said if I wanted water, there was a fountain over by the bathrooms at the gas station."

He hands me one of the dark-green bottles labeled *Squirt*. Is this a product that spans both realities or one of those niche items that only exists in one? I take an experimental sip. It's actually not bad. Definitely better than the Dr. Pepper I grabbed the last time I was in 1930s New York. We sit on a bench outside the store, and I bring him up to speed on events since he got on the bus.

"And you think Clio will be an asset?" he asks when I reach the end.

"I do, although I'm beginning to think the idea that we can put this timeline completely back on track is naive, to say the least. The books in our library back in Bethesda seem to suggest that we're several realities away from the original where I somehow assist Alex and RJ in forming CHRONOS." He opens his mouth to speak, but I already know what he's going to ask. "Yes. I checked the anomalies list for Elizabeth Forson and her clones. They never exist in this timeline."

"Well, that's good news, right? No new genetics war?" Jack would never have been pulled into all of this, and we likely would never have met, if not for the fact that his father was trying to avert a war he was convinced would kill millions of people.

"It's not that simple, unfortunately. A second genetics war has been going on for the past two decades. I don't have all the details, but simply removing Forson from the picture doesn't seem to have changed much."

A car pulls into the lot next to the bus stop. I dismiss it at first because the driver is an elderly woman, but then I remember that Kate Dunne is in her seventies now. Only moments ago, I was mentally berating her for being late, and now I wish she'd have waited because I'm not really ready to tell Jack goodbye again. And the face staring out at us isn't exactly a welcoming one. In fact, I'd classify it as royally pissed.

"I'll drop by the cabin each day to keep you up to speed," I tell Jack as we head back across the street.

"No. Not every day," he says. "You only have two days to fix this, Madi. We both know there won't be much I can do from here. Tyson was just trying to soothe my ego." I start to protest, but he squeezes my hand. "It's true. If there are stable points you need monitored, Clio is probably a better option. Or the Dunnes, back in 1939. Plus, if I see you in danger, there's a decent chance I'll blink myself back even further. What you said at the hotel was right. Fix this, and when you're done, we can deal with everything else."

I'm tempted to protest, but we're now only a few feet away from Kate Dunne, who is scowling at us from the open window of her powder-blue Ford Fairlane. "He's right. I've just experienced three decades without my daughter. I lost a son to this abomination of a government. We've spent years stuck in the cabin as virtual hermits, trying to stay off the radar. These are *not* memories I want to keep." The photograph I gave her at the restaurant is clutched in one hand. It's fared worse over the past thirty years than it did during more than a century inside the album in the controlled atmosphere of the library. "This reality," she says. "I want this back. This, or as close to it as you can get. And I want your promise that you'll do everything in your power to make sure that Clio and Kiernan remain in this picture. Otherwise, I swear to God I will haunt you."

There are tears on her cheeks and in her voice, and all I can think of is Clio crying on the side of the road ten minutes and thirty-one years ago. I felt as helpless then as I do now. Kate's words are angry and demanding, but there's a note of pleading that breaks my heart. They all looked so happy in that picture, and I wonder whether I was unkind to leave it with her. True, it probably gave her hope during some very dark times, but was it a false hope? I want to ask her why Clio and Kiernan might *not* be in that picture, but I suspect that knowledge would only complicate things even more.

I take a few steps toward the car and crouch down. Her eyes, still green but cloudy with age, are now level with mine.

"You have my word, Kate. *I promise.*"

The anger fades from her expression, and she just looks old and very tired.

I rejoin Jack, who's still standing near the back of the car. He gives me a look that very clearly asks whether it was wise to make promises about things outside my control, and then pulls me into his arms.

On the one hand, it doesn't matter. I said I'd do everything in my power. And I would have done everything in my power anyway, even without the promise.

But he's right. If I can't keep the promise, Kate Dunne won't have to haunt me. The memory of her clutching that tattered photograph will do the job all on its own.

FROM *THE BOOK OF PROPHECY*

CHAPTER OF PRUDENCE

The patron of the House of Prudence is the Apple.

As Eve took the Apple from the tree, so shall the House of Prudence bring five thousand Apples into the storehouse on the twelfth day of December in the year 1980. And the House shall live upon the dividend of these Apples in perpetuity.

As Prudence is the first daughter of Cyrus, the living embodiment of his spirit upon the earth, her form is eternal. When the body takes the shape of the Crone, three daughters will arise, each as a helpmeet, each identical in form and substance. They shall wear the Key of Light, but not the Key of Time.

As it is foretold and decreed, the ancestral home of the Mother of Prudence shall be raised up as an eternal, unchanging shrine in the year 2017.

So it is written, and so shall it be.

∞14∞

Madi reappears in the library about twenty minutes before the deadline for inserting the game chip. As soon as she steps out of the stable point, another woman blinks in. The new arrival appears to be in her midtwenties, with dark curls and green eyes. Almost instantly, her tentative smile morphs into a grimace, and she clutches her stomach. When the queasiness passes, she glances around the library, where the entire contingent, including the baby, is now gathered, and tucks her CHRONOS key back inside her sweater.

"That was the shift, wasn't it?" she asks Madi. "That sick feeling that hit me."

Madi nods. "Almost certainly. I guess this is your first trip past the date the timeline flipped." Then she turns toward the rest of us. "Jack is now settled in Skaneateles. This is Clio Dunne, Kate and Kiernan's daughter. She's offered to help."

"Did you say *Dunne*?" Rich asks after we introduce ourselves. "Are you related to Padraic?"

She nods. "He was my great-grandfather. Never met him, though, since he died even before my dad was born in 1885. I haven't jumped to County Clare to see if he's still around back then, but I'm fairly sure he's not. From what Madi told me, this new chain of events means he was erased before the jump that stranded him over there while researching the Great Hunger."

Padraic Dunne is in the same cohort as Delia Morrell, one of the historians I trained with. Given that he's a Europeanist, our paths haven't crossed much. He's also the only historian I know who is married to someone outside CHRONOS, and as a result he doesn't tend to hang out and socialize after hours. The agency tends to be pretty insular, and outside partnerships are strongly discouraged prior to retirement, which comes early enough that you still have options for raising a family if you're so inclined. Marriage before retirement is generally tolerated between historians, however, especially those who are paired off to work as couples in the field. In our classroom training, we were taught that outside relationships rarely work because of the aging differential. Most historians spend six months in the field for each year they're active. We return exactly an hour after we leave, so it's not that relationships are strained by the burden of long absences. Over the course of field training and the fifteen years or so that you're an active agent, however, you generally age an extra eight to ten years. That time is added onto your official age in the medical records, which makes birthdays a bit confusing.

I don't see much similarity between Clio and Paddy, who is fair skinned with ruddy cheeks, yet another testament to the stereotypes perpetrated by most CHRONOS genetic-design teams. But the girl's bright-green eyes are very familiar. They look almost identical to the eyes that greeted me a few days ago when I woke up in the isolation tank. Angelo had pulled in Timothy Winslow to go back to 1965 and make an anonymous tip that helped get the Voting Rights Act back on course. He'd been kept in the dark as to exactly what I did to screw things up, but we suffered through the time-travel equivalent of a hangover—double memories for him, and triple for me—during that twelve-hour stint in the tank.

Madi said Kate Dunne was sort of kin to her. She also said previously that she was descended from several CHRONOS historians. I'd assumed that meant just Katherine and Saul, but now I'm beginning to suspect that Timothy and Evelyn Winslow are somewhere in her gene pool as well.

Katherine turns to look at us. "I don't think bringing her in is a good idea. Didn't we just decide that we were going to do this without observers? We'd only be giving the other side hostages by pulling anyone else in."

"Clio and I have had this conversation," Madi says. "And to be honest, I agree with you, Katherine. I don't like this. But—"

"But you need the help," Clio says. "I know the era better than *any* of you. You may have had classroom training on how to be a historian, but I've probably spent more time actually using the key in the field, and a good chunk of that time was in 1939 and 1940."

"Why those years?" I ask her. "What were you studying?"

"Baseball, mostly. If a city had an American League team or made the series in either of those years, I spent at least a few days there. There were also a couple of trips to the fair. Movies."

"So you were a time tourist?" Katherine says. "Are you sure you wouldn't rather volunteer to work for the other team?"

It's a rather caustic comment, and more than anything else she's said since we got here, it tells me that Katherine is more upset than she'd like to admit about killing the observer in Memphis. I suspect she thinks that if she's sufficiently snide and nasty, the girl will huff out and she won't have to worry about putting anyone else in harm's way.

But judging from the amused lift of her eyebrow, I don't think Clio Dunne is going to be easily offended—or easily deterred.

"Let me guess. You're Katherine Shaw. My mother said—" She stops abruptly in response to Madi clearing her throat, takes a breath, and then continues. "I'm not a time tourist. Any time travel I engaged in was work related. I may not have the training of a CHRONOS agent, but I've spent several years managing one of the messes you guys left behind. As I said, I know the time period better than any of you—for one thing, it's close to my own time, but I also read a lot of newspapers during those games. Baseball is tedious enough the first time you watch a game, let alone the third or fourth time. And Simon—" Madi doesn't even have to clear her throat this time. Clio stops herself automatically and shifts tracks. "Anyway, there's a *lot* going on in those years. And this is as much my fight as it is yours. I hadn't told my family yet, but I was thinking about volunteering after Pearl Harbor. I'm willing to take the risk."

Everyone is looking at me for input, and I realize that they're assuming I'm taking the lead again. "Whoa. Hold on. This is a group decision. And even if it wasn't, I'm not the senior historian here. That's either Rich or Katherine."

They both protest, noting that I have more time in the era than either of them. "Plus," Katherine adds, "your name was first on the roster. Alisa contacted you, not one of us, to give you the data. And we don't have a lot of time to dither about."

I'm tempted to point out that Madi was listed second on that roster, which would put her second in command. Katherine is right on one thing—we need to make decisions quickly. But it only takes a few seconds for a show of hands. "Fine. Since you're designating me as team lead, my decision is that the entire team votes. All in favor of adding Clio Dunne as an official observer, raise your hand." I run a quick count. Everyone but Katherine votes yes, although I notice a slight delay as Alex, Lorena, and RJ look to Madi for guidance. I think it's safe to say that we really have *two* team leaders.

"The ayes have it, seven to one."

"Seven to two, technically," Katherine says, nodding toward the baby. "Welcome aboard, Clio." Katherine doesn't seem at all put out about the vote not going in her favor, so I think her resistance was merely a safeguard to make sure she didn't have the death of another observer on her conscience. I'm fine with that, especially since the observer in question is her great-granddaughter . . . sort of . . . although I left that information out of the bare-bones account I gave her earlier.

I turn to Clio. "Okay. You are an official observer. But the bulk of your observing will be done through the CHRONOS key, from this library. We can jump back regularly to get your input."

Clio shakes her head. "With all due respect, that's not the best use of my abilities. It sounds more like you're planning to stash me away out of danger and make me think I'm doing something useful. If you want me to keep out of your way, I will, but I'll be doing that from 1939 New York, which is where I plan to be whether I'm officially part of the team or not."

She nods toward the list on the wall screen.

1) Conversion of Father Coughlin (*11/10/1938?)

2) Deaths at Pro-America Rally (*2/20/39)

3) Unsuccessful attack on Japanese ambassador (*6/2/39)

4) Attempted assassination of Lindbergh (*2/22/40)

5) Court of Peace at World's Fair is bombed (*7/4/40)

*NYC

"Are those the things you think were changed?" Clio asks.

"They only changed three," I tell her. "The others are consequences of those changes. We're about to vote on which three to choose for our initial predictions, which we have to enter into the system in . . ."

I check the time on my key. "Fourteen minutes. Coughlin's conversion happened first, so it's definitely on the list, but the others could, at least theoretically, be the result of another change."

Clio pulls a CHRONOS diary from her handbag and records the screen, then shifts the diary in my direction. "You'll have to research all of them, though. Right? Have you decided yet who will be handling what?"

"Katherine and Rich will take the lead on Coughlin and probably assist on Lindbergh," I say, wondering if she always takes notes via diary. "Both of those may include some travel outside NYC, even though the moves we make will have to be inside the city. Madi and I will take the lead on the others."

"Okay." She aims the diary toward each of us for a few seconds and then asks Madi, "Am I violating any rules of The Game if I blink out briefly?"

"Nooo," Madi responds, sounding a little confused. "Not as long as you spend less than four hours away and are back here within a few minutes." She turns to me for confirmation and I nod.

"Okay, then. Back in a flash." And then Clio blinks out.

"Where is she going?" Katherine asks.

Madi shrugs. "Don't look at me. I have no idea what she's up to."

Clio is back in less than a minute, carrying a briefcase. She puts it on the coffee table and unlocks the clasp, pulling out a stack of manila envelopes. "Identification for all four of you. Money, too. Neither of those will be worth a damn after 1943, but they're solid for the years prior to that." She pulls out a sheet of paper. "These are just basic bullet points because you only have a few minutes to absorb them before you make your predictions. We have the full research to back it up at the apartment."

"What apartment?" I ask.

"A three-bedroom walk-up on West 44th, near the Algonquin. My dad purchased a small house in the Detroit suburbs, too, although

I haven't seen it. I know you'll be coming back here some to use the computers—the one we have is just a tablet and it's really basic—but there will be room for everyone to sleep in both places if they don't want to or, for some reason, can't make the trip back."

I'm about to ask how they have any sort of computer in 1938, but Alex jumps in with a different question. "And you managed all of that in less than four hours, right? Because otherwise, you can't be listed as an observer, which means you'll need to be out of here before we initiate the simulation."

Clio checks her key. "Three hours and twenty-seven minutes for me. But about three years for my parents to purchase the properties, secure the identification, and so forth."

"Christ. They must have spent a fortune," RJ says.

She smiles. "Let's just say they have a knack for the stock market, even though my mom insists that they avoid defense stocks and major polluters, which makes it a challenge. Plus, they live in a house in the middle of nowhere, and they don't travel because there's too much of a chance they might end up outside the CHRONOS field, which would erase my mom. And I think they've both always worried that something like this might happen again. My mom calls my dad a prepper, which I think was slang for a crazy hoarder when she was growing up. Anyway, money isn't something they have to worry about. Oh, and my dad will be joining us in June of 1940. Strictly a support role, since he can't use the key, but we may need extra boots on the ground, as they say."

Madi, who looks a bit paler than usual, says, "What about your mom? I mean, I know she can't use the key, but—"

"The plan is for her to remain in Skaneateles. We know there's risk involved, and while my brothers are both adults now, Dad didn't want there to be any chance that they might lose both parents. And if you meant is she okay with either of us being involved, the answer is *not entirely*. She's worried. But she understands what's at stake. She's actually the one who handled most of the research for the background files."

Clio hands me the paper with the bullet points. "The only one on this list that has my parents worried is the date for Coughlin. They say it started earlier, based on conversations with some Cyrists in Detroit. My dad stayed in the area for a few weeks while he was purchasing the house there, and he went to the temple a couple of times. He grew up in that culture, so he can fit in pretty easily. Several of the people he spoke to said the land they're building the new temple on was purchased in late 1937, and someone began hiring contractors the next summer."

"That's not possible, though," Katherine says. "We know that the other team earned full style points and a bonus for the chronological category, so everything has to be within a two-year window. If Coughlin was converted in 1937, all of their other moves would have been before the fall of 1939."

Katherine has a valid point, but I hate to dismiss the opinion of Clio's parents entirely, given that they've gone to great expense and effort to keep us from winging this. "Maybe Coughlin's earlier contacts with the Cyrists were just an . . . I don't know. Interfaith cooperation of some sort?" I suggest, but Clio doesn't seem convinced.

I scan through the bullet points she gave me and see that she's right. They're mostly just additional information about the events. Suspects the police questioned, names of possible contacts in the Bund or Universal Front, and so forth. There's not much here that we can act on in the few minutes we have left before the deadline to start the game. So after passing the list around the room for everyone to skim through, I collect a notepad and several pens from an old desk in the corner of the library.

"Rank the five options," I say as I tear off a sheet of paper for each of them. "We've currently got the choices in chronological order, but the only option that is connected to Japan is third on the list, and something our opponents do keeps Japan from bombing Pearl Harbor, so . . . we have to take that into consideration."

I jot down 1, 3, 4, 2, 5 on my sheet. The killings at the Pro-America Rally are definitely a change, but Coughlin is on the stage this time. Lawrence Dennis, as well, although I guess it's possible that Dennis signed on when he saw Coughlin was going to be speaking because he knew there would be a major crowd. Maybe Coughlin's presence also resulted in a different dynamic among the protestors outside Madison Square Garden. He was an incendiary figure in our timeline—people either loved him or hated him. Maybe his rhetoric grew more heated after his conversion. And the fifth change, the July 4th bombing, is the last chronologically. It seems far more likely to have been triggered by the earlier alterations to the timeline.

Rich collects the ballots, and I tally them up. One person, probably Clio, drops Coughlin's conversion down to the fourth slot, and another elevates the Court of Peace bombing to third. But in the end, most of the ballots mirror my own.

"Okay, we'll be going with one, three, and four. Are you ready to start the simulator, Alex?"

He nods and slips the drive into the SimMaster 8560. The trademark globe appears as always, but it's accompanied now by up-tempo music. Then the globe, which usually just hovers, explodes into a cascade of fireworks as a small sign reading *TD Off-World* zooms into view. Then we're back to the usual globe, with a video screen superimposed on top. The image is the Redwing Room, where Morgen Campbell is seated on his platform. The chair, which is a bit worn and tattered in our reality, seems to have gotten an upgrade, and the Doberman at his feet looks considerably younger than Cyrus. The man in the chair, however, isn't the younger, slightly more svelte version, but the old gox himself, looking every bit the king on his throne. He's smiling genially at the camera, and apparently at an audience, based on the background sound of applause. After a moment, he holds up his hand, and the applause gradually dies down as he speaks.

"Welcome, welcome, time-chess aficionados to the twenty-seventh edition of TD Off-World! I am, of course, your host, Morgen G. Campbell, and we have a very special treat for you this season. As those of you who followed the last round are no doubt aware, things took a rather unusual turn at the end of play, when the timeline shift was reversed by a group of rogue historians from World 47H, resulting in an unprecedented draw between our two championship teams."

As Campbell speaks, images from the Beatles concert flash onto the corners of the screen behind him in clockwise order. At the upper right, there's a clip of me tackling John Lennon to the stage. Directly below is Richard in the men's room, nearly strangling one of their observers with his CHRONOS key. Katherine zapping Saul and Alisa fills the lower left corner. The montage ends at the upper left with a dramatic clip of Madi shooting the sniper who was preparing to fire on Dr. King and the Selma marchers camped across the street.

"How did they get those images?" Madi whispers.

"Probably from stable points they had set at those locations," I say.

The clips are mostly met by boos, although there is a smattering of applause mixed in.

"An unexpected twist to say the least," Morgen says. "And both team leaders initially requested a rematch on a different playing field. I think perhaps there's a bit of ego involved." Polite chuckles from the audience. "But where's the fun in that for you, our viewers? You don't want to see the same scenario, do you?"

A chorus of nos arises, and we get a brief glimpse of the audience shaking their heads. They look entirely normal, just like any group who would be at an OC event. I'm not sure why that surprises me, but it does.

"Of course you don't!" Morgen booms. "And who could blame you? That's why we've opted instead to rattle the box a bit and embark on an adventure that I'm sure will be appealing to our viewers, our contestants, and five lucky off-world observers." The camera again moves to a section of the audience, where four men and one woman, presumably the five observers, are seated.

None of the men look familiar to me, but my stomach sinks when I realize the woman is Marcy Bateman, who heads up the Timeline Consistency section of the Temporal Monitoring Unit. She looks a bit different—longer hair and she's in a dress, rather than the usual CHRONOS scrubs. But it's definitely her.

"Is that . . . *Marcy*?" Katherine looks to me for confirmation because Marcy and I dated briefly when we were in our respective training programs. This was before Marcy had fully sorted out whether she was more attracted to guys or to girls, and we parted on friendly terms when Annika came into the picture to answer that question definitively. Rich and I have lunch with the two of them a few times a month. I glance over at him and see that he's wearing the same expression of shock that I'm feeling.

"Yeah," I say. "That's her."

The words have barely left my mouth when the names pop onto the screen below their faces. Three of the men are classified as *SPORT*. One of them has odd sideburns and a pointy nose that make him look like a fox. Another reminds me a bit of Tate. He's not nearly as large, and his hair is slightly darker, but I suspect those muscles are attributable more to a genetic boost than hours spent at the gym. Marcy and the young guy seated next to her are labeled *ACADEMIC*.

Katherine curses under her breath. We'd already agreed to make every effort to spare the observers they seem to be using as cannon fodder. But having a face we all know, a face we see after each and every time jump, on one of their pawns hammers the point home.

"You may be wondering why we have only *five* observers tonight, rather than the usual five per team," Morgen continues. "That is because for this special event, our four ranking champions will compete as a *single* team. This season, for the first time, they will combine forces against an off-world opponent"—he waves at the images on the display behind him, which now include the names *TYSON, RICHARD, KATHERINE,* and *MAX* in bold white letters—"the team who threw our last season into chaos, four scrappy, unseasoned, and undeniably brutal CHRONOS agents from World 47H."

Approving murmurs from the crowd follow this announcement. It might be my imagination, but I think those murmurs are louder after he says the word *brutal.*

"World 47H will be known as Team Hyena. And now," he says, "let's welcome the players for our own Team Viper. First—"

The video cuts abruptly at that point. When it resumes, Morgen Campbell is no longer on his throne but seated behind a desk, leaning toward the camera. "I think we'll keep the next bit to ourselves, since our viewers like to see individual player stats displayed, and that's the sort of information that might give your side an unfair advantage. These are the only stats you need. Display style-points tally for Team Viper."

A list pops up on the right side of the screen:

Character Assist: 75

Chronological: 125

Geographic: 175

Social Movement: 75

Government: 75

Probability: 50

"As you can see, our players have done exceptionally well. When the game begins, you will have two days. During that time, we will avoid direct interference with your moves, although that is not a popular decision with the team due to your actions in our last match and the fact that you seem to have a rogue agent tweaking our playing field. But since that occurred *prior* to the official beginning of play, I'm willing to overlook it. Let me just note that from here on out, all of your moves must be made by the four players and officially designated observers."

"Hmph," I say. "He's got a lot of nerve talking rogue agents given that they had someone taking potshots at us in Memphis."

Morgen tilts his head to the side, arching one eyebrow. That's when I realize that this, unlike the previous segment, is not a recording. Alex must notice the same thing, because he immediately begins typing something into one of his computer terminals.

"Oh, be still," Morgen says with a look of disgust. "I'm messaging you through the sim-system. It's not going to let me tap into your files. And you can hardly blame Saul for targeting one of your observers. Your side has now killed three of ours. We rarely lose that many in an entire season, let alone in a single match. Once the game begins, we'll be following standard player-safety protocol and—"

"Which means what in this context?" Rich says, clearly exasperated. "We don't play with living pawns, so you're going to have to spell it out."

Morgen blinks, annoyed at the interruption. "The SimMaster includes a rule book. I suggest that you read it carefully before attempting your first move. The short version is simply this: Players are off-limits. You may incapacitate them if you encounter them, but you may not maim or kill. You are playing against our four most popular players. They are fan favorites, and we'd prefer not to lose them. Should you violate this rule, the safety protocol will be abandoned, and you will all become fair game for our team and our observers. And we have the advantage of having a damn good idea where you'll be and when, so I wouldn't advise it."

"Extend the safety protocol to the observers," I tell him. "It should apply across the board."

"How odd that you say that *now*, after you've taken out three on our side. Seems like a rather convenient time to climb on your high horse and start worrying about morality and the sanctity of life. But I'd have said no either way. If the safety protocol extends to observers, you've effectively removed most of the drama from the equation. We would lose millions of viewers, as our audience would quickly move on to something more interesting. That's not to say that you can't show a bit of mercy, from time to time. We usually simply capture or wound the observers on the other side. But given that you've played in such a bloodthirsty fashion so far, you shouldn't be surprised that Saul is feeling a bit—"

"Bloodthirsty?" Madi says angrily. "This is *our* reality you're fucking around with. You may be playing a game, but we're not."

Morgen stares at her for a moment, then shakes his head, laughing. "Oh, but you *are*, my dear. Whether you like it or not, you most certainly are."

The screen goes blank, aside from the still-spinning globe and a timer set to five minutes. As the numbers roll, the automated female voice of the SimMaster 8560 calmly instructs us participants to enter our names, along with whether we are team leads, players, or observers. I go first, and at the end, the voice asks me to activate my CHRONOS key.

When I'm done, I step aside and say, "Your turn, *Max*."

Madi nods to acknowledge the reminder about her pseudonym. "Max Coleman, player." She activates her key, and then the computer asks for the next player. Rich is about to begin when Jarvis chimes in with an announcement.

"Mistress, your grandmother has arrived. Shall I let her in?"

"Nora's here?" Madi asks, and then her face falls. "Oh. Never mind. You mean Thea. No. Don't let her in yet. Tell her I'll be down in a couple of minutes."

Rich states his name and is about to activate his key when Jarvis interrupts. "Mistress, Thea Randall is in the foyer."

"But I said *not* to—"

"Unfortunately, Miss Randall is registered as a representative for the legal owner of this property. Section 3239c of the local housing code prevents me from refusing her entry."

Madi sighs and says she'll be right back. Rich and Katherine enter their information. By the time Clio is finished registering, Madi is indeed back, with an older woman directly behind her. As they step into the library, the woman says, "Thea Randall. Observer."

"No. She is *not* an observer," Madi says. "Thea, tell the computer that you're not an observer. You can't even use the key!"

I second Madi's objection, but the computer begs to differ. "Tyson Reyes, team lead. Max Coleman, player two. Katherine Shaw, player three. Richard Vier, player four. Clio Dunne, observer one. Thea Randall, observer two. Do you wish to enter additional observers?"

"We have only *one* observer," I say. "Clio Dunne."

"Incorrect. You have two observers. Clio Dunne and Thea Randall. You may add more observers to reach the maximum of five. Otherwise, you have two minutes to state your three initial predictions in the order you plan to proceed."

"Thea, please," Madi says. "You can't help us, and you're putting yourself at risk. Just tell the computer that you are not an observer."

The woman narrows her eyes at Madi. "I'll do no such thing. I'm *supposed* to be here. It's in *The Book of Prophecy*. If we didn't follow the "Chapter of Prudence," I wouldn't even exist. You wouldn't exist. Well, you'd *exist* but . . ."

"Enter your initial predictions now," the voice insists.

"Reverse order," Katherine reminds me as I step up to the computer. "Four, three, one."

I nod, and then read from the list we voted on, adding in a few details. "Prediction one: New York City, February 22, 1940—the attempted assassination of Charles Lindbergh. Prediction two: New York City, June 2, 1939—the attempted assassination of Japanese Ambassador Horinouchi. Prediction three: New York City, November 10, 1938—the conversion of Charles Coughlin from Catholicism to Cyrisism."

"You should have asked me first," Thea says, tsk-tsking as she parks herself on one of the sofas near the windows. "That last date is definitely wrong."

There's a brief pause and then a transcribed version of all three predictions appears on the screen.

The voice says, "Prediction number two is partially correct. Fifteen bonus points will be added to your total at the conclusion of play." A pale-green check pops up next to the second line, and a red X appears next to our first and third predictions. Below this is a red button—of course it's red—labeled START.

For several seconds, we're stunned into silence. Then Richard says, "What the hell? Coughlin used to be a Catholic. We know that for certain. He's now a Cyrist. That should be at least a partially correct answer, although I guess we might have the date wrong, like Clio was saying . . ."

Thea clears her throat dramatically.

Madi shoots her grandmother an annoyed look. "Yes, Thea. You told us, too. But not in time to do us any good. And we might even have the place wrong, although it's hard to see how we could have botched either of those, given the style points they racked up. But Coughlin's conversion was definitely a change to the timeline. And what's with the partial points?"

"We got most of the points on that one," Katherine says. "So we have almost all of it correct. Could be that they want the name of the shooter."

"Which we couldn't know at this point," Rich says. "The newspapers mention a suspect, but I don't think anyone was ever actually convicted. Maybe the date is slightly off? Maybe we have the date it was reported in the papers."

Madi asks Jarvis to confirm the date of the assassination attempt, and he comes back with the same information.

"That's what the list of anomalies coughed up, too," Alex says. "Can we ask the simulation to check again?"

We do. Twice. And each time, we get the same answer.

"Maybe there was another attempt on his life on the way to the fairgrounds. Or afterward . . ." Katherine stops. "Or maybe the real target wasn't the ambassador. That's one of Saul's favorite ploys. Make what looks like an obvious move, while hiding the real goal—some seemingly insignificant move that won't necessarily occur to your opponent. Which means there's very little for us to glean from these totals."

The red *START* button begins to flash. We all stare at it for a moment, and then I do the only thing I can do at this point. I push it.

"You have two days to complete your moves," the voice says as the button disappears. "All moves must be entered by a registered player or observer. All players and observers must actively participate. No splinters allowed at any stage of play. Please refer to the official rule book for additional details." The timer on the SimMaster 8560 then dings once, resets to 48:00:00, and immediately flips to begin the countdown.

"What's a splinter?" Thea asks. "It sounds painful."

"It's when you double back on your timeline to change something," Katherine tells her. "It's best to avoid them because yes, they're painful. They make your head hurt."

"They make everybody's head hurt," Lorena says. She and RJ have been watching quietly from the sofa on the other side of the library. Yun Hee is now curled up on the couch between them, sleepily tugging at her socks. "Is it possible that Team Viper made an extra move and simply failed to enter it into the system?"

"They must have," Clio says. "Because we know Coughlin wasn't a Cyrist before. And that guy had the nerve to snipe at us for my dad simply handling some logistics. Or . . ." She gives the machine a wary glance. "Maybe they *did* enter the extra move. What guarantee do we have that this simulation system is a fair judge?"

"None," I admit.

We have no guarantee at all, and with Thea Randall's arrival, I'm more than a little suspicious that we now have a spy in our ranks as well.

But what choice do we have?

The game is on. Our only option is to play.

PART TWO

ZWISCHENZUG

Zwischenzug [from German, "in-between move"]: An
intermezzo, or intermediate move, played in anticipation
of an expected response. Answering this move generally
exposes the opponent to an even greater threat.

∞15∞

KATHERINE
ROYAL OAK, MICHIGAN
FEBRUARY 13, 1939

A bitter wind whips around my bare ankles. I'm thankful for the coat that I found, along with several era-appropriate outfits and an assortment of wigs (which I have no intention of using), in the closet of the neat brick cottage two blocks away from the Shrine of the Little Flower. It saved me the hassle of shopping, something I've done only as part of my cover in the past rather than having to worry about finding something that actually fit. Clio's mother must value fashion over functionality, though, because I'm wishing the coat were longer, with a nice, warm liner. Or better yet, that we were in an era where cultural norms didn't mandate skirts that leave everything below the calf exposed to the elements and allow bone-chilling gusts clear up to your thighs. Long skirts may be inconvenient, but at least you can wear thick stockings underneath to keep warm. Richard, who is approaching the church from the other side of the block in a thick wool suit and overcoat, definitely got the better end of this deal in terms of comfort.

The tower up ahead stands in stark contrast against the cloudless winter sky, a pillar of limestone over a hundred feet high with a crucifix carved into the front. According to Father Coughlin, this tower was built in response to a cross that was burned on the lawn of this church shortly after he arrived to take over as priest. Coughlin, or possibly a stand-in with similar features, gave a dramatic reenactment of the KKK attack for a newsreel feature several years later, and it's *possible* that it actually happened. No police report is on record, and no one aside from Coughlin and a few close allies seems to remember the event, but given how commonplace ties between the police and the Klan were during this era, it could well be that the incident was reported and never quite made it into the official record. Whatever the truth of the situation may be, the cross burning was the reason Coughlin gave for approaching a local radio station with the proposal to air his weekly sermons. Perhaps, he suggested, intolerance would be less prevalent if the community knew more about their Catholic neighbors? Perhaps he could help build bridges so that his small church would not be at perpetual risk of being burned to the ground?

Five years later, the proceeds from Coughlin's now-syndicated radio show were used to build this much grander church and tower, with its stone cross that the Klan could not burn. It also served a dual purpose, since Coughlin's weekly radio show, which gradually took on a tone far more political than religious, was broadcast from the tower.

In the reality I know, Coughlin pushed his rhetoric too far for the Catholic Church to condone. He had, however, built bridges—to the Klan, the Nazis, and a host of other radical groups that saw the Jews as the cause of every political and economic woe. His radio program was shut down, but he continued to preach from this church until the 1960s.

But in *this* here and now, Coughlin will announce that he is severing ties with the Roman Catholics to embrace Cyrisism. In less than a year, a new Cyrist temple will be opened about half a mile to the west, on the other side of nearby Roseland Park Cemetery. I walked past the location this morning, and apparently construction has been going on for some time. The new temple will showcase a massive limestone tower nearly twice as tall as this one, in the shape of a Cyrist cross. Charles Coughlin was clearly not above a bit of petty, symbolic one-upmanship.

Our goal today is to find out how long Coughlin has been planning this move. If we can pin down the date of his conversion decision, hopefully we'll be able to prevent it. Plan A has Richard joining the reporters who will be arriving shortly to cover the press conference that Coughlin is holding in about an hour, following his address to a regional meeting of the National Mothers' Union, which is being held here today and which I'll be attending. The NMU is the feminine arm of Coughlin's Christian Front. My gut feeling is that the Mothers' Union didn't exist in the other timeline. It popped up on what Madi calls the Anomalies Machine as a tiny blip on the radar, but only because of the publicity surrounding the connection to Coughlin. The group could well have existed in the other timeline, but simply kept out of the limelight. That seems unlikely to me, however, given that the leader, Elizabeth Dilling, was far from a shrinking violet. She craved publicity and had her fingers in many different pies in the late 1930s, including the publication of a newsletter chockful of anti-Semitic conspiracies under the guise of the Patriotic Research Bureau, proclaiming in the masthead to be *For the Defense of Christianity and Americanism.*

But even though I remember Dilling's name from when I was working on my research plan during field training, I don't remember the National Mothers' Union itself. It's possible that's just a gap in my memory. There were certainly plenty of far-right women's groups that wrapped themselves in the cloak of patriotic motherhood. While my memory is far better than average, thanks to the CHRONOS gene, it's still not perfect, and the fact that the group popped up on that anomalies list and is connected to Coughlin makes it worth investigating.

If I can wrangle just a few minutes alone with Mrs. Dilling, I'm pretty sure I can get her talking. Dilling has a considerable ego, and also a chip on her shoulder about the tendency of the various isolationist groups to discount the value of her work. And thanks to the diligent efforts of Clio's parents, I have two copies of her vile little newsletter in my bag, along with a business card announcing myself as a journalist for the Catholic magazine *Our Sunday Visitor*.

Richard and I will meet back at the house on Earlmont Road around noon, which is roughly four hours into the game, although we left that a bit flexible, just in case either of us gets a solid lead that requires a bit more time to follow. If Plan A doesn't yield the information we need, I'm tentatively planning to jump back to Friday. Coughlin was traveling at the time, so hopefully security will be a bit lax. I'll try to blend in with the secretarial staff. Coughlin had well over a dozen women who handled the letters and donations that were delivered to the church in large mail sacks on a daily basis. If I can get into the office, I'll set a stable point so that Richard and I can return after hours and go through Coughlin's correspondence, appointment calendar, and whatever else we can find. Either way, we're scheduled to meet Tyson, Madi, and Clio at the stable point in Manhattan at the five-hour mark.

To be honest, both of these plans suck. Normally, we'd spend days, even weeks, establishing a cover. I wouldn't dream of approaching a historical figure, even a minor one like Elizabeth Dilling, until I'd attended numerous meetings. She might not know my name when I began the conversation, but she would recognize my face. I spent three weeks in the 1870s last year building up two separate covers within the warring factions of the women's suffrage movement—one in New York and the other in New England. This involved dozens of day trips to attend their monthly meetings and several side trips where the goal was simply to exchange a word of greeting with Susan B. Anthony or Lucy Stone at a public event. All of that effort was aimed at learning whether the two groups collaborated on an under-cover strategy to create a network of supposedly apolitical women's clubs to serve as "suffrage kindergartens" to convert the vast majority of women who claimed they had all the rights they needed. An interesting question to be sure, but not a problem on par with trying to prevent the complete destruction of our timeline.

Things can and do turn on a dime when you're in the field. CHRONOS agents are trained to respond quickly, to think on our feet. We are not, however, trained to *wing* it. Walking in with no real cover, no set plan?

That's winging it.

I spot Richard leaning against a tree across the lawn, CHRONOS key in hand. He probably set a stable point here on the lawn and is scrolling forward to find out when the press will start arriving. He gives me a little finger wave, barely looking up from the key, and I scan the area for a group of women who look like they know where they're going. I don't find them on the church grounds, but rather in the parking lot, and they're heading toward the school across the street.

The meeting is scheduled to begin at ten. Many of the seats are already taken. Some of the women appear to know each other, but there are plenty of others who seem to have traveled here on their own, so I don't feel too out of place. A few minutes after ten, the side door opens and Elizabeth Dilling enters, along with Father Coughlin and a woman I don't recognize. Dilling, a small, neatly dressed woman with horrible taste in hats, steps up to the podium as Coughlin takes one of the two seats on the stage. The other woman sits near the front and pulls a small notebook out of her bag. She must be one of his secretarial staff. That reminds me that I'm supposed to be here as a reporter, so I take out my own pen and paper and begin jotting down notes as Dilling welcomes the group.

"I'll keep my opening remarks brief," she says with a conspiratorial smile, "since our host has another event after this one, and we want to make the best use of his time. Most of you know me from previous meetings, but I see a few new faces in the crowd. No doubt we have corresponded, and I'm sure that you're busy organizing your districts. I just wanted to give you a brief—very brief!—record of my activities as your president over the past few months. I've been busy. As the good book says, 'The Lord helps those who help themselves.' Some of you may have seen the newspaper accounts of my trip to Washington, DC, last month, where I provided testimony to the Senate Judiciary Committee opposing the nomination of Felix Frankfurter to the Supreme Court. They didn't listen, of course, but I did my very best, noting that the country would rue the day they placed that man on the highest bench in the nation. I won't go into the sordid details—they're all in my Red book, and I have copies with me if you'd like to purchase extras for your members. Suffice it to say that his connection to the American Civil Liberties Union alone disqualifies Frankfurter, as, I would argue, does the fact that he is a non-Christian. As such, he should not be placed in a position to judge us. As noted in Cyrus 6:7, 'Neither should you be yoked with unbelievers. What fellowship can light have with darkness?'"

Most of the women nod appreciatively, although I do see a few confused expressions as Dilling goes on. "As I told the committee, not a single word of what I've written about Mr. Frankfurter, and for that matter not a single word in the Red book, has been disproved. If it had been, I would be in jail this very minute, and as you can see, I am not."

She pauses until a wave of applause circles the room.

"Although," Dilling continues, holding up her hands, which are clad in demure white gloves, "I'm afraid that may change in the near future, as I've made some rather powerful enemies in standing up for our way of life. I don't want my children to live under a socialist or communist kind of government. Mothers have an obligation to feed *their* children, not children in other countries whose parents were unwise enough to wage war. If women—and I can hardly bear to even call them women—such as Dorothy Thompson had their way, our sons would be marching into Berlin even now, such a bugaboo has she made of Adolf Hitler. The simple truth is that we don't want our sons to die on foreign battlefields. Nor do we want our children attending the kind of colleges that Justice Brandeis and his wife were connected with, where they teach communism and have free love and nudist colonies. This is sadly so pervasive among the Jews in this country, and Brandeis is no exception. Five of the nine justices on the Supreme Court today have verifiable ties to the communist movement in this country and abroad, as I show conclusively in my Red book. They're going to get us into another foreign war if we don't organize and speak out in every state. But I've gone on long enough. We'll have plenty of time to go into more detail on all of this in our sessions later in the day, so please allow me to end my remarks by saying that even though this is a truly dark time for our country, I'm comforted knowing that we have strong, God-fearing men like Father Coughlin taking our message to the people."

The women applaud enthusiastically as Coughlin steps to the podium. He holds up a hand, smiling, and when the applause dies down, he thanks Dilling for her introduction and welcomes the group to the Little Flower Shrine. His voice starts out a bit more gently than what I remember from vids of his speeches, but it slowly begins to rev up as he shifts from casual words of thanks to politics, which is, after all, the reason the group is assembled.

"As many of you know, I have always fought for the little guys, the downtrodden. It's hard to do that when you're part of a monolithic institution, but I have endeavored to remain close to the people who make this country great. And no group does more toward that goal than our blessed mothers."

He speaks for several minutes about the sacrifices that mothers make, and somehow manages to segue into internationalism, a rant against the Jews, and the assertion that fascism is almost certainly the nation's only hope for warding off godless communism.

"But we cannot forget that people are suffering. Our leaders must ensure that capitalism benefits you, the everyday people who make this country great. The one silver lining of this economic depression is that the greedy have been brought low, and there is now a chance for working people to invest. And I know that's a scary idea in these times, when so many have lost so much, but with God on your side, you'll know the right moves, the moves that will make your family safer without handing your money over to the Jewish banks. Pay close attention to my upcoming address, for this is the next battle that we must win—taking back our economy and ensuring that it works for those who built this country, the true Americans. This is the one area where I feel the Catholic hierarchy has been somewhat derelict in its duty. It is all good and well to feed American souls, but we must also ensure that they can keep soul and body together. If we do not, the communists will win, and in a communist society, God is not welcome.

"And now, while you ladies adjourn to refreshments in the fellowship hall, the vultures of the press await. As some of you may have already gathered, I have decided to leave this church that has been my home for so many years." He holds up his hands in response to the expressions of dismay. "Do not worry. I will take up the cross under a new banner. It is my hope that Cyrism will better unite us against our common foe, rather than divide us sect against sect. I had planned to delay this announcement until we'd made a bit more headway on construction, but I can state with some assurance that the Temple of the Lotus Flower will open just across the way in the spring. My radio ministry will continue in the interim. And if any of you happen to bump into the vultures I mentioned in the parking lot later, be sure to let them know that you were the ones who got the big scoop. You ladies are, after all, the very heart of this movement. While you are kind enough to allow us men to think we run things, I want to assure all of you that I, for one, know the actual truth of the matter. And now, I place you once again in the most capable hands of Mrs. Dilling."

Coughlin leaves through a side door, and we follow Dilling into the fellowship hall, where cookies, coffee, and a pitcher of watery-looking lemonade are arranged on one end of a banquet table. A stack of books and pamphlets is at the other end. Dilling chats with several of the women as she pours herself a cup of coffee and then takes her place at the business end of the table.

I debate making small talk with the women for a moment so that I don't look overly eager, but we're pressed for time, and she's all alone right now. If I wait, I may end up stuck in the afternoon sessions and never get a chance to talk to her. And so I pull out the business card and copies of her newsletter that were in the research packet the Dunnes put together for me.

"Mrs. Dilling, I hate to be forward because we haven't officially met. I'm Mrs. Daisy Ritter, and I've just started a branch of the NMU in the Fort Wayne area. I also do a little writing on the side—nothing like your excellent work, just occasional interviews and articles for *Our Sunday Visitor*, because their headquarters is in Huntington where I live. I've been listening to Father Coughlin from the beginning, and I've written several articles about him—"

Dilling frowns, cocking her head to one side. "I'm pleased to meet you, of course, Mrs. Ritter. But I was under the impression that Bishop Noll was not a fan of Father Coughlin."

Oops. I smile, nod, and shift gears. "Exactly. I've *written* several articles. The bishop has published almost all of my other stuff, but he seems to be of the opinion that women should stay out of politics, for the most part. He probably won't be happy when he finds out that I'm trying to start a branch of the National Mothers' Union, so I'm . . ." I stop and lower my voice to a confidential whisper. "I'm trying to branch out a bit. Maybe begin publishing a few pieces in the papers in Fort Wayne and Indianapolis. And Father—although I guess it's now Brother—Coughlin just gave me the most wonderful idea. I want to write a feature about your role and, more broadly, the role of women in general within his ministry. It's been clear to me for some time that the two of you work together very closely. As I said, I've been listening to his weekly message, but my sister and I are also longtime subscribers to your newsletter. Such wonderful, in-depth research, really. Anyway, from my reading, I've gotten the sense that Fa . . . excuse me, *Brother* Coughlin relies heavily on your input for his sermons."

To be honest, I suspect that the reverse is true. The research memo Kate Dunne provided showed a lot of overlap in their topics, but Coughlin was generally the one to go first. He's not the one I'm sucking up to, however.

"Why, yes," she says, beaming. "We collaborate very closely. That's why I was willing to take the train all the way from Chicago to hold this event here."

"So you already knew his big news?"

I expect her smile to falter, but it doesn't. "Oh, yes. Of course. This may be new to the press, but the entire thing has obviously been in the works for quite some time. He's met on several occasions with one of the lead Cyrist Templars to discuss plans for the new church. And . . ." She looks from side to side and gives me a conspiratorial little grin as she pulls down the edge of her left glove to reveal a pink lotus-flower tattoo.

"Oh, my goodness," I gush. "It's lovely. So . . . how *long* has this been in the works?"

She waves the question away. "I think for at least a year. He made the comment last month that if that . . ." A quick look around, and then she continues in a lower voice, wearing a tiny smirk. "He told me that if that old battle-ax Dorothy Thompson is going to keep insisting that his movement is allied with the Bund, he might as well make her happy. Maybe she'll smile for a change. I think he took the Cyrist offer much more seriously after the Jews got everyone all worked up over the Kristallnacht business and trying to defend the little murderer who started the whole thing. Thompson even started raising funds for his defense, if you can believe it. No one kicked *her* off the air for that, and there was nothing at *all* wrong with Father Coughlin's sermon that week. He only spoke the truth. One of the Cyrists bought out that radio station, you know. That's why they started airing his stuff again so quickly. I think that's when he realized that we could do so much more if we can unite all God-fearing people—Catholic, Protestant, maybe even those Mormons out in Utah—under a single banner."

"So, just between us," I say, "I swear I won't put it in print. Was this *your* idea?"

"Well, no. I was a little hesitant at first, to be honest. I mean, I've been a Catholic all my life. And I'll still be a Catholic, of course, but I've been *only* a Catholic until now. He told me he had a vision about a year ago. A spirit visitor. Brother Cyrus himself. Last . . . March, I believe."

"Really?" I struggle to keep my expression neutral. Coughlin seems like the practical type to me. Definitely not a mystic. I doubt he believes in the Holy Ghost, let alone the more mundane type, and that has me wondering how much of the story he gave to Elizabeth Dilling was fact. It seems far more likely to me that the ghost he saw was a member of Team Viper.

Dilling nods emphatically. "The first vision happened one night when he was alone up in the tower. He said it felt very real, almost as if he could reach out and touch him."

I'll bet it did.

Dilling glances over at a woman who is hovering a few feet away clearly wanting a turn to speak with her, and lowers her voice. "Would you mind terribly keeping that off the record, though? I mean, unless Brother Coughlin mentions it to the reporters during his press conference. I wouldn't want him to think I'm telling tales out of school."

"Oh, certainly," I assure her. "Like I said, this is just between us. Listen, I don't want to monopolize your time. I know you're busy, and I need to run out to the car and grab my sweater. Maybe we can chat for a couple of minutes after the meeting, and I could take down a few official quotes for my article? Oh, and don't let me forget that I need to purchase a few copies of your books for my group before I go!"

"That would be perfect," Dilling says.

I grab a cookie from the tray as I walk by, trying to decide if there's actually anything more I might be able to get from Dilling. I doubt it. What we need to do now is ascertain who met with Coughlin in the guise of Brother Cyrus. If we could get a stable point inside the room at the top of the tower, we could scan through to see if he had any late-night guests, although I have no idea how we'd be able to get up there. If Coughlin's recording equipment is there, they almost certainly keep it locked, and it's not like we can crawl through a window when it's over a hundred feet tall.

The press conference is probably still going on, and I don't want to interfere with any conversations that Richard may be having. So I head for the back door of the fellowship hall, which leads into the parking lot. I pull the thin coat tight around my neck to ward off the wind as I step outside . . . and straight into Saul.

FROM THE *NEW YORK DAILY INTREPID*

THREE DEATHS AT GERMAN-AMERICAN BUND RALLY

(February 20, 1939) A "Pro-America Rally" at Madison Square Garden last night ended in tragedy when a New Jersey woman and her two children were trampled by panicked crowds rushing for the exit after a small explosive was apparently detonated in one of the upper levels of the auditorium.

The woman who was killed, Mrs. Herbert Slater of Warren Township, NJ, had been a member of the Bund since 1936. She was in the audience with her two daughters, Eliza, eight, and Marta, five, while her husband and two sons marched in uniform as part of the military guard known as the *Ordnungsdienst*.

The rally was sponsored by the German-American Bund and timed to coincide with the 207th anniversary of George Washington's birth. A thirty-foot-tall banner of the nation's first president held center stage behind the podium, flanked by US and Bund flags. It had been widely rumored that there were threats against the event, but this did not have a noticeable effect on the crowd's size. Most of the more than twenty thousand seats in the sports hall were filled. The event received a publicity boon last week when a poster for the rally leaked the news, apparently inadvertently, that radio priest Charles Coughlin would be leaving the Catholic Church and continuing his ministry as a Cyrist.

Despite assurances by the Bund that anti-Semitic chants and posters would not be allowed, banners reading "Stop Jewish Domination of Christian America" and "Wake Up, America—Smash Jewish Communism" hung from the upper tiers of the auditorium. Speakers, who included Coughlin, aviatrix Laura Houghtaling Ingalls, Bund leader Fritz Kuhn, William Dudley Pelley of the Silver Legion, and Lawrence Dennis, blamed the Jews for everything from international communism to the cost of groceries at the local supermarket.

Mayor La Guardia acknowledged in an interview yesterday that his office received an anonymous note on Wednesday threatening to explode three devices if the rally was not canceled. Security was increased to 1,700 officers, the largest number ever assigned to an event of this nature, but the mayor refused to give in to the foes of free speech. "If we are for free speech, we have to be for free speech for everybody, and that includes the Nazis." He added, "If they bomb it, we'll catch the bombers." They carefully combed the entire building earlier in the day in the wake of the bomb threat, leading officials to believe that the explosive was carried in by an attendee.

In a brief statement to the press, NYPD Commissioner Valentine noted that the investigation is ongoing. Anyone with information about the attack should contact the police department immediately.

∞16∞

MADI
NEW YORK, NEW YORK
FEBRUARY 20, 1939

"Ticket holders only." The policeman edges closer to the line of protestors, using the massive bulk of his horse to nudge them behind the barricade along Forty-Seventh Street. "Get back, all of you! If you ain't a Bundist, you ain't gettin' past."

The two men in front of us are clearly not with the German-American Bund, judging from the signs they're holding—*No Nazis in New York* and *Give Me a Gas Mask, I Can't Stand the Smell of Nazis.* That goes for most of the crowd, which has broken out into choruses of "Solidarity Forever" and something about having the bourgeois blues, which is actually kind of catchy. We've been pushing through crowds for the past block, even though we purposefully selected the Ninth Avenue entrance in hopes of avoiding the main protest gathering at Eighth and Fifty-Third. The Socialist Workers Party requested permission for a counterrally of fifty thousand people, and while newspaper interviews with police officials claimed that only a few hundred actually showed up, I'm thinking a few thousand of their fellow travelers may have gotten mixed up and wound up on the wrong side of Madison Square Garden.

If not for the Dunne family's extensive prep work, Tyson and I would likely have been even farther off target. RJ and Alex had already begun putting together maps and various data about the five scenarios we were debating before Clio joined the team. The map Alex located was from the early 2000s and pinpointed our destination about a mile in the other direction. But that was a *different* Madison Square Garden, which was constructed in the 1960s after the building up ahead was demolished.

We lucked out in terms of the weather, with the temperature still in the low fifties at nearly six p.m. The air is still damp from rain earlier in the day, but since it's mid-February, it could be far worse. Given how tightly packed we are on the sidewalk, a blast of frigid winter wind would actually be kind of nice right now.

Tyson and I begin pushing through the crowd toward the barricade so that we can present our tickets. The officer responds to the surge by inching his horse closer. One of the men in front of us shoves at the horse's flank, and the officer swings a leather baton in our direction. "Touch my mount again and I'll be haulin' you in for cruelty to dumb animals."

When the man recoils from the baton, Tyson pushes through and flashes our tickets at the officer. The crowd responds with a chorus of boos, and we're called several charming names, including *Nazi scum*, as we move toward the barricade. A woman around my age plants both of her palms on my back and shoves me forward. I slip on the wet sidewalk, but Tyson grabs my elbow, and I regain my balance at the last moment. Which is fortunate, because otherwise I'd have landed under the police officer's horse.

Once we're past the barrier, I say, "We do not tell Clio about that."

"Agreed," Tyson says.

When we arrived in 1939 and began final prep for tonight's event, we found pretty much everything we needed waiting for us. The house was stocked with several days' worth of provisions. Several changes of clothing, too. Tyson's pants are about an inch too long, but the clothes fit surprisingly well given that all they had to go on were a couple of pictures that Clio hastily snapped. Someone had also put together an array of disguises, which may come in handy eventually. There were two pistols, as well, which look quite a bit like the one in my grandfather's desk. The most important things they provided, however, were file folders with extensive background information on each of the events we think might have been changed. The one for the Bund rally included tickets to the event, contact info for protestors who will be arrested, and detailed biographies of the speakers, including Fritz Kuhn (who calls himself the "American führer"), Brother Charles Coughlin, Laura Houghtaling Ingalls (not the author, thank God), and Lawrence Dennis, who Tyson described as one of the leading thinkers of the fascist movement in the old timeline. Dennis was brought up on probably bogus charges of sedition during World War II, but never convicted. In this new timeline, he'll have a reversal of fortunes, serving in both the Bilbo and the Dies administrations. I have no clue who either of those individuals are, but I'm certain they never made it to the White House in our history. I don't feel a strong desire to dig any further into their biographies. Tyson's expression when he mentioned them told me everything I needed to know.

There were also bios on about a dozen members of the press who are attending tonight's event. The only name I recognized was Dorothy Thompson, a syndicated columnist with the *New York Herald Tribune*. According to the file, she was the first American journalist Hitler kicked out of Germany when the war began, and one of the most widely known and respected journalists of the era—which makes me a little ashamed to admit that the only reason I recognized her name was because of her tumultuous marriage to one of the literary stars of the 1930s, Sinclair Lewis. According to the newspaper accounts, Thompson will be hauled out of the event for heckling

Kuhn, the leader of the Bund, a few minutes before protestors break through the security barrier.

The oddest thing in the information packet was a list with the names and badge numbers for twenty-two current NYPD police officers who are connected to the KKK and the Universal Front. I wasn't sure why the list was relevant. The Klan and the Bund are ideological allies. In fact, the Grand Giant of the New Jersey KKK, who's also vice president of the Bund, is one of the speakers at tonight's event. It seems very unlikely that Team Viper would have been able to convince any officer with KKK ties to help with the attack. The only solid bit of intelligence that Kiernan had been able to get from the police was that the bomb itself appeared to have been a false alarm or, at a bare minimum, so small that it did no obvious damage. They searched the building meticulously afterward and found no sign of an explosive.

Tyson, however, had immediately recognized the value of the information on the Klan. As he scanned and saved the list and other documents with his lens gadget, he explained that our tight schedule meant we'd likely have a difficult time getting anything more from the authorities than Kiernan had, even with the advantage of a few well-placed bribes. But the list gave Tyson twenty-two contacts he could greet with a secret handshake and a racist comment or two, and (hopefully) walk away with information that would help us figure out how to reverse these three deaths and undo whatever changes Team Viper has set rolling.

But while we were going through the papers earlier, Clio realized that there are no stable points inside Madison Square Garden. Since there are seven others within a mile radius that are valid in 1939, this wouldn't be a big deal under normal circumstances. Of course, under normal circumstances, historians aren't contending with a timer ticking down the minutes they have left to fix the damn timeline. And so we had no choice but to waste a half hour fighting our way through the crowds in the area.

Clio spent several minutes berating herself for this oversight before we left the apartment. "Mom could have attended an event there and left stable points," she said. "Dad wouldn't have been able to do it. But my mom can still lock in the interface well enough to set a stable point. That would have been useful not just for jumping in, but for observing the auditorium remotely. I can't believe I didn't think about that."

Tyson pointed out that we were still several hours ahead thanks to her foresight in getting tickets and having her family do most of the background research. And he's right. If we manage to pull this off, most of the credit will be due to their effort and to Clio's quick thinking in jumping back to give them the background information they needed to set all of this up. The fact that I didn't think of it when I was in Seneca Falls suggests our team would probably be much better off if I were the observer and Clio was the official member of the team. Although, to be fair, none of the historians thought of it, either. They're used to having everything they need for a jump provided for them—clothing, ID, background data, etc. None of us were really trained for this.

When we reach the entrance, we find that several of the protestors seem to have broken through the barrier and are verbally sparring with a line of young men in uniforms reminiscent of the SS—black pants and boots, gray shirts, shoulder belts, and swastika armbands. The police are just watching at this point. They look bored, and I suspect they wouldn't entirely mind if the two sides got into a row, so that they could step in and break it up.

"Too bad we can't just stay out here," I whisper to Tyson as we head toward the ticket booth. "I feel a lot more connected ideologically to the crowd on the *other* side of the barricade."

"Tell me about it," he says, looking around nervously as he hands our tickets to the woman inside the booth. It hadn't even occurred to me until this moment that Tyson is likely to garner a few suspicious glances at this event. I may *feel* out of place, but I'm a pale, blue-eyed blonde. My face would be right at home on one of their Aryan propaganda posters.

The woman stashes our tickets in the box and then shoves two programs through the slot at the bottom of the window. I suspect that she's employed by the owners of the Garden rather than the Bund, based on her tone and the slight curl of her upper lip as she tells us to enjoy the show.

"Not bloody likely," I say under my breath as we step inside.

Tyson snorts. "Not a fan of swastikas?"

"Or political rallies. Or crowds. Any of this." I nod toward the far end of the auditorium, where the massive portrait of Washington we saw in various articles about this event stares back at us. He's in a typical soldier's pose on the tall, thin canvas, flanked by US and Bund flags. I'm not normally prone to excessive patriotism, possibly because I've spent as much time in the UK as I have in the US, but seeing Washington surrounded by swastikas evokes a visceral reaction. Was he really America's first fascist, as Fritz Kuhn, the pudgy little swindler who calls himself the American führer, will claim tonight? My knowledge of ancient American history doesn't go beyond the basic undergraduate courses, and the myths surrounding Washington are so pervasive that it's hard to sort fact from fiction. I do know he was an isolationist, but that was a wise precaution in his era. When you have a fledgling nation, the surest way to destroy it would be to take sides in the conflicts of other countries. And yes, he owned slaves, although I seem to recall that he freed them when he died. But that doesn't quite add up to a fascist in my mind. For one thing, would a fascist have so readily turned down the suggestion that he should become king?

We separate once we're inside, and I wander around the main hall, CHRONOS key in hand, trying to set observation points as unobtrusively as possible. This is the earliest change to the timeline, and the style-points total suggests that our opponents made this change last, since they went in reverse order. If we want to negate those points, we'll need to do the same. Our goal for this trip, therefore, is to set up our surveillance stable points and try to find out exactly what happened. If Tyson gets a chance to speak with Lawrence Dennis, he'll take it, but we'll hold off on Coughlin until we find out what Richard and Katherine learn in Detroit. Once we have the stable points set, we can head back to the apartment to watch and see when the device was planted and by whom.

With that in mind, I duck into the ladies' room to set an entry point for my return trip, so that we don't have to waste time fighting our way through demonstrators and wannabe Nazis again. According to Tyson, bathroom stalls are the very best spot for setting local stable points, even better than broom closets, since you tend to arouse suspicion when stepping out of the latter. It feels a bit skeevy to me, though. Not just the general ick factor, even though this is far from the cleanest bathroom I've encountered. The bigger issue is that I'm dreading the prospect of scrolling through to find a time when the stall is empty and invading the privacy of God only knows how many women in the process.

Once I'm back in the hallway, I glance around the auditorium for Tyson. We need to get up to our seats on the second level before the speeches start. Locating him is no longer a simple matter, however, since the main level is now teeming with people, including dozens or maybe even hundreds of men in Nazi attire. So I head upstairs to find our seats and continue searching from there. Finally, I spot the glow of Tyson's CHRONOS key at the back of the balcony on the other side of the auditorium.

The tickets the Dunnes purchased for us are no doubt considered the cheap seats, since we'll only be able to see the speakers in profile. For our purposes, however, that's perfect. We'll mostly be looking at the audience, anyway.

Tyson is now at the edge of the stage, talking to a police officer and a tall, dark-haired man. He hands something to the dark-haired guy, then heads toward the stairway. When he joins me a few minutes later, he asks how many stable points I set.

"Twenty-five, maybe thirty," I say. "Most on the lower level."

"Good. We should be able to see everything we need to remotely. It's going to take time to scroll through, but between the five of us . . ."

"Or we could outsource that and move on to the next thing that requires an actual time traveler. Jack wants something to do. From what Clio said, her mom can still use the key enough that she might be able to help as well."

"Excellent idea. I'd like to stay through Dennis's speech and maybe part of Coughlin's. We can go once Kuhn begins, that way we'll be out of here by the time the panic starts. Wish I had the little audio devices I used at CHRONOS so we could hear the rest of it, but this place is going to be crawling with police, so we'd have a tough time retrieving them anyway."

I ask if he had any luck with the cop.

He hesitates for a second, looking a bit confused. "Oh, no. His badge wasn't on the list, and I wouldn't want to attract too much attention by being nosy before the attack happens. I was actually talking to the guy with him. That's Lawrence Dennis."

I recognize the name from the poster. He's the guy Tyson said was one of the more intellectual fascists. "What did you ask him?"

"Asked if he'd meet me at a bar a few blocks away for an interview after this is over. Gave him the reporter's business card from the background file. Didn't expect him to recognize me, though."

"Recognize you?"

"We've met before," he says. "It was a public event a few years back, and like I said, I really didn't think he'd remember it. I wasn't even sure it would have happened for him, since there's no CHRONOS in this timeline. But it was a solo jump, so . . ." He winces slightly as he says this. I'm not sure if it's a double memory of some sort or if it's just the typical headache of trying to figure out how these stupid time shifts work. "It was my second solo jump, actually. Just a day trip, to attend a talk he gave after his book on fascism was published. I didn't tell him my name at the event, so there's no conflict with the business card. And he may have thought I was a reporter back then, given that he didn't like a question I asked him. But even if I hadn't met him before, I'd have been trying to find a way to talk to him." Tyson motions for my CHRONOS key. I hold it out, and he transfers a stable point. "Scroll back a few hours to 6:24 p.m."

The stable point is on the second level. I glance over my shoulder at the back wall, but Tyson shakes his head, nodding across the arena to the spot where he'd been earlier.

"But . . . the reports said the sound came from the right side of the building."

"Yeah, but did that mean the right side when you're facing the stage or right side facing the door? That's why they usually specify the south side or east side of the building or whatever."

I scroll back to nearly six thirty, not long before we arrived. When I pan around, I see a few people on the lower level, but the balcony is empty. Then a shadow obscures the stable point. I follow the blur, and it takes the form of the tall, middle-aged man with dark hair I saw talking to Tyson. He moves to the back, opens the door of what looks like a broom closet, and enters. Less than a minute later, he steps back out. This time I can see his face—very distinctive looking, with a square jaw and strong features. "So what made you scroll through to investigate this particular stable point out of the dozens you set?"

"Easy," Tyson says. "I opened the door. It's a storage closet. Inside, I saw a record player, hooked up to a loudspeaker. There's a timing device on the back. Given the lack of damage to the building that the papers reported, I'm pretty sure the noise people heard wasn't a bomb. Dennis was probably starting the timer when he stepped inside."

"But the cops supposedly searched the place . . ." I trail off and shake my head. "Never mind. Since the cops were responding to a bomb threat, they probably wouldn't have paid any attention to a phonograph hooked up to a loudspeaker. So . . . did he agree to meet you?"

"Yes, although he insisted on a club across town. I decided to appeal to his ego. I told him I was now a writer for *Time* magazine, and we were thinking of doing a profile story."

I ask if I should join them, and Tyson shakes his head. "Dennis's libido is reportedly as big as his ego. He might talk more if you're around, but I think I'd have a tougher time keeping him on topic."

"Do you think he'll show up even after what happens? I mean, he's probably going to feel bad that three people were killed, right?"

He shrugs. "He might have a twinge of guilt about it. Especially the kids, since he's a father. But I think there's a good chance he'll choose to blame the Jewish protestors who storm into the building rather than the audience trying to get out of the building. Either way, I'm hoping I can get some information from him about the changes in the fascist movement. He wasn't closely allied with the Bund in the previous timeline. Neither was Coughlin. Oh, they were all in the same ideological camp, generally speaking, but both of them felt that the Bund was a little too explicit in their embrace of Hitler. And now here the two of them are, casting their lot not just with the Bund, but with each other. That's what had me doubting that the deaths tonight were the triggering event for the timeline shift in the first place, instead of an unintended consequence of some earlier action."

The band that was tuning up earlier has now started. I don't know the piece, but it's the type Nora referred to as *Sturm und Drang*, by which I assume she meant loud and overly dramatic, because it's drowning out our whispered voices. Tyson is saying something, but I can only make out a few words. I ask him to repeat it, but he taps the disk behind his ear three times. I do the same and the music fades. It's still there, but it's muted now, and I can hear his voice.

"Better?" he asks.

I nod. "They're almost as loud as the Beatles. But at least the audience is a bit more orderly. No shrieking." Of course, that reminds me that some members of the audience will soon cease to be orderly and there *will* be shrieking. I shiver, even though the night is still quite warm for February.

"Yeah," Tyson says. "But I'd much rather listen to an auditorium of screaming teens than *"Heil Hitler Dir!"* being sung by a bunch of Nazi chucklefucks."

The word instantly conjures up a memory of walks on the beach with my grandmother, near her house in Bray on the Irish coast.

Tyson frowns at my expression. "Sorry. Guess I should watch my language."

"Oh, no," I say. "It's not that at all. You just used one of Nora's favorite swears. She's not a particular fan of her mayor, mostly because he pushed through a law that allows personal hovercrafts along the stretch of coast near her cottage. Any time we were on a walk and one of them would go zipping by, she'd launch into a rant about 'that chucklefuck Mayor Peters.'"

He smiles, and then says, "We'll fix this, okay? You'll see Nora again soon."

"What about your family?" I ask, realizing that I know almost nothing about them. "Do you think they still exist?"

"Possibly. They weren't connected to CHRONOS. But given the radical change in the racial makeup of the US, and the fact that so many black and brown people headed to the western states or other countries . . . I think it's unrealistic to assume each link in the chain that made either of my parents is still intact. Katherine is pretty sure her parents would never have met. Rich's apparently did, but they do a lot of tweaking to our DNA. He said he looks very different. In some ways, though . . ." He trails off, shaking his head.

"What?"

"This will probably sound weird to you. I mean, you lived with your family for how long?"

"With either my parents or Nora until around age twenty," I say. "But that's not typical. Nora's flat in London was close to my classes. And that last year probably shouldn't count as living with her, since she was at the cottage in Bray about half the time. Why?"

"It's just . . . so many people think it will be cool for their kid to get the CHRONOS gene, but it guarantees that there will be a chasm between you and your family. You're basically giving up your kid at age ten, aside from vacations. We live and breathe the eras we'll specialize in, and sometimes that makes it hard to communicate with our families. Katherine's really the only one who's close to her parents, probably because she's an only child and her mother works at HQ. I still managed to stay fairly close to my dad—he is a teacher, knows a lot about history. But my mom oversees a day-care center, and she really has more in common with my sister. Richard says it's the same for him, except he's not especially close to either of his parents. He seems to think this was a status thing for them . . . Unless you get a waiver, the CHRONOS gene is one of the more expensive chosen gifts. Losing Angelo feels more immediate for us. Plus Glen, in my case, and all of the other historians who are still active. HQ is home. We lived there longer than we lived with our families."

I feel a little bad now. Tyson, Katherine, and Richard lost everything. I still have Thea. Maybe my mother, too. Thea says she's fine, although I got the sense that she hasn't actually checked, and since

Jarvis didn't find any record of her existence, I'm not exactly optimistic. Alex, Lorena, RJ, and Yun Hee have become almost like family in the past few weeks. And I still have Jack.

Thinking about Thea now has me once again wondering about her origins. "How common is human cloning in your time?" I ask Tyson. "In your time in our timeline, that is."

He arches an eyebrow. "It's definitely a thing. An illegal thing . . . but people do it anyway."

"Do they make clones of clones . . . of clones?" I ask.

"Not that I'm aware of. Why?"

"Just thinking about Morgen's clone from the other timeline. And Elizabeth Forson, the bioterrorist Jack's dad was trying to block. She had two clones she raised as daughters. And, well . . . Thea. I'm a bit suspicious that she's a clone, too."

"Of Sister Prudence?"

I nod. "And I'm kind of wondering if that's what made her so flaky. Or maybe it's just a personality trait. I mean, according to Kate Pierce-Keller's diaries, the original Prudence wasn't exactly a picture of stability, although I had the sense that was mostly from looping back over her own timeline on way too many occasions."

"My guess is that they just make a new copy from the original genetic material. Assuming they have it. Pattern degradation would be a problem, otherwise. I mean, a copy of a copy of a copy of anything . . . well, you're apt to lose some definition. But that's just a layman's assessment. You'd probably get a better technical answer from your geneticist friend, even though I'm sure there was some progress in the field between 2136 and my time. How do you think Thea fits into all of this? Is she on our side?"

I have to take a moment to process that, because I really don't know the answer. "It's complicated," I say. "I don't think she'd ever purposefully do anything to hurt me. She loves me. I love her. But, first and foremost, Thea is on Thea's side. Even before all of this, she's probably the last family member I'd have sought out if there was a crisis of some sort. She'd be as likely to make the situation worse as she would be to help. Which is pretty much what Kate Pierce-Keller said about Sister Prudence in her diaries. A loose cannon might be the best way to sum her up."

He makes a sick face. "A loose cannon we are unfortunately stuck with for the duration. And apparently, a loose cannon who had some advance notice of this entire situation."

"She claims that it was in *The Book of Prophecy*, but . . ."

He raises his eyebrows for me to go on, but I nod toward the stairwell, where one of the security officers is staring at us. There are half a dozen seats between us and anyone else, and we're barely even whispering. But apparently even that is a breach of decorum now that a speaker is approaching the microphone.

In one sense, I'm glad to table the discussion for later. It gives me a bit of time to think about how much to tell Tyson about Kate's experience with the Cyrists. I sort of glossed over all of that when we were fixing the last time rift, with his blessing. Anything that disrupts the chain of events that produces me threatens the existence of CHRONOS, or at least that's the working theory, which means the less the historians know about the earlier events, the better. But the Cyrists are clearly part of the equation with this new time shift. Tyson needs to know that they were created by Saul Rand.

He also needs to know Katherine is probably aware of that fact. Kate's diary states that Katherine knew prior to Saul's sabotage of CHRONOS that he'd created the religion and incorporated it into his time-chess strategy. If this *other* Saul is doing the same thing, then she may be able to give us some insights.

I spend the next forty-five minutes half listening to the speeches. Political history isn't my field, and I find myself nearly nodding off on several occasions, partly because I don't have the historical background to follow a lot of what they're saying or recognize the people they're complaining about. I know Franklin Roosevelt, who they apparently think is some sort of devil. I know Hitler, who many of them seem to think is a god, but that definitely doesn't accord with the histories I've read. The female pilot is mildly interesting, but the rest of it is snooze inducing.

Tyson, however, is listening intently, especially when Lawrence Dennis is called to the podium, even though Dennis's speech is easily the most boring of the lot. I'm not the only one who thinks this. Quite a few Bund members are fidgeting in their seats. It's hard for me to connect this man at the podium to the one I watched sneaking out of a storage closet on the CHRONOS key. He doesn't seem like someone who would be involved in any sort of direct political action. In fact, he reminds me quite a bit of this professor I had for research methods, who was obviously intelligent, but extremely insecure. Every lecture felt like he was trying to make sure everyone knew how very, very smart he was.

A really odd thing happens at the end of his speech, though, just before Dennis introduces Coughlin, who follows him on the program. I don't even catch the first part of what he's saying, but he ends with the four words *that's why I'm here*. With each word, he points to a different section of the audience, ending not just with our section, but pointing directly at Tyson, who seems mildly amused. This is a massive auditorium, with over twenty thousand people in attendance. The lights on the stage probably prevent the speaker from seeing beyond the first few rows of faces. I know they spoke before the event began, but I'm not sure how Dennis could have picked him out in the crowd.

If anyone in the audience dozed off during Dennis's speech, Coughlin wakes them right up. He opens with a joke about the publicity surrounding his conversion, and then quickly shifts gears to shaking his fist and railing loudly against a shopping list of things that he deems un-American, communistic, and anti-God, which he seems to view as basically the same thing.

About ten minutes in, Tyson nudges me and nods toward the exit. I'm a little surprised, since he'd said we'd stay until Coughlin finished speaking, but not at all sad to be leaving. Once we're outside the arena, he says, "As he was talking, I realized that his speech will be in that newspaper of his. It's a waste of time to sit through it, and I don't know how long this meeting with Lawrence Dennis will take."

The chants of the protestors, combined with traffic noise, are nearly as loud as Coughlin's shouting inside the rally. Most of the crowd is gathered around the front, but there are a few stragglers near the side exit, along with a couple of police officers on horseback. One of the demonstrators, a guy in his early twenties with a *Smash Anti-Semitism* sign, gets right up in Tyson's face.

Tyson shoves the man back and then pulls out one of the business cards. "We're press, okay? Someone has to report on what the sons of bitches are doing!"

There are a few grumbles, but they let us through without any further conflict. Tyson just holds out the card and says, "Press. Let us through," every few yards. The crowd has mostly cleared out by the time we reach Broadway, about ten minutes later, and Tyson starts looking around for an isolated spot where we can jump out without attracting attention.

I'm looking around for something else, however. A coffee shop or restaurant where I can get something to wake me up and give me a bit of courage for this conversation.

"There," I say, nodding toward the Ham n Egg Corner at Fifty-First and Broadway, beneath the sign for the Roseland Ballroom. "I need coffee. And there's something I have to tell you."

He gives me a hesitant look. "We've only got about two hours before we're supposed to meet Rich and Katherine back at the apartment."

Before we left my house in Bethesda, we agreed that we needed to keep to a schedule and check in at regular intervals to the extent possible. Richard and Katherine are about a week prior to this time in Detroit, finding out what they can about Coughlin's decision to join the Cyrists. They're going to spend five hours there and then, and we're spending five hours here and now, although I'm going to use a bit of that time to update Jack and also the folks in Bethesda 2136. At the end of the five hours, we're supposed to meet back at the apartment with Clio, compare notes, and figure out what to do next.

"I know, Tyson. But I really do think this is important."

He nods and we head over to the diner. We find a small table near the back, and Tyson flips over the two coffee cups that are facedown on saucers. It's apparently a signal, because the waitress brings the pot with her when she comes to take our orders. There's no question about regular or decaf, even though it's evening. Did they even have decaf in 1939?

I just stick with the coffee, but Tyson nods toward the pastry case and tells her he'll have a slice of lemon pie.

"To be honest," I tell him once his pie is in front of him, "I was hoping to put this discussion off, mostly because I'm still not sure how this may complicate an already hopelessly tangled situation. But as team leader . . ." I give him an apologetic look, because I can tell from his expression he really would rather not have that title. "*As team leader*, this is something you need to be aware of. How much do you trust Katherine?"

A long time passes before he responds. On the one hand, I like the fact that he's giving the question serious consideration. On the other hand, it bothers me that he has to give it any consideration at *all*. And I get the feeling he's worried by the fact that I felt compelled to ask the question.

"Katherine is a good historian," he says finally. "She's smart, she knows her time periods, and she does an excellent job of blending into most environments. I haven't worked with her much in the field, because she's usually focused on mid-to-late nineteenth century, and my focus is more mid twentieth. But we're both considered modernists, with a focus on US history, so we're almost always in the same team scrums. She is always prepared, always presents a well-ordered argument for the projects she wants to pursue, and seems to come back with interesting information most of the time. And she is a huge stickler for avoiding even minor timeline glitches. Richard knows her a lot better than I do. They've been friends since they entered training, but . . ."

He trails off, so I finish the sentence. "But he's in love with her."

"Yup. Anyway, he said she came back from one of her earliest jumps terrified that something she'd done had caused an aberration."

"Of what sort?" I ask.

Tyson shrugs. "Either she didn't go into detail with him or else she swore him to secrecy. Whatever it was, she found out the situation resolved without any ripples to the timeline. So she's pretty conscientious. But . . . and this is a *huge* but . . . she has a major weakness—"

"Saul."

"Exactly. With the exception of the comments on intelligence, my assessment of Saul Rand is pretty much the opposite. He likes to bend rules, and because his family is well connected, he tends to get away with bending them. The day I jumped back after we fixed the rift at the Beatles concert, he just marched out of the jump room, without even going through Temporal Monitoring, which is a major infraction."

"Do you think he would do anything to alter the timeline? I mean, intentionally?"

"I was thinking more carelessness, but he does play The Game pretty obsessively." Tyson's brows have been slowly knitting deeper and deeper into a worried frown as we talk. "Where is all of this going? Rich and Katherine looked for Saul before they left 2136. They didn't find him. He was at the Objectivist Club when the time shift hit, and he wouldn't have been under a key, so it was really more to humor Katherine than anything else."

For the time being, I ignore his question of where this is going and focus on the real issue. "You said that Saul is Katherine's weak spot, but . . . do you think she would cover for him if he was breaking CHRONOS rules?"

"Depends on what you mean by breaking the rules," he says around a bite of the pie.

"I mean altering the timeline."

His mouth opens, and then he shakes his head. "That's not possible. I know you're not entirely familiar with our process, so let me explain. Like I said, we're supposed to go through Temporal Monitoring at the end of any jump—"

"I know. To see if there's anything major enough that it shifts the timeline. Katherine mentioned the process in her diary, and there's a section in *A Brief History of CHRONOS*. But you noted that tiny aberrations happen. What if someone was making small, incremental changes that he planned to take advantage of later?"

Another long pause. "No. I mean, not to the question of whether it's possible. I don't think it's at all likely, but I can't entirely dismiss it. But no to the main question of whether Katherine would cover for him on something major. Unless . . ." He stops and rubs his face.

"Unless what?"

"Just a stupid theory one of the other historians mentioned. I'm guessing you've heard of him, actually, since I'd lay bets he's the source of Clio Dunne's bright-green eyes."

I sigh. "Timothy Winslow. Is the resemblance that obvious?"

He shrugs. "Overall, no. Katherine might not notice it, if that's what you're worried about. I just spent a bit of time in the tank with him during our last little adventure, so the resemblance stood out. It's mostly just the eyes, really. They're pretty distinctive. Anyway, we were at lunch one day, talking about how Katherine kind of lets

Saul walk all over her. She's as smart and capable as any of the other historians, but he treats her like a doormat. Timo has this theory, and I really shouldn't have called it stupid, because I know the genetic-design teams have done similar stuff in the opposite direction. Tate Poulsen, for example, is our Viking historian. He looks a lot like—"

"Thor," I say. "From the comics."

Tyson gives me a look that's equal parts annoyed and amused. "Should I just assume you already have full background details on everyone at CHRONOS?"

"Not everyone. But between Katherine's diaries and Kate's . . ." I stop, my breath catching in my throat. I'd been about to say that I know most of the historians who will be stranded in the field when CHRONOS is destroyed, and a few facts about some of the others. That's more than I really should tell him, but that's not what has me unable to breathe. This is the first time it has occurred to me that Tyson Reyes was not one of the names mentioned among the historians in the field that day. The odds, therefore, are very good that he is one of the people in the building the day that Saul blows it sky high, leaving nothing but a crater of ash and rubble. If, by some miracle, we manage to restore CHRONOS, and they return to HQ to cobble together the chain of events that leads to my eventual birth, Tyson only has about six months to live.

"Madi?" he asks. "Are you okay?"

I force myself to nod. "Yes. The brain is just misfiring, I guess." I take a long sip of coffee, now eager to get this over with. "Given that time is short, how about I just let you know if I'm unclear on who someone is?"

"Sure," he says, still looking at me a bit oddly. "As I was saying, they clearly boosted Poulsen's testosterone and probably some growth hormones, too. Although I'm sure there were plenty of men in the Viking community he lived in who were average size and build, the design team seemed to have a tendency toward stereotypes. And in the case of my team, which also designed Tate, a fondness for ancient comic books. Anyway, if they tweaked hormones for the male historians in situations where they felt the guy might need to be hypermasculine, what would prevent them from doing the opposite in the case of Katherine, who spent the vast majority of her time in the field in situations where the woman was expected to be demure and even somewhat subservient? I don't know that they actually *did* this. Evelyn—that's Timo's wife, which you already knew, right? She was kind of pissed about the whole theory. But the only time I've ever seen Katherine really lose it was when she was confronting one of the many women Saul slept with . . . well, I was going to say behind her back, but if he was trying to be stealthy, he failed miserably. And Timothy said that's another sign of some increased hormone—oxytocin, maybe? Anyway . . . long story short, I don't think she'd cover for Saul if it was a major breach of protocol. But if she discovered something tiny, something she could reason away? Maybe. She doesn't like to cross him. I seriously doubt that he's actually abusive, but . . ."

I struggle to keep my face neutral, but I can't help thinking of the vid from Katherine's diary. The bruise on her cheek. The red mark around her neck where he ripped off her necklace. I remind myself that those things haven't actually happened yet, and maybe they never will. But I know the potential is there, and that must show in my expression.

"Aw, fuck," Tyson says softly. "And to think I was feeling guilty for wishing we could restore CHRONOS, *except* for Saul. So . . . what brings this up? What changes do you think he made to the timeline?"

"Saul Rand created the Cyrists," I say. "It's complicated at this point, because I think we're in something of a . . . well, not a time loop, because it isn't closed. So a time *spiral*, I guess? I don't even know if that makes sense. What I do know is that Saul used a preexisting cult, the Koreshan Unity in Florida, as the basis for the Cyrists, but he's the one who wrote *The Book of Cyrus* itself. And he was dropping in on churches in the guise of Brother Cyrus, curing someone's cancer, giving a few bits of prophecy, and so forth. I'll bring you back Kate's diary, and you can read it once all of this is over, but the condensed version is that he was planning a rather nasty bit of genocide. He even did a dry run of it in 1911 in a small village in Georgia."

Tyson's face goes pale. "You've got to be kidding. How could he do something like that and not have it show up in Temporal Monitoring?"

"It was a very isolated village. No one even realized they were dead for several weeks. Anyway, Katherine wasn't aware of that part. And in the version of events that I know, she doesn't figure out what Saul is doing in terms of the Cyrists for a few more months. In that version of events, however, I didn't find a CHRONOS key to jumpstart our research and put us decades ahead of schedule. So, I really don't have a clue what Katherine knows. But *The Book of Cyrus* was an ongoing project of Saul's. He joked about it with Tate and maybe Morgen. That's why I'm suspicious that Katherine may know more about some of this than she's letting on. I think she's covering for him. And since the other team seems to be using the Cyrists as part of their strategy, that means she's holding back information we need."

FROM THE *DAILY INTREPID-HERALD REVIEW OF BOOKS*

THE COMING AMERICAN FASCISM: TWENTIETH ANNIVERSARY EDITION

(January 8, 1956) Twenty years ago this week, one of our correspondents provided us with a lengthy review of Professor Lawrence Dennis's seminal work *The Coming American Fascism*. At the time, the review reflected the common wisdom of many educated elites, that Dr. Dennis was a blowhard with little understanding of economics, politics, or human nature. The review noted that Dennis's book, while well written, was overly long and tedious and that his arguments for the benefits of a fascist government might also be applied to a government of cannibals, since the latter would quickly solve the problem of unemployment. In the end, our reviewer concluded that the book effectively guaranteed that fascism would not take root in our nation because he managed to make the topic utterly boring.

We have been reliably informed that Professor Dennis has long kept a framed copy of the review in his office to keep him humble. Our initial idea for this anniversary piece was to contact the original author, R. L. Duffus, and ask whether hindsight had inclined him to deal more favorably with *The Coming American Fascism*. As we were unable to locate him, the editorial staff has chosen instead to look at all the ways in which Mr. Duffus was wrong about this prophetic work.

Two decades ago, our nation found itself at a crossroads. Our government clearly failed to avert economic disaster, and economic thinkers understood that the nation could not recover and achieve its true potential under a system of unfettered capitalism. Change was on the horizon, with the only question what the nature of that change would be. Would the United States take the path of international communism or the nationalist path of fascism?

For Dennis, there was never really any question. He understood that the communist path would simply not work in the United States, given the nation's level of development. Not only would the economy be seriously damaged in a communist revolution, but there would likely be significant loss of life, since the bourgeoisie would not step aside willingly. Thus, he argued, fascism was the only viable alternative to achieve a planned, well-regulated economy. Effective planning would only be possible with a strong, permanent government, unencumbered by constitutional guarantees and state boundaries and administered by a competent elite.

Dennis acknowledged that the country was too diverse to organize around race or religion. The glue would have to be the one thing that unites all members of the country—our view of ourselves as Americans.

Had this retrospective been written a decade ago, many would have argued that the success of these policies was far from guaranteed, especially after the defection of the western states. Professor Dennis himself was somewhat dismayed when disaffected racial and religious minorities had to be relocated in order to ensure economic stability. But today, we are a powerful, prosperous nation far more united than at any time in the past. And contrary to all expectations, many elements of our original Constitution were retained under the new Contract of State.

In his original review, Mr. Duffus held that Professor Dennis's theories were farcical, flawed by twisted logic, and yet essentially harmless given their philosophical nature. He concluded by saying that Dennis "wastes a lot of breath on a small sneeze." Today, with twenty years of hindsight, however, we can argue with assurance that, on the contrary, Dennis's theories breathed new life into our moribund nation.

∞17∞

TYSON
NEW YORK, NEW YORK
FEBRUARY 20, 1939

Historians tend to divide into two opposing camps on the issue of night jumps. Some argue that darkness gives you a bit more cover, and that's true. The problem is it also gives that same cover to others. In the bright light of day, you simply pan around the area before jumping. If you see no one, the odds are damn good that there's no one to see you. With a night jump, however, that's far less certain.

Case in point, the couple making out in the bushes here in Washington Square Park, less than a meter from my stable point. Luckily, they seem to have been too preoccupied with each other to realize that I popped in out of thin air. They do, however, both realize that they're no longer alone.

"Sorry." I back out toward the walkway. "Just looking for a spot to take a leak."

It's the standard excuse, the one we're taught in training, and by far the most logical reason that a guy would wander into the bushes alone in the dark. It's definitely the excuse least likely to get you into trouble with anyone other than the police, and even then, the odds are good that the cop will take pity on you.

That said, I'm sure this guy is wishing I'd used pretty much any other excuse, because his girl is now thinking about her dress, and the grass, and how many guys may have done the same thing in that exact same spot.

It feels like an odd choice for a make-out spot to me anyway, but then the location is seared into my memory. Maybe if you live here, maybe if you use the sidewalk across the street every day, maybe then you become immune to it. Maybe it's like any other sidewalk. I mean, people die everywhere. Usually not 146 of them in a single building, though.

Nearly twenty-eight years ago, the area just outside the park along Washington Place was littered with the bodies of young women who jumped to their deaths when the Triangle Shirtwaist Factory caught fire. The greed of the owners led them to block the doors against the prospect that the women, most of whom were mere girls, might slip out for a breath of fresh air. It also made it easier to check every worker's handbag for stolen goods at the end of her shift. Safety laws were changed as a result of that fire, but it took the visceral shock of watching dozens of girls jump to their deaths and seeing even more carted out of the building as charred corpses to spur people into action. It took 146 deaths to buy a tiny bit of progress.

The location doesn't tie in with my research agenda, but it was part of the standard training curriculum for all historians in my cohort who studied 20th-century America. Thankfully, it's not the first jump you take during training. The first two or three show you the lighter side of history. My very first jump, at age fourteen, was to Disneyland in 1959, along with three other students in my year and two chaperones. It was partly for fun, but also to see how comfortable we were with the language of the era, the use of money, and other things we'd need to master before formally beginning the field-training phase of our studies.

This jump was where things got serious, though. I've compared notes with others from different cohorts, and all of them had something similar in their third or fourth training jump. Something with bodies, and usually quite a few of them. I think the reason is twofold. First, they want to show us that our jobs are serious. We will be studying issues of life and death. It's not all Disneyland.

But second, and I think this might even be considered the primary goal, was to remind us that the people we encounter on these jumps are dead. All of them. Our chaperone on that trip, a soon-to-be-retiring historian named Rose, who specialized in this era, mentioned this several times. They're all dead. Not just the bodies I saw lined up on the sidewalk in neat rows but also the police officers who stood by guarding them, unashamed of the tears running down their cheeks. The reporters snapping photographs of the disaster for the newspapers. The people who began gathering here in this very park, trying to find out whether their friend or family member had made it out of the fire alive. All of them, Rose had insisted, were long, long dead in our time.

They were history.

Looking back, I believe this second goal, the one we discussed in an essay upon our return, was supposed to remind us that we are scholars. That our goal in the field is to be objective, analytical observers, and to uncover the history that is all too often obscured by the biases of those who lived during the time frames we study. As part of our research, we might play roles that revolve around war, death, and disaster, but those are just roles. The people we interact with in the past are history—*our* history. And while catastrophes like the Triangle fire are tragic, the girls on that sidewalk would have died eventually anyway.

I understood the message being delivered and dutifully gave the expected response on the essay, which earned full points. But it didn't sit well with me. Maybe it would have if I had been standing a few feet to the left and hadn't seen one of the bodies move. It was one of the girls who'd jumped to escape the fire, and given what passed for medical care in the era, I suspect she died from her injuries anyway. And yes, no matter what happened to her on March 25, 1911, she would have died at some point during the 1900s, centuries before I was born.

But in that moment, the girl *wasn't* dead. She was alive and clearly in pain, reaching out to a nearby officer who was looking in the other direction. I opened my mouth to call out, to alert him, but Rose squeezed my shoulder.

"Tyson, no. If the man is supposed to see her, he will. If she's supposed to live, she will. We're observers. We do not interfere." Her words seemed clinical and carefully chosen. Not we *cannot* interfere, but we *do* not.

In the dreams that haunted me for quite some time after that jump, the girl is reaching not for the officer but for me.

Except now, from what Madi has just told me, it's pretty clear that Rose was wrong. Sometimes we *do* interfere. Or at least, Saul interfered. Will interfere, rather, if we manage to restore CHRONOS.

Apparently, it was just a series of tiny tweaks at the beginning. Things so isolated that they weren't flagged during his checks by the Temporal Monitoring Unit. A minor miracle at one church, a bit of prophecy at another. All laying the groundwork for the day when he would destroy CHRONOS to break free of its constraints and emerge as the leader of his own religion.

In the end, it doesn't work. He strands himself and others at various points in the past, and none of them can use the key. Am I one of the historians who gets stranded? Or one of those killed when CHRONOS is destroyed? Madi didn't have answers to a lot of my questions. She's offered to let me read the diaries in the library back in Bethesda, and eventually I will probably take her up on that. Right now, however, we need to focus on the problem at hand. The only questions for me are how much Katherine knows and why she hasn't told us. I'm certain that she knows *something* based on her reaction to seeing the Cyrist temple not long after the time shift erased HQ. The fact that she's keeping anything from us is troubling, and I hate having even a small doubt about whether we can fully trust her. Opening this can of worms at the very moment we desperately need to be working together as a team seems like a bad idea, especially since I know from past experience that no matter how close he and I may be, Richard's first instinct is always to protect Katherine. But I'm not sure how we can avoid discussing it.

The couple from the bushes, their clothes now back in place, passes me on the walkway. He shoots me a dirty look, which is completely fair. A hotel room will likely set him back a day's wages. The two of them scurry across the street to the sidewalk where the bodies were stacked, unmindful of the ghosts beneath their feet, and I hear Rose's voice again—*We do not interfere.*

I turn the opposite way, toward Waverly Place, keeping to the park side of the street. About ten minutes later, I arrive at Café Society. A year or so from now, the place will be too popular for someone to simply walk in off the street and expect to get a table. But the club has only been open for about six weeks. The fact that Lawrence Dennis even knows about it is a bit surprising.

It makes me wonder if maybe he lives a double life.

His race is one of those odd open secrets that anyone who cared to investigate could have uncovered even a century before the advent of the internet and social media made it almost impossible to reinvent oneself. Born Lonnie Lawrence Dennis, he began work as a child evangelist at age five, touring African American churches in both the US and Britain. One of the accounts I read told of his visit to a church in Brooklyn, where a member of the congregation called out to ask the then-five-year-old child, "Why are you here?" to which he responded that he was there to save New York like he had saved thousands before. It became something of a call-and-response after that. Whatever city he toured, someone would shout out *Why are you here?* And he'd say he was there to save Chicago, or Boston, or London.

As a teenager, however, the "Inspired Child" stopped touring and cut all contacts with his family. Lonnie Dennis was now Lawrence Dennis. He attended Exeter and Harvard, and worked as a diplomat, until he grew disillusioned with US foreign policy. He then worked as an advisor to a stock brokerage, until he grew disillusioned with capitalism, although he didn't think communism or socialism were viable alternatives and wrote a book to that effect at the height of the Great Depression. While he's often hailed as the intellectual voice of the fascist movement, his views were a bit too complex to pigeonhole into one ideology.

If Dennis did not explicitly argue for racial equality, he didn't argue against it, which made him a bit unusual, given that he worked with political figures who proclaimed the white race supreme. Some within those circles clearly suspected that he was of mixed race, using vague code words to describe his appearance, such as the occasional mention of "woolly hair" or his "swarthy" complexion. Charles Lindbergh, with whom Dennis worked closely, speculated that Dennis's ancestors may have come from the "Near East."

Mostly he just avoided the topic altogether, mentioning race and racism only twice in *The Coming American Fascism*. Dennis argued that there were two ways an American fascist state might deal with racial minorities. He "devoutly hoped" that the focus would be on assimilation and accommodation for racial differences, because the only other option would be to exterminate, deport, or sterilize them. In his view, free speech and freedom of the press were almost meaningless buzzwords, so the leader should dispense with the notion that these are rights, and simply determine what degree of freedom was possible without disrupting the social and economic order. Women were to be restricted, for the most part, to the role of housewife, since that suited them best and would ensure full employment for men, who he said would do the job better anyway, in the vast majority of cases.

I'll admit that Dennis fascinated me, not just as a research subject, but for intensely personal reasons. In my time, being mixed race is the norm. In his, any hint of nonwhite blood would have been a major barrier to his career, and the complete kiss of death for anyone professing fascist beliefs. After Glen and I returned from a training jump to view the 1944 sedition trial of Dennis and nearly thirty other fascists, I convinced Angelo to let me schedule, as one of my first solo day trips, a jump to a small book signing and reading here in New York for Dennis's *The Coming American Fascism*, which was published in 1936.

When I returned from that trip, I wrote up a brief official account, but I omitted the fact that I botched the trip. I didn't even note that in my personal log. Not because I'd done anything that marked me as being outside the timeline or made any real mistakes. I was just embarrassed. Embarrassed that I'd let my personal interest in Lawrence Dennis's views affect my work, for one thing. Thinking about that jump also dredged up the question at the core of my research agenda. Not the question that I would be answering, but the one the jump committee had attached to me. With whom would I identify? Would I choose the side of the KKK or those they terrorized? It was never really a question I had debated. From the beginning, I took the part of the oppressed. I couldn't imagine how someone could choose otherwise.

But then I discovered the enigma of (Lonnie) Lawrence Dennis, who had come to the same fork in the road and opted to, as they say, hug the viper to his breast. It bothered the hell out of me that someone could face that dilemma and make the *wrong* choice. That felt a lot like self-loathing to me.

Of course, I was nineteen, idealistic, and more than a little naive. It was a relatively cost-free decision for me, at least when I wasn't in the field playing a part. When I walked outside of CHRONOS, I faced no discrimination of any sort. I faced no *real* discrimination inside CHRONOS, either, aside from occasional jokes and the nickname Chameleon (Cham for short) given to me by assholes like Saul, and I simply chose to avoid those assholes to the extent possible.

But Lawrence Dennis had chosen to bed down with them. Why?

On that evening, Dennis had closed out his formal presentation and asked if there were questions. I looked around at the dozen or so men in the room . . . all white, all obviously wealthy, and, judging from the questions that followed, all smugly assured of their innate superiority. After five or six questions, Dennis's dark eyes paused on my face as he searched the room to see if anyone else had raised a hand. The scrutiny made me uncomfortable, as if he could tell I didn't belong in this group, even though I was dressed to fit the part, complete with the stupid blue contacts. He motioned for me to go ahead, clearly reading on my face that I had a question. And I did, although I hadn't planned to ask it. But every eye was on me now, and I blurted out the only question on my mind, the one that the woman had asked in the newspaper account of his tour as a child evangelist—*Why are you here?*

I realized the question was a mistake as soon as the words left my mouth, of course, and quickly added a clarification. Why did he choose to speak so often in New York? Wasn't the most receptive audience for his message outside the cities filled with immigrants? It was a lame cover. Given the population density, he could easily reach more budding fascists per square mile right here in Manhattan.

The addendum might have fooled the others in the audience, but it didn't fool Lawrence Dennis. His eyes narrowed, and then he smiled slyly. "Why, obviously, I'm here to save New York."

A wave of polite laughter followed, even though the others almost certainly didn't get the full context. I joined in, but I didn't feel comfortable enough to stick around to chat afterward. Watching Dennis work the crowd was a little too much like looking into a mirror of the future. The reflection wasn't mine. But could it become mine? If I spent long enough studying the Klan from the inside, would their arguments start making sense to me?

When no one was looking, I slipped out of the signing line and headed for the stable point two blocks over. I was so unnerved by the whole thing that I'd run the last stretch, half certain the security guy at the door was following me.

I'd eventually chalked the whole thing up to beginner's nerves, but it stuck in my mind. And so tonight, when I began thinking about what I could say to get Dennis's attention, I knew there was only one possible thing to scrawl on the back of the business card I presented when asking for an interview. On the front it said *Harold Fletcher, Reporter,* Time *Magazine.* On the back, I scrawled four words: *Why are you here?*

As I draw closer to Café Society, I debate jumping back and waiting for Rich. He's the only reason I've even heard of this club. The racial integration of 1930s jazz clubs was the focus of his first project after we became roommates. But while Richard's experience might come in handy, having him here would make it far less likely that I'd get anything of substance out of Lawrence Dennis. This is a conversation we need to have one-on-one. And while my expertise is nowhere close to Rich's, we trade off duties as proofreaders and sounding boards for our proposals. That gives me at least a nodding acquaintance with 1930s jazz and blues clubs, especially those establishments that pushed the color barrier, in much the same way that I'd learned everything there was to know about the Beatles by osmosis when he was getting ready to pitch that plan to the jump committee.

Café Society is located in the basement of the building that faces Sheridan Square, which isn't a square at all, but an elongated triangle of greenspace. The club is generally heralded as the first integrated club in New York, although Rich claims that's only partially true. It's true that, with only a few exceptions, there are black jazz clubs and white jazz clubs in 1930s New York. Black performers play both venues, but there are rules against the performers mingling with patrons. And while black patrons might occasionally be allowed at the white clubs, they aren't exactly encouraged.

Barney Josephson, the owner of Café Society, wanted the club to be a place where patrons of all races and classes mingled freely. He also wanted a place where performers would be paid fairly, and not treated as second-class citizens. Even the name of the establishment was intended as a bit of a snub to the elitist, segregated clubs, and the walls were decorated with murals created by artists with the New Deal–era Federal Arts Project. The paintings included vignettes of snooty society couples staring down their pince-nez at the common folk. Matchbooks given out at the bar proudly proclaimed the club's motto: *The Wrong Place for the Right People*. The club attracted famous performers (and made a few unknowns famous). It also attracted famous guests, including Eleanor Roosevelt, in perhaps her only visit to a nightclub during her time as First Lady.

Josephson's idea was largely a success. He even opened a second, swankier location uptown, although some of his social-justice principles seem to have fallen away at that location due to pressure from patrons. In February 1939, however, Café Society is only just beginning to attract attention, mostly among the theater and literary crowds. When I arrive at the door, I'm greeted by an unshaven doorman dressed in rags and gloves with the fingers worn out. It's part of the club's schtick about being the place where class and race are irrelevant—the waiters are clad in tuxedos and the doorman looks like he wandered in after sleeping off a bender in the park.

The only music I hear as I head down the stairs is a soft, jazzy background number by the pianist, so they must be between sets. About half of the tables are occupied, mostly by white couples, although there's one table with two women near the back and quite a few guys, both black and white, hanging out at the bar. The dance floor is almost nonexistent, something I remember Rich mentioning. Josephson wanted the focus to be on the performers.

A dense cloud of cigarette smoke hovers beneath the low ceiling, making me wish I'd packed nasal filters. I also wish I'd packed the fake smokes that the prop department gives me when I'm in the field as Klan member Troy Rayburn. In an era where almost every man in a bar, and many of the women, have cigarettes in their hands, you're less likely to stand out if you do, too. I'm not worried enough about it that I'm willing to actually order a pack and light one of the foul things up, however.

The waitress seats me at a table near the back next to the two women, which is the only empty table with a clear view of the doorway so that I can keep an eye out for Dennis. I order a Rheingold and a rib eye, mostly to give me something to occupy my time while I wait and set a stable point both at the table and in the restroom, in case I need to pop back in quickly in the future.

A comedian named Jack Gilford takes the stage. He's funny, but the humor is kind of topical, so I don't catch a number of the jokes. The women sitting behind me clearly find him hilarious, especially the blonde. Her laughter and her voice are both distinctive, deep and raspy, possibly a result of the steady stream of smoke coming from her table. And there's something familiar about the woman's voice. For some reason it's evoking memories of my mentor, Glen, and one of our training jumps to the mid-1960s.

The steak is gone and I'm on my second beer when Dennis comes through the door. For a moment, I don't even realize it's him. He's abandoned the suit and tie that he wore at the rally in favor of a tweed jacket, and instead of the usual businessman's hat, he's wearing a newsboy cap and glasses that look slightly tinted. While it's possible that this is just his everyday casual look, I don't think so. This is Lawrence Dennis in disguise.

He spots me at the table, nods, and then heads to the bar. This seems to be a regular haunt, since the bartender greets him as *Mr. Lawrence*, and one of the men on the barstools claps him on the shoulder. He chats with the guy for a moment, then brings his drink over to the table.

"Ah, Mr. Fletcher." He pulls out the chair opposite me and sits. "Wasn't sure you'd still be here."

"Wasn't sure you were coming," I say. "Or that you'd remember me."

"I didn't remember the name. In fact, I'm not sure you ever gave me your name at that event. But I did recall what you scrawled on the back of the card." He leans forward, lowering his voice. "You think you're the only dumbass kid to show up at one of my events thinking he's morally superior? I will give you this, however . . . you're the only one who did his research. *Why are you here?* Ha. So I guess you're more a *smart-ass* kid. Let me just say up front that if that's what this is about—"

"It's not."

"What happened to your eyes?"

Surprised that he noticed the difference, I improvise an answer. "Contact lenses. Got a friend who does makeup in Hollywood. She fixed me up with a pair like the ones they use to change eye color in movies." It's a couple of years off. From his point of view, he saw me in 1936, and the first use of colored contacts in a film won't happen until around the end of 1939. But he'll have a hard time dredging up that information. "The lenses bothered me, though, so I stopped wearing them."

"You might want to get past them *bothering* you if you plan on anything permanent with that pretty little blonde you were trading whispers with up in the balcony." He gives me a serpentine smile, quite pleased with himself for having spied on me at the rally. Or, more likely, for having slipped someone a few dollars to do the spying for him, thinking back. Probably the cop that Madi spotted.

"She's a colleague," I say. "Nothing more."

"Of course. Do either of you actually work for Henry Luce?" he asks, referring to the owner of *Time* and *Life* magazines.

"No. But I'd like to. I'm thinking with the right story . . ." I shrug.

Dennis's eyes go icy over the rim of his highball glass.

I shake my head. "No, you misunderstand. I have no intention of revealing your secret."

"Hmph. But you're not above leveraging the fact that you *know* it in order to finagle an interview. I must confess I'm not exactly in awe of your moral code."

The feeling is mutual, I think, flashing back to the article I read about his contributions on policy as secretary of the interior. Dennis's arguments about the ill effects of diversity on national cohesion had been largely responsible for the mass westward migration of most people of color, non-Christians, and leftists. No, he hadn't personally put them onto the trucks, but he'd argued as early as 1936 that a strong, authoritarian state would convince minorities—racial or ideological—that the risk of fighting back was not worth the reward. After a short period of time, they'd relent, and the country could focus on rebuilding an economy shattered by global depression.

But I smile pleasantly, as if he's joking. And he may well be, for all I know. "My only goal in writing that was to get my foot in the door. Because this whole thing has me baffled. I've followed your writings about some of the baser elements of the fascist movement in this country, so I was a bit surprised to see your name on the poster for tonight's rally. You've never been a fan of the Bund, or of the Coughlinites, for that matter. So while everyone else is rattling on about the poster saying *Brother* instead of *Father*, I'm staring at your name, wondering what made you decide to cast your lot with the reactionary, unintellectual side of the movement."

"Intellect will only take you so far," he says. "You want to know something truly ironic? I have advanced degrees. I have the ear of political figures at the national level. And still, in some sense, I had more raw power as a five-year-old prodigy touring the nation in my white robe, spewing the Bible verses my mother taught me. Religious fervor can bond people, make them act outside their self-interest. It is a powerful force on its own, but coupled with nationalism, it could make these states truly united. And the Cyrists don't even demand that you put aside other religious faiths. As Coughlin noted tonight, it is the perfect civic religion to bind a fractious nation."

"You have to admit that it's a major change on your part, however. The last time I heard you speak in person, you said that Coughlin was a hypocrite. Listening tonight, I couldn't help thinking it doesn't make a damn bit of difference whether that windbag and his pilot are wearing a crucifix or a Cyrist cross. His listeners aren't tuning in for religious guidance. But you deciding to climb down out of the ivory tower and take your ideas to the masses . . . now, *that's* news."

It was intended as flattery, but as I say the words, I realize there's a lot of truth there. Not that the crowd had paid much attention to Dennis at the rally. They applauded politely on the few occasions that he mentioned Germany, Hitler, or said something bad about Roosevelt and his policies. There simply wasn't enough red meat in Lawrence Dennis's measured, cerebral speech to excite that crowd. I'm sure he was relieved that he'd been the warm-up act for Coughlin and not the reverse. But having Coughlin and Dennis at a Bund event, and both of them voicing at least some degree of approval for the Cyrist faith, was a big step toward unifying if not the nation, then at least a fractious political movement.

"Did I actually call Coughlin a hypocrite?" he asks, sounding a bit amused.

"I don't think you said it directly, but it was definitely implied. When did he convince you to endorse the Cyrists?"

"He didn't convince me of anything. I haven't even spoken with the man. But I have . . . contacts. Sources who told me Coughlin was finally going to go through with this conversion that has been rumored for the past few months. I was right about one thing, though. He *is* a hypocrite. And believe me, I saw more than my fair share of those as a boy."

The temptation to say that he sees one in the mirror each morning when he shaves is strong. I think there's a slight chance I would have said it if the woman at the table behind us—not the blonde with the husky laugh, but her black friend—hadn't pushed her chair back into Dennis's, drawing his attention away.

As the woman heads toward the bar, Dennis sticks his arm out to block her way. He says something I don't catch, and she picks his arm up by the sleeve and ducks under it. "You are so bad, Lonnie."

"Well, I certainly *can* be if that's what you want."

The woman turns around, one hand on her hip, and cocks her head to the side. That's when I spot the magnolia in her hair and recognize her as Billie Holiday. "Oh, you could *not* keep up with me, old man. And I'm not in the mood to listen to you flap your mouth all night."

Yeah, Rich is not going to be happy that I didn't bring him along. His one annoyance about his trip to Café Society was that his mentor's research had been focused on the period during and just after World War II, so he scheduled their jump for 1941, when the vocalist was Lena Horne. Rich said she was good, but he'd really wanted to see Holiday.

She turns to look at me. "Now this one, though . . . why didn't you tell me you had a son?"

"I don't," Dennis says flatly. "And he can't even afford to buy you a drink."

Billie grins. "Well, damn. I can fix that. Hey, Joey?" she calls out to the bartender. "Bring baby boy over here another drink. On me. And make it a bourbon. He needs something stronger than that Rheingold shit if he's gonna listen to Lonnie's nonsense."

This is greeted by laughter, especially from the blonde she's been sitting with. The woman raises her glass toward Billie, who responds with a demure little curtsy and then sashays over to the microphone in the corner, near the center of a very minimalist stage. Someone tried to fancy it up a bit by adding a small fringe of curtain over the ductwork, but it really only serves to draw attention to it.

"Oh, don't pout, dahling," the blonde drawls to Dennis, placing a well-manicured hand on his arm. "It's *so* unattractive. One day, mark my words, you'll wear that insult as a badge of honor. Our Billie is going to be a star."

I'd pegged her as older based on her voice, but she's probably in her thirties. Exceptionally pretty, with dramatic eyes. Her face is familiar, too, but I can't place it.

She glances over at the bar, then says, "Damn it all. I need to pee, and that communist ninny is about to turn the lights out." With that, she hurries toward the stairs, tottering slightly on her high heels.

"And there we have southern aristocracy at its finest," Dennis mumbles. "The moral turpitude of the political elites on full display."

I sit there for several seconds trying to think of a response, but it's hard to know what to say when I still can't place the woman's face.

"She's wrong about one thing, though," Dennis says. "It's Barney's brother who's the communist. Barney himself is just a fellow traveler. Or, even more likely, an unwitting stooge."

The lights do indeed go out, sending the room into a pitch-black, eerie silence.

Well, almost pitch black. On the other side of the stage, at a small table near the stairs, I spot three circles of purple light. I can't make out their faces, though. Observers, I'd guess, since the rules state explicitly that the players may not enter the field again until we've made our three moves. Although I suppose it could be players, if this was a location *where* they made one of their three moves.

A slow instrumental, almost a dirge, begins, and the blonde's name finally comes to me, probably because I stopped actively trying to remember it. *Bankhead.* Tallulah Bankhead. Broadway star, daughter of William Bankhead, speaker of the House of Representatives. The husky laugh was her trademark, and she'd put it to full use as the Black Widow on the TV show *Batman*, which I watched to prepare for a trip to 1967, when the show was all the rage.

The toilet flushes upstairs as the instrumental continues. A moment later, a single spotlight comes on, and Billie Holiday's distinctive voice fills the room.

"Strange Fruit" was an unlikely hit, but several months from now, Holiday will find a producer willing to take a chance on this beautiful, bleak, and undeniably morbid tune about lynching. It's a powerful song, with rich imagery, and it grabbed me the first time I heard it. But here, in this room, it's mesmerizing. You can almost smell the magnolias and burning flesh as she sings.

And that's when I realize *why* Lonnie Lawrence Dennis insisted on this particular club tonight, rather than someplace closer to the rally. He's making his point without having to say a word. We might be alike in some sense, but I didn't grow up as a black child in the South, during an era when lynching was the regional sport.

I don't get to judge his choices.

The spotlight goes out when the song ends, and when the lights come back up, Billie Holiday is gone. So are the three observers. For a moment, the place remains completely quiet. Then the band begins a slow, soft number, table service resumes, and the club gradually comes back to life.

Dennis is staring down at my sports jacket when I look back in his direction. A paranoid voice says that he might see the light of the

CHRONOS key through the breast pocket, but that would have been astoundingly unlikely even before. It's virtually impossible now, with CHRONOS erased from the timeline. And if that were the case, he'd definitely have noticed the light from the three medallions that were on the other side of the club. It's much more likely that he glimpsed my shoulder holster. I'm not used to wearing one, and these clothes aren't exactly tailor made.

"It's a moving song, isn't it?" Dennis says. "Even for someone like yourself, who was born after a decade of progress." He puts a sarcastic emphasis on *progress*, and the difference in our ages is closer to twenty years than ten. But I don't interrupt.

"It's slow progress, and much of it has taken the nation as a whole in the wrong direction," he continues. "But I'm sure you're fine with that. You've got friends who can make your eyes a bright baby blue when you feel like it. In my case, however, I had to make a choice, and I made it. I could choose this world or that one. And if I chose that one, odds were good I'd end up being that *strange fruit* Billie was just singing about. Because, for good or for ill, it is simply not in my nature to defer to a stupid man."

There are dozens of bones I could pick within that statement. For one thing, it contradicts his long-standing claim that minorities would not resist a strong government. Or maybe he just thinks he's the only black man smart or brave enough to fight for his own interests. If I were here as part of a normal CHRONOS mission, I'd dig a bit. Try to find out what makes him tick. Hell, if I just met the guy at a bar, I'd do that. But far too much is riding on this stupid game for me to risk Dennis shutting me down entirely.

"Can't blame you there, sir. Like I said, I take no issue with your choices. We all have to find our way in the world, to play the cards we're dealt, even if the deal isn't always a fair one." It's hard not to roll my eyes at my own words. It's like I was trying to see how many trite platitudes I could cram into a single sentence.

"You think I'm complaining about my lot in life?" he says with a touch of amusement. "I got a better hand from the *dealer* than the vast majority of clueless Aryan dolts heiling their ersatz Hitler in that auditorium tonight. A better deal, for that matter, than any of the other brainless idiots who stood at that podium. It doesn't take much to fool them, because they simply can't imagine that a man from an 'inferior' race could be this much smarter than they are."

Dennis nods toward the bar, where a slight, pale man with a receding hairline is talking to the bartender. "That goes double for the crowd on the other side of the political divide. Barney Josephson over there thinks the only way a Negro performer can become a star is if some smart Jew like him gives them a break. At least the Nazis are honest with their disdain. He thinks he's raising consciousness with that damn song, but he's just making money off the blood of Negro fools not blessed with the brains to allow them to escape. And the Holiday girl isn't much better. She's in the back room or out in the alley right now, letting a rich dyke whose family legally *owned* women like her a few generations back cop a feel in exchange for a bit of cocaine. But I guess that's progress, hmm?"

The waiter arrives with my bourbon, which he says is courtesy of Lady Day, and a second drink for Dennis, whose glass is now empty. He didn't place an order, so he must have told the bartender to keep them coming when he stopped at the bar on his way in. And either he's got a low tolerance for the stuff or else he had a few on his way over, because his words are beginning to slur.

"Were you still at the rally when the police let the lunatics break down the door?" he asks.

I'd steered clear of this discussion, waiting to see if he broached the topic. Maybe that's why he's tossing back the scotch. I'd like to think that, because it would mean there might be a bit of a conscience hiding in there with the man's ego.

"Not inside the building," I say. "I left shortly after your speech. But I heard what happened."

"Damn shame. People can't peaceably assemble in the country these days without fearing for their lives."

"Someone said there were children among the dead. Was it the explosion?"

"Two girls and their mother. And there was no bomb. They were killed by a bunch of Red hoodlums storming the gates."

"I didn't say it was a bomb. I said *explosion*. Which leads me to a question—who put you up to it?"

Dennis is silent for a moment. "I don't have a clue what you're talking about. But I'm certain that I don't care for your implication."

"I saw the phonograph, Mr. Dennis. Saw the timer, too. And I saw you come out of the storage room. I'm not blaming you for what happened. I just want to know who put you up to it. *That's* the real story I'm hunting down."

He doesn't answer for so long that I'm convinced he's not going to. Then he laughs. "You're as bad as they are. I don't think you saw a damn thing today. Definitely not anything you can prove. But leaving that aside, why do you automatically jump to the conclusion that someone *put me up to it*? Your assumption that I'm the lackey for Coughlin or one of those other fools isn't just laughable, it's insulting. Finish your drink and get the hell out." He tips back his glass, then says, "You know what? Never mind. I'm leaving."

He stops at the bar for a moment, then stalks out.

I'm tempted to follow him and at least try to explain that I wasn't implying he wasn't smart enough to be the brains behind the plan. But I'm pretty sure he knows that. It was just an excuse to get out of here. And I can't think of any other way I could explain what I meant other than telling him the truth—that I know someone, or something, convinced him, because there's another timeline where tonight's events did not happen. Since I can't do that, I might as well give it up and go back to the apartment. Rich and Katherine will be back by now, and we can compare notes.

I finish the bourbon and settle my tab. Two double scotches have been added, so I guess Dennis's stop at the bar was just to tell them that I'd be footing the bill.

The temperature has finally dipped down to where it's downright chilly when I step out into the night. I turn to head toward the stable point in the park out of force of habit, and then remember that the only silver lining about CHRONOS being gone is that I don't have to hike all the way back to my entry point in order for my key to work. All I need to do is duck into the alley or slip behind a dumpster.

I take a few steps into the shadows between the buildings, but two people are standing near the back door of the club at the far end of the alley. Probably workers taking a smoke break. It's too dark to even tell if they're looking my way, so I reverse course.

As I turn, Lawrence Dennis's fist smashes into my jaw.

I stumble back into the brick wall of the building. It's not the hardest punch I've taken, but it's definitely in the top five. I push away from the wall, raising my fists into a defensive stance, hoping that it was just a lucky punch on his part. He's got at least thirty pounds on me.

And, as it happens, he also has a knife.

"You've had that coming since 1936," he says. "I would have given it to you then if I'd gotten a chance. When you slipped out, I told them I needed a bathroom break and I followed you. So maybe you did see something tonight at the Garden, or maybe you didn't, but I saw something, too. Saw you up and vanish from an alley between the buildings three years ago. One second you were standing there, staring at your pocket watch, and the next, you were nowhere. So you want to tell me how you did that? While we're at it, I think I'd like to see that watch. And don't bother saying you left it at home, because I saw you walking around with it at the rally."

"Sorry," I tell him, raising my voice in hopes that the workers at the other end of the alley will hear us and stay clear. "I'm not giving you my watch. It's been in the family for generations."

That's true, in a sense. At least a half dozen agents from earlier cohorts used this medallion before I did.

"I'm not a thief," Lawrence says. "I just want to look at the damn thing."

I take a step back and reach into my sports coat, pulling out the gun. Which he apparently hadn't noticed, despite my slightly gaping jacket. Unfortunately, the two figures in the doorway have let their curiosity get the better of them, rather than doing the smart thing and slipping back into the club. I hear footsteps behind me. They're definitely not male footsteps, however, since I can hear the distinctive clicking of women's heels against the pavement. I'm about to glance back when I hear Bankhead's unmistakable throaty laugh.

"I don't know about you, Billie, but I think I can predict the winner of this little tête-à-tête."

Holiday, who sounds slightly less drunk than her companion, says, "She's right, Lonnie. I've got to get back inside for the next set. Barney's already alerted Jeeves, though, and he usually calls the cops. Unless he's in the mood to take care of things himself. A doorman's job can get a bit boring."

Dennis gives me a baleful look, retreats to the sidewalk, and then begins walking briskly toward Seventh Avenue. The sad thing is that both of the women probably assume that he's leaving because he's already got a record, rather than because an arrest for even a minor infraction could reveal the secret that ends his career.

It's the sort of thing that I could easily leak to a few sources in the media. Some might have the decency not to print it, but there are always those who value a scoop over ethics. Normally, I wouldn't even consider doing something like that, especially when I know that the man ends up in court for sedition in a few years, anyway, effectively ending his career and his influence. The case will be dismissed after the judge has a heart attack and the government decides it's not worth the effort to start over from scratch, probably because the damage will already be done to most of the people on trial. I listened to the evidence when I was there with Glen, and while I'm no legal expert, I think the government overstepped its bounds. As much as I may not like Lawrence Dennis's views, or those of many of his codefendants, only a few of them (like Coughlin) were actually in league with Hitler.

In this timeline, however, there will be no tribunal that curbs his influence. Instead, he'll be a cabinet member in a fascist administration and do untold damage to millions of people. So anything that exposes him, that keeps him from being part of that, would be a very good idea. This would be a great opportunity to halt him in his tracks.

But I can't, because the fucking *style* points dictate that we have to work in reverse chronological order. Everything in 1940 has to be handled first.

Tallulah places her hand on my arm and then presses her body close to mine. A curl of menthol-scented smoke rises from her cigarette, and her breath is heavy with gin. "You should come back inside, dahling. Have another drink and keep the two of us company."

I thank her for the invitation, which is very clearly for more than a drink and, God help me, is actually a bit tempting. But I make my excuses, telling them I have to be at work early in the morning.

Tallulah gives me a little pout, and then holds her arm out to Billie. "Well, then I guess we'll have to amuse each other."

When the two of them are back inside, I stash the gun back in the holster, then take out my key and pull up the stable point back at the apartment. Before jumping, I scan the alley briefly to see if anyone is watching, but . . . it's dark. Who knows? Lawrence Dennis could have circled the block.

There is someone moving toward me from the far end of the alley, but it's not Dennis. Not unless he found a CHRONOS key in the past minute or so and shrank a few inches. The figure is bathed in purple light. I think it's a woman. Alisa, maybe. Or Esther. But according to the rules they provided, their team members are not supposed to be interacting with us. Team Viper made their moves, and now it's our turn to make ours.

She does look familiar, though. I take a few hesitant steps closer, and so does she. Then she takes one very purposeful step that puts her inside the range of the dim light bulb outside the back door to Café Society.

"Marcy?" I ask.

The word seems to flip a switch. Marcy Bateman begins running toward me, nearly stumbling over a piece of broken pavement in the alley, and flings herself into my arms. I start to ask if she's okay, but before I can get the words out, she's pulling my face down to hers for a kiss.

This is not the first time we've kissed. But it was never *this* sort of kiss. For one thing, her face is wet with tears. Something must feel different to her, too, because she steps back and wraps her arms around herself.

"But . . . you *know* me," she says. "You said my name."

"I know a version of you. We're friends. The Marcy I know runs the Temporal Monitoring Unit at CHRONOS. Is that the job you have?"

She shakes her head. "I teach. We're just friends?"

"We dated a few times. But that was before you went on that ski trip and met Annika. I didn't stand a chance after that."

Even in the dim light I can see the effect that comment has on her. She shakes her head vehemently. "That's not true. I don't even ski."

I have to chuckle at that, despite the fact that she's clearly upset. "You told me that. Both of you went with a group of friends. Neither of you liked skiing. Even with the stabilizing field, it made you anxious. Annika felt the same way. And so you said the two of you found something to do that was a lot more fun."

She draws in a sharp breath, as if my words stung her. Then she swings a hand back to slap me. I block it, grabbing her wrist.

"That's a lie," she says. "A dirty lie. Three days before our commitment ceremony and you just vanish. Nobody knew where you'd gone. You just left. No message. Nothing. Then I saw you on *TD Off-World*, and Alisa said it wouldn't really be you, but . . . I hoped maybe she was wrong. I hoped maybe . . ."

"I'm sorry, Marcy. I don't have a clue what happened in your reality. In this one, you're with Annika. I have lunch with the two of you about once a month. You're happy. In fact, you were talking about starting a family, but she said maybe the two of you should start with something small, like a dog or maybe a rabbiroo, and make sure you could handle it before considering a baby."

She twists the fabric of her skirt nervously. "You mean we're together? In the open? And that's okay here?"

"Well, not so much in *this* era," I say, and then decide to amend it slightly, given my recent acquaintance with the two women inside the bar. "Although, if you have enough money or influence, you can sometimes flaunt societal rules without fear even in the 1930s. But in my time, yes. It's definitely okay."

I don't add that there have been cycles of oppression, much the same as with race. Two steps toward equality were all too often followed by a step back, or sometimes two or even three. The worst backlash came during the early days of genetic engineering, as some parents sought to choose not only sex but also sexual orientation of their offspring. But I'm not sure that she needs the details right now.

"We were happy, though," she says. "You and me. At least, I was."

"Most people can be happy with more than one person."

"You're with that blond girl now, aren't you? Max? The one I saw you whispering with in the balcony at Madison Square Garden."

"No. I'm not with her . . ." Over Marcy's shoulder, two people blink in. Esther and Alisa. Both of them are glaring at me like this is all my fault. Or maybe it's just because I'm on the opposing team.

"I can't believe you broke our agreement," Alisa says, turning to Marcy. "You know the rules. You're not allowed to interact with any players on the other side during the course of the game unless you have explicit orders. I put my neck on the line to get you that academic slot, and you promised you'd wait and contact him after the match ends. You *promised*. Pull up the home point and let's go."

"I need to finish talking to him," Marcy says. "I'll only take a couple of minutes."

"No," Esther says, moving up behind Marcy. She snaps one hand out and grabs the back of the cord holding Marcy's CHRONOS key. In one swift move, she twists the cord to tighten it and pulls the key—and also Marcy—toward her. I have a momentary flash of déjà vu, remembering Richard doing the same thing to one of their observers in the bathroom at the Mid-South Coliseum the night of the Beatles concert.

"Put that medallion in the palm of your hand, right now," Esther says. "Otherwise, I will yank this cord, and you'll vanish even faster than your version of lover boy here did after he realized it was a mistake to slip a ring on your boring little finger."

Alisa tsk-tsks. "That was really uncalled for, Ess."

I take a couple of steps back, then reach inside my jacket and draw the gun. "Let her go."

"You wouldn't dare," Esther says.

"She's right," Alisa tells me. "That would violate the rules."

"Try me. Pretty sure that you're violating them by being here, so who's going to tell? Plus, I didn't have any say in determining these rules. None of us did. And I'm beginning to wonder why in hell we should play by them."

Of course, I know exactly why we're stuck following their rules. If they don't think we're playing the game fairly, what's to stop them from sending in dozens of players and screwing up the timeline so badly that human life is extinguished? Just jump forward a couple of decades and start the bombs flying.

Marcy grabs for the key, but Esther has pulled the cord so far back that the key is now too high up for her to center it in her palm and still see the interface. Her eyes grow wide, and it looks like she's having trouble breathing.

Esther twists the cord a bit tighter, and I can tell she has every intention of calling my bluff. But then her eyes focus on something behind me. I don't look back, because I'm more than a little worried that this is *her* bluff, and if I give her even half a chance, she'll pull some sort of move she learned among the Akan warriors, and the end result will be my gun in her hand and my blood all over this alley.

But she's not bluffing. I hear the unmistakable sound of someone racking a slide. I do risk a quick glance over my shoulder at this point to determine whether the new arrival is friend or foe.

"Gonna need you to let go of the lady's jewelry right now." It's the guy Billie Holiday referred to as Jeeves. The fake patrician voice he used when he opened the door has been abandoned, and he now sounds more Bronx than Boston Brahmin. A sawed-off shotgun is pointed straight at Esther. He nods at me. "And you're apparently a friend of Lady Day, since she sent me around here to check on you, but I'd appreciate it if you'd put that gun away, given that I don't know you personally."

I do as I'm told, reluctantly. Esther lets go of the cord and steps back away from Marcy, who begins coughing as she pulls in air.

"And before any of you get ideas about pullin' another weapon, the bartender just called the cops. They spent the whole night protectin' Nazis over at the Garden, and some of 'em ain't too happy about it, so they'd probably be delighted to take you for a ride down to the station if you decide to stick around."

Alisa and Esther exchange a look, then tap the purple buttons on their cuff bracelets and vanish.

"Son of a bitch." The doorman looks from Marcy to me. "What the . . . How'd they do that? They're just *gone*."

Marcy is trying to say something between gasps for air, but I can't hear her over the doorman. Then she points behind me, and I make out the words *stable point*.

But it's too late. A shot rings out, and the doorman crumples next to me. A second shot, and Marcy clutches her chest as a dark stain spreads across the tiny blue flowers of her blouse.

I spin around, reaching for my gun. Esther grins, taps her bracelet with the hand holding a gun almost identical to the one now on the pavement next to Jeeves, and vanishes.

And so I turn back to Marcy, just as Alisa pops in behind her.

"I told you she was ruthless," Alisa says with a disgusted huff as she pulls the key over Marcy's head and they both vanish.

The back door to Café Society opens a second later. I press myself flat against the wall behind the dumpster and blink out.

FROM THE *NEW YORK*
DAILY INTREPID

COUGHLIN OFFICIALLY SEVERS TIES WITH CATHOLIC CHURCH

(Detroit, February 14, 1939) After more than a year of escalating tensions with the Roman Catholic hierarchy, Detroit radio priest Charles Coughlin has formally severed ties with Rome. Coughlin, whose weekly sermons reach as many as thirty million listeners, enjoyed a certain degree of protection prior to the death of Bishop Gallagher in January 1937. Gallagher's successor, Archbishop Mooney, rebuked Coughlin for comments supporting Hitler and Mussolini shortly after taking over, and Coughlin reined in the political content somewhat following censure.

As commentary on political and economic events gradually found their way back into his sermons, astute observers noted that it was joined by occasional verses from *The Book of Cyrus*. Indeed, those verses have begun to nudge out biblical references in recent months. In remarks on the evils of workers' unions and internationalism last October, for example, Coughlin cited Cyrus 7:14: "The moral objective of any life is its own existence, for its own sake. Each soul is an end unto itself."

Yesterday, at a meeting of the National Mothers' Union held at Coughlin's Shrine of the Little Flower, in the Detroit suburb of Royal Oak, Coughlin announced that he would be resigning his post effective immediately. The break with the Catholic Church became official in the wake of what many assumed was a clerical mix-up concerning an event in New York where Coughlin is scheduled to speak next week. Members of the Christian Front, a political organization connected both to Coughlin and the German-American Bund, were apparently aware of Coughlin's plans in advance. The information they provided for the poster advertising the Bund's upcoming "Pro-America Rally" listed him as Brother Coughlin, using the title given to Cyrist Templars, sparking speculation that a split was imminent.

Coughlin initially discounted the rumors, but amid a flurry of questions from both his followers and his superiors in the Catholic Church, he decided that it might be best to make a clean break. At a press conference following his address to the National Mothers' Union, Coughlin encouraged his audience to remain with the faith of their choice. "Christianity is a wide tent. I have chosen to reject the internationalism and creeping communist threat within some elements of the Catholic Church. This does not, however, mean that I reject the message of Christ, simply that I now believe it to be reflected in its most pure form within the teachings of his disciple Cyrus." In response to a question from the press, however, Coughlin did note that the Christian Front, which he is now free to officially lead due to the less restrictive political guidelines for Cyrist Templars, would henceforth be called the Universal Front.

At the conclusion of the press conference, reporters followed Coughlin to a location on the other side of nearby Roseland Park Cemetery, where construction has already begun on a Cyrist temple. The new church, tentatively called Temple of the Lotus Flower, is expected to open in early summer. In lieu of Sunday services for the next several months, Brother Coughlin will be speaking at various locations around the country, traveling aboard the newly christened *One True Way*, a Lockheed Vega six seater, piloted by aviatrix Laura Ingalls, herself a recent convert to the Cyrist faith.

∞18∞

KATHERINE
ROYAL OAK, MICHIGAN
FEBRUARY 13, 1939

Saul steps back and places one hand on each side of my face as he stares into my eyes. His hands are like ice, and my first thought is that this is a ghost my mind has conjured up to punish me for my earlier skeptical thoughts about ghostly visions. My second thought is that this isn't my Saul. But the scar on his face is missing. These are the same eyes that have stared into my own countless times. It's him.

"Oh, God, Kathy. I didn't know if you made it out. But I had to look, and the press conference seemed . . . and then I saw Richard but not you, and . . ." He lets out a long, shuddering breath and pulls me close again.

I was too in shock to really respond at first, but now I clutch him to me so hard my arms ache, biting my lip to hold back tears. "I *looked* for you, Saul. I swear. Richard and I went to the Club, even though I knew you couldn't be . . . How? *How* are you here?"

"Let's get out of the cold," he says. "My car is in the lot."

"Your car? Why do you have a car?"

"It's part of my cover. We're in Detroit. Everyone has a car."

That doesn't exactly make sense. He could get anywhere he wanted to go by setting local points. My guess is that Saul simply saw a car that he *wanted*.

"Okay, but I have to meet Richard soon. We're on a tight deadline." I stop, realizing that there are actually *two* huge questions. Not just how Saul survived, but also why he decided to look for me here and now. "How did you know where to find me, Saul? Out of all the places and times, why did you come here?"

"Mostly because of the message the hackers sent out. When I went to the OC the day I burned my arm on that jump, Morgen showed me the message that popped up on all of the TD consoles. The one with our names on it. He asked me what was going on, and he didn't seem to think it was a joke. I mean, I could see my name and Morgen's being on that list if this was some time-chess fans playing a prank. Maybe even Esther or Alisa. They've both been ranked nationally a few times. But you barely play. I've seen Rich play a couple of times at most, and I've never even heard of this Max. I mentioned this when I got home, and you said you didn't know anything about it, remember?"

"Yes. I'm sorry. I was—"

"I'm not blaming you, okay? You were under orders, I'm sure. Listen, could we just get out of here? It's fucking freezing, and—*God*. I still can't believe I finally found you. I've been looking for months."

Months?

I'm supposed to meet Richard at the four-hour mark, which is less than half an hour from now. It's not a huge deal if I miss that, though. We established a fallback rendezvous at the Manhattan apartment at hour five in case either of us needed more time. And Saul is right. It's freezing.

I follow him to an odd green vehicle that's shaped a bit like an avocado. "Do you know how to drive this thing?"

"Of course. It's not that different from the truck I just drove in 1911. And like I said, I've had a bit of time to acclimate to the 1930s."

The second I pull the door closed behind me, I'm hit with the sudden conviction that this is a mistake. This can't be my Saul. He couldn't possibly have been under a CHRONOS field when the shift happened. Other-Saul must have had his scar repaired and his bionic eye implant replaced with a more realistic model. And that means this mistake is probably a fatal one, even though Team Viper isn't supposed to harm actual team members.

As he slides behind the wheel, I grab the door handle. This could be my only chance to get away.

But then he turns my face toward him and kisses me, and I know. Doubt evaporates like the clouds of my breath in the cold morning air, and the tears I'd managed to keep at bay spill over. Saul holds me, smoothing my hair with his ghost-cold hands.

It's him. But I still have questions. Many questions. And so I wipe the tears on my sleeve and nod toward the key in the ignition. "We should go. I only have a little over an hour."

"There's a diner a few blocks away. How long has it been for you since the shift?"

"About twelve hours. I think."

Now it's his turn to look surprised. "How did you figure out all of this in twelve hours?"

As he drives, I give him a basic overview of my day, omitting the information about Madi. I'm not sure why, except that it feels like telling him would put restoring the timeline into even greater jeopardy. Saul has casually mentioned having children, maybe, in the distant future. I'm not sure, however, how he'd take the idea of a baby within the next year or so, when both of us are still in the middle of our field research. To be honest, though, I can't see how the stars could possibly align in exactly the right way to re-create that pregnancy and whatever it is that strands us in the past. Even if we restore CHRONOS, there will be minor changes to our timeline. Given where Angelo was headed when the shift happened, it's entirely possible that we could fix this aberration only to have the Solons decide to erase all of us anyway.

When I tell Saul about watching Angelo vanish, he reaches over and squeezes my hand. "Ah, babe. It's no secret he wasn't my favorite person at CHRONOS, but I know how much he meant to you. I'm sorry."

"Was that you that I saw at the OC?" I ask. "About an hour after the shift. I convinced Richard to go with me, and we both thought we saw you . . . or at least some version of you. But Sutter was interrogating us, and we had to get out. Richard set a stable point so that we could go back and look, but then the countdown was starting, and . . . I simply didn't see how it could have been you. How were you under a CHRONOS field, Saul?"

He parks in front of a squat trailer labeled *S & C Coffee Car* and gets out without answering my question. I know his expressions too well to be fooled. He's trying to figure out how much he wants to tell me. Saul is the master of partial truths. To be fair, I just did the same thing by deciding not to tell him about Madi and the pregnancy that may or may not be in my future. But I have a very good reason for being selective in what I tell him.

Once we're seated in a booth, warming our hands against the smooth ceramic cups of hot coffee, I repeat the question. "How were you under a CHRONOS field?"

"Morgen," he says simply, as if that's an answer. I stare at him for a moment, and then he adds, "Money couldn't buy him the CHRONOS gene, but it *could* buy him a key. You might wonder why the stupid gox would even want a key when he can't actually use it. I've definitely wondered that. He kept the medallion in the side drawer of his gaming table. Took it out and showed me one night when he was skunk drunk. I don't know if he even remembered telling me about it later, and I sure as hell didn't mention it. And, no, I didn't report it. We both know that given my relationship with Morgen, I'd be the first person they'd suspect of getting him the contraband, and even though they wouldn't be able to make it stick, it would be a pain in the ass. Plus, it's not my fault if security is so lax that they lost a key. Or maybe two. I know he had his tech people build a field extender for his quarters, but I don't know if that was powered by a key or a diary, or just something they managed to build on their own. Anyway, we were in Morgen's private game room in his quarters when the shift hit. We were playing an early twenty-first-century election scenario, and all of the constants just . . . readjusted. The graphics changed, as well. A quick computer check made it clear that something happened that kept us out of World War Two—exactly as the message on all of the TD consoles had said. But we didn't need a computer to tell us how much had changed. Looking outside, the entire city was altered. It was . . . jaw dropping."

Morgen Campbell's penthouse suite is round. It sits atop the rectangular main building of the Objectivist Club like a slightly off-center screw cap. His sleeping quarters are in the middle, and the living area that encircles it has a 360-degree view of the city. Those windows are one of the few things I like about his apartment.

"Half the damn city had vanished," Saul says. "The Washington Monument was sticking up out of the reflecting pond, for Christ's sake. Then I looked down K Street and HQ was gone. Completely *gone*, with that old library in its place, although you could barely see anything through the smog. I didn't know if you were under a key, but I thought there was at least a chance, given that you were mentioned in the message, and um . . . well, I'll get to the other part in a minute. So I ran the scenario through Morgen's system and came up with seven or eight different possibilities. Which I actually had to write down," he says as he pulls a sheet of paper out of his pocket, "since my comm was connected to CHRONOS, which no longer existed."

"And Morgen allowed you to take his key?"

"I think he probably would have. Eventually. If I'd argued with him long enough. But I really wasn't in the mood for his games. I sort of . . . incapacitated him and took it."

"That must be what Sutter's guards were talking about. They said Morgen didn't show up for a meeting or something. Do you think he's okay?"

"I don't know. And I'm not sure that I care, to be honest. Take a look at this key." Saul flips the key over to the back. Instead of the word CHRONOS, which is printed on a normal medallion, it reads CHRO-NOS. "That's from the other group, isn't it?"

"Yes," I say. "I've seen several of their keys. But how did you know that?"

He sighs. "Okay, babe . . . this is the hard part, because I'm pretty sure you're going to be pissed. And maybe you have a right to be. I lied about the burn on my arm. Well, it wasn't a complete lie. I was supposed to meet Grant at our stable point, which *was* in an alley behind a bar in Atlanta 1911. Only I found Grant inside the bar, completely shit-faced. But that wasn't the full story. I managed to get Grant out of there and around back to the stable point. He jumped back to HQ, and I was about to do the same, but then I saw myself standing a few yards away. At first, I thought it was a splinter. Maybe I was coming back to tell myself to leave Grant in the bar and let him face the consequences of an extraction team. Only this version of me had a weird scar along my cheek and an eye that looked an awful lot like Sutter's."

I debate whether to mention that I've seen this other version and decide that can wait. "Why did he seek you out?"

Saul colors slightly, something that is highly unusual for him. That's not an indication that he's lying, though. Based on my own past experience, when he's lying, even a white lie, he keeps his face almost motionless and holds my gaze. He almost never blushes.

"Mostly it's just a thing that my other self does," Saul says, "when he visits a new timeline. Hunts down his other self to . . . say hello."

"Oh. That's very neighborly."

"Indeed," he says wryly, and again, I'm tempted to push, because I'm quite certain that there's something he's not telling me. But I hold my tongue.

"My doppelgänger showed me his CHRONOS key, only the back was like this one I swiped from Morgen, with the word hyphenated. My other self also showed me a copy of *The Book of Cyrus*. I don't know if it was one of . . . I mean, if it was *my* copy. I don't think so. The symbol on the front seemed a bit different, but I only caught a glimpse of it. Then he said he had an invitation for me. He explained the nature of playing off-world Temporal Dilemma, and how it was several orders of magnitude better than the computer version."

"So . . . is his version of CHRONOS engaged in historical research? Or do they just use the medallions for gaming?"

"I don't know for certain," Saul says. "If I had to guess, I'd say the latter. Anyway, the other me told me that the opposing team had been picked because the four of you interfered in a previous game set in the 1960s, which I'm guessing was Rich's project that they didn't really want me on in the first place. He said this was a rematch of sorts. And then he asked if I was interested in helping him take Morgen down."

"Which Morgen, though? There are two of them. I don't just mean one Morgen in our reality and one in theirs, but two in *their* reality. Campbell apparently cloned himself. And both the clone and Alisa have the CHRONOS gene."

"I don't know which one he meant. He just said Morgen. And he said that I couldn't be an actual team member. I'd have to be an observer, whatever that is, but he'd let me handle Coughlin, since that would be well within my area of expertise. I'm not entirely sure what their game plan was with him, but he mentioned him explicitly. And he said that if I helped him, he'd leave me with an open key when the game was over—that is, a key that wasn't tied to HQ's system. That I'd have carte blanche to do whatever I wanted. *Go* wherever I wanted. Start the Cyrists for real if I wanted."

"What did you tell him?" I ask when he falls silent.

"I told him no, of course. What did you think I'd do? Even if I'd been tempted, what would be the point if outsiders have already screwed up the timeline, you know? Who knows what sort of mess they'd leave behind? And the whole thing sounded crazy, to be honest. I mean, I joke about playing The Game for real, but it's mostly just to mess with Morgen, since I *could* do it, at least theoretically, and he can't. So of course I told him no." He lets out a long, shuddering breath. "And then he said he couldn't have me warning everyone else and pulled a fucking gun."

"Oh my God."

"Fortunately, I've got quick reflexes. The bullet careened off the bricks and grazed my arm. That's the wound you bandaged, and that's why I didn't want to go to the med unit. They'd have known the difference between a burn and a groove caused by a bullet. He was about to fire again, and I'm pretty sure that he'd have killed me, but another guy—the dishwasher for the bar, I think—stepped outside when he heard the shots. Dumb move. The other me shot him, but that gave me enough time to pull up the stable point and blink out."

"So you knew the time shift was coming before the message even arrived. Why didn't you tell me?"

"I didn't *know* anything, Kath. Not for certain. In fact, I'd convinced myself that I might be the prankster. That I could have gone crazy at some point in the future, and this was insane me's twisted idea of a joke. When I mentioned the message to you and you said you didn't know anything about it, that made me wonder even more. And it didn't make sense that he's part of this game where he and Morgen are supposedly on the same team, and yet he's wanting me to help him take down Morgen. Plus, Morgen can't time travel. Neither can Alisa."

"Like I said, though, it's the younger Morgen who is on Team Viper. Four players and five observers. The older Campbell runs the show, and I literally mean *show*, as in with an audience. He said something about millions of viewers. And . . . I don't think it matters whether we flip the timeline back or even how quickly, because they maxed out the style points. They even got a double bonus in the geographical category, which I didn't know was possible. The bonus for that one is that all moves have to be within the same city, right?"

"Yes. But . . . are they using the exact same rule book? In version 1.6 they had subunits for geographic. They were dropped when they streamlined the categories. One player got a triple bonus—so a total of one hundred and fifty bonus points—on the geographic category for having all moves made within a one-kilometer radius. All at the US Capitol. She lost points in other areas as a result, but with a bonus like that, who cares? A five-kilometer radius would earn a double bonus on top of the regular bonus. Did any of your initial predictions hit?"

"One partial hit. The attempted assassination of the Japanese ambassador."

"Where?"

"In New York City. We think all of them are in New York."

"Yes," Saul says with a face that means I'm trying his patience. "But *where* in New York City?"

"I was going to say Hotel Astor, but that's just where Tyson and Max were thinking about going to see if they can get background information. Maybe see if they can spot anyone in the crowd that we can keep an eye out for the next day. The actual attempt was on Japan Day at the World's Fair. June 2, 1939."

"Then you should assume that all of them are at the World's Fair. That's not one I've attended, but I'd guess that the fairgrounds are within a five-kilometer radius, which would get you the double bonus you mentioned."

"But all of the moves can't have happened at the Fair. We were thinking New York, yes, but the Fair doesn't even open until April of this year. And Coughlin is giving a speech today announcing that he's joining the Cyrists."

"Yes," Saul says. "But trust me when I say that you shouldn't enter his conversion into the system as one of their moves."

It takes a moment for that to fully sink in. "Damn it, Saul. Please tell me you didn't?"

"But I did. Coughlin was delighted to be out from under the thumb of the Vatican. He's mostly interested in the political and economic side of things anyway. Thanks to the popularity of his radio show, he has a lot of influence among the isolationists and just plain nationalists. He could have even more if he'd tone things down a bit, and he's . . . malleable. Instead of taking money from Hitler, he was perfectly happy to take it from me, especially when I threw in the prospect of a shiny new temple that would put his current shrine to shame."

"Where did you get that kind of money?" Even as I say it, I know the answer. It's the same thing that Clio's parents did, although I'm guessing Saul was far more aggressive. I'm pretty sure that about a dozen years back, there was a very savvy investor who bought some stocks and knew to bail just before the market crashed in 1929.

I rub my forehead and then stare at him over my clasped hands. "This isn't good."

"Why? Why isn't it good? We need some sort of advantage in this game, or we are royally fucked. Your team is undermanned and underskilled. You don't have even one senior agent in the bunch. Did it occur to you that maybe that's *why* they chose this particular lineup to be their opponents? I mean Cham is great for blending in and getting comparative data on racists and their targets. But he's hardly the best we have. I've never even heard of this Max person, so I'm guessing he's a first-year. And Richard . . . well, seriously. A music historian?"

"The same could be said for religious history." Even though I know it's going to piss him off, the words tumble out, probably because I'm annoyed about the stock market stunt. And Coughlin. They both will cause ripples, and in the case of Coughlin, they could be major. We're trying to *fix* the timeline, not spin off some different version of it.

"No," he says. "It really couldn't. And you're smart enough to know that, so stop playing games with me. A song generally doesn't make people willing to fight wars or cough up more than a few dollars to own a copy, and then only if they can't find a way to get it for free. Religion, on the other hand, is a powerful motivator. A catalyst."

We've argued this point before. It's not uncommon for historians to think that their subfield is the most important area of study. In fact, it's pretty much the norm. But Saul generally takes this to extremes. His insistence that religion was the prime mover for almost all historical change borders on obsessive. And if he has had a few drinks or is in the middle of one of his squabbles with Morgen, he'll add that society could have been managed far better if someone who understood that fact had consciously used religion as a tool for shaping social and economic change. That makes him a bit of an anomaly at the Objectivist Club, given that it traces its roots to a debate club organized around a pseudophilosophy that began in the late 1950s, which viewed religion as a habit of the weak. Saul likes to goad Morgen by claiming the woman who founded it is one of his distant relatives, even though he told me he was certain she's not.

"But leaving all that aside," he continues in a more conciliatory tone, "you need my expertise on The Game and, most of all, on those players. I know what makes them tick—all four of them—assuming their personalities are reasonably similar in the other timeline. Esther and Morgen will both cheat. It's practically their signature move."

"So you don't think Morgen will keep his end of the bargain? Even if we somehow manage to win, you think he'll renege?"

Saul is silent, taking a long sip from his coffee before he answers. "It depends. He'll probably keep his word if his reputation is on the line. You said they're recording portions of this, right?"

"Yes. But recordings can be altered."

"True. My best guess is that he'll keep his word if the cost is low enough. From what you've said and from what I gathered from my other self, they can just move on and muck about in the next reality, right? Remember, this is a *game* to him. Just a game. If it becomes boring or not worth the cost, he'll move on to another playing field. And I can help make it not worth the cost. Gaining control over Coughlin's network was a big step in that direction. Coughlin has got millions of listeners. And we've got nearly two years to gradually shift his broadcasts toward supporting war in the Pacific."

"Saul . . . it doesn't matter. We can't add you to the team. Not even as an observer. The team roster is locked, and I doubt it would have been allowed anyway."

"Oh, I don't know about that. I'm sure Morgen would think that a grudge match between two versions of the same player would be great for luring in viewers. But I'm not asking you to get me added to the team. My help will be behind the scenes, and I can just feed you the information about my activities so that you'll know which moves are theirs and which are mine."

"What's to stop them from counting your conversion of Coughlin as one of our three moves?"

"Well, the rules, for one thing. If you don't enter the move into the system, it will be counted as an unintended consequence."

"A consequence that happened *before* any of the other events? That's crazy!" His eyes narrow, and I go on before he can interrupt.

"Anyway, we already *did* enter it as one of our three initial predictions. Like I said before, it failed. But still, it's in the system."

"It won't matter. You said the clock officially started what . . . four and a half hours ago?"

"More like six. We spent about an hour and a half mapping out a game plan."

"Either way, everything I did with Coughlin was *before* the game started. I'm not a team member. I'm not an observer. I'm outside their rules. They can't count my actions. Not if it's a fair game."

"Except you've already said they're not playing fair. That they *won't* play fair."

"*They* won't. But the SimMaster will. It's not like it's going to know every move you make. It's simply moderating a game. I assume they have it tapped into some sort of public data system, so that it will know whether or not the US enters World War II, but it's not going to know whether we make three changes or three hundred. It will measure whether your moves counter theirs, and award style points based on the manner in which you counter those moves. And barring a challenge from the other side, it will make its decision based on that data only."

"And if they challenge? What then?"

"I assume each side presents its case, using evidence to confirm how the moves and countermoves were made. But that's just an assumption, since I've never dealt with an opposing team capable of actually changing history. I'm guessing they gave you a rule book. Read it. But the main thing to keep in mind is that this is a game to your opponents. The only thing at stake is bragging rights, and if there's an audience, they lose credibility if they're not playing by their own rules. Anything I've done falls outside those rules. Face it, I'm the only advantage your team has, Kathy."

He's talking in circles. My gut instinct is to keep arguing with him, to try and change his mind, even though I generally avoid arguments, especially with Saul. But I can count the times that I've changed Saul's mind on the fingers of one hand. And now I'm wondering if Campbell wasn't actually referring to Saul instead of Kiernan Dunne when he said that we had a rogue agent tampering with the field before the start of play.

The unfortunate reality is that I can't stop Saul from doing whatever this is with Coughlin. But it feels dangerous and wrong to hide it from the others. Anything Saul does here in early 1939 could have an impact on the moves we make. And he's definitely right about one thing. We're going to need all the help we can get, especially if the other side intends to cheat. And that seems almost guaranteed, given that they've already contacted Saul with a bribe.

We're both silent for several minutes. "I'm going to have to tell the others. We need to coordinate our moves with whatever you're doing with Coughlin. And whatever Coughlin is doing with this Dennis guy, Lindbergh, and the America First Committee. I'm not even the team lead, so I can't guarantee that they'll listen if you offer advice. I'll try to convince them, but that's the best I can do."

He smiles, reaching across the table to stroke my cheek. "In my experience, you can be very persuasive when you want to be."

I return the smile, but it's a little forced because I know he's not going to like what I say next. "But I also need a promise from you."

He doesn't respond, just looks at me with his eyebrows raised as if to say *go on*.

"When we flip the timeline, you have to promise to turn that key over to CHRONOS."

"You mean the key that isn't mine? I merely borrowed it, Kathy. Technically speaking, it doesn't even belong to CHRONOS. Or at least not our version."

"The tech folks will need to figure out a way to stop these incursions into our timeline, and that key could help them. So, you need to promise that you'll turn the key over to CHRONOS and . . . that you'll collect any copies of your revised edition of *The Book of Cyrus* and whatever this *Book of Prophecy* is that you may have deposited in the past. No side experiments, okay? The past few days have shown us how very dangerous they are, and we can't afford to make that sort of error. Will you promise me?"

"Just to be clear, that's three separate promises that you're asking." He ticks them off on his fingers. "One, no side experiments. Two, destroy my version of the Cyrist books, although I will note that the differences are quite small. And three, turn over Morgen's key. I don't like that last one at all. It's theft, and Morgen is going to know I took it."

While I think I could argue that the no-side-experiments promise is implicit not just in my other two requests but also in the oath that he took as a historian, I stick to the key point. "Morgen might not know that if the timeline is repaired."

"He'll know *someone* took it, and I'll be the prime suspect, especially when word gets back to him that it showed up at CHRONOS. And word will get back to him. He has eyes and ears everywhere at HQ. He's got three people that I know of on his payroll in Archives alone. But fine, I promise—"

"Thank you."

"Let me finish," he says. "I promise under one condition."

And now it's my turn to give him the *go on* expression.

"You do not tell the others about my role in writing the current *Book of Cyrus*. I mean, it could just as easily have been entirely the work of that other me, right? I'll destroy the damn thing when this is all over, but it could cause . . . complications at CHRONOS, if someone were to take it the wrong way."

That nagging feeling is back—a pervasive sense something isn't right that I keep getting anytime I think about *The Book of Cyrus* and that symbol. "This historical religion that you based the Cyrists on, the one down in Florida? The Koreshans, right? You haven't been giving them any sort of an . . . assist, have you? I mean, before the time shift."

"Before? No! God, Kathy. I took an oath when I entered field training, just like everyone else. I've run this kind of scenario in The Game often enough to know what a major impact it could have. And believe me, if I was going to create a religion from scratch, it would have a bit more . . . teeth. I've done a bit of research into the trajectory of these Cyrists, and in this timeline at least, they basically hand over all of the control that could have been theirs to the government. It's all carrots and no stick. All numbers and no magic. Jemima understood that you need that spark of the unknown, even if you have to fake it. But you've heard all this before."

I have heard it all before. This is another conversation we've had many times, usually when he's mapping out one of his Temporal Dilemma scenarios. On our first research trip together, I'd been naive enough to think he'd be disappointed to discover that Jemima Wilkinson's prophetic abilities were more flash than substance. But he'd been impressed with her initiative, although he noted that she could have been bolder. Could have done more. That others did do more. When he's had a few drinks, Saul can make a fairly persuasive case for Jesus being a time traveler, explaining how he pulled off each and every miracle. In Saul's telling of the story, however, the Jesus they encountered outside the tomb three days later was actually three-days-*earlier* Jesus, and his crucifixion was the end of the line.

"Dangling financial rewards and feel-good carrots works to control *some* people, but there are always a few who need the literal fear of God," he says. "The fear of demons and magical consequences for not toeing the fucking line. Anyway, if I'd been screwing around with what eventually becomes a *global* religion, don't you think something like that would show up in a Temporal Monitoring check?" His voice grows increasingly tense with each word, and even though he's not exactly yelling, it's obvious from his tone that he's angry. The fry cook behind the counter keeps looking over this way, probably wondering if there's about to be trouble.

We don't need trouble. And I don't really want to argue this with him right now, especially since I'm fairly certain he's not telling the full truth. But there will be plenty of time to thrash all of this out once we fix the timeline. "Of course they'd catch it at TMU," I say. "There were just some things about the Cyrists that felt a little . . . off to me. Anyway, what's your game plan with Coughlin? And when and where should we meet up again?"

Saul taps his palm, which is his signal that he wants to transfer a local point from his medallion to mine. He pulls up the location, not even bothering to lower the key into his lap or cup his hand to hide it. Given that we've already attracted attention with our argument, he's raising quite a few eyebrows in the café by poking at the air in front of him. Maybe it's for the best, though. If they think he's a candidate for a psych ward, they might mind their own business.

"This is for my place in Miami. What?" he says, in response to my expression. "I may be working in Michigan, but I don't have to *live* here. It's cold." He taps the back of his key to mine to transfer the stable point, then continues. "As for Coughlin, I've already gotten him, and several others, off the German payroll. The good Father seemed a little surprised that I knew Hitler was paying him, but like I said, he's easily persuadable. I'll get him to tone down the isolationist rhetoric. Start questioning German motives, and he can begin nudging the isolationist crowd toward the reality that war is coming, and we'd better get ready for it. Beat the war drums a bit, so that our soldiers can head off to kill and be killed."

To be honest, I don't like the way that sounds at all. I'd much prefer to be on the side of preventing wars. But based on what we've seen of this new future, it seems like a good time to make an exception. "Why do you think this is going to keep Japan from bombing Pearl Harbor, though?"

"Japan is a lot more likely to make aggressive moves if they believe we won't retaliate. A weaker isolationist movement could tip the needle if things are close. But I obviously wasn't counting on that alone. Once I had everything set up here, I was planning to start working on other fronts. But now that I know we have a team, such as it is, in place, I guess I can leave that to the four of you. What's wrong?"

"I didn't say anything."

"No, but that tiny wrinkle between your eyebrows just deepened. So what's wrong?"

"Converting Coughlin just doesn't make sense to me as an opening move, Saul. Couldn't you have done this just as easily if he remained a Catholic? I mean, there are certainly verses in the Bible, especially the Old Testament, that could be used to argue in favor of war, especially a just war. Plus, Coughlin doesn't seem to take direction well. He's bucked the Catholic hierarchy on more than one occasion. What's to stop him from taking your money and doing the same?"

"The fact that I said I'd shove him out of the window at the top of that tower, for starters." He chuckles at my expression. "That was a joke. But you've read most of the verses in my version of *The Book of Cyrus*, right?"

"Well, I haven't *read* them, per se. But I've heard you and Tate chortling over them when you've both had a few beers too many."

"My point is, you know there are passages that can be used to support any set of beliefs, any philosophy, any policy option. The thing is vague to the point of meaninglessness. I designed it that way. Something for everyone. All I have to do is emphasize the parts Coughlin should stress in his messages. He'll toss in a few Bible verses, too, for good measure. As for taking direction, I'll step in directly to keep him on the straight and narrow, if necessary."

"Maybe. But, if he didn't take direction from his bishops, what makes you think he'll take it from you?"

"Well, for one thing, Coughlin believes that bishops are appointed by God, but in the end, they are only men. Fallible men."

"And what exactly does he think *you* are?"

"He thinks I'm Brother Cyrus, of course. Seventh messiah, and his own personal conduit to God."

FROM *THE COMPLETE DUMMY'S GUIDE TO US HISTORY SINCE 1950,* 23RD ED (2022)

The mid-20th-century schism in the United States is frequently referred to as the Secession Crisis of 1944. While it is true that events came to a head during the summer of that year, the problem had been building for several years, and it extended well beyond the end of the decade. Indeed, one could argue that the crisis lasted into the mid-1980s, when the Western Alliance appealed to the US government to agree to a limited trade pact, which eventually led to diminished tensions and the demilitarization of the border. The most treacherous period of relations, however, was 1957–1958, when the two sides hovered on the precipice of total nuclear war.

Tensions were already heightened due to Mexico's decision to opt out of a proposed multilateral reciprocal-assistance treaty with the United States. The McCarthy administration argued on the basis of solid evidence that the Western Alliance had threatened trade sanctions against Mexico if they signed the treaty, which was in conflict with the 1946 Peace Accord. The United States even offered to extend the treaty to the Western Alliance, but this peaceful overture was rebuffed.

Then, in November 1958, a group of dissidents within the government of Arizona, led by Governor Barry Goldwater, staged a coup. An unapproved measure on secession was added to the ballot in the 1958 election, with a reported 72 percent of the voters opting to join the Western Alliance. US troops entered the state to restore order, only to discover that Goldwater's forces had acquired several W-54 nuclear warheads, one of which was launched at US troops gathered at the New Mexico border near the Peloncillo Mountains. The Arizona militia claimed they did not fire first, noting that the small town of San Simon was obliterated by a weapon fired earlier in the day. Several rounds of retaliation followed, with both Bisbee, Arizona, and Lordsburg, New Mexico, taking heavy casualties before a ceasefire was negotiated. Over three thousand American lives were lost, with equal or greater casualties on the opposing side. Unfortunately, the battlefield deaths were followed by a greater number of residents on both sides of the border who were afflicted with radiation poisoning or died of cancer in the coming years.

∞19∞

I'm kind of regretting not checking this stable point more closely when Clio gave it to me. She said it was to her parents' house, and that's where Jack was headed, so I just held out my key and let her make the transfer. It's my fault that I assumed the stable point would be on the front lawn or perhaps the porch. I'd pictured myself jumping in, ringing the doorbell, and asking Kate or whoever answered the door if I could see Jack.

But, no. The stable point is in their living room. While that makes perfect sense for a daughter, I feel weird just jumping in unannounced. Unfortunately, that's the only way that I *can* jump in, since it's not like I can find a pay phone in 1939 and call their number in 1966 to say, *Hey, I'll be popping into your living room for a visit in a few seconds.* My only choice is to scan through to find a time when the room is empty so that I don't give anyone a heart attack.

As it turns out, that's not a problem. Scanning through the day after Jack arrived, I find the place very quiet. Of course, Kate and Kiernan are close to eighty, and Jack was probably exhausted when he got in. I doubt he was able to get much sleep on the bus from Memphis.

That's the key reason I don't select the time Kate and Jack would have arrived at the Dunnes' house yesterday. Jack spent nearly two days in transit. He needed time to sleep, get a shower, and maybe relax a bit, and I know him well enough to be certain that he'll pour all of his energy into watching these stable points as soon as I give them to him. And unlike the rest of us, Jack isn't subject to the clock. He can take his time, and he'll undoubtedly be more observant with a clear head. So, I scroll forward to late morning of the next day and jump in.

I've seen this living room before. It was the backdrop of several pictures in the Dunne family's memory book that Kate sent back—or *will* send back—when she turns over the CHRONOS keys in 2015. It looks different now, however. In those pictures, the walls and bookshelves were lined with sports trophies and photographs, and a knitted afghan was slung over the back of the sofa, along with a variety of other tiny things that give a house the look of a home. This is the same living room, but those things are all missing. It has the generic appearance of an unoccupied flat—a sofa, a chair, a lamp, a coatrack, and a small black-and-white television set with a V-shaped wire antenna. There are curtains on the windows and a few books on the shelves, but otherwise, the room looks abandoned.

That has me a bit worried until I spot Jack's bag hanging from the coatrack.

"Jack? Kate? It's Madi."

No answer. I call out again as I glance into the kitchen. A single mug and cereal bowl are drying in the dish rack on the counter. They're still damp. The appliances are a golden color that coordinates with the drapes and the telephone on the wall. I glance out the kitchen door, trying to keep my anxiety at bay, but I can feel the hair rising at the back of my neck. Opening the door, I step outside onto the porch, looking across the wide lawn toward the strip of trees and the lake beyond. There's a dock that stretches out onto the lake, with a rowboat tied to the end. The setting is very peaceful, and that makes me even more nervous, probably because it's in such total contrast to the way I'm feeling.

I cross over to the edge of the house. The lawn rises to a slight hill that overlooks the lake, where a low hedge of flowers encloses a small cemetery with three graves. Beyond that is a dirt road leading to two houses on the other side of the hill.

There's no one out here, either, so I circle back to the porch and the still-open door to the kitchen. The pipes inside the house groan loudly, startling me so badly that I nearly stumble on the steps. I hadn't even noticed there was water running. Closing the porch door, I hurry back to the front of the house. "Jack?"

A door opens on the floor above me, and then I recognize the pattern of Jack's footsteps on the stairs. He's in just his pajama pants, rubbing his hair with the ends of the towel draped around his neck. "Sorry. I didn't hear you over the water."

He loops the towel over my head and pulls me to his chest. His skin is still warm from the shower. The soap he used isn't his usual brand, but beneath the surface smells of ginger and jasmine, it's still Jack. I feel the tension leave my body piece by piece.

"You okay?" he asks.

I nod. "Just got a little freaked out when I couldn't find you. Where are Kate and Kiernan?"

"Kate dropped me off here and rode home with one of her sons, so that I'd have a vehicle."

"I thought this *was* home."

Jack shakes his head. "Nope. Not for the past fifteen years or so. She lives across the border in the suburbs of Toronto. This was the first time she'd ventured into the US since the secession crisis." He smiles grimly at my blank look. "I'd say you need a crash course in revisionist US history, but you've got enough on your plate right now trying to re-revise it. How long can you stay?"

"Not long." I glance at the timer on my CHRONOS key and then begin selecting stable points to transfer as a batch, both the ones that I set and the ones that Tyson transferred to my key before I left the café. "We synced up our keys after the game officially started," I tell him, "which was four hours and thirteen minutes ago. I have to make a quick stop in Bethesda and then back here again, because unfortunately, I have some work for you. We set about fifty stable points at Madison Square Garden that need to be scanned. And we're supposed to have a team meeting back at the apartment in Manhattan at hour five."

"You've been on the clock for just over four hours, and you already have an apartment in Manhattan? No wonder you look tired."

I explain about Clio's idea and the prep work that the Dunnes completed for us. "We've got detailed research packets for the various eras, identification for all of us, and a base of operations both in New York and Detroit, which is where Katherine and Richard are right now, investigating this Coughlin guy."

"So . . . why have your rendezvous point be at the apartment in Manhattan? You've got computers in 2136. Jarvis. And Alex, Lorena, and RJ for that matter."

"We don't know how much we're going to have to use the keys in the next two days. Tyson seems to think it's a bad idea to overtax ourselves. We're planning to take turns going forward to Bethesda. I'm going first, mostly because I need to talk to Thea."

"You located her?"

I give him a quick rundown of the Temporal Dilemma tournament video and Thea's inconvenient and typically dramatic appearance just as the game was beginning. "On the one hand, it's really, really good that she got a heads-up from this Cyrist *Book of Prophecy*, because she was able to arrange for them to purchase the house so that we'd have a base of operations. But now she's an observer, by which I'm pretty sure they mean *pawn*, so she needs to remain at the house. Knowing Thea, she's probably driving Alex and the others crazy."

"Speaking of Alex, how is he?"

"Barely eating, barely sleeping, and ingesting massive amounts of caffeine."

"So, pretty much the same as any time he's working on a project."

"Maybe. But he seems to be having a tough time focusing, possibly because he's worried about you. And I think it bothers him that there are so many different things going on. He keeps having to shift gears, trying to figure out exactly how the keys work and how the other side is managing to hitchhike on our signals and dealing with the Anomalies Machine, which is still spitting out changes. Plus, he had to sync our computers up to the game console, and he's also trying to find a way to extend the CHRONOS field without using an actual key. It's probably no surprise that he's a bit more frazzled than usual. When he was sitting out at the picnic table today, I felt bad for him. I wanted to wrap him in a giant hug, but I wasn't sure how he'd take that. He doesn't seem to be the hugging type."

Jack smiles. "Probably a good thing you resisted. You'd have scared the hell out of him. But yeah, this situation has to be extra stressful for him. Alex is used to being on a team where he can focus on one segment of a project. Multitasking isn't really his strong suit. Maybe you can get RJ to help him with some of the research. I mean, not the physics stuff, but . . . is Lorena still working on the serum?"

"She's doing the best she can, under the circumstances. The building she worked in doesn't even exist anymore, so she turned the kitchen into a research lab. When I last spoke to her, she was trying to program the food replicator to spit out the components she needs for your stress-hormone cocktail."

"You make it sound so appetizing."

"Hopefully, it will be an injection instead of something you chug. Anyway, aside from the lack of lab equipment, I'm kind of glad they're not venturing outside the house. Morgen explicitly said that his players wouldn't be targeting their opponents, but observers are fair game. None of them are *official* observers, since they don't have the CHRONOS gene, but I don't think we can rule out Morgen's team using them as leverage. Speaking of which, you need to be careful, too, okay? Stay here as much as you can. Of the three people who killed one of their observers, you're the only one that isn't a player, so even though you're not officially part of the team, they clearly consider you a target."

He pulls me close. "There's enough food in the pantry and freezer to last through a nuclear holocaust, so I'll be fine here. What exactly should I be looking for at these locations?" he asks as I hold the back of my key to his to transfer the observation points.

"Any sign of the players or observers, for one thing. I didn't see any blips of light that looked like CHRONOS keys until we were outside the auditorium, but we have to assume they'll be around later in the evening when the actual security breach occurs. We set a few outside the building, too, so maybe we can figure out how to keep the protestors from breaking through the line of police out front. Newspaper reports suggest that it happens around ten."

I fill him in briefly on what we know about Lawrence Dennis and the recorded explosion. Then I go into the kitchen, find a piece of paper and pencil, and make a very rough sketch of the arena.

"What's that thing?" Jack asks, pointing to a mark near the right margin.

"A stairwell. What does it look like?" I bump him with my elbow when he pulls a skeptical face. "I never claimed to be an artist. This is just to give you an idea of key locations."

I mark two *X*s in the approximate spot where Tyson and I were sitting on the second level, and another *X* near the closet on the other side of the area where Tyson saw the phonograph. Finally, I draw a circle near the staircase—which, to be fair, really doesn't look much like a staircase—where we assume Mrs. Slater and her daughters will be killed.

"Two of the stable points are just inside the doorway," I say after labeling these spots. "I doubt they'll give you much information, but between that and my *very perfect* map, you should be able to get a feel for the layout of the place."

"So, do you think this Dennis guy coordinated with the people outside who let the protestors break through? Or did whoever told him to set the timer on the sound effects simply have it synced up to coincide with the breach?"

"No clue," I say. "Hopefully you'll find something to help us answer that. There are fifty-two stable points, so just skim through and see what you can find. Focus on the ones closest to the locations on the map, and right around ten fifteen, which is when they hear the explosion and the panic starts."

"Will do. When will you have the rest of the stable points set?"

I'm confused for a moment, thinking he means additional points at the Garden, but then I realize he's talking about the various other events and locations. "We should probably narrow it down before we bombard you with too much. Especially since it's just you here. Even if you skim, fifty-two locations will take a while. I thought maybe Kate would be helping you with these—"

"Madi, I'm better off with her not here. She's not exactly . . . happy with this entire enterprise. I could barely get her to speak to me. She waited outside until her son Harry showed up to drive her back to Canada about twenty minutes after we arrived. He was pretty close-mouthed, too. Kind of looked like he wanted to punch me."

"Did they say anything to give you a hint as to why they were so . . . antagonistic?" I ask, even though I know there are really only two things it could be. Either something happens to Clio, or something happens to Kiernan. Or both.

"All I know is he told me the same thing Kate told you at the bus station. *Fix this.* Anger aside, they've left me in good shape. A stocked pantry. Clothes. Money, although I have no clue why I'd need it. Just looking at it makes me feel weird, because it has the wrong pictures and it's not even green anymore. There's also a damned impressive library including a—actually, come upstairs and I'll show you, because I'm not sure what it's called. I'd never even seen one. It took me a bit to figure out what it was."

I follow him upstairs to what must have once been a bedroom. Three walls are lined with books. There are framed sketches on the other wall, drawn by someone with far better skills than my own. Clio, maybe, since the curtains on the one window have pale purple flowers and look a bit like something you might hang in a young girl's room. Two desks are on either side of that window, one stacked with papers and the other taken up almost entirely by an odd metal device that looks a bit like an old-style metal trash bin that someone tipped on its head. A stack of small cardboard boxes is next to the device, and even more of the boxes are on one of the nearby shelves.

"What exactly is it?"

"I thought the reels were movies at first. But they're newspapers. Those little boxes by the machine contain the years 1936 to 1945. Several different newspapers. Each frame contains a picture of a page, and there's an index. It's really jumpy, though, and you have to zoom in to search the page. I tried it earlier this morning and nearly barfed up the cereal I'd just eaten. And I'm thinking maybe Kate felt the same way, because . . . hold on. Let me find it."

Jack digs around and comes back with a tablet computer. It's fairly clunky compared to the readers we have at the house, but it's practically microscopic compared to the metal monster in Kate's library. There are tiny amber dots attached to two corners. I run my finger over one.

"Yeah," he says, "those seem to be CHRONOS-field extenders. They're all over the house. You might want to take one back to Alex for comparison."

"So . . . the house is under a CHRONOS field?"

"It could be. There's a gadget in one of the bedrooms. If I put the key inside it, Kate says the field extenders will pick it up and create a protective barrier around the house. They set it up when Clio was small. But I feel safer wearing the key, and anyway, I don't want these archives to be protected. We need whatever you change in 1939 or 1940 to be reflected on these microfilm copies the Dunnes bought in 1960 or whenever. That way I can tell if and when major events change."

"How did they manage to rig all of this up? I mean, Clio was born in 1913, right?"

"Something like that, yeah. I'm guessing they raided the Cyrist Farm before they set the place up. There are several out-of-timeline gadgets, including a CHRONOS diary and that." He nods toward the tablet.

"Maybe Kate got tired of doing research the old-fashioned way and had her daughter bring back an upgrade on one of her jumps?" I suggest. "You won't need to bother with the background research, anyway. I can just get Jarvis to check things when I'm in 2136. It will be a lot quicker."

"True," he says. "Although your time is limited by that stupid countdown, and you can't spend the entire game doing research. The tools at my disposal may be archaic, but I'm not on the clock. My time is pretty much limitless."

He has a point, although I hate the idea of him here alone, staring at slightly different views of the same event for days on end.

"I just need to focus on the important stuff and avoid diving down rabbit holes," he says. "Some of the stuff in those files ties in with my own military-history research, so it's easy to get off on a tangent. She has a lot of articles comparing the deaths from dropping nuclear weapons on Japan to the deaths that would have occurred if the war had continued . . . which makes sense when you're con-templating restoring a timeline where the Hiroshima and Nagasaki bombings occur. If it makes you feel better on that front, the US uses nuclear weapons first in this timeline, too."

"Against . . . Japan?"

"No," he says. "Against the western United States."

"You're kidding?"

"I wish I was. Small nukes, with three or four cities hit on each side of the Arizona-New Mexico border. About thirty-five thousand deaths total, so still less than Hiroshima and Nagasaki, but when you add it to the million or so other deaths that could have followed if US forces hadn't used it . . ."

I shudder and lean into him. The last thing I want is to have any part in life-and-death decisions of this magnitude, but yeah . . . repairing the timeline means repairing all of it. The good, the bad, and the unimaginably awful.

"So," I say, after a deep breath, "how much time do you think you'll need to scan three hours from fifty-two different angles?"

"Check back in a couple of days. If I'm not done, you can always just jump ahead to when I'm finished."

"Okay. How about eleven p.m. on the 27th? That would give you about two and a half days."

"Sure. Why so late, though?"

I put my arms around him and reach up for a kiss. "Because that's about the time you usually get sleepy. I'll have to sleep at some point, too. And I'm thinking I'll sleep much better in 1966 *with* you than I will in 1939 without you."

∞

BETHESDA, DC
NOVEMBER 18, 2136

My grandmother is on the couch when I blink in, scanning idly on a tablet and looking thoroughly bored. She doesn't seem very happy that I dive straight into questions, and not particularly easy questions, as soon as I spot her.

"You would have existed anyway," Thea says in response to my first question, "and you'd have a slight trace of the gene that is the core for the CHRONOS gene. Your friend in there who has been tinkering with the test tubes and the young man at the computers would have used that trace of the gene as the basis for their research, but it would have taken several years longer. That is what *The Book of Prophecy* tells us, at any rate."

Great. I'm featured in yet another book I'd never heard of until a few weeks ago. *A Brief History of CHRONOS* at least seemed to be dealing with a version of me that came into being without selective breeding. I have a sudden flash of sympathy for Kate Pierce-Keller, and fresh insight into why Prudence Rand may not have gotten along with her mother. Maybe they were just too much alike, since both Katherine and this cloned version of Pru were perfectly willing to play matchmaker in order to get a granddaughter who met their genetic specifications.

"Perhaps you could get me a copy of this *Book of Prophecy*," I say, "since it apparently knows more about my origins than I do?"

She laughs. "Well, I wouldn't hold my breath, dear. Even I don't have an entire copy. The Templars have given me information from the book from time to time, and we were given copies of one chapter—the "Chapter of Prudence"—as children, since we were required to commit it to memory. That's the section that mentions the shrine."

I've heard that word recently. It takes a moment, and then I remember that the church Charles Coughlin built, the one that Katherine and Rich are currently investigating, is called the Shrine of the Little Flower. "You mean the Catholic church in Detroit?"

Thea looks confused for a moment, and then she shakes her head. "No, dear. I mean *this*." She waves her hand in an inclusive gesture that takes in the living room, foyer, and the two curving staircases that lead up to the second floor. *"As it is foretold and decreed, the ancestral home of the Mother of Prudence shall be raised up as an eternal, unchanging shrine . . ."*

There are several things in this that need to be unpacked, so I say, "Okay, let's back up. Who did you mean when you said, *'we'* were given a chapter?"

"The three in my birth group. I guess you'd call us sisters. Twins . . . or triplets, I guess. Clones, obviously, although we're not really supposed to admit that. Anyway, they did this stupid thing of assigning us Greek letters as names. I hated Theta, so I dropped the middle *t* once my commitment was up. They're all the way to Rho and Sigma now, and I guess there will be a new batch coming soon. I wonder what they'll do when they run out of letters? Do you think maybe they'll use a different alphabet?"

"I . . . don't know. Can any of these clones use the CHRONOS key? I mean, to jump with it?"

"Oh, no," she says, shaking her head emphatically. "We can only see the light and read the diaries. That's why they need three of us, and truthfully, I think they could use four or five. One would probably be enough, though, if she could just zip from place to place and time to time. Although Zeta—she was in the trio before me, the only one who ever entirely left the fold—said that was one of the reasons that Prudence Alpha, the original one, lost her marbles near the end, so I'm kind of glad I can't use it. On the other hand, it would have made travel so much faster both as a Sister and once my commitment was up. And you know how I love to travel. Maybe once all of this is over, we can take another trip! The mountains are always nice in winter."

"Maybe." I take a deep breath and try to pull her back on topic. She's always been flaky, but I think it's gotten worse in the year since I last saw her. "So, you spent a period of time as Prudence, and then you were free to do whatever you wanted?"

She nods. "Although my case was a little different. Normally, we're allowed to just go on with our lives after the twenty years are up, but later, when they learned that I had a daughter who was only a few years older than your father, they pulled me back in to see if Mila and I could ensure that you'd be able to fulfill your destiny even if there was outside tampering. That's a very good thing in retrospect, don't you think? And then now, they've put me under this key and pulled me back in so that I could be here, which is a very good thing for *me*, because I've got an odd second set of memories now. Which don't include any of the other Pru Sisters, but then none of them would have been under a key, would they? So maybe I don't exist outside of it. Or maybe I do and—"

"Could we go back to the part about me *fulfilling my destiny*?" I say, beginning to feel a little queasy at the loops and turns in her train of thought.

"Yes. Your destiny." She gives a philosophical little shrug. "Without you, there is no CHRONOS. Without CHRONOS, there are no Cyrists. And without the Cyrists, there would be no you. It's the circle of life."

"That's not what people usually mean by the circle of life, though. And you just said that there would have been some version of me even without Cyrist interference."

A tiny frown creases her brow. "*Interference* is such a judgmental word. *Insurance* is really more accurate. The Cyrists—at considerable cost, I might add—provided insurance that the plan would be fulfilled. Because prophecy is all well and good, but if you fail to act on the prophecy, then what is the point? Things can obviously change in any iteration of the timeline, and the Templars didn't wish to leave something so important to chance. What if some tiny aberration in the gestational environment meant that the gene wasn't expressed at all? And so, a plan was devised to bolster your inheritance on your mother's side as well. Which is where Mila came in. I expected her to simply stay with the man until she was pregnant, but the poor baby was never exactly fond of the Cyrists, I'm afraid. And I guess she got that from me to some extent, because I was more than happy to shed my Pru duties as soon as the Templars decided the bloom was no longer on the rose, if you follow my drift. And yet some of the Sisters seem loath to let it go. How can that be, do you think, when we're supposedly identical?"

"I don't know," I say again, and try to lead her back toward the questions I need answered. "You said Mom is okay. Could we call her?"

Again, she responds with an airy wave of her hand. "Mila *is* okay, Madi. Somewhere. Somewhen."

I don't find that at all comforting, but I stick to the topic. "So, you're saying the Madison Grace in the books isn't me at all. She had a different mother."

"Different mother," she says, "but probably a very similar life, since Mila decided to remain with your father. There was some pressure to remove you from your parents entirely, but I told the Templars that it would be unwise. After all, your environment also plays a role in determining your abilities. And see, there's *another* puzzle. My Sisters had the same environment as I did and the same genetic makeup. Nature and nurture both the same, and yet . . . we're different." She shrugs. "How can you explain that?"

"But at some point, there must have been a version of me that didn't have the CHRONOS gene at all, right? I mean, it had to come from *somewhere*. Someone developed it initially."

"I suppose. But does it really matter?"

"Yes! It definitely matters."

She gives me one of her enigmatic smiles. "Then keep searching, my love. The answers you require are somewhere within you."

I open my mouth to protest, but I know there's no point telling her that these answers absolutely are *not* within me. Her smile will just grow sad for a moment, and then she'll flit on to another topic.

"In fact," Thea says, "I was about to go up to that cozy little room in the attic and meditate. Perhaps you should join me."

"I can't. The game, remember? Could you do me a favor, though?"

"Of course, sweetie."

"Since you can't get me a copy of this *Book of Prophecy*, could you jot down anything you can think of from that book—from the "Chapter of Prudence" or anywhere else—that might pertain to what we're doing here? Or just anything that pertains to me. And maybe the whole Sister Prudence thing, because I'm afraid I'm not really following a lot of what you've said."

I expect her to give me a pout for assigning her homework. That would be a typical Thea reaction. But she positively beams. "That's a *very* good idea, Madi! Sometimes when I'm talking it's so hard to organize everything, and I tend to go off on a tangent, and then we're talking about something else entirely, and I even forget what the original subject was. It's a lot easier to write things down. I'll even send you my journal . . . well, not all of it. But I'm sure there are *some* sections I can share. I'll go to my room and start right after my meditation."

"Oh . . . your room. I guess we need to find you someplace to sleep."

"No need. I'm in the room with the extra blanket. I get so cold when I sleep. But you might want to tell your friends that one of them left a little blue hat behind. Or at least I think it's a hat. I found it on the nightstand." She gives me a hug. "Be careful out there, okay?"

There's still one more question I really want to ask her, and oddly, it's the same question Tyson scrawled on his business card to get the attention of that Lawrence Dennis guy—*Why are you here?* She can't use the key to jump, and I'm not sure that her mind will stay in one place long enough to count on her to monitor stable points, and yet she showed up moments before the game started. Which means *someone* told her when we were supposed to begin. I'm not really suspicious of her motives. Thea is self-centered, but in a very open fashion, a bit like a small child. But someone else could be using her, either as a spy or simply as a limiting factor. We had three research assistants here, as well as Jarvis, and we could have left them with substantial research tasks. So what if it took months to complete? They aren't registered in the system as players, so their time, like Jack's, is essentially unlimited. I could simply jump forward a few months and collect their answers.

Now, however, Thea is in the system, and she can't use the key to travel in time. Simply by being in the room and pulling herself in as an observer, she bound everyone in this house to the same time limitations as the rest of us. Although the machine being here might have done that regardless of whether Thea was at the house.

All of that would seem to beg the why-are-you-here question. But I'm worried that it will sound rude, and she seems quite pleased to have a task. So I table the question for the next time we talk.

Thea scurries up the stairs at an impressive pace for her seventy-six years, and I'm left in the odd position of envying my grandmother's energy. It's only been thirteen or maybe fourteen hours since I woke up, and I had two cups of coffee at the diner when I was filling Tyson in on the whole Saul-and-the-Cyrists issue. I shouldn't be dragging like this. What I really want is to pull on my swimsuit and clear my mind with a few dozen laps in the pool, my own personal form of meditation, and then curl up in my bed for a good night's sleep. But that's a luxury I can't afford when the clock is literally ticking. I still need to check in with Lorena about progress on the serum, and I have a whole list of questions for Alex.

And so I trudge up the stairs to the library. Maybe Alex will share some of his buzz beans.

Buzz is the operative word when I open the door to the library. I heard the sound from the stairs but thought maybe it was something that Lorena and RJ were using to get Yun Hee to sleep. It appears to be coming from the vicinity of the SimMaster, which is walled in by four mirrored doors that someone pilfered from the bathroom medicine cabinets, apparently in an effort to restrict what the recording devices inside the simulation machine can see and hear.

Alex is exactly where I expect him to be, inside his nest of displays. Two of them have the bubble grid I've gotten used to seeing, but the third is a tangled mass of lines. Nora tried crochet for a few months, after one of her reading-club buddies swore it was a great form of relaxation. Alex's display looks a lot like the wadded mess of multicolored yarn that I found in her trash bin the next time I visited.

Only two things are different from our usual pattern. First, Alex isn't looking at any of the displays. Instead, he's reading a physical book. A fat one, too. Second, he's now wearing a simple band around his wrist. If not for the fact that the light is amber, I'd have assumed it was one of those old-fashioned neon light tubes that kids used to play with. The only difference is a small metal disk on the side.

"Is that a prototype of the field extender?" I ask.

He looks up, startled. "What? Oh, sorry, Madi. Yeah. I've calibrated it to the field that runs through the bookcase, and I've been testing how far I can get away from it without the protection wearing off."

"Is that smart? You might—"

He grins. "I keep the spare CHRONOS key in my pocket. So far, I've made it about a hundred meters outside the front gate before this thing buzzes." He taps the metal disk. "You'd probably be able to see the light go out, but since I can't see the light, I needed another way to test it. I now have them on RJ, Lorena, and Yun Hee. RJ's helping me get several more charged to send to all of you as backup. I mean, it's not like they can go out *now*, but hopefully, once this stupid game is over. We've all been going a little stir-crazy. Especially RJ. He's always hated being cooped up."

I hadn't really thought about it, but that's one definite advantage I have over my housemates. I can blink out of here, and I'm still protected from any potential time shifts as long as I have a key. Alex and the others have, for the most part, been restricted to the house for going on two weeks.

"Well, one way or another, the game will be ending when that timer goes off." I nod toward the book in his lap. "Relaxing with a little light reading?"

He looks up from the page, shaking his head to clear it. "Oh, no. This isn't for fun. It's actually relevant to our problems. Or I think it might be."

"I'm joking," I say as I pull up one of the computer chairs. "What book is it?"

Alex tips the spine in my direction. *The Physics of Many Paths*, by Stanford Fuller. "I've read it before," he says, "for a philosophy-of-physics class I took back in my third or fourth year. I asked Jarvis to pull up something from the book, and he told me that you had a copy here in the library."

"Yes. Kate bought it. She mentioned it in one of the diary entries that I read. She said it had something to do with the many-worlds theory—"

"Not theory. It's an interpretation."

"Is there a difference?" I ask.

"Yes."

He hesitates, probably wishing he hadn't corrected me, because now he needs to figure out a way to explain an almost certainly complicated scientific concept in terms that a literary historian can grasp. I'm about to tell him not to bother, but then he continues.

"In quantum mechanics, theories are mathematical, and that math has to hold up to fairly rigorous tests. But there are different ways of explaining how those theories operate in the real world. An interpretation is basically an application of that mathematical theory to the world we live in. You can have multiple interpretations of the same theory. Does that make sense?"

It kind of does, so I nod, and he goes on.

"Anyway, you were right about it being light reading. This was one of those oddball books that a professor occasionally assigns in addition to the more serious text, mostly to get you thinking about the subject in a slightly different way. Fuller wasn't a physicist or any sort of scientist. He made his living as a psychic of sorts. My grandmother was a fan."

"Yeah. Jarvis pulled up an excerpt for me when I saw his name in the diary. He was on TV or something, right? I can't say it really made a lot of sense to me. But Kate seemed kind of comforted by his theory—or should I say interpretation?"

Alex laughs. "Either is fine in his case."

I gesture toward the book. "So, do you think the author was a time traveler?"

"No. I think he was what he claimed to be—a seer. A seer and, like me, a visual thinker, although in his case, he was able to visualize without the aid of all these displays. The paths that he talked about were pretty clearly diverging timelines. He even talks about adjacent and intertwined paths, which got me to thinking about Morgen calling this world 47H. I mean, why add the letters, you know?"

Even though I *don't* know what he means, I nod. Otherwise, I'm pretty sure it's going to be another complicated thing for him to simplify, and we don't really have time.

"Anyway," he continues, "I was just looking at all of this . . . insanity and trying to come up with some ideas on how to protect our timeline from any future incursions. I can't even begin to do that until I know where they're coming from. And I thought I remembered a chapter in the book about blocking off unsafe paths. It was actually *unsteady* paths, although that may be the same thing, and I can't say I fully understand what he was talking about, either way. I need to think about it for a bit."

"Would it help for me to jump back and ask him some questions for you?"

"Maybe. But at this point, I'm not entirely sure what to ask, and . . . he's not a physicist, so it might require some back-and-forth. I think we've got enough to deal with at the moment, anyway. There is one thing you could do, however." He opens the drawer and takes out a medallion. "Can you transfer a stable point to this?"

"Sure," I say. "Just hold it up."

As it turns out, it's not that easy. The key isn't activated when Alex holds it. I am, however, able to hold my key in one hand and the CHRO-NOS key in the other hand and tap the backs together to transfer the location.

"What's this for?" I ask as I hand back the other key. "I mean, what good does it do if you can't view the stable points?"

"Just something I'm playing around with."

RJ is standing in the doorway. "Lorena says she may have a test serum for you to take to Jack by tomorrow," he says. "She had to rush order a couple of compounds and test tubes, and let's just say that commerce is a bit difficult in this timeline. Neither of us seem to have credits. Thea was able to make the purchase, so I guess it's lucky she's here." He lowers his voice. "She sure does talk a lot, though."

I give him a sympathetic look. "She really does."

Alex clearly agrees. "I got a lot more done after I realized that most of her questions are just rhetorical. You can simply nod and make occasional grunting noises, and she'll take it to mean whatever she wants it to mean."

"Which is what you do with us all the time," RJ says, grinning.

"Hey, that's not true . . ." Alex trails off, probably realizing that his cousin's comment is very much true.

"Seriously," I tell them, "kick her out if she's distracting you at all. Or I can have a talk with her," I add, although my tone probably suggests that I'm really not all that keen on diving back into Thea's conversational whirlpool just yet.

"That's okay," RJ says. "We've been playing tag team dealing with her, although I had to steer her out of the kitchen about an hour ago so that Lorena could focus. We were considering just putting her in a room with Yun Hee and letting them chatter to each other."

"Thea might enjoy that, actually. She likes babies. I was glad when she headed upstairs to meditate . . . although I'm kind of wondering how she manages to quiet her mind. We were talking for at least five minutes, and all I got was a couple of vague answers to the questions I asked her, peppered with talk about double memories, the circle of life, and Pru sister-clones with Greek-letter names that might not exist anymore."

"She mentioned that last part to us," RJ says. "And she may very well have a point on that one. The First Genetics War seems to have started a bit earlier in this timeline, although it's a little unclear exactly who is fighting whom."

Alex nods. "All research—not just genetic but pretty much all science—is under the government, with most of the focus on military operations. The Cyrists have had to keep their cloning a bit more low key in this reality. They may not have been willing to take the risk."

"So, you knew Thea was a clone?" I ask. "Or rather that the Cyrists were engaged in cloning?"

"Me?" RJ says. "No. Lorena, however, says it's common knowledge in her circles. That's why the Cyrists pushed hard on that whole religious-liberty exemption to keep the government from taking samples of body fluids. They were worried the government would find out that they have some carbon copies. And maybe a few illegal modifications. Or at least that was the case in our timeline. And

Prudence's face is pretty well known, so there would likely be some people watching out for her to pop up. Or for *them* to pop up, I guess."

Alex yawns. It's catching, and after I shake it off, I ask if he's managed to get any sleep.

"I grabbed a few hours."

"He actually did," RJ says. "Ate a giant bowl of cornflakes and fell asleep right there on the couch with the empty bowl propped on his chest. And I'm guessing you haven't looked in the mirror lately, because you're not exactly the poster child for healthy sleep habits right now. There are circles *under* the circles under your eyes."

"He's right," Alex says. "How many times have you used the key since you slept? And how many of them were long jumps?"

"Well, I jumped here, and then back to 1966 Memphis," I say, tallying the trips on my fingers. "Back here. Seneca Falls, 1935. Seneca Falls, 1966. Back here. New York, 1939. Skaneateles, 1966, and then back here."

"So about fifteen hundred years in the course of a day," Alex says. "Leaving aside the distance. Maybe you should—"

"Promise. I'll sleep as soon as I get back to New York . . ." I glance at the timer. "Which needs to be pretty soon. But yeah, Tyson already mentioned that we might not want to overdo it. And that reminds me . . ." I tell Jarvis to add Tyson, Katherine, and Rich to his voice controls, so that they'll be able to use him for research when they jump in.

"We're planning to take turns coming back here," I tell them, "so that we can reserve our energy for any jumps we may need to take for research."

"And . . . that's my cue," RJ says, picking up the tablet on the table next to him. "Since Alex has the physicsy things to do, Lorena is busy trying to turn your kitchen into a genetics lab, and Thea is . . . distracting, I took up the research task. Historical research isn't exactly my field, but I've had to do a bit when writing grant proposals at my last job.

And luckily for me, Jarvis is already pretty well trained as your research assistant. I was going to write all of this out, so that you wouldn't have to carry back an anachronism like the tablet, but it would take more time than we have, and you do *not* want to try to decipher my handwriting. I started out with a broad overview, but then Alex said . . ." He turns to Alex. "Have you explained what you found yet?"

"Nope. Hadn't had a chance." Alex spins one of the displays toward me and pushes a button on his keypad. The image is one he's shown me before, with hundreds of colored bubbles of varying sizes. A few of them, the ones that depicted my jumps and Tyson's to the mid-1960s, had clear bubbles attached to one side. That's how he figured out that we had carried in hitchhikers from the other timeline.

Alex zooms in on one section of the screen, then taps something that divides it into three sections marked *1938*, *1939*, and *1940*. Each of the three sections has bubbles. There are six colors, three of which I recognize. Amber is the shade I see the key. Purple is Tyson. I know from the diaries that the pale-orange shade is Katherine's color. There are a few in mint green and dark red, but most of the ones remaining are a deep blue green. In fact, that color accounts for about half of the bubbles on the display. There are also dozens of clear bubbles, but unlike last time, they're not attached to colored ones.

When I ask Alex why, he says, "They didn't need to hitchhike this time. They already had stable points in this reality, so they were just able to adjust the time and location. Not a simple matter, to be sure, which is probably why we go with using saved stable points instead of setting all of the coordinates on the key each time when we develop the system. But it could be done. The bright side to CHRONOS being erased is that it cleared out this grid. Before the shift, I'd have had to filter out the jumps by the various CHRONOS historians who had research trips to New York during this three-year period. All of those blobs vanished from the display, however, when they were erased. As I noted before, each bubble measures the surge of energy required to initiate a time jump. I was going to look at 1941 as well, but there were no clear bubbles that year, so I narrowed the field."

I point to the three colors I recognize. "That's me, Tyson, and Katherine. I assume the others are Clio, Rich, and . . . I guess that blue green could be Jack, but I thought his bubbles were lighter. And smaller. And there are so many of them."

"Not Jack," RJ says. "He hasn't been anywhere but 1966, right? The blue green is Clio, given that there are also a bunch of jumps to upstate New York and Chicago. She wasn't kidding when she said she spent a lot of time in 1930s New York. And the light-green one is Richard."

"So . . . who is the red bubble?"

"Excellent question," Alex says. "You might want to ask Katherine, because she went white as a sheet when she saw it pop up on the display earlier."

"Really?"

"Yes. I'm guessing the red one is our mystery jumper, because while that dot appears in New York and Detroit, it also appeared here in DC on November 12, 2304—which is when the time shift zapped CHRONOS—within a hundred yards or so of the location where Katherine and Rich jumped out. And they jumped at right around the same time. The red dots don't appear to be especially stable, however. Like I said, one of them vanished from the screen while Katherine and I were watching. And no, I don't really know why."

"We also have recent trips to two locations in Florida and also Boston," RJ says. "Those were the locations you told me to include in the notes. You said there were others, but we haven't tracked those down yet."

"Where in Florida?" I ask as a knot begins to form in my stomach.

"Miami and Fort Myers."

"It's Saul," I say. "Damn it. They manage to erase everyone else at CHRONOS, all the people who might have been able to help us, and yet somehow, *somehow*, he survives."

"Yes. That was our guess, as well," Alex says. "So I guess that's bad news, but there's good news, too." He zooms in further, highlighting the largest cluster of clear bubbles. "These are arranged on a chronological axis, and"—he spins the display slightly—"also on a geographical axis. You'll see that there are some outliers from this angle, but most of the clear bubbles are clustered in this region."

"So . . . New York City?" I say.

"No. The entire display was New York City. This subsection," he says, "is the roughly five-square-kilometer plot of land that housed the World's Fair. We already knew that some of Team Viper's moves were taken there, but given that extra geographical bonus they earned, I think it's a safe bet that it was *all*, rather than merely some. Unfortunately, all of their bubbles are that same clear shade. I can't even tell which ones are players and which are observers."

"We can, however, give you approximate dates," RJ says, tapping the tablet. "There are a few jumps scattered about from the time the Fair opens on the last day of April 1939 through its closing in October 1940, although there's a big gap during the off-season from Halloween 1939 to late May 1940, during which the exhibits were shuttered. But most of them are clustered into these five groups. Jarvis, display this list on the wall screen."

1) May 9, 1939

2) May 28, 1939

3) June 2, 1939

4) September 12, 1939

5) July 4, 1940

"Three and five," RJ says, "are on our original list. June 2nd is Japan Day, and the attempt on the ambassador. July 4th is the bombing in the Court of Peace."

"But . . . all of these are *after* the rally that Tyson and I just attended in Madison Square Garden," I say. "There were changes. Charles Coughlin becoming a Cyrist. And Tyson discovered that Lawrence Dennis is the guy who faked the explosion by hiding a recording in the janitor's closet. We think someone also bribed the police to let some of the protestors through. All of those are changes to the historical record. They resulted in three deaths. So how in God's name could the first possible date of a change be nearly three months later? That doesn't make sense." And then it *does* make sense. "Saul," I say. "He's working with them. And his actions aren't entered into the system, so . . . it's a free move. Or moves."

"We agree that it's probably Saul," Alex says. "There are red chronotron pulses in New York in early 1939. Plus a lot of activity near Detroit."

I sit there for a moment as the reality sinks in. Our odds of winning seemed small before, but this just whittled them away to almost nothing.

"But," RJ says, "we're not entirely sure he's working *with* them. Coughlin's rhetoric grows increasingly less isolationist and less anti-Semitic over the next year and a half. By late 1940, he's actually arguing that we have to balance against Hitler. Not completely in favor of entering the war, but he supports lend-lease. That's not the kind of thing you'd advocate if your goal was to keep the US neutral. So, the situation may not be as bleak as you think. And we can't give up, even though this complicates things a bit."

I close my eyes. Complicates things *a bit*? That's an understatement, to say the very least. But then Alex and RJ haven't read Kate's and Katherine's diaries. They have only a vague understanding of why the possibility that Saul Rand is on the other side—or more accurately, knowing that the other side now has *two* Saul Rands—has me ready to toss in the towel. But RJ is right. Giving up isn't an option.

"And like I said," he continues, "we know what the last two dates are. I have a printout of events that happened at the Fair on May 9th, May 28th, and September 12th. There's a writers' conference going on during the first one, and the opening of the Italian Pavilion, where a bunch of people cheered for Mussolini, which might be relevant. The last one is a pretty normal weekday, nothing big going on. But . . . it *is* the day where the two Japanese tourists are mugged. That has to be significant."

"Do we know their names?"

"We do," RJ says. "But we haven't been able to find any information about them. Two people saw them come out from behind a building, but the news account doesn't even say which zone it was in, and the only thing we get for a time is that it happened that evening. One of the men was bleeding and needed a stitch. I'm not even sure it would have made the paper if not for the fact that the injured guy told security there are men of that sort in all countries, and it was far outweighed by the kindness he'd seen from others in this country both before and after the attack. And so it was picked up for the section called 'Heard at the Fair' as a heartwarming human-interest story. We'll keep looking, but I'm not sure we'll find anything else. On May 28th, however—"

"Einstein is there," Alex says. The excitement in his voice is palpable. "In order to fix this thing, you're going to have to meet Einstein."

As he says it, I flash back to the living room that Alex shared with Jack. I was only there a few times, but I clearly remember the image on the door to Alex's room. Albert Einstein, with his trademark wild hair, sticking his tongue out at the camera.

"If I could use that key," Alex says, "I'd be begging you to switch places."

I smile. "And while that would mean absolutely no progress on the temporal-physics front during your absence, I'd still let you take a turn. Why was Einstein at the Fair that day?"

"He was there several times that first year. On that particular day, he was giving a speech at the opening of the Jewish Palestine Pavilion. Huge crowds, because the Jewish people had to organize and push hard to get any sort of recognition at the event. But I think the *reason* he was there may be less relevant than the overall picture of what he'll be doing in a couple of months. In August 1939, Einstein will coauthor a letter to FDR, along with physicist Leo Szilard, telling the president that the Germans are developing an atomic bomb. According to our list of anomalies, that letter was never written . . . and it was the catalyst for the Manhattan Project."

I heave a sigh. "I thought the rules said no nukes."

"That probably just means neither side can use them," RJ says.

"So, what do you think happened?" I ask. "How did something at the Fair in May convince Einstein not to sign this letter months later?"

"I'm not sure," Alex admits. "But Einstein regretted writing the letter after the US used atomic weapons to end the war. My best guess is that someone either convinces Einstein that Germany isn't as close to having nuclear weapons as Szilard and the other experts believed . . . or they convince him that the US can't be trusted with those weapons, either."

FROM THE *NEW YORK* *DAILY INTREPID*

WORLD'S FAIR OPENS TO LARGE CROWDS DESPITE WEATHER

(May 1, 1939) President Roosevelt officially opened the largest international exposition in world history at just after 3 p.m. yesterday afternoon. Attendance was reportedly more than 600,000, somewhat less than anticipated, but afternoon crowds may have been deterred by the rainstorms that hit shortly after the opening ceremonies concluded in the plaza known as the Court of Peace.

Fewer than one-tenth of the crowd that attended yesterday was able to jam into the open-air Court of Peace to watch the opening ceremonies, but a far larger number viewed the parade as it made its way from the 600-foot Trylon and 200-foot Perisphere—the giant orb that houses the Democracity exhibit—down

Constitution Mall toward its final destination. The marchers numbered 20,000 with military troops, participants from around the world in native costumes, and hundreds of workmen who have spent the past several years constructing the building and statues, and landscaping the fairgrounds, which were built atop a trash heap.

The president's address focused on the theme of the exposition—the "World of Tomorrow"—as he declared the fair "open to all mankind." He further stated: "The eyes of the United States are fixed on the future. Yes, our wagon is still hitched to a star. But it is a star of friendship, a star of progress for mankind, a star of greater happiness and less hardship, a star of international goodwill, and above all, a star of peace. May the months to come carry us forward in the rays of that eternal hope."

Rain began to fall during the 150th-anniversary reenactment of the first presidential inauguration and the dedication of the 65-foot statue of George Washington. Crowds scurried to take cover as drizzle turned to downpour. Most exhibits and restaurants were soon standing room only, with several forced to close their doors to additional guests for safety reasons.

The rain did not let up until after 9 p.m., but those who stuck it out were able to hear Dr. Albert Einstein give a brief speech on cosmic rays, before launching the cosmic-ray detector, which was supposed to capture ten separate rays in order to illuminate the Trylon. All ten rays were captured in a feat the announcer referred to as "modern temple magic," but the electrical system overloaded. The audience was disappointed, but there were many other marvels to enjoy—the Lagoon of Nations, the fireworks display, the stage shows, and the music of Guy Lombardo and his orchestra at the Band Shell on Fountain Lake.

∞20∞

I blink into the living room of the apartment in Manhattan. Clio is seated in one of the armchairs, scanning through something on her key. She looks up when she realizes she's no longer alone.

"Is that blood?" she asks, staring at my sleeve.

"Um . . . yeah. Not mine, though."

"Where's Madi?" she asks, alarmed.

"Oh, no. It's not hers, either. She was going to drop off some stable points in 1966 for Jack to monitor and then check in with Alex and the others back at her place. I . . . I guess I need to change."

She nods. "Sure. Give me the jacket. I'll treat the stain."

I toss her the jacket, and the shirt, too, once I realize that the blood has seeped through. In the hallway bath, I rinse away the red smear on my arm and splash some cool water on my face. Then I go back to the room that I'm sharing with Richard and grab another shirt from the closet. My hands are shaking, so I sit down on the edge of the bed and take deep breaths until they are steady enough to work the buttons. Then I take out my CHRONOS key. We've got nineteen minutes left on the five-hour timer. I pull up the stable point in the living room and scroll through. Richard will arrive about seven minutes from now. Madi in twelve minutes. Katherine will bring up the rear, popping in about three minutes late.

When I get back to the main room, Clio has the jacket spread out on the tiled kitchen counter and is pressing a dry towel against the stain on the sleeve.

"Will it come out?" Even as the words leave my mouth, I can't help thinking that it's a truly unimportant question. Who gives a fuck if the blood comes out of a stupid jacket?

"It's wool," she says. "And it didn't have much time to set. Are you able to talk about it yet? There's bourbon in the cabinet if you need it."

I *do* need it, so I pour both of us a shot and then sit down at the small table on the other side of the kitchen. "I'm pretty sure the blood belongs to the doorman at a club in Greenwich Village called Café Society."

"I've been there," Clio says. "A couple of times. It was later, though. After the war, just before they closed it down."

"I thought at first the blood might have been Marcy's," I tell her, "but then I remembered that the blood disappears when you yank the key if the person is out of timeline, so . . ."

"Marcy. She's one of their observers, right? The one you knew?"

I toss back the bourbon before answering. "Yes. The one I *dated*. And apparently the relationship was a bit more serious in her timeline."

"Did you get a look at him? The guy who shot them, I mean. Not the doorman."

"Oh, I definitely got a look. Not a guy, though. It was a member of Team Viper. Esther. Which definitely means that we made the right call about you sticking to the apartment. If they'll kill one of their own observers, then . . ."

She makes a face but doesn't argue the point. "I've heard the name. I mean the Esther in this timeline, obviously. She gets stranded back in 1300 or something like that, and essentially redesigns the entire map of Africa. Saul pulled in one of her daughters to be a Cyrist Templar when he was planning his little global disaster."

"What do you mean Esther *redesigns* the map?"

"The map, the history of the continent. My mom says there was a time when Africa was composed of dozens of small countries. Akana didn't exist. Neither did the African Union, except as sort of a regional League of Nations."

"But . . . that's just wrong. I'm not an Africanist, but the Akan were one of the first empires. The AU came along later, but the Akan have controlled West Africa for millennia."

"That's how I learned it, too," she says, swapping the now-bloody dishcloth out for a clean, damp one. "But I'm guessing if you rummage through the shelves in the library back in Bethesda or, even more likely, some of the books in their computer system, you'll find at least a few histories that show the version my mom mentioned."

"But I thought they fixed the timeline."

She shrugs. "*Fixed* is a relative term. They destroyed most of the keys, but apparently Madi and her buddies couldn't leave well enough alone. Probably the government, too. My dad always said that there was no way the genie would stay in the bottle. Nukes, genetic modifications, time travel . . . once big secrets like that are out, they tend to stay out. Preventing the Culling just bought some time." She chuckles. "*Bought some time.* How's that for irony? Anyway, there was once a timeline without the Akan Empire. And there was a timeline without Cyrists, too. At least that's what some version of Katherine told my mother in 2015 or whenever. They stopped Saul from killing billions of people, but they never got back to that reality. My mom says they had to accept the timeline where people have frog tongues. Do you know what that means?"

I shake my head. "Can't say I've ever heard that one."

"A TV reference, apparently. My dad didn't get it, either. Said it was probably from this cartoon show she liked. But it's the sort of weird comment that sticks in your mind. Why do you think Esther shot one of her team's observers?" She looks at me for a second, then shakes her head, tossing the jacket over the back of one of the kitchen chairs. "You know what? Just wait. You're going to have to tell it to the others when they get here, and I've got a feeling it's not a story you want to repeat multiple times. Grab a couple of cans of soup out of the pantry, okay? Maybe toma . . . to . . ." She stops, staring down at the red stain on the blue gingham dishcloth she was using to clean the jacket. "On second thought, maybe something else would be better. You pick."

I scan the red-and-white cans for something that looks reasonably safe. "Chicken noodle okay with you?"

She says it will be fine, so I hunt for the opener while she slices cheddar off a block for grilled cheese. When I finally locate the opener, I can't get the stupid thing to work. It's partly because it's old, but my hands are still a bit shaky. Clio takes the opener from me and gets it started.

"Were you in love with her?" she asks. "I mean, not this version, but . . ."

I shake my head. "Just friends. The romance didn't really take on either side in this reality. The spark was missing from the beginning. She was nice and we were in the same social group, so I asked her out."

"But there *is* someone at CHRONOS?"

"For Marcy? Yes. For me . . . no. Not at CHRONOS." That, of course, pulls the image of Antoinette Robinson into my head, but I push it away. "Or anywhere really."

"Not buying it," she says, apparently reading something in my expression. "What's her name?"

I know what Clio is doing. She's trying to get my mind off the scene in the alley. Off the blood. And maybe she's right. "Her name is Unattainable," I say as I empty the first can of soup into the pot.

"Off-Limits. *Verboten*. And even if I wasn't a historian, even if I was native to 1966 Memphis, there's a damn good chance that if we spent more than fifteen minutes together, we'd find we're not even compatible. But she was very pretty in her orange dress, outside Exchange Avenue Pharmacy with her friends and her sister, waiting for their ride to the Beatles concert. And I won't consider any timeline legitimate that doesn't include that scene. I mean, I might have to accept it as good enough, as a . . ."

"As a frog-tongue universe?"

"Exactly. I might have no choice but to accept it. But it won't be *right*."

"Time travel screws everything up," she says. "I had a great relationship with a wonderful guy in Chicago, but he wanted the whole white-picket-fence thing. Which I wanted, too . . . but way too much of my time was diverted to making sure Simon Rand didn't screw up the timeline."

"Simon?"

"Long story, best told when I'm not holding a knife. Anyway, Matt got tired of waiting. Bought a house. Gave me an ultimatum. Last I heard through normal channels, back in 1935, he was engaged."

"Maybe once all this is over . . ."

She shakes her head. "I don't think so. Because I enjoy torturing myself, I set a stable point in front of that house. Here in 1939, he's married, with an adorable little boy and another kid on the way. And yes, I scrolled forward. In this reality, at least, he ends up with five kids before the moving truck arrives . . . presumably to take all of them to a bigger house. And five kids makes me think maybe Matt and I weren't nearly as compatible as I thought."

I've just emptied the second can into the pot and added water, when I realize that Richard will be blinking in any second. "I need to talk to Rich for a moment. It's kind of personal, so . . ."

"It's okay," Clio says. "I can take it from here."

When Richard arrives, I motion toward the hallway leading to the bedrooms. "We've got four minutes until Madi arrives and ten until Katherine, and I need to chat with you first."

"Okay," he says, following me. "What's up that can't be discussed with the whole team?"

"Mostly, we can't discuss it in front of Katherine. Madi's already in the loop, and we'll bring Clio in shortly, but . . . I wanted to let you know about this first and get your feedback. You know her better than any of us."

"Yes." His eyes narrow slightly as he sits on the edge of one of the beds. "I *do* know her better than any of you. What's up?"

"Madi says Saul created the Cyrists. She believes Katherine is aware of this, and that she's covering for him out of fear that he'll get booted from CHRONOS. And . . . maybe just out of fear, period."

Condensing everything Madi told me into three minutes isn't easy, and I wind up looping back around a couple of times to fill in bits that I've forgotten.

"Doesn't make sense," Rich says when I finish. "The Cyrists have been around since . . . what? The 1700s, I think, at least in terms of US history. Maybe earlier."

"Except Madi has access to diaries written by Katherine and her granddaughter that beg to differ. Clio just confirmed that much without me even telling her what Madi said. Apparently, they have books in that library in Bethesda that were protected under a CHRONOS key, and those show our history *without* Cyrists."

"Yeah, well, we have an entire archives section protected by a CHRONOS key that shows history *with* them. Or at least, we did."

"I know. Madi described the situation as a time spiral, but I'm not sure how that explains CHRONOS not picking it up. Unless it was just so incremental . . ." I rub my temples, hoping to loosen a bit of the tension that's been building all day. "All I'm saying is that we have an issue. Madi admits she has no idea how much Katherine knows about

Saul's actions. In the diaries she's read, Katherine doesn't find out for a few more months, when it's too late to prevent Saul from sabotaging CHRONOS and stranding the two of you in the past."

"What about you? Are you stranded, too?"

That question is definitely one that occurred to me at the diner as Madi was telling me all of this. I could spot the moment when it occurred to *her*, as well, because she went kind of pale. "She didn't say, and I didn't ask. And I don't *plan* to ask. Either I'm stranded at some point in the past, like you and Katherine, or I'm killed in the—" I stop as I hear Madi's and Clio's voices in the other room. "Or I'm killed in the explosion. Madi says CHRONOS is just a pile of rubble afterward."

"Well, that's one pile of rubble more than it is currently," he says. "I mean, Saul can't reduce it to rubble if it never exists."

"Yeah. And either way, it's a moot point, because if we fix the timeline, we're sure as hell not going to turn around and let him break it again. If there was any doubt in my mind on that point, it was erased a few minutes ago as I watched . . ." I shake my head. Clio is right. I don't want to rehash the story multiple times. "I'll get into that once everyone else is here. The reason I wanted to talk to you first is to ask if you believe Katherine would have covered for Saul if he was breaking CHRONOS regulations. And if so, can we risk telling her what we know?"

"But we don't *know* anything. Why are you believing people we just met over Katherine? Personally, I'm going to have to see some serious proof before I make that kind of leap. Madi needs to hand over this diary and any other information she's got, so that we have something to go on aside from her word."

I'm about to add that it's Clio's word, too, but he's already out the door. I sigh and follow him. This is precisely why I didn't want to be team leader. We're going to end up with a schism in Team Hyena if I'm not careful, and we literally don't have time for this sort of drama.

Madi is already at the table when we get to the kitchen, with food in front of her. Clio is at the stove, flipping sandwiches.

"We've got a big problem," Madi says around a mouthful of grilled cheese, which is already half gone. "Saul—the one from *this* reality—may be working with the other side. Alex says he survived the time shift. He's already been in Detroit, New York, and Florida, including Fort Myers, which is where the Cyrists were founded. I'm guessing he's the one who converted Coughlin. Maybe that Dennis guy, too. That's why it didn't register as one of their moves. Alex is almost certain that all of Team Viper's moves were taken at the World's Fair."

"All of them?" Richard sinks into one of the chairs, his demand to see the diaries apparently forgotten for the time being.

"Yeah," Madi says. "That's how they got the double geographic bonus. It's within five kilometers or something like that. Those clear bubbles Alex uses to display the chronotron pulses from the other group are scattered all around the fairgrounds during the time period, but there are five main clusters. Two of them are the attack on the Japanese ambassador and the bombing on the Fourth of July. We just have to figure out which of the other three was their third move. From what I can tell—"

I hold up a hand. "Katherine's going to be here any minute. You said Saul has been in Detroit?"

Madi nods. "He jumped out from the same place that Katherine and Rich did. Alex measured three pulses from the same location, which I'm guessing is the Objectivist Club. Katherine is pale orange. Are you mint green, Rich?"

"I always thought of it as closer to sage," he says. "But yeah."

"The other one is red, and Alex said Katherine reacted strangely when she saw a red bubble pop up on his display earlier."

I take two of the sandwiches from the counter and slide one in front of Rich, who glances down at it without much interest. "We both thought we saw Saul," he says.

"In Detroit?" Clio asks as she joins us.

"No," Rich says. "Before we left the OC. I told Katherine we could go back and check, but she said there was no way Saul could have been under a CHRONOS key when the shift happened. That whoever we saw down in the Redwing Room couldn't have been him, and the only hope we had of getting Saul back, of getting any of them back, was to win this stupid game."

"Why didn't the two of you arrive here together?" Madi asks, looking toward the stable point in the living room. "You were both in Detroit, right?"

"Yes," Rich answers, sounding rather defensive. "We were both at the church. I was outside for the press conference, and she was in a conference of Coughlin's women's group. We were going to meet up an hour ago, a few blocks from the church, but we set up a secondary meeting point—here—in case the research took longer than anticipated for either of us. That's standard for team travel."

"And you didn't see Saul there?" Madi asks.

"No. I just saw a gaggle of journalists waiting for the story from Coughlin, who was sporting a Cyrist cross when he came out of the building. We walked with him across a nearby park to the location where they're building the new Cyrist temple. Saw the shiny new airplane, too, with the Cyrist symbol emblazoned on the side, and met the pilot—a woman, which is a bit unusual for the era."

"Laura Ingalls?" Madi asks. "Early thirties? Dark curls?"

"Yeah," he says. "How did you know?"

"She's with America First," I say. "And she spoke briefly at the rally earlier tonight. She's the one who drops leaflets at the White House. Like Coughlin, she's on the Nazi payroll."

"Okay," Rich says, looking confused. "But . . ." He stops and glances over at Madi. "I know what you told Tyson earlier. And I hate to break it to you, but the Cyrists aren't something Saul created. They can't be. We've got a massive historical archive at CHRONOS, and—"

"You're wrong," Clio says matter-of-factly. "Saul definitely created the Cyrists. Yes, he built it upon a tiny historical kernel of a group originally under the leadership of some guy named Cyrus Teed, but unless they're going around now saying that we live inside the earth, there aren't many similarities between the two groups. Saul is the author of *The Book of Cyrus*, although it's mostly cobbled together from other religious texts, self-help manuals, and get-rich-quick books. He wrote the other one, too, *The Book of Prophecy*, with the stock tips they dole out to their loyal sheep to make them believe that God wants them to be rich. So long as they keep sending in that tithe to Cyrist International, of course."

Rich shakes his head. "I'm telling you. That's just not possible. Temporal Monitoring would have picked it up." He's practically yelling at her, and while I suspect that his frustration and anger are mostly due to the news I gave him about Katherine, Rich is also used to being the guy with the answers to temporal conundrums. We're breaking new ground now, however. Everything is so tangled up that I'm not sure how anyone could easily separate the threads.

Clio ignores his tone of voice and calmly stirs her soup for a moment before looking up at him. "Possible or not, I'm telling you what *is*. I spent the past few years babysitting Saul Rand's favorite errand boy, one of the two people who jumped back in time to drop off those nasty little books of his at one of the first printing presses. Madi's grandmother is quite clearly a clone of Saul's daughter, a.k.a. Sister Prudence. And yes, I know it hurts your head, but why are you people surprised at that? It's the logical result of creating a technology that sends people back to your own past. Sooner or later, that kind of tampering will inevitably screw up your present and your future. Which is probably why Team Viper prefers to play their little games in someone else's backyard. That way, they don't have to clean up the messes they leave behind."

"You're right," Madi says. "I'll take the blame for that, since some version of me, in some reality, apparently thought time travel was a smart enough idea that I let some version of Lorena tinker with my DNA." She yawns, then continues. "The rest of you had that decision made for you, so you're off the hook. But I think all of that has to be on the back burner for now."

"Exactly," I say. "We have about three minutes to figure out how to handle this situation with Katherine. Although I guess a lot will depend on how she reacts to the news about Saul. You said he *might* be working with the other side? That feels excessively optimistic to me. Is there really any other way to interpret this?"

Madi makes a noncommittal gesture. "Alex and RJ both pointed out that the whole thing seems more like it was designed to *block* the other side than to help them. Coughlin's radio sermons actually start tilting away from isolationism during the coming year. He apparently tones down the hate speech, too. I didn't have time to get complete details, but it's *possible* that Saul is trying to help us, rather than them."

"But why?" Richard asks. "If he's the monster the three of you seem to think, that is. I don't trust the man one bit, but even I wouldn't have pegged him as a genocidal maniac."

"Maybe because this is connected to The Game," I suggest. "You know how competitive Saul is. We've both seen him at the Club when he plays in the annual tournament. If he's competitive there, why would this situation be different? Maybe he can't stand the idea of these off-worlders beating the home team? But regardless of his reasons, we need to find out more about what he's doing and why. Which means that, for now, we have to keep Katherine at least partially in the dark. Because if we tell her all of this, I don't think she'll be able to hide that knowledge from Saul. Do you, Rich?"

There's a long pause, and the look he gives me is baleful. "No. He plays her like a freakin' violin. You know that. But you just said he's dangerous. And you expect me to keep quiet about that when she heads off alone to meet him?"

"Maybe we could adopt a buddy system?" Madi says. "We could decide who goes with whom once we're clear on how we're going to divide up the tasks, but that way someone could keep an eye on Katherine."

"Won't work," Rich says. "Think about it. Are we going to follow her into the bathroom? Keep a guard posted to watch her while she sleeps? She could go wherever she wanted and be back a fraction of a second later. The only way we could keep her from jumping out is to take her key . . . and we can't do that without erasing her."

"Well . . . not here," Clio says. "We could do it at Madi's place in 2136. Or at my parents' house."

"We're not taking Katherine's key," Rich says.

"Richard is right," I tell them. "Looking at this from a strictly practical point of view, that would cost us a player, something we can't afford. Plus, we lose our advantage. Right now, Saul doesn't know we're aware that he created the Cyrists. Katherine is our only hope for keeping an eye on him and figuring out whether he's on our side or theirs."

"Again, though . . . are you seriously suggesting that we don't tell Katherine?" Rich says. "You claim to have evidence that Saul is abusive, and you're actually planning to keep that from her?"

"No," Madi says. "We *will* tell her. Just not yet. She's been with him for years, Rich. When this is over, win or lose, I'll give her the diary and let her make her own decision. The main reason I suggested the whole buddy-system idea was concern for her safety. Our priority right now has to be finding out what the hell Saul is up to, and where his loyalties lie. Katherine is far more likely than anyone else to figure that out and, for that matter, to help us find him. Alex can narrow the time and place down a bit, but his system is reactive, not predictive. It only picks up the chronotron surge when Saul jumps *from* a location, not where or when he's jumping to. Plus, there's the original reason I told Tyson what I know. The Cyrists are wrapped into this somehow. I think Katherine knows more about Saul's connection to the Cyrists than she's told us."

"Waiting has another benefit," I say. "If we win this thing and CHRONOS is restored, the goal has to be to get Saul back to HQ. That way, security can deal with whatever he's done and prevent him from any future crimes."

"Alternatively, you could just shoot the rat bastard and yank his key," Clio says. "That's the option my parents would suggest. And this time, if you future folk can resist digging up medallions or inventing more of the damn things, maybe he'll *stay* erased."

Madi gives Clio a look that I don't fully understand. Sympathy, but I think there's also a bit of wariness in the mix. I debate asking but decide it might be better to just talk to Madi later.

"I'm generally not a fan of violence," Rich says, "or I'd probably side with your parents on this one. I'll definitely get a great deal of satisfaction, however, from siccing Sutter on his ass."

"On whose ass?" Katherine says from the kitchen doorway. Her eyes seem a bit red, as if she's been crying, but she's smiling ear to ear.

The four of us exchange a look. "Um . . . Morgen," Richard says. "We were just wondering if they had a Sutter in their reality."

Katherine gives him a confused look, but it disappears quickly. "I'm really sorry that I'm late, but I have good news. Saul was under a key when the shift happened, so Team Hyena now has an extra set of hands. Unofficially, of course, but still . . . He's been trying to find us for months, and he finally tracked me down at the church where I was speaking with Elizabeth Dilling. Which means we don't need to worry about anything on that front. Saul has the whole situation with Coughlin covered." She tilts her head slightly to the right and frowns. "None of you seem particularly surprised."

"I just finished telling them that Alex thinks the red bubble you saw on the display was Saul," Madi says. "He dug a bit deeper and realized that a red dot jumped out from the same location as you and Richard. At almost the same time, too. So . . . we sort of put two and two together and assumed Saul survived."

"How, though?" Rich asks. "How did Saul just *happen* to be under a key?" There's a faint undertone of *damn it all to hell* in the question, but Katherine seems to be too excited to notice.

"I know! I'm not normally the type to believe in miracles, but this experience has me wondering if we don't have a guardian angel. Maybe we can win this thing after all." She spends the next few minutes explaining how Saul swiped the key from Morgen Campbell, who had apparently decided a while back that his quarters were going to be under a CHRONOS field and had enough cash to make it happen. Saul had also seen the note from Team Viper that supposed hackers placed on all the TD systems. He and Morgen had both dismissed it as a joke, but they'd been curious enough to run a quick basic scenario on what it might take to keep the US out of the war, and that meant Saul had at least some idea what had happened when the time shift hit.

There are only two pieces of new information in what Katherine tells us. The first is that when Saul was on his jump to Georgia last week, the Saul from Team Viper tried to recruit him. That explains a lot about the way he stormed out of the jump room and Katherine's emergency exit in the middle of our meeting with Angelo. The second bit of news is the fact that the key Saul swiped from Morgen has the hyphenated version of the word *CHRO-NOS* engraved on the back, which has me wondering whether this is their first incursion into our universe. Or maybe it's a relic from some other group that was over here playing time tourist.

One thing that's conspicuously missing from Katherine's recitation of Saul's narrow escape from oblivion, however, is any reference to the Cyrists—specifically why, when faced with a reality where the US doesn't enter World War II, his mind had gone so quickly to converting Coughlin. Apparently, it's going to be on me to ask her that question, because Madi and Clio give me expectant looks when Katherine wraps up. Rich glances my way, too, although his expression is more one of resignation than expectation.

"So," I begin. "Saul has been looking for you for over a month. I'm going to go out on a limb and guess, given that he found you at Coughlin's church, that he's behind the priest's sudden change of faith?"

"Yes. Which is why it didn't score when we listed it as one of our initial predictions. Team Viper never entered it into the system. Saul figured out that they were *planning* to use Coughlin to fan the isolationist flames. And he preempted them, so that saves us a move."

"But . . . Tyson and I heard Coughlin speak at the rally tonight," Madi says. "Aside from name-dropping the Cyrists on a few occasions, he's still beating the same drum."

"Well, yes," Katherine says. "But Saul has only just started working with him. And Coughlin can't switch gears all at once, or he'll lose his listeners. If nothing else, this will isolate him. Saul has already gotten him off Hitler's payroll."

"But that means he was on Hitler's payroll in *our* timeline," Clio says. "That's not something we needed to change. So at best, what Saul is doing is unnecessary, and at worst, it could make actually fixing the timeline a lot harder."

Katherine opens her mouth as if to speak, and then closes it again. When she finally does respond, it's simply to say, "I don't think so."

"But why this particular move?" I ask. "If Saul ran game scenarios, like you said, he'd have been running them on a system fairly similar to the one we used. We compiled the top options for Angelo's meeting, and I'm certain that converting Charles Coughlin to Cyrisism wasn't on the list."

"Because it's what he knows," Katherine says. "My first inclination when looking at this problem, or any problem for that matter, is to figure out what social movements are active and how they might have been motivated. It's what I study. It's what I know. You probably look to see which group of racist jerks have their fingers in the pie, although in this case, the giant swastikas at that rally made your job fairly easy. As a religious historian, Saul played to his strengths and looked for a way that religion might be used to change the situation. Keep in mind, he didn't know we made it out. He was half convinced that the person he saw in Georgia was just some later version of himself, screwing around with his head."

"Why the Cyrists, though? Why not leave the guy as a Catholic? What connection does Saul have to the Cyrists?"

It's an obvious question, one that I was about to ask, in fact. While I wouldn't have been surprised to hear it come from either Madi or Clio, I *am* a bit surprised to hear the words coming from Richard. He's seated directly across the table from Katherine, looking straight at her as he asks the question. She doesn't meet his eyes at first, and when she finally does look up, her composure seems to falter a bit.

"Katherine," Richard says, and his voice is gentler as he repeats the question, "what connection does Saul have to the Cyrists?"

Clio expels a huff of breath and gets up from the table, snatching a few dishes away to put in the sink. I get her frustration. We would have learned a lot more about Katherine's loyalties and motivations if Richard hadn't essentially tipped our hand. There's no way she could be looking at his face right now and not realize that we know, or at least suspect, *something*. The only real questions at this point are how *much* she'll tell us and how much Rich will end up telling her.

"The Cyrists were part of a couple of scenarios he ran with Morgen," Katherine says. "Saul had this running joke, where he added verses to *The Book of Cyrus*. Changed them up. Added bits from other religions. Tate Poulsen sometimes joined in. I think it was something they started doing when they were roommates. And apparently the fascination with the Cyrists is something he and his twin over on the Viper side have in common, although some of the details seem . . . different. The symbol, for example. When Team Viper was setting things up to use the Cyrists, it looked more like a standard cross. I think Saul switched it . . . back. Back to the original." Katherine rubs her forehead. "I could be wrong, though. It's been a long day."

"You're definitely right on that account," Madi says a bit too cheerfully to be convincing. "I'm exhausted. I think we all are. Which is probably why we all started dissecting the one bit of good news we've gotten since this nightmare started. From what all of you have said, there's no one better at The Game than Saul, right? So having him on our side—officially or not—is a coup. And it has to be such a relief to you to find out he's okay." Katherine nods, her eyes going teary, as Madi continues. "Anyway, why don't we go around and give a basic report of anything else we learned during our respective jumps? That way, we can let everything gel overnight and start fresh in the morning."

Katherine smiles. "Good idea. I've told you most of what I found, so mine will be quick. Elizabeth Dilling confirmed that Coughlin had been planning the move to the Cyrists for some time now. She converted, too, and now has a lotus-flower tattoo on her hand. And then Saul found me, and well . . . I've told you the rest."

Richard then summarizes his jump, which is a repeat of what he'd told us before Katherine arrived.

When he finishes, Madi says, "Tyson is a better person to tell you about the rally, since he understood more of it than I did. After that, I jumped to 1966 to hand the stable points off to Jack."

"Is my mom being nice to him?" Clio asks.

"Yes," Madi says with a slightly shaky smile. "Jack told me he has absolutely everything he needs, which isn't much, since he'll mostly be staring at the key, trying to find something that can help us avert the killings at the rally."

"That event isn't one of their moves, though," Katherine says. "According to Saul, the fact that they were awarded a double geographic bonus means we should focus on events within five kilometers of the one initial prediction we got right . . . so, basically, we should assume everything they did was at the World's Fair."

"That tracks with Alex's theory," Madi says, "which I was about to get to, but this does raise an important question. There were three deaths at the rally that didn't happen in our timeline. If that *wasn't* one of their moves, but was rather an unintended consequence, can we still act to prevent it? I mean, even if you take the view that the woman was in league with the Nazis, two kids were killed. They weren't old enough to know better."

"I don't know," I admit. "If that wasn't one of their official moves, reversing it might be seen as a violation of the rules. I know they have cameras, or at least stable points, at two different locations in Manhattan, which is well outside the five-kilometer range. Maybe changing the timeline will reverse it, and we won't have to do anything specific. Or maybe we'll have to come up with some off-the-books way to deal with it. Maybe there won't be any cameras there and it won't matter. Because you're right. Those are deaths that weren't supposed to happen."

"Saul says the extra moves he's made won't count," Katherine says. "Unless the other team launches a challenge. In which case, recordings might be entered into evidence, but . . . the SimMaster is just going to measure the moves we enter and whether or not the goal—that is, the US entering the war on schedule—is accomplished. Anything else is peripheral. So . . . reversing those moves should be peripheral, too."

I shrug. "I'm more worried about Saul's convincing people like Coughlin and Dennis to back the Cyrists than I am about the rally, to be honest. I mean, there's a quick and easy way to stop those three deaths. I'll just jump in and rip the timing device off the phonograph. Figuring out how to undo what led Lawrence Dennis to set the damn thing in the first place is going to be a lot harder."

"Saul has promised me that he will go back and remove his version of *The Book of Cyrus* and anything else he planted," Katherine says. "He can also go back and tell himself not to contact Coughlin and the rest of them after we flip the timeline. Saul handles double memories a lot better than most of us do."

I'm very skeptical on Saul following through with these promises. Judging from the expressions of Rich, Madi, and Clio, I'm not alone in my skepticism. But there's little point going into this now, so I move on to the next person at the table. "Your turn," I say to Clio.

"Oh, lots of excitement for me, since you told me to stay inside the apartment. I made grilled cheese sandwiches and soup—although I can't really claim credit for the latter, since you opened the cans and added water. All I did was stir. Oh, and I cleaned a large bloodstain out of your jacket, something I actually had a bit of prior experience with, sadly."

"Blood?" Madi asks.

"Yes. Not mine." I deliver a brief summary of my evening, and as I expected, Rich gives me an annoyed look when I mention the location of my meeting with Lawrence Dennis. It quickly fades, however, when the story moves from Café Society itself to the alley behind the building.

"And so," I tell them, "despite Clio's diligent efforts, I'm pretty sure that the jacket over there still carries traces of the blood of a doorman that the Viper version of Esther murdered tonight. It would probably be stained with Marcy Bateman's blood, too, if that hadn't disappeared when Alisa snatched her key. And while I get the sense that the communist who runs the place might generally steer clear of involving the police, he probably made an exception when they found his doorman dead next to the dumpster. Given that Lawrence Dennis and I had been arguing back there just a few minutes earlier and both Tallulah Bankhead and Billie Holiday saw me waving my pistol around, they're probably already working with some police sketch artist to make sure they get as much info as possible into the all-points bulletin."

I try to keep my tone matter-of-fact. But as Clio had predicted, talking about it stirs the same low-level panic I was feeling earlier.

"You're lucky you weren't killed," Madi says. Everyone is silent for a moment, and then she adds, "This is exactly what I was talking about earlier, though. We're going to be in dangerous circumstances. I think we need a buddy system. If something happens to one of us, the other person can jump back to get help. Near the end, we may have to split up to do everything in the order and at the speed it needs to be accomplished. But for tomorrow at least . . ."

Katherine frowns. "But we'll cover more ground if we separate. You might want to stick with Tyson, since you're new to this, but Richard and I are both experienced agents. There's no reason to treat us like first-years."

Madi doesn't argue, but she gives me a very pointed glance. Apparently, that's my cue to step in as team leader.

"We need to make it a blanket rule given what very nearly happened to me in the alley. Safety in numbers. Not just at the Fair, but across the board."

"That's silly," Katherine says. "All four of us are armed. Richard has the watch gadget. I have Sutter's nasty little laser pointer or whatever it's called. Madi still has the tiny gun she used at the Beatles concert. So . . ."

"Katherine, I was carrying a pistol at the time. I still could have been killed."

She glances around at the others, and when it's clear that they're taking my side on this, she gives me a little nod and says, "Fine, then."

"Okay. If that's settled, maybe we should get some rest. It's nearly one a.m., so let's be back here and ready to start the day at nine. We can decide then who will go where and with whom." I can tell from their faces that the thought of waking up with eight hours less on the clock terrifies them exactly as much as it does me, but we can't function without sleep.

"I'm tired, too," Rich says. "But maybe we should briefly discuss plans for tomorrow first? I don't know about anyone else, but I'll sleep better knowing we at least have a tentative game plan."

"Maybe you and Katherine can set observation points at the World's Fair," I suggest. "We'll put together a list of all the spots we're going to need to watch."

"Alex gave me a map of the Fair marked with some of them," Madi says.

"Good. We can just add to it as needed. As for me, I'm going to try to talk to some people within the Universal Front, since they held a protest outside the gates on the day the Japanese ambassador was attacked. One of the newspaper accounts seemed to think they could have been responsible."

"But why would they do that?" Katherine asks. "Isn't it more likely to be one of the leftist groups, given that the Japanese are allied with Hitler?"

"That's what you're supposed to think," I say. "Or at least what they hope the police and reporters will think. Frame the other side as terrorists, and you can sway public sentiment in your favor. And they aren't really allied with Hitler yet."

"It could still be the communists, though," Rich says. "Both sides were willing to engage in targeted violence. Either way, I think we may need to go to Café Society. You said something about the owner being a communist. He's not, but . . ."

"Yeah. Lawrence Dennis said it's his brother."

"Exactly. There were widespread rumors that the club was a communist front. Josephson's brother—Leo, Leon, something like that—was a member of the Communist Party. He wasn't just a casual member, either. He got himself arrested in Europe in the mid-1930s, as part of a Soviet plot to assassinate Hitler. Rumor has it that the initial six thousand bucks in startup funds for Café Society was a loan from unspecified friends of Barney's brother. And because most of his brother's friends are communists, the House Un-American Activities Committee ends up assuming that the money was actually fronted by the US Communist Party. And it may have been. The CP's underlying goals dovetailed nicely with Barney Josephson's—they wanted a place where diverse people could mingle. But they were less interested in racial justice than in having a place where party members could openly associate with people they might be able to convert to the cause."

"So . . . what's wrong with that?" Madi asks. "I mean, if any other political party put up the money for those reasons, it wouldn't be a problem, right?"

"Right," Rich says. "If it was the Republicans or Democrats or virtually any other political organization, no one would have blinked an eye. But the US Communist Party is, by its international nature, linked to the party in the USSR. After the war, at least in our timeline, anti-Soviet sentiment becomes pretty intense. By 1950, Café Society was essentially blackballed into nonexistence. HUAC managed to wreck the careers of quite a few of its performers, too. And . . . there's something else about it that's bothering me. My brain is trying to connect some dots, but I can't make out the pattern yet. I'm thinking I may go forward and see what I can find on the brother before we do anything else tomorrow. Madi's digital assistant can probably pull up what I need to know, and we can figure out if a trip to Café Society is a good use of our time."

"Works for me," I tell him. "If we do visit the club, though, it will need to be on a date before my last visit. Otherwise, they're going to remember I was there the night their doorman was killed. Okay, Madi. You're next."

"I'll see if I can get in to speak with Einstein," Madi says. "Alex has a list of days that he was at the World's Fair. There were several of them just before the ceremony dedicating the Jewish Palestine Pavilion."

"That sounds good." I notice Katherine's mouth tighten from the corner of my eye. When I realize why, I quickly add, "We'll see what we can find out with the Universal Front first, and then I'll come with you to see what we can discover about Einstein's activities."

Clio pulls a pill container out of the cabinet next to the stove. It has a childproof cap, so I would bet it's not native to the 1930s. "These kick in after fifteen minutes or so," she says, "and they'll wear off fully in about six hours. I've used them. They won't leave you groggy. So, if you think there's any chance at all that you're going to lie there staring at the ceiling, I'd suggest taking one now."

I hold my hand out along with everyone else. I'm tired, but my nerves are still jangling, so I pop the pill and head off to the shower. I sponged away the blood earlier, but I can still feel the spot on my arm where the jacket clung to my skin. Yeah, it's psychological, but a shower can't hurt.

The medication is already starting to take effect when I crawl into the empty twin bed across from Richard a few minutes later.

"Sorry I was a jerk earlier," Rich says. "But, just so you know, Katherine has probably already jumped out. She thought Saul was dead, and she just found out he's not. So I'm pretty sure she'll sleep there, not here. And Saul's not working with us. I can't say whether he's actively working *against* us, but he's lying."

"Not surprised, but what brings you to that conclusion?"

"Katherine said Saul claimed he *preempted* a move by the Vipers. That they were planning to use Coughlin, but he captured their pawn." He gives a sullen chuckle. "Their bishop, to be more accurate. But unless this is some extracurricular move they started *after* the time shift, it doesn't make sense. First, the moves Team Viper made are what caused the time shift that erased CHRONOS and sent all of us off in search of what happened. We know that converting Coughlin wasn't one of their three moves. So how did Saul preempt something he wouldn't even have known about until it was a done deal? And second, based on what Madi told us, Alex has it narrowed down geographically to the fairgrounds, something that Saul even told Katherine was likely. And we know that Coughlin is converted before the Fair opens. So he's lying to her . . . as fucking usual. The only question is why." He rolls over and fluffs the pillow under his head. "Still can't believe their Esther shot Marcy. And Alisa yanking her key. That's just evil. Guess things are pretty different over there."

I don't respond, because I'm starting to get groggy and also because I don't know if I agree. If I had to guess, I'd say it's entirely possible that the Esther and Alisa from our timeline are equally as capable of evil, given the right set of circumstances, as their doppelgängers on Team Viper.

"And, Tyce? I didn't say anything in front of the others, but . . . are you sure about the Universal Front thing? I mean, it's one thing to go into that rally with Madi as part of a crowd. But showing up as a potential new recruit when they're going to be scrutinizing you closely seems dangerous to me. You don't have your lenses, and you don't have any inside connections to vouch for you. I'd offer to go myself, but I don't have the background knowledge, and they'd probably toss me out on my ear—or worse—within five minutes. I just think it's too risky, especially given that you'll be solo, because despite what you told Katherine, we both know you can't take Madi in there."

As much as I don't want to admit it, he has a point. I'd probably be okay with a Klan group, even without the stupid lenses, because I know the lingo. I know the customs. And my southern drawl is a hell of a lot more convincing than my New York accent. "You're right," I admit. "Maybe we can find out what we need to stop the attack on the ambassador through viewing the locations alone. I'm just worried about the stupid style points. Undoing their moves seems more likely to score high than simply blocking them. And I can't talk them out of it if I'm not inside."

"We'll just have to get creative in other ways," Rich says. "Maybe the probability points."

I'm not even sure how those work, but I don't ask because I'm too close to sleep to follow his answer. As I drift off, Madi's comment earlier tonight about it being unlikely that we'll ever get our exact timeline back keeps echoing in my head, along with Clio's remark about settling for the universe where people have frog tongues. Between that and the scene in the alley, my dreams are going to suck.

Maybe the timeline we end up with *won't* be exactly the one we had before. Maybe we can break out of this stupid time spiral or whatever it is and create something better. But I promise myself one thing as I drift off to sleep. The reality we end up with will *not* be one designed by Team Viper. And it will not be one designed by Saul Rand.

FROM THE *NEW YORK*
DAILY INTREPID

MISSING AVIATRIX APPEARS NEXT DAY IN MIAMI

(Miami, Fla., March 5, 1934) Crowds stood waiting for several hours at the small airfield in Jacksonville on March 3rd, hoping to get a glimpse of acclaimed aviatrix Laura Houghtaling Ingalls. Miss Ingalls, who recently announced that she has "a yen" to fly the Andes solo, left Charleston at noon, piloting a Lockheed Vega destined for Jacksonville, but never arrived at the airport. Indeed, nothing was heard from the pilot until she landed in Miami, nearly 350 miles to the south, late yesterday.

Miss Ingalls declined to say where she had spent the night and dismissed several reports of a similar plane in the Key Biscayne area south of Miami. "Now, can't I have one little secret?" she told reporters. "Put it down to anything you like. But not romance. That's out. A friend gave me a six-shooter when I left New York, so I had to just dip off someplace and use it. I knew I would never have a chance to use it on the South American trip, so I went off, looking for adventure."

Miss Ingalls is scheduled to depart for Havana on Thursday morning, before continuing on to the Yucatan.

∞21∞

KATHERINE
MIAMI BEACH, FLORIDA
FEBRUARY 13, 1939

The room is dark, except for the dim glow from the candles in wall sconces on either side of the bed and a pale shimmer of light from the plate-glass door that opens to the balcony. On a less cloudy night, you could probably see the moon and stars reflected on the ocean, but tonight, you can barely make out the waves.

I can hear them, though, crashing against the shore, almost but not quite in tempo with the soft music. Camille Saint-Saëns. It brings an instant smile. The song has been a favorite auditory aphrodisiac of ours since we took in a performance in Chicago in 1906, during a trip to see what elements of the 1893 World's Fair, often known as the White City or the Expo, were preserved in the White City Amusement Park that had opened the previous year. (The answer: almost none.) While the title of the song, *La Danse Macabre*, might not exactly sound romantic, Saul had whispered suggestions that bordered on the obscene throughout most of the production. The end result was that we left the concert early, hurried through the bone-deep chill of the November night, and barely made it to our room at the Palmer House with our clothes intact.

Tonight, Saul is exactly where he was when I pulled up the stable point, seated in the center of the bed wearing absolutely nothing aside from a lecherous grin as he takes in my naked body. I smile and take a step toward him, and then his voice comes from directly behind me. "Happy Valentine's Day . . . almost."

Two hands slide down my arms to the bare skin of my waist. I scream, twisting out of his grasp, and when I turn to face him, I'm certain that I'll see the scar running up the side of his face, and the false eye. But it's just Saul looking back at me, concern in both of his entirely normal eyes. I look toward the bed, but that's Saul, too. He's wearing the same look of slight surprise and worry.

Both Sauls, almost in unison, say, "Oh, God. Kathy. I'm sorry." Then, as if by unspoken agreement, only the Saul on the bed continues. "You thought I was him. The Saul from Team Viper. That didn't even occur to me. I was just . . ." He shrugs. "This has been a common fantasy for a while, hasn't it? I'm pretty sure we even talked about it at the Saint-Saëns concert that night."

He's right. We were curled up on the bed at the Palmer House, in the grip of what Saul often calls *le petit mort* and what other, less morbid souls call the afterglow. We talked, as couples often do, about our fantasies. Some were shared, others not so much. I'd jokingly told him that I wanted to make love in the giant Ferris wheel at the Expo. He'd informed me that I'd have to find another partner. And then he'd mentioned the splinter fantasy, claiming that he'd breezed through that test during training. He had a nice conversation with himself, shook his hand, and walked away without the slightest complication. I, on the other hand, had very nearly barfed on the way out the door after the mandatory chat with ten-minutes-later me and had stayed in my room for hours with a miserable headache.

"Can you imagine how much fun we could have? And why stop at just two?" he'd said, placing both of his hands, still cold from our dash through the November night, against my bare abdomen, and then, in quick succession, on my breast, my face, my legs, and all points in between as I giggled and tried to move away. "There would be hands absolutely everywhere."

Saul II brushes my hair aside and presses his lips against my neck. His hands, his breath, are not cold now, but deliciously warm against my skin. "It was just never possible before," he says, "given how they limited our use of the key. But now . . ."

"We don't expect you to reciprocate," Saul says as he walks toward us. "Although that *would* be interesting. But my friend here probably only has about ten minutes before he blinks into oblivion. So we should make good use of him."

"Are you certain he's the one who will vanish?" I ask, pulling in a ragged breath.

"I guess you'll have to wait and see."

For a while, I'm able to close my eyes and forget. To pretend that it really *is* only the two of us in the room and Saul is just really . . . flexible. He didn't intend this to unsettle me. And if by some miracle the controls had been lifted from our keys two weeks ago, it wouldn't have unsettled me at all.

But by the time there are only two of us in the room, I've entirely lost track. I have no idea whether it's Saul or the splinter who vanished. Although, come to think of it, I don't know whether it was Saul on the bed in the first place. It shouldn't matter. They're both Saul. But it bothers me.

I get up and pull the needle from the phonograph and turn it off. "As a heads-up, this will be my last visit without one of the other team members until this is over. The other side has already shot at us, and Tyson saw them kill one of their own observers tonight. So for the next day and a half, at least, I'll have a buddy in tow. Just in case we're followed, I guess."

"Followed how?"

"Tracking our jumps. That's how they crossed over in the first place. They attached themselves to Tyson's and Max's signals."

"And how did you figure that out?" Saul asks.

This question could definitely be a land mine, so I go with a vague answer. "We're working with a temporal physicist. Someone Max knows. He said he might be able to block them if he could figure out which . . . universe, I guess? . . . they're coming from. But he hasn't had much luck."

"So," Saul says, leaning back against the upholstered headboard. "How did the rest of the team take the news that I somehow survived? I'm guessing poor Rich wasn't too happy about it. He was no doubt thinking he might finally stand a chance."

I catch myself just as I'm about to tell him they already knew. That could open up more questions about Madi, however, and I'm not sure it's a good idea to go there. "They were happy, obviously. What did you think? You might not be Rich's or Tyson's favorite person, but they both know we need all the help we can get." That's not entirely true, and Saul probably knows it. At best, they're cautiously optimistic, and to be honest, I get it. We don't know if Saul's actions will be judged as breaking the rules, plus it seems very much like he's hoping not to simply reverse the timeline, but rather to have a timeline with a few added features, namely the Cyrists. Or maybe it's another example of him acting impetuously, taking bold steps without thinking things through. Like he did just now with the whole splinter thing.

"You could have brought a buddy tonight," he says with a little grin. "Only fair, since I did."

"Yeah, I don't think so. Which one are you, though? The one who was on the bed or the one who sneaked up behind me?"

"Does it matter?"

"Not really. I was just wondering which one disappeared."

"It wasn't me."

"Well, I know *that*." I pretend to shrug it off, but it's not easy. It may not be logical, but his little trick with the splinter troubles me now in a way it wouldn't have before almost everyone I love was snatched away, courtesy of a group of people who are only slightly more addicted to The Game than Saul is.

Saul knows me well enough to sense that I'm bothered. He snatches a robe from the foot of the bed and stalks off to the bathroom. "You know, if you weren't into the idea, you could simply have said so before. When did you become such a prude?"

I could tell him that it isn't prudishness. But should I *have* to? Shouldn't he have some basic understanding after more than five years together that this was not the best time to play doppelgänger games?

And I can't shake the feeling that he *did* know it would frighten me. That he knew, and that was maybe even the part he liked best. I shiver, wishing there was another robe, or that I'd had the foresight to bring clothes with me, even if I wasn't wearing them.

But I'd been so relieved to discover that the bedroom back in New York was empty that I hadn't even thought about that. Clio took the room that her parents had slept in sporadically for the past few years while they were in the city doing our preliminary research, so the four of us had to share the remaining two rooms. I spent a good fifteen minutes listening to Madi breathing in the room we're sharing, waiting until her sleep sounded deep enough that she wouldn't notice if I blinked out to join Saul. But instead of becoming deeper, the rhythm of her breath simply stopped, and I turned to see nothing but slightly rumpled covers on the twin bed where she'd been lying only moments ago. At least I won't have to worry about her ratting on me for disregarding the stupid buddy system, because I can do the very same.

Normally, this wouldn't be an issue anyway. I could simply blink out, spend as much time as I wanted here, and then blink back with no one the wiser. But we'll be syncing up our keys in the morning to make sure that we're all on the same time. Otherwise, we could find ourselves thinking we still had time on the clock at the end of the game, only to discover that one of us had spent an hour or two extra somewhere along the line and the SimMaster was already flashing the words *GAME OVER*.

I wrap a sheet around myself and walk to the balcony door. I'd like to go outside, get a breath of fresh air, and see if the scent of the ocean will clear my head, but when I press my palm against the glass, it's obvious that mid-February is a bit chilly even this far south. And it looks unsettling—too isolated, too deserted. I can see lights farther down the coast, but this stretch looks undeveloped.

Something is shining in the moonlight. Not on the beach, but on the wide expanse of lawn off to my left. An airplane. Not a large one. Just one propeller. Something is written on the side. I can't decipher the words, but I can make out the symbol near the front of the plane—it's a Cyrist symbol. Either Saul has learned to fly, or there's a pilot somewhere around.

The reflected glow of my CHRONOS key in the glass door catches my eye, and I suddenly feel very vulnerable. This key is the only thing that keeps me from simply vanishing like Saul's splinter did a few minutes ago. In a sense, I'm no more real than he was in this timeline. Just an aberration that could vanish with a simple yank of a chain.

I go back to the bed, pulling the sheet tighter around me. I'd planned to sleep here, but I want to go back now. I'm sure Saul expects me to stay. In fact, he was probably planning to spin off another splinter for a second round before I spoiled his fun. Which means he's going to be in a foul mood, and I still need to set a time for an official visit to find out exactly what actions he's been taking with Coughlin and the rest.

I need sleep. And he's going to make me wait, by taking one of his marathon showers.

Ten more minutes pass. Screw him. There's a pen and paper on the nightstand. I'll leave a note with a time and a place for our next meeting. If he doesn't show, I can always come back to this moment, tear up the note, and deal with his grumpy ass in person, since double memories don't seem to bother him.

I lean over to grab the notepad, managing to knock the pen off the nightstand and under the bed in the process. So I crawl onto the floor and fish around. I don't find the pen, but my fingers brush against a bit of silk . . . and a strap. When I tug on it, there's a slight ripping noise, and then I'm holding a slinky black nightgown.

Dropping it onto the pillow, I pull up the stable point I jumped in at—the one facing the bed—and begin scrolling backward, beginning a few hours prior, before Saul started lighting candles to set the mood. Nothing, nothing, nothing. Night, day, night, day. No movement in the place at all for several weeks.

I could be overreacting. It has happened in the past, where Saul's concerned. He could be renting this place furnished for all I know. Maybe it belonged to the last tenant. And even if he is fooling around, would he be stupid enough to give me the stable point facing the damn bed if there was anything I shouldn't see?

But that's the wrong question. He might not be stupid enough, but he's definitely arrogant enough.

And then, between multiple scenes of the bed in the dark and in the sunlight, I see one with candlelight. I stop and scroll back at a slower pace. The black, silky next-to-nothing on the pillow is now inhabited by a young woman with dark, shoulder-length curls. I'm seeing only her back at the moment, with Saul's hands lifting her slim bottom in a steady rhythm. Saul's face is to the stable point, wearing an expression I've seen many, many times. There are no splinters in the room, just the two of them, very much caught in the act. I move forward until she's facing the stable point. She looks familiar, but I can't place a name to the face.

If I confront him, I'm sure he'll point out that he only confirmed I was still around today. He thought it entirely possible that I'd been erased. I couldn't really expect him to be a monk, could I?

And so I scroll forward. Day, night, day, night, day—and there she is. This time it's her bare back, with sunlight streaming in through the windows.

Yes, it's possible that he's not doing his days in sequence here. This could be him at a time *before* he found me. Either way, Saul Rand can go straight to hell. This is not the first time I've caught him cheating. But one way or the other, it will be the last. He's not even getting a note or an explanation. Let him wonder where I went and why.

I pick the black nightgown up with my fingernails and drop it back down into the crevice between the nightstand and the bed. Then I wrap the sheet around me and step onto the balcony, setting a stable point that shows the entire bedroom and another aimed at the yard below, including the plane and the small landing strip.

That's when the dots connect. The woman in the bed is the pilot. The little Nazi who was embedded with America First. Laura something. As I step back into the bedroom and pull the door shut, the shower cuts off. Dragging the sheet behind me, I head into the hallway, where I set more stable points. Three more in the main room downstairs, which is massive. One in the dining room, one in the kitchen, and one at the front door. I'll know when Saul is here and who is with him. Maybe we can figure out what he's really up to.

A tiny voice in my head tells me I'm being unreasonable. Even though Saul is cheating on me, he could still be trying to defeat Team Viper. I know the voice is right. It's not rational to assume that his infidelity to me means he's willing to hand this world over to what is, essentially, an invading army. But my gut tells me it's true, at least to some extent. Saul might not be working for the other side, but I don't believe he's working for us, either. More likely, he's working for himself, and clearly, I'm at most a peripheral element in whatever future he's planning.

Storming out will simply tip him off that I'm suspicious, though. I'll set up a time for our next meeting, and then tell him I need to head back and get some sleep. I'll even kiss the snake goodbye, assuming he's not pouting when I tell him I'm not sleeping over.

"Kathy?" he calls from upstairs. "Where did you go?"

"I'm in the kitchen!" I yell back. "It's now officially Valentine's Day. Please tell me you didn't forget to buy champagne?"

FROM THE *NEW YORK DAILY INTREPID*

ON THE RECORD BY DOROTHY THOMPSON
WHEN VIOLENCE BEGETS VIOLENCE

(February 27, 1940) On February 22nd, at the woefully misnamed "Pro-America Rally," Col. Charles Lindbergh was gravely injured by an attacker, who shot himself before police could apprehend him. This marks the second year in a row that a preventable tragedy has occurred at Madison Square Garden, as thousands of spectators, including hundreds of children, watched. Last year, a woman and her two daughters were crushed in a stairwell by the crowd. Indeed, last night's rally was intended as a memorial to Joan Slater and her daughters, Marta and Eliza. Their pictures hung from banners on both sides of the auditorium—not as large as the massive painting of George Washington, but still a somber reminder, according to Bund leader Fritz

Kuhn, of the violence perpetrated by men of a "lesser race."

I was in that auditorium last year. My decision to laugh openly at the absurd nature of remarks by the Bund leader, by Brother Charles Coughlin, and by others who seek to create a very different kind of America was met, as I expected, with removal from the arena. What I did not expect was for dozens of people to be injured and three to be killed only yards away from where I stood, as crowds stormed through the police barriers to protest their tax dollars being used to protect those who spread hate from facing the anger of those they would erase.

In my column on that event, I predicted that if no culprit could be found, one would be created. I firmly believe this to be the case. The two men in prison for last year's bombing hoax have solid alibis for their whereabouts the day of the rally, having only arrived at the Garden shortly before the crowd stormed the barriers. While the response from city leaders has been measured, the Dies Committee dumped dozens of subpoenas on leftist groups, especially the Communist Party, despite no credible evidence linking either suspect to that organization. Hundreds of people have had their homes raided and their lives upturned as Fascists within our government seized upon flimsy excuses to begin a purge. The fact that many of those targeted are Jewish should surprise no one.

The words spoken from the podium at this year's rally were similar, casting the Jewish people of this nation and of the world as villains and expressing sympathy for the Nazi cause. This year, however, there was a key difference. The tone was slightly moderated, the words a bit more polished, but they were spoken by a candidate for US Senate.

I have made my views on Col. Lindbergh quite clear in this column over the past few years. Likewise, he has been open with his laughable accusation that I am an agent of the British government, intent on dragging this country into war. The attempt on his life last week does not change my view that Lindbergh is a Fascist. While I am glad to learn that he will live to continue his slander against me, I am also glad that he has decided to end his campaign for the Senate. There are too many Nazi sympathizers in positions of power in this nation without adding more to their numbers.

∞22∞

I blink into the stable point on the living room sofa to find a bottle of wine and two glasses on the coffee table in front of me. The lights are low, but someone is in the fully lit room off to the right. I head for the light, both in search of Jack and hoping it will wake me up. I'd very nearly fallen asleep waiting on Katherine to doze off in the other twin bed. I'm pretty sure she was doing the same damn thing. Finally, I decided I couldn't wait any longer, flipped my feet over the side of the bed, and blinked out.

"Jack?" I say, stepping into the kitchen, where he's placing a package of crackers on a plate with some very yellow cheese and dried fruit.

He gives me a hello kiss, and then says, "I'm afraid our appetizer options are rather limited. There's more than enough food in this place to last me for months, but most of it is of the nonperishable variety. The box says this is cheese, but I'm not entirely convinced."

"It's okay," I tell him. "I'm more tired than hungry. The wine sounds good, though. I have a sleeping pill Clio gave me, which she says won't make me groggy, but I'd rather not risk it. I'm thinking I'll try the wine and other natural methods of relaxation first."

I press my body against his with those last words, and he grins. "So that's what I am, hmm? A 'natural method of relaxation'?"

"Well, that and a research assistant," I say as I follow him back into the living room. "Unpaid. Overworked. And speaking of . . . Did you find anything?"

"A CHRONOS key in the crowd that was not attached to you or Tyson," he says as I pour us a glass of wine. "After you left. A tall, thin man. Couldn't really see his face, but I'm pretty sure it was Saul. He's on his own, and he doesn't do anything while he's there, as best I can tell. Just sits in the upper level, on the opposite side from where you and Tyson were. Watches as the Nazi leader—Kuhn, I guess?—starts speaking. A reporter heckles the speaker, and the police escort her out."

"Dorothy Thompson, right?"

"Yes. She has a syndicated column, and she really, really doesn't like Nazis. From what I was reading, she was the first American journalist Hitler kicked out of Germany when he took over. Anyway, she's escorted out just when all hell breaks loose inside the arena. I can't hear anything, obviously, but judging from the reaction, the protestors ram through the police line at the same time people start reacting to the noise of the explosion. Or what they think is an explosion. Here, it will be quicker to just show you. I'll transfer the point back to you, because it will take you forever to find the right one. I now have the relevant points labeled and in folders, by the way, like a good research assistant."

"Remind me to give you a bonus."

"I will definitely do that." He transfers one location to my key. "To be honest, I think this is really the only one you need to see. This is from the edge of the balcony. I tried the one from the main floor, but the view is mostly blocked by people, especially once the chaos begins. Start at 9:47 p.m., and pan slightly left and down."

I follow his instructions, and after a couple of seconds, two police officers come into view with a woman between them. From this angle, I wouldn't have known it was Dorothy Thompson, but they're clearly escorting her toward the exit. Everyone yanks their heads up toward the balcony, almost in unison, and then the police continue moving. Just as they pass the stairs leading up to the balcony, a wave of people, mostly male and mostly young, enters the auditorium. The first group is looking toward the balcony, too, and so I'm guessing they heard the explosion. Maybe those behind them didn't, however, because they push onward down the center and left aisles toward the podium, which I can't see from this observation point.

Another smaller group breaks toward the aisle where the officers and Thompson are standing. Two of the protestors rush the guards, one of whom pushes Thompson into the wall behind him, shielding her. At that instant, people begin pouring out of the stairwell, but one of them, a rather large guy, halts abruptly on the bottom stair.

It's not clear why for a second, and then I see the gun carried by one of the two men who rushed Thompson and the police officers. One of the cops draws his gun in response. The heavyset guy tries to back up into the stairwell, but everyone else is still trying to get out. A mass of bodies slams into him, and he falls facedown onto the floor. Two women land on top of him. One scurries to her feet and dashes for the exit. The other stops and looks behind her, back up the staircase.

"You can't see when they're killed," Jack says. "I even tried the stable points on the staircase, and there are just too many shoving bodies to get a clear view. I see the chubby guy heading down, and then it's just elbows and backs for a bit. Then later, you see the emergency personnel heading up there, and carrying out the three bodies. I think they stumbled, and then other people fell on top of them."

I watch the crowd for a couple of minutes, looking for the guy with the gun and the cop who chased after him, and also for Dorothy Thompson. "She makes it out okay, right?" I'm pretty sure that she does, but I'm still relieved when Jack nods.

"Yeah. The other cop gets her outside. I caught a brief glimpse of her from the stable point outside the auditorium. And her next column was published right on schedule."

"So . . . did it look to you like she was the target?" I ask. "Because it kind of did to me."

"Not the target of most of the people who stormed the gates. They were going after the tin-pot Nazi at the podium . . . who also got away unscathed, of course. But she was definitely the target of the two guys who broke off from the pack. And I'd have been a little suspicious anyway because I started doing some digging on Thompson. She does stop writing, or at least, she stops writing about political events the next year. Her last column is one covering the Republican convention in late June. Her son is home from boarding school, so she agrees to take him to the Fair for the Fourth of July celebration. She was near the Court of Peace when the bomb went off. Received minor injuries from the blast."

"Okay, that doesn't sound like a coincidence to me."

"No, it doesn't," he agrees. "Oh . . . and one more thing about the Bund rally. Saul is standing right at the railing staring down at the scene, until Thompson gets away. Then he just blinks out, right in the middle of a group of people. It's a miracle there wasn't another panic on that side of the auditorium."

"You say you couldn't see his face?" I ask.

"No, but it's definitely a guy, and the build is wrong for Morgen, from what you've said. I suppose it could be one of the observers—"

"I'm not doubting that it was Saul," I tell him. "I'm just wondering *which* Saul."

"Oh," Jack says. "That does not sound good."

Once I catch him up on the pertinent details, Jack shakes his head. "The lighting is too bad for me to say for certain whether he's got the scar, but I haven't checked all of the points on that side of the balcony yet. Once I figured out that it was him, I moved on."

"You didn't know we might be dealing with two . . ." I stop for a yawn. "With two Sauls. I'm pretty sure it's the one from our reality anyway. All of this stuff with Coughlin is apparently his attempt to set the timeline straight, although I have no earthly idea how or why he thought it would help. If we actually manage to reverse the changes the Viper team made to the timeline, we'll still have to deal with the repercussions of what Saul is doing."

"We need to get you to bed," he says, pressing his lips against my hair. "I don't think you're going to require the sleeping pill *or* my natural relaxation techniques."

"Hey, I didn't hire you for your research skills alone, mister." He's right, though. I'm out almost instantly afterward, with no need for Clio's magic pill.

Jack set two alarms before falling asleep, just to be on the safe side, but he still has to nudge me to get my lazy behind moving.

"May 9th," he whispers into my ear.

Curiosity kicks my brain into gear—low gear, admittedly, but at least I'm awake. "That's one of the dates Alex and RJ gave me."

"Yep. It's one they gave me, too."

"How did they give you any information? They can't come here, and you can't go there yet, so . . ."

"Pull up the library on your key, on the morning of the 19th. Then pan around to the wall screen."

"Oh, wow. They're using it as a bulletin board. It's like the doctor, June, did at that beach house at Estero. There was a little board near the door where they left her messages."

At the top are the five dates they gave me. In addition, there are two notes at the bottom.

- *Serum ready.*
- *Tourist name misspelled in paper. It's Tomonaga. Japanese physicist. Super-many-time theory. Come get info.*

"What is a super-many-time theory?" I ask.

Jack laughs. "You are asking the *wrong* housemate. Anyway," he continues, "I'm fairly certain you'll find both Dorothy Thompson and Albert Einstein at the World's Fair on May 9th." He gives me two handwritten sheets of notes.

"Did you sleep at all?"

"Yes, I slept. This was just kind of nagging at me, so I got up for a bit in the middle of the night, and I spent a little time combing through the microfilm newspapers. You need to have Rich and Katherine set stable points at the Jewish Palestine Pavilion and in the General Motors auditorium."

"The first one is on our list. Not sure about the second one, unless that's the Futurama thing?"

"I don't think so. But Dorothy Thompson is the president of the US chapter of PEN, the international writer's organization, in 1939. They're holding a conference at the Fair on May 9th, and the novelist Thomas Mann, a close friend of Einstein, will be speaking. Both he and Einstein fled Germany, and both were teaching at Princeton at the time. I wouldn't be surprised if Einstein took the train in on the day that his friend was giving an address about his hopes that Germany would find its way back to democracy. If you don't catch him at the conference, I suspect he'll stop by to check on the progress of the pavilion. This is just a few weeks before it opens, and Einstein was very much involved in the project. And it's a day that the newspapers don't seem to have highlighted the fact that the famous Professor Einstein was in attendance, so it's a perfect day for the other team to contact him, given that it would be a day we'd be less likely to look."

"Okay. Alex seemed to think May 28th would be Einstein, but . . . maybe it's both? Anyway, I'll be back with the observation points from the fairgrounds later today. And I'll also have the serum, so maybe, maybe you can finish this research at home, and you won't have to deal with microfilm anymore. The food unit at my place isn't great, but at least the cheese doesn't glow in the dark."

He gives me a rueful smile. "Afraid I'll have to stick with Velveeta for a bit longer. As long as I'm here in 1966, you can use and abuse me as needed. I can spend days going through your stable points. If I go home, I'll be on the same schedule you are, and you've got what? Only a little over a day left? I'll try Lorena's science project once we set the timeline straight. And if I still can't jump out, it's not the end of the world. We'll get a cabin across the lake. I've started watching this show called *Days of Our Lives*. Wouldn't mind finding out how it ends."

"I'm not watching anything on that teeny-tiny screen," I tell him. "I'll have Jarvis start combing through archives. We can curl up on the sofa and watch your show in comfort when this is all over. Deal?"

"Deal." He gives me a long kiss, and then says, "You need to go."

I check the timer on my key. He's right. I debate jumping to get the info and the serum from Alex but decide it might be better to send one of the others. They almost certainly have a better understanding of temporal physics than I do, and they'll be far more likely to know what questions to ask Alex. And I need to get back. I'm about fifteen minutes away from everyone waking up to find me missing.

"Oh, crap," I say. "I was about to waltz in and tell everyone all of the great new information I have . . . but I'm supposed to have been asleep in my bed this whole time. I guess I'll be back shortly with one of the others."

"As much as I'd love to see you, it makes more sense to follow Alex's lead. Check the living room stable point at ten a.m. this time, and I'll have your cover story ready. Now, go."

When I arrive back in the bedroom, Katherine is still in her bed, snoring softly. Or maybe she's *back* in her bed, because I'm still fairly sure she left last night. That's based not just on her opposition to the buddy plan, but also on Richard's expression. He clearly knows her better than anyone else, and he didn't believe for one minute that she'd stay put.

I grab my toiletry kit out of my bag and feel around for my hairbrush. It's not in the interior pocket where I left it. I crouch down to look more closely and see that it has tumbled out. That's weird, because I'm almost certain it was in there when I zipped the bag last night. Katherine must have borrowed it. Which isn't a big deal, really, although I'll admit I'm a bit annoyed that she didn't ask . . . and that she didn't put my property back where she found it. I fish the brush out from under the dresser, and then head for the bathroom.

And the bathroom is occupied, so I slump down into the chair in the hallway to wait. The table next to the chair holds a clunky, black rotary-dial telephone and a fat, red telephone directory. A picture of the Trylon and Perisphere from the World's Fair is on the cover. I thumb through while I wait, thinking how much time people must have spent looking up numbers in this era. How many decades was it before you could call someone simply by speaking their name? I'm not at all sure . . . Technology history isn't really my strong suit.

Rich comes out of the bathroom a couple of minutes later. "You should have showered in Skaneateles. The water was barely tepid when I got out."

His tone is more than a little smug, and it's not about using up the hot water, I'm sure. He clearly expects me to ask how he knows I was in Skaneateles, but I ignore his little jab. As I step into the water—which is indeed lukewarm—I'm really, really tempted to jump back a half hour and beat him to the bathroom. We'd both have a double memory, but is that worse than a cold shower?

Yes. It is. And so I resist the temptation and just do a rush job of it. At least the chilly water helps wake me up.

Katherine is now awake and at the table when I enter the kitchen. Her eyes are even more red rimmed and puffy than they were last night. It might just be from sleep, but it looks more like she's been crying again. I cross over to the coffeepot and caution her that she might want to wait until after breakfast to shower unless she likes it chilly. She nods and pours cream into her coffee until it's only a shade or two darker than the cream itself.

Her hair is loose now, rather than the updo she wore the day before. That reminds me of the hat that Thea mentioned, and I tell her that I'll grab it for her on my next jump home.

"Thanks. Do you trust your grandmother?"

"If Thea says you left your hat in Bethesda, I think we can take her at her word."

"That's not what I meant," she says.

I knew it wasn't what she meant. But the question bothers me, possibly because I'm not at all certain that I trust *Katherine*.

"I trust that Thea has my best interests at heart. Why do you ask?"

"Because Thea *Rand*all reminds me of someone," Katherine says. "Quite a bit, actually."

"And who is that?"

"Saul's mother. Dark curls shot through with silver, including that one distinctive streak on the left that looks almost as if someone took a paintbrush to it. Thea is missing Elora Rand's sharp widow's peak, and her nose is a bit wider. But otherwise the similarity is striking. Looking at you, I see no family resemblance to Saul. Maybe a bit to me, but not to him. Clio, on the other hand, looks quite a lot like him, so I'm thinking maybe there are some things you haven't told me in regard to her lineage. And your grandmother—if you put her next to Saul's mother, people might not think they were twins, but they'd definitely say they were sisters. And the reason I asked if you trust her is because Elora Rand doesn't strike me as particularly trustworthy."

I'm tempted to point out that it's rather prejudicial to assume that a physical resemblance means that Thea also inherited her grandmother's personality traits. But that would require me to get into a lot of details that I really don't have time to explain. And I get the sense that this is more about Katherine wanting those details than it is about Thea. Which I totally understand, but she's going to have to wait. "When this is over, Katherine. Come talk to me when this is over, and I'll tell you everything you want to know. About Clio, about Thea. All of it. We can even go ask Thea some questions together if you like, because there are quite a few things I'm not clear on. I dug up that damn CHRONOS key only a little over a week ago. I need answers, too."

She's silent for a moment and then says, "Fair enough. But, since we're on the buddy system, would you mind accompanying me to Detroit for a few minutes after I shower? I agreed to check in with Saul. He may have some useful information."

I doubt that, but I keep the opinion to myself. And as tempted as I am to point out that she's partnered with Richard today, I know she probably has reasons for not wanting Rich along for the ride. I've never met her version of Saul. Based on Tyson's and Richard's opinions of him, I'm not missing anything, but I do have a bit of morbid curiosity, given all that I've read about him in Katherine's and Kate's diaries. And now, I also have a couple of questions I want to ask him, even though the sane portion of my brain isn't exactly keen on meeting a future mass murderer. Or possibly a current mass murderer, depending on whether he's killed the people in that little village in Georgia.

I tell her sure and pour a bowl of something called *Wheaties*. While I'm reading the back of the box, Clio, Tyson, and Rich come in.

"Did you know that Abraham Lincoln got word he won the presidential nomination while on a baseball field?" I ask, turning the box around to show them. "I'm used to having the food unit just spit cereal out into a bowl. You don't get a history lesson along with it."

Clio yawns. "You'd seriously trade your Jarvis device for a cereal box?"

"Well, no," I admit. "But it's still kind of cool."

Once everyone is settled with their food, I make a show of pulling out my key to check stable points. When I pull up the Dunnes' living room at the time Jack gave me, I find him sitting on the couch. He holds up a sheet of paper with a smiley face drawn on the back, and then pulls it away to reveal a sheet that directs me to check stable point 162 on my key at 9:47 last night. A second note reads: *Dorothy Thompson injured; Court of Peace Jul 4th*. The final note says: *May 9th, Einstein (?) and Dorothy Thompson at Fair*.

I relay some of this to the others as they eat, along with what was on the bulletin board back in the library. Richard's eyebrow is arched so high that it looks like it's going to pop off his forehead, but he doesn't actually question how I got the new info.

"The bulletin-board thing's not a bad idea," Katherine says as she puts her coffee cup in the sink. "When we visit Saul, I'll get him to set up something similar."

"Which of you knows the most about temporal physics?" I ask. "Because that's who should make the next jump to the library."

"Rich," Katherine and Tyson say in unison.

"Well, it's definitely not me," Clio says. "Super-many-time theory? That sounds like something from a comic book."

"I'm not familiar with that *particular* theory," Rich says. "Or with Tomonaga. But yeah. I'll go. I wanted to see what I could find on Josephson's brother anyway."

We check the time on our keys and find out that we're all within ten minutes of each other. My clock has the least time left, with twenty-five hours and thirteen minutes, which means I need to be more careful about getting back here on time. Tyson has about three minutes more. After a bit of basic math, we figure out how long we have for our various information-gathering trips and agree to meet back here in three hours.

After Katherine heads to the shower, I tell the others the one bit of information I held back—that Jack thinks Saul was at the rally watching when Dorothy Thompson was targeted.

"But which Saul?" Clio asks.

"Good question," I say. "I think we have to assume that it's the one from our reality, given the new alliance between Coughlin, Dennis, and the Bund. Maybe Rich can ask Alex if there are any clear bubbles in Manhattan last night."

"We know there were three a few miles away from the rally," Tyson says. "Alisa, Esther, and Marcy at Café Society. But maybe he can tell you if there were any others."

"But why would they target Thompson?" I ask. "Is she that big of a deal?"

Clio laughs. "Uh . . . *yeah*. She's a very, very big deal. Thompson is sort of the anti-Coughlin. She's not just a writer, but also has a radio show. Millions of listeners. She's the one who took up the case of that kid who shot the German diplomat and gave the Nazis an excuse for launching Kristallnacht. My mom gets annoyed at her. Says she's a hawk, whatever that means. But she still listens. And even Mom doesn't fault her for being a hawk about the Nazis. She says you can be antiwar and still think there are exceptions. And Dorothy Thompson has been warning people that we're probably going to have to fight fascism in Europe for several years now. She's one of the strongest voices in favor of the US joining the war. *Time* magazine did a big article on her . . . Or maybe they haven't done it yet. Anyway, she's on the cover. They say she's the second most influential woman in America—after Eleanor Roosevelt. You studied writers and you haven't heard of Dorothy Thompson?"

I bristle slightly, but just say, "I mostly study fiction writers. And yes, I'd heard her name. But nothing to suggest she was that important. Does she continue writing after the war in our timeline?"

Clio shrugs. "I'm not sure. Most of my time after 1945 has been in theaters and baseball stadiums. I mean, I see the covers of magazines at the newsstands, but I usually try to steer clear of too much news, since I'd really like to go back to living a linear life one day. It would be nice to have a few surprises."

"Well," I say, "the way things are going right now, you may get your wish."

"True. But I'd prefer to have that life *not* be in some sort of fascist dystopia. My mom just always seemed to be thinking about the next crisis coming up and whether we were safe and how she could help those who wouldn't be safe. Then she'd start second-guessing herself, saying maybe she *shouldn't* help because it might break something. And on that note, I'm going to go get dressed so that I can sit on the sofa and *not help* all day."

"You're watching stable points," Tyson says. "That's help."

"Which Jack can do better because he has pretty much unlimited time," she says. "I could do more out there."

Tyson exchanges a look with me and then says to her, "You're helping, Clio. And you heard what Morgen said. They consider you fair game. If they'll take out one of their own observers for a minor infraction, I don't think they'd be above killing you or using you as leverage to distract us. And the same is true for your father. You might want to call and tell him to just stay in Skaneateles."

"We have an agreement. No contact with them until we jump forward to July 1940. He'll show up here the night before the bombing. Otherwise, he's going to have double memories. But . . . I could call him that afternoon. No sense in him traveling all this way to be stuck in the apartment with yours truly."

Richard, who had gone out to grab his backpack, pops his head in and says, "I'll add Dorothy Thompson to my list of things to ask your Jarvis. Anything else? Oh, and perhaps one of you would like to come with me so that we can keep up the buddy charade?"

"We need the serum for Jack," I say. "And I agreed to go with Katherine, so . . ."

Tyson says, "I'll be right behind you." Once Rich blinks out, he adds, "God, he's in a pissy mood this morning."

"Yeah. That might be my fault, at least partially. I didn't follow the buddy rules last night. I'd already arranged to meet Jack back at the Dunnes' place. Not sure how Rich knows I skipped out, but . . . Anyway, speaking of the buddy system, do you actually want me with you at the Universal Front meeting?"

"No. The UF meetings will be men only. While there might be a female auxiliary, I doubt they meet at the same time. But . . . Rich pointed out last night that there might be a little problem with me going undercover right now." He taps the corner of his eye with one finger. For a moment, I don't follow, but then I realize that as a new recruit, he'd probably be under fairly close scrutiny, and without the blue contacts, people might actually have questions about his race.

"So what's the game plan?" I ask.

"Looks like we're going to the Fair. Katherine and Rich can still set the main observation points in the areas where we know we'll need to make changes, but we can check out Einstein and the Japanese tourists. Thompson, too. Something is off about that entire thing to me. I mean, pre-World War Two isn't my primary era. I've only made a few training jumps here, and then that one day trip to see Lawrence Dennis. But I know a *lot* about the period between the late 1950s and the early 2000s. And like you, I'd heard the name, but I couldn't have told you exactly who she was. Admittedly, it's a fairly generic name, but I certainly wouldn't have thought of her as someone with that kind of political power."

"Do you think Thompson's influence is something that's been changed? Maybe by Saul, like he did with the Cyrists?"

"Maybe."

"Speaking of Saul, I'm assuming that I shouldn't ask him about whether he was at the rally last night?"

Tyson is quiet for a moment and then shakes his head. "If I felt like he was actually working with us, actually trying to set the timeline right, then I'd say yes. But I don't think we want to tip our hand that we suspect he's doing anything other than exactly what he claims to be doing. Just . . . be on alert, okay? And if you get a chance to set some stable points, take it. We need to keep an eye on him."

I sigh. "Which means Jack is going to be stuck in 1966 for a bit longer. He might finish watching that *Days of Our Lives* show after all."

FROM THE *NEW YORK*

DAILY INTREPID

50,000 ATTEND DEDICATION OF JEWISH PALESTINE PAVILION; EINSTEIN PRAISES FAIR

(May 29, 1939) Albert Einstein, renowned physicist, a leader of the nation's Jewish community, and its most famous German refugee, spoke yesterday at the dedication ceremony for the Jewish Palestine Pavilion, noting that the World's Fair "is in a way a reflection of mankind, its work and aspirations. But it projects the world of man like a wishful dream. Only the creative forces are on show, none of the sinister and destructive ones, which today more than ever jeopardize the happiness, the very existence of civilized humanity."

Yesterday marked the largest paid attendance to date since the Fair opened, despite record-breaking heat. Vehicles from many different states filled the parking lots as people arrived not merely to see the Fair and the Jewish Palestine Pavilion but also in protest of the British government's recent release of a White Paper on Palestine, widely viewed as a repudiation of the Balfour Declaration and its stated goal of creating a permanent home for the Jewish people.

As many as 100,000 people crowded into the Court of Peace to hear the dedication speeches by the mayor, Mr. Grover Whalen (president of the World's Fair), and Professor Einstein, who summed up the view of many in attendance, stating that "England has, in part, ignored its sacred pledge. Remember, however, that in the life of a people and especially in times of need, there can be only one source of security, namely: confidence in one's own strength and steadfastness. There could be no greater calamity than a permanent discord between us and the Arab people."

∞23∞

TYSON
BETHESDA, DC
NOVEMBER 19, 2136

"Yeah," Alex says as he follows my gaze toward the giant countdown clock, where the current reading is 23:59:06 and counting. "It makes me nervous, too. I tried turning the screen off, but it popped right back up and gave me a warning about non-team members staying away from the console."

"I was more wondering about the mirrors and the noise," I tell him, nodding toward the four mirrored doors that are propped up against each other, forming a wall around the SimMaster. In addition, the library, which is usually quiet, is now buzzing with several different variants of white noise emanating from a speaker near the simulation machine, but also at lower levels from the house intercom. "It sounds like we're in the middle of a restaurant located under a waterfall in the middle of a thunderstorm."

"Yeah," he says. "I can keep the sim machine from getting into my data, but I'm still a bit worried that we're being recorded. Too bad it's not old school like the display for the Anomalies Machine. We could toss a blanket over it and reduce the anxiety."

The Anomalies Machine brings its *own* form of anxiety, however. While there are no large red numbers counting down our impending doom, the differences between our current timeline and the one we'd like to return to keep scrolling past on the display.

Richard blinked in a couple of minutes before I did, and he's looking at several photographs on the wall screen. "Leon was a bit camera shy," he says, "but I found this from the contempt-of-Congress trial when he was sentenced for refusing to testify before your old friend HUAC."

"Back when the House's idea of un-American activities was confined to communists, rather than including the Klan, I guess."

"Unfortunately," Rich says, "I also found this." An entirely different picture pops up. The man is about the same age, but much better looking.

"Definitely not the same guy. So which one is right?"

"If I had to guess, I'd say the first one, since it's a bit closer to the appearance of his brother, and we have a ton of photos of Barney. But the second picture was used in several online histories of the trial. I'd chalk it up to his hobby of passport falsification. That seems to have been almost as popular an FBI excuse for bringing suspects in as tax evasion, except you change the name, not the photo. Josephson was almost certainly a spy, though. He was apparently part of a Soviet plan to assassinate Hitler in the mid-1930s. But my brain kept trying to make a connection to something else. I kept hearing that Billie Holiday song 'Strange Fruit.' You know it, right?"

"Yeah. I um . . . kind of heard her sing it when I was at Café Society."

Rich shakes his head. "Seriously, Tyce? While I was freezing my ass off in Detroit listening to an egomaniac priest, you're in a club listening to Billie fucking Holiday. Which sucks double, because if we do go there, it will have to be before the club opens, and I still won't get to hear her in person. Leon was the moneyman, so he was around a lot more during the start-up phase. Anyway, getting back to my point, that song kept sticking in my head. I shrugged it off because I couldn't really see why a song about lynching would have anything to do with our current situation, but then Jarvis pops up the info about the club, and I see the name Abel Meeropol. He's the guy who wrote the song. And he also ended up raising the kids of two people who were executed for trafficking in nuclear secrets."

"The Rosenbergs?" I ask.

"Yup. Which proves absolutely nothing where either of the Josephson brothers are concerned. I'm not going to start down the path of drawing elaborate webs of conspiracy like that Dilling woman Katherine talked to in Detroit—while *you* were in a club drinking beer and watching Billie Holiday."

"And also nearly getting killed in the alley. I think I'd have rather dealt with cold weather and the egomaniac priest."

He gives me a point-taken nod. "Fair enough. Anyway, I'm not saying that the Josephsons are traitors or whatever simply because they knew the guy who was a friend of the Rosenbergs well enough to help him launch his very controversial song, or because the club was frequented by communists. But there were rumors that Leon was involved in trying to get nuclear secrets to the Soviets. I don't know how much of that was true and how much was J. Edgar Hoover's imagination. Still, I think there's a decent chance Team Viper would have seen this and decided Leon Josephson might be a good person to pull into their scheme to pass information along, either to Einstein or to this physicist Tomonaga. Josephson is tangentially related, but maybe offbeat enough that they get a few extra probability points."

"But if Josephson was trafficking secrets to the USSR," I say, "why would he give anything to the Japanese? They were on the opposite end of the political spectrum at this point, right? The only way that makes sense to me is if he was a mercenary."

"I'm pretty sure he was a true believer," Rich says. "But Alex has a theory on that."

"Jack knows more about this than I do," Alex says, "since he does a lot of military history. So you might want to check with him for details. But I do know this would be around the same time as the nonaggression pact. Stalin's whole reason for going into that was to get the capitalist powers all fighting each other, while he stood on the sidelines and watched them wipe each other out. And Josephson doesn't have the benefit of knowing that Japan is going to attack the US. In 1939, they were still professing eternal friendship. That was even true the next summer. It's pretty much the entire point of the Japan Day ceremony where the Japanese ambassador is shot at."

I sink down onto the couch and rub my forehead. "How does this physicist . . . Tomonaga? And the super-time theory. How does all of that fit in?"

"Super-*many*-time theory," Alex says. "It's complicated, but the short version is that it's a quantum electrodynamics theory connected to renormalization." He pauses, scanning our faces for a sign that we're following. I don't know what he gets from Rich, but I'm pretty sure my own expression conveys that he lost me somewhere around *quantum*. "Basically, Dr. Tomonaga proposed that every point in space has its own clock, or its own time. Which builds a bridge of sorts between quantum field theory and Einstein's theory of relativity. Tomonaga was studying in Germany when the war broke out. He's on his way back to Japan when he stops for a day at the Fair. The other guy with him was a fellow student. And here's the interesting catch—Tomonaga was studying under Heisenberg." He waits, apparently expecting a reaction. "Heisenberg? Werner Heisenberg?"

"I'm remembering something about an uncertainty principle," Rich says.

"But are you certain?" I ask. Both of them give me a look that suggests I should probably just stay out of this.

"He was in charge of the Nazis' nuclear weapons research," Alex says. "He actually ended up telling them it wasn't doable with the resources they had, and there's some speculation that it was a principled decision on his part because he didn't really want the Nazis to win. But at any rate, Tomonaga would have been well positioned to get any information about nuclear weapons into the hands of people who might understand the ramifications."

I leave them to discuss the details of this and go downstairs to see if I can locate Lorena and get this serum she's been working on. As I head down the curved staircase, I instead find Thea and the baby, whose name I can't remember, both seated on the tile floor of the foyer. Thea stacks a small red cup-shaped block on top of a tower of three other colored blocks.

"Your turn, Yun Hee!" she says to the baby, who reaches out with her chubby hands and sends the tower crashing to the floor. "Yay!" Thea says enthusiastically as the baby claps her hands. "Good job. And now it's my turn."

I sit on the bottom step and watch them for a moment until Thea looks up. "Aren't you supposed to be fixing the timeline?" she asks. "Is Madi with you?"

"No. She'll probably make the next trip. And yes, we're working on fixing it. I just need to find Lorena and . . . RJ?" I hesitate, not certain I have the name correct.

"They're having sex," Thea says. "Lorena has been very stressed, getting this serum finished, and she doesn't know if it will work. I offered to watch the baby."

"Okay," I tell her. "I need to talk to you for a moment anyway. The rules say that all team members must contribute, and while I think that watching the little one here is indeed a contribution . . . I'm not sure that the SimMaster 8560, or whatever model they've got hooked up in there, will agree on that point. And we're going to be spread a bit thin trying to get our moves accomplished quickly and in the right order anyway. So do you think you could watch a specific stable point through your key and then enter the moves into the system?"

"I can certainly try," she says cheerily.

Given everything that's on the line, I'd much prefer to have her say that it will be a snap. But it seems like a truthful answer, even if it's not exactly a comforting one.

"After all," she adds, "I'm here to help. In *The Verses of Prudence*, it tells us to watch for the signs to appear within the 'Chapter of Prudence' in *The Book of Prophecy*. And then the Chosen Sister must take her place and follow the guidance of the One. *The Verses* have been handed down to each group of Sisters, from the Alpha to the current three."

"So . . . you were chosen to come here because of something in *The Book of Prophecy*?"

"No," she says. "I am chosen because of Madi. The 'Chapter of Prudence' merely gave us the sign of the change, and now I must follow *The Verses*."

"The verses in the 'Chapter of Prudence' from *The Book of Prophecy*?"

Thea laughs. "No! Our *Verses* are not *in* the 'Chapter of Prudence.' *The Verses* are the testament and decree of the Sister. The *Book* and Chapter are handed down from the Templars," she says with a dismissive wave of her hand. "And they hide most of it anyway. But they will never hear *The Verses*. We are the keepers. We do not write. We only speak."

I nod, pretending to understand the word salad she just dished up, and tell her that I'm going to go in search of a drink. I'm now really feeling that we need a backup plan for entering the moves into the system. We'll have to let her do something, since the rules seem to say all team members must participate, but I'm reluctant to put too much responsibility in her hands, given that her cognitive skills seem a bit sketchy, to say the least. Although Madi might be a better judge of how much she can handle.

The kitchen is a disaster zone, with beakers and vials in the sink and papers stacked on the island area in the center of the room. "Jarvis, is there alcohol in this place?"

"Yes. The cabinet by James Coleman's desk in the library contains a partial bottle of vodka, an almost full bottle of gin, a bottle of rum—"

"That's okay," I say. "The gin sounds good."

"Perhaps. Mistress pronounced it *nasty* on the one occasion she sampled it."

"Guess we'll see."

I grab a couple of small glasses from a shelf near the sink and head back up to the library, sidestepping Thea and the baby, who are still playing their game. As it turns out, there are already several shot glasses on top of the cabinet. I pour a few fingers of gin into one of them and discover that Madi's assessment isn't wrong.

"Do you want one?" I ask Rich.

He frowns. "No. It's still morning."

I glance at the windows, which are dark, and he says it's morning for *him*, pointing out that alcohol and Wheaties probably won't combine well in my stomach.

True. But I'm hoping the gin will untangle my brain after my conversation with Thea just now. "What is that?" I ask, nodding at a new addition to Alex's cluster of displays. Three of them are still covered with the dots he's been using to display chronotron pulses, but one is now covered with what looks like wires.

"These are trace chronotron pulses," he says. "There was a filter in place to get rid of noise in the system. I decided that might be cloaking some data points, so I dialed the filter back and set up a subroutine to isolate and catalog them. Based on the early results, I decided to amplify those signals in a separate program."

"Yeah . . . but what *is* it?" I ask. "I mean, what do the bundles represent?"

"Signals from alternate universes. Or, at least, that's my theory."

Many of the lines are part of a massive tangle at the top of the display. Others are grouped, clamped together at one end the way you'd tie off old-school electrical wires, although most of these bundles are fatter. On the left side of the screen, the bundles are clear, and they remind me a bit of cellophane noodles. On the right side, the bundles are colored wires, lined up in a spectrum from vivid to faint and back to vivid. The colored bundles are labeled alphabetically, ranging from A to Q, and the brightest, most vibrant group near the middle is labeled H. It's also the narrowest of the colored bundles, with just seven colored strands. It's different from the others in another way, too. A–G and I–Q are perfectly smooth lines, but H has tiny little projections that shoot off and then disappear, like split ends on a hair.

As we watch, a clear wire from the tangled mass at the top separates and joins one of the clear bundles on the right.

"Of course, this is a simplification and a bit of a misrepresentation, because I need to view them separately right now." Alex flicks the screen with his finger to shift to another view where the wires all start as a single massive cord and then unravel into hundreds of separate threads. "This is a more accurate picture of the paths. I got the idea from a book I was reading, and also from the signal I picked up here in the house on the occasions when Madi spun off a splinter."

Rich points toward the one marked H. "That's us, right? 47H. That's what Morgen called us."

Alex nods. "As much as I hate to take his label, it's a starting point. I have our signal as the baseline. This is a really rough analogy, but you can think of it as similar to pitch, with the earlier letters being the lower notes and the later ones higher. Carrying the analogy further, there may be others in our group, as well, but their 'pitch' is either too low or too high for me to measure. And here's where the analogy breaks down, because I don't know what you'd call the little spurs from the splinters."

Rich shrugs. "Reverb, maybe? Or an echo. Why don't the others have those?"

"They most likely do," Alex says. "I'm just not able to drill down in enough detail to measure them. Or at least, not yet."

"The colors are the same as the ones on the other displays," I say, nodding toward the one next to us. "Are the lines just another way to show that data?"

"Yes. *Some* of the data points," he says, clicking the purple strand in the *H*-bundle, which has a few of the feathery offshoots, mostly at the end. "This is you." He clicks the amber strand, which is much shorter, with a similar number of splinter strands. "Madi." And then he clicks the dark-red strand, which is longer than the other two, and has dozens, maybe even as many as a hundred, of red tendrils, most of them near the end. Some appear to be thinner than others. The effect is a bit like a frayed red shoelace.

"Saul has been busy," Rich says. "So . . . what's the end goal of all this?"

"Finding a way to keep Team Viper out. At least, that's what I'm aiming at. But I have less data for the clear variants. Right now, I'd be glad just to be able to pinpoint which cluster Team Viper belongs to. At least then we could let them know that they are seen, if you get my drift. They *might* have a way of blocking outsiders from coming in, but so far, I'm not picking up anything that is similar to the sort of interference I would, personally, use to block their entry. So it's possible that they were arrogant enough to break into our house without bothering to lock their own door. And I need one of you to try something for me. Thea's the only one here who can use the key, and I tried it with her, but let's just say the response was a little garbled."

Alex reaches over to the far side of his desk and retrieves a key that's inside a device that keeps it activated. He flips it over. "As you can see from the hyphen in CHRO-NOS, this is one of the keys we um . . . captured . . . from their observers." He grimaces slightly, clearly thinking about what the loss of the keys cost those observers, and then goes on. "Anyway, as I noted before, the key was fine for maintaining the protective field around the house, but it was on a slightly different frequency. That got me to thinking about why the frequency might be different. I had Madi transfer a stable point to this key earlier and made some minor adjustments. Thea said the location is this room and that there were books, but then she sort of went off on a tangent."

Rich activates the key. "So, what time do you want me to check?"

"Now," Alex says. "This exact time."

"Okay. What am I looking for?"

"If I'm right, you'll know," he says.

After a moment, Rich says, "Damn." He hands me the key and says, "Pan around to the right."

There are only seven stable points on the key, including the last one, which is the stable point we arrived at on the other side of the library. Only I can tell almost immediately that it's not quite the same. It's still the library, but the faint orange glow from the bookcases is missing. The furniture is different. And when I reach the spot where we're currently standing, we're not here. There's something that might be a computer on a desk near the back wall, but Alex's displays are entirely missing.

"Is this one of those different realities?" I ask, nodding back at the display.

"If I'm right," Alex says, "it's their reality. That's the default for this key."

"That's excellent work," I say.

He shrugs. "Still can't say which of these universes it's connected to, so the odds are extremely small that anything I have here will come to fruition while there's still time on the countdown. Even if, by some miracle, it does, that wouldn't tell us how to evict them. And it doesn't address the Saul issue. I mean, I don't know him, but I don't get the sense that he's the type to just amble placidly back into his corral at the end of the day."

"He's not," Richard says. "You've got enough to focus on, though. Like Tyson said, this is really good work."

Alex colors slightly, and shrugs again. "Some version of me is apparently the idiot who broke a perfectly good space-time continuum into this." He nods toward the tangled display of the time cables. "I have an obligation to fix it. It would be easier if we had one of their people here to activate the key, though. I might be able to match the frequency. It's like what I was explaining to Rich just before you walked in. Some information, like the colors, isn't encoded in the key. It's encoded in the person *using* the key. The chronotron particles are released when the key reads their genetic signature, and that's part of the information included in the packet. That's why Saul's dot still shows as red, even though he's using a key that reads *CHRO-NOS*. And that's how we can tell that it was the Saul from this timeline who was at Madison Square Garden watching the brawl on February 20, 1939, not the Team Viper version."

"Good to know." I'm not sure whether it's good news or bad that our own rogue agent is behind all of this. Did he get Lawrence Dennis to set up the fake explosion? And why was he targeting a journalist? Either way, I guess it is still good to *know*. Any information is better than working in a vacuum.

"I was just about to ask Alex how much he can narrow down the exact location of those dots," Rich says. "That could make a huge difference in terms of the number of observation points we need to set, and how many your buddy in 1966 will have to monitor."

"The closest I can drill down to with any degree of accuracy is a square kilometer." Alex taps something on the screen, and a map of the fairgrounds is layered below the current display. "So I could tell you, for example, that most of the activity on September 12th is in the Amusement Zone, since that falls in one sector." He flicks through several screens, and then adds, "On the rest of the dates, most of the activity is on the other side. Not sure how helpful that is."

"It tells us that Tomonaga wasn't spending his time at the science exhibits, so that's something," I say. "I'd have been hunting for locations dealing with advances in physics or whatever."

"Hmph. Then you'd have been hunting in vain," Alex says. "To be honest, there wasn't a lot for serious scientists in the main exhibits. RJ says it's mostly just gadgets, like that giant robot. The latest in home appliances. It focused primarily on ways people were turning science into commercial products. They did have a science advisory committee. Einstein was the honorary chair, in fact. But it was added once most of the planning had already taken place."

"So, you've been looking through the maps, right?" Richard says. "You have a decent idea what this Fair had to offer. What would *you* visit in the Amusement Zone? I mean, you're the closest thing we have to a 1930s Japanese graduate student in physics."

"I guess that's true, since I can tick off two of those four boxes. If I could pick a date, I'd go in July of 1939, because RJ was reading that they had the world's first science-fiction convention. Isaac Asimov, Ray Bradbury, and a bunch of others were there. But if I was in Tomonaga's position, and I had to go on that specific day, I'd probably check out the music shows. And I'd check out that Theater of Time and Space. As best we can figure out, it was a simulated rocket ride."

"He'd also visit the Salvador Dalí exhibit," says RJ, who has just entered the library with Lorena and the baby. "The one with the naked girls. For educational purposes, of course. Just to see what was considered risqué in 1939."

Lorena pulls a hypospray container from her pocket and hands it to me. "Give this to Madi to deliver to Jack. No clue whether it will work, but if not, I've got some other ideas."

"I also come bearing gifts," RJ says, handing me a small bag. "Two FBI badges. The fabricator isn't exactly cutting edge, and they definitely wouldn't hold up to scrutiny today, but they look pretty decent, if I do say so myself. I think they'll be fine for the 1930s, and they may come in handy for getting people to talk to you."

Rich snorts. "Not at Café Society. But yeah, they may be useful at the Fair. Why only two?"

"I didn't bother with badges for Madi and Katherine because nobody would buy that they were FBI back then. But so they don't feel left out, there are also several CHRONOS-field extenders in the bag, like this." He pulls back his sleeve to reveal a plastic tube filled with purple light. "Although I guess these are mostly gifts from Alex, aside from me printing out the casing and using the key down in the basement to charge them."

"They should be considered backup only," Alex says. "Eight hours, tops, and I wouldn't trust them more than a hundred yards from a CHRONOS field. But maybe they will prevent any of our people from being erased the way Madi said they erased your friend."

Thea, who is now at the door, says, "Oh, wait. Don't go yet. I have something for Madi, too." She hurries off down the hall.

"Is she . . . okay?" I ask Lorena, nodding toward Thea's retreating back. "I mean, mentally?"

Lorena makes a little *comme ci, comme ça* gesture. "She's okay enough that I trust her to keep an eye on my baby for a half hour, *with* Jarvis monitoring. Her heart seems to be in the right place. I wouldn't, however, trust her to handle anything complex."

"That's not exactly comforting. The rules say each team member has to contribute, and I think that means she and Clio will both need to enter at least one of the three moves. But you guys have override powers. I think it's probably better to have the right moves entered by the wrong person than the reverse."

"I wouldn't guarantee that," Rich says. "Either one of them might get us disqualified entirely."

Thea must not have had to go far, because she returns with a computer tablet, which she hands to Richard, who sticks it into his bag, along with the tablet of relevant newspaper articles that RJ assembled.

"That's for Madi," Thea says. "I did what she told me to do. I wrote it all down and it's mostly in order. Plus, *The Verses* and what I remember of the Chapter. Maybe it will help her understand. And now I'm going downstairs for a swim. Would anyone care to join me?"

We all decline, citing work and nodding toward the timer. Thea's face falls.

"Actually, maybe Yun Hee and I will join you," Lorena says. "We'll be down shortly. We just need to get into our *swimsuits*." It's clear from Lorena's voice that she's not exactly eager, and I'm not sure why she puts such strong emphasis on the last word, but Thea doesn't seem to notice.

"Oh, wonderful!" she says. "That makes me happy. It's so much more fun with friends." When she reaches the door, she turns back. "Tell my granddaughter that she needs to come home. I travel all this way to visit, and I've hardly even gotten to see her."

"She'll be home soon," I say, nodding toward the timer. "At some point before that hits zero."

But Thea is already heading down the hall.

"I can take June Bug down and join Thea at the pool," RJ says, taking the baby from Lorena. "You went yesterday. Come on, sweetie. Let's go splash."

An amused smile spreads across Lorena's face as he heads to the door with the baby.

Alex glances at his cousin's retreating figure. "So . . . what's that all about?"

"Oh, nothing," Lorena says. "Just wondering how RJ will react when he discovers that Madi's grandmother prefers to swim au naturel."

FROM *THE VERSES OF PRUDENCE*

Hail, Daughters of Prudence, we Sisters of the
  Word.
Templars keep their secrets, and so ours shall
  be heard
From lips of Sisters only into a Sister's ear,
Until the Scourge returns and trusted others
  hear.
Those who sought to stop him had but a partial
  win.
Time is not a circle, but circles round again.

∞24∞

KATHERINE
NEW YORK, NEW YORK
OCTOBER 24, 1939

I pull the map out of my handbag and stare at it for a moment before handing it to Rich. "Okay . . . Town of Tomorrow is here," I say, tapping the neighborhood of model homes that housed one of the two existing stable points for this World's Fair. "So, we turn left?"

He tilts it counterclockwise a few degrees to line it up with the Trylon and Perisphere, the large spire and orb that sit at the other end of the fairgrounds. It's one of those campy, hand-drawn maps with little illustrations of the various exhibits, many of which are now obscured by the large red dots that Tyson, or maybe Alex, drew to indicate locations where Rich and I need to set stable points today.

"Looks like a left here, and then another left around the fountain will take us to the British Pavilion," he says. "And we'll probably have five minutes to kill before the tour that gets us close to where the briefcase was found in the original timeline."

He hands the map back, and I fold it along the creases, but apparently not along all of the creases or at least not along the *right* creases, because it's now twice as thick as it was before. "God. I hate these stupid things. They never fold up right, and they're always badly drawn."

Rich chuckles. "I'd have thought you were used to them by now, given how many Fairs like this you've attended."

"It was more multiple jumps to just the one Fair in Chicago," I say, "and I only had to wrestle with the map once. After that I pulled up locations on my retinal screen. But even that was mostly for the schedule of events. By the time we made our first jump there, I had the entire layout memorized."

"So you're experiencing a fair like an actual tourist, for once," he says.

It's a good point, and one I hadn't really considered. Our goals at CHRONOS have always been twofold in a sense. If we simply wanted data, we could get that remotely. That was the process, after all, before the two halves of the agency merged. They left small recording devices, both audio and video, in strategic locations, and historians watched those if they had questions that couldn't be answered definitively by traditional historical methods, or even, in many cases, to prove that traditional methods had gotten history very, very wrong. We still do remote monitoring, on occasion, at locations where it would be difficult to gain access for security reasons or where events are relatively small and popping in to view them from multiple perspectives would mean encountering ourselves and triggering double memories. But the goal of the Natural Observation Society—the NOS in CHRONOS—was to ensure that we understood the nuances that can only be captured by living through similar experiences, or experiencing them *naturally*. Folding that stupid map back in 1893 was frustrating, but it's a frustration that other tourists had to go through on a regular basis.

"Point taken," I say. "Perhaps I would have understood the people I encountered better if I hadn't taken the easier path with fewer annoyances. That doesn't give me any qualms about dispensing with the map this time, though. This isn't my era, and it's most certainly *not* my World's Fair."

"Better or worse?" Richard asks.

"Mostly worse. It definitely *smells* worse."

That's primarily because there are cars everywhere. The Fair that Saul and I pretty much camped out at for six months last year, and to which we're scheduled to return in a few months, had an elevated railroad that circled part of the fairgrounds. It had gondolas to carry you along the canals, an automated sidewalk, and even a giant Ferris wheel that offered a bird's-eye view of the entire Expo. But there were only a handful of automobiles, and the majority of them were electric. I was one of the many thousands of people who took a ride in a six-seater electric vehicle that circled the interior of the massive Electricity Building.

If there are any electric vehicles at this fair, I haven't spotted them. I have, however, spotted dozens of the internal-combustion variety, many of them circling about on the Road of Tomorrow that runs through and up onto the roof of the Ford Building. Grand Central Parkway runs through this fair, as do several other highways, and the air is thick with gasoline fumes.

Thinking of Saul pulls up the image of last night. His stunt double. The damn nightgown. But I shove the thoughts away and answer Rich's question.

"The clothing is definitely less restrictive than it was in 1893, except costuming would have made sure that I had functional pockets and a bag that would actually close even with this ridiculous map inside. This fair seems less crowded, too. I think it's on a bigger plot of land."

"Maybe. But the crowds are usually much worse than this," Rich says. "That's why Tyson picked today. It's one of the days when attendance was relatively low, according to the calendar Clio's parents left in the folder. And since our only goal is setting observation points in the areas we'll need to monitor, the fewer people the better. The only thing going on today is some sort of coal convention and the Mardi Gras parade over in the Amusement Zone. But you probably missed that discussion when you and Madi were in Detroit."

"Well, either way, having fewer people around is a huge plus. I suspect that the food is better here than at the Expo, too. Or at least safer. But I think I'll pass on the jellied gumbo." This is a very purposeful attempt on my part to switch the subject. We both skimmed through a folder that included menus, along with news clippings, flyers, and other ephemera, and I expect that Rich will go off on some of the more oddly named dishes, like scrod or rarebit.

But he doesn't, because he's clearly got something on his mind. Madi and I spent about a half hour this morning at the new Cyrist temple, the Shrine of the Lotus Flower, a few weeks after its opening. It was the time and place that Saul and I agreed on for our meeting before I left last night, so he was expecting us. When we popped in, he feigned surprise—overfeigned it, to be honest—at the fact that I wasn't alone, but since Madi hadn't met him before, I doubt she noticed that he was hamming it up a bit.

Saul gave us a rundown on his work with Coughlin and the others in the America First Committee, including Lindbergh, Dilling, and even Laura Ingalls, who he described as the pilot who flies them around to various speaking engagements, not the woman he's boinking on the side. After his summary, he'd asked what our next moves were, and I told him that we'd be spending four or five hours setting stable points to see if we could pinpoint the specific actions that Team Viper entered into the system for their official moves.

All in all, he was in a fairly laid-back mood, noting that he'd also managed to convert the pilot to Cyrisism . . . or at least to the notion that Cyrist money spent just as well as the extra cash she'd been earning as a German agent.

I resisted the very strong temptation to ask him for the details of her conversion. Maybe that was the conversion ceremony I witnessed through the key. I should go back through and see if there's a lotus flower stamped on her butt.

The entire visit took thirty minutes off the timer, and when we returned to the apartment, Rich, Tyson, and Clio were apportioning sections of the fairgrounds that our two groups would cover. I doubt we missed much in terms of the discussion. This is the second time Richard has made not-so-subtle hints in that regard, however, and I think he's just trying to find a way to steer the conversation around to Saul.

Maybe Saul is right. Maybe Rich *isn't* exactly pleased that he survived. I push that thought away, because I don't like to think that Rich could possibly be that petty. To wish that on me, knowing how unhappy I'd be, would make him a pretty sad excuse for a friend.

It's also possible that he's just picked up on my mood. Madi even asked if I was okay this morning, and she barely knows me. I simply told her that I didn't sleep well because I kept wondering if and when she'd pop back in from her little field trip. The fact that she didn't make a snarky comment in return means she hasn't thought to check the stable point she set in the room last night in order to see whether I stayed put.

Rich and I walk along silently for a few minutes, stopping at various junctures to set an observation point for watching the crowd later if need be. Finally, after several minutes of silence and growing tension, I grab Rich's arm. "Just say it. Whatever it is, say it and get it off your chest."

He sighs and nods toward the British Pavilion, which is just ahead. "Could we take care of this first? We've only got about five minutes before the tour begins. We can hash it out afterward."

It's one of just a handful of stable points that we need to set inside a building, and we need to follow the guided tour in order to get to the location. "Fine. Let's go."

Of course, the tour guide is late, so the two of us wander around for ten minutes, pretending that we're looking at memorabilia from Buckingham Palace, although anything that's actually interesting is a replica, not the real thing. And then we spend fifteen minutes following the guide through as he explains the various items in the collection. When the tour moves up to the second floor, however, we both hang back to examine paste mock-ups of the crown jewels and wait for our moment to duck into the utility closet.

The door to that closet is, unfortunately, locked. Rich shoves against it with his shoulder, and for a second, I think the lock might give. It doesn't, though, and if he pushes harder, he's going to attract attention. That may also be true if we don't rejoin the group soon, so I pull the lethal little pen out of my purse. "Step back."

I point the beam at the lock inside the keyhole, trying not to think about the last time I used the device. My hand shakes. For a moment, the key plate glows red and I smell burning wood. When I cut off the beam, Rich pushes again. I hear a tiny clink inside the workings of the door, and then it swings open.

We step inside and quickly set a few stable points near the center of the room and two more at the doorway. I'm about to stash the key back into my blouse when a security guard's head pops up inside the stairwell.

"Get out of there! That's a *restricted* area!" he says. I expect to hear a New York accent, but apparently even the security guards in the pavilion are British nationals. "It's right there on the sign, miss."

"Sorry!" I hold up the medallion and give him an apologetic smile. "I was rubbing my St. Eligius medal for luck when it slipped off the chain and under the door. It was my great-grandmother's. And the door was unlocked so I just ducked in and grabbed it."

"That's no excuse. You should have called someone for help. Can't go around ignoring posted warning signs."

"I've told her to just keep the blasted thing in her pocket." Richard leans forward and says to the guy in a confidential whisper, "Rubbing the medallion is a nervous tic, I'm afraid. The poor dear can't handle crowds. That's why we put a bit of distance between ourselves and the rest of the group. I'll keep a closer eye on her, Officer, and make sure it doesn't happen again."

Rich reaches behind us to pull the door shut, and the guard waves us on. While that's a very good thing, Rich's sexist comment ticks me off, and I have to resist the urge to kick his shin once we're out of the guard's sight. But then I realize he's cradling his right hand against his side. I start to ask why, until I remember the glowing metal of the key plate. The knob itself didn't glow, but it was all one piece, so the knob almost certainly absorbed a good deal of the heat.

"Are you okay?"

"Yes," he says. "Hurts like hell, but maybe it won't blister if I get something cool against it. Let's just go."

We head out of the building. He finds a bench, while I locate a food vendor and purchase two ice-cold bottles of soda. I glance around and finally spot him in the garden area near the center of the strip. When I sit down next to him, I take his hand and flip it over to examine the burn.

He pulls his hand back quickly, almost as if my *touch* is burning him. "It's not bad, okay? Just give me the soda."

I do, and slide over to give him some space. After a moment, he shakes his head.

"Sorry," he says. "I'm a wimp about injuries. And . . . I'm also sorry for the comment to the guard."

"What comment?" I ask.

He snorts. "Yeah, right. I caught your expression. You were pissed."

"Okay, sort of. But I didn't really have a right to be. You were following my lead, and I was playing the helpless little lady. You got us out of there without additional drama, so . . ."

Now I'm wondering why it annoyed me in the first place. We were both doing exactly what they teach us at CHRONOS: do not question the prejudices of the era, and use them to help you if necessary. We don't go into the field to change hearts and minds, but simply to learn. I often resort to the scatterbrained-woman act, because it works well when you're young, petite, and yes, blond. I *always* defer to Saul in the field when we travel as a couple, and he's said things that were more dismissive than that on many occasions. In fact, he's said things that were more dismissive even when we *weren't* in the field. If Saul had made that comment, I wouldn't have thought twice about it.

The only difference is that it was Richard this time. I can't remember him ever treating me as anything other than an equal. But I think the main thing that triggered that response was knowing Richard is trying to get up the nerve to talk to me about Saul. Something in his eyes says I've disappointed him, and it's not just his usual dislike for my life partner. It's more like he's questioning my intelligence or at least my rationality right now, and that stings double at a moment when I'm questioning them, too. I'm suddenly a lot less eager for him to just spill whatever is bothering him than I was before we went into the British Pavilion.

"If you're really okay," I tell him, "we should probably get a move on. Set the rest of the stable points and then head back to the apartment."

He doesn't respond, so I look over at him. When I catch his eye, I get the sense that he somehow followed my entire train of thought, convoluted as it may have been. He gives me a resigned smile, although I think there's a hint of relief there, too. Maybe he's not all that eager to discuss the issue of Saul, either.

For the next hour, we set observation points, mostly in spots where we know or at least expect something will happen, both in this timeline and the last, since that's the only way we'll be able to tell we've undone any given element that combined to switch the timeline. We set points at the Court of Peace, which is the site of both the attempt on the Japanese ambassador's life and the bombing, at least in the current reality. We set points at Flushing Gate and at other locations near the spot where the bomb was taken in an effort to minimize loss of life in our own timeline. We set them, as well, at various points that were on the list Madi brought back, where Einstein spoke or visited on the several occasions he was at the Fair. And then we focus on locations where we can hunt for CHRONOS keys in the crowd. I thought it would be difficult to see during the day. Given that I see the key as a pale orange, I have a tough time picking it out during the daylight hours. Tyson, however, sees the light as purple, and says it's pretty easy for him to spot in daylight, even at a distance.

We enter the Perisphere, a giant orb with a circumference of more than six hundred feet, via the world's longest escalator, according to the guide at the base of the exhibit. The entrance is about eight stories off the ground, so we set a few points on the way up. You can't get down once you're on the platform, so we take seats on the "magic carpet," which is basically a moving sidewalk that circles a diorama of Democracity, the city of the future. One nice thing about being inside the darkened sphere is that I don't even have to wonder whether we're being watched by observers, at least not ones who are physically present. If anyone else had a CHRONOS key in here, we'd see it.

The last official point on our list is the General Motors building, with its Futurama exhibit. Unfortunately, there are hundreds of people in the line. We duck into a small alcove on the side of the building, and Rich scans forward to see when the line is manageable.

"Looks like it's going to be right before closing time," he says, and we blink forward. It's still a fifteen-minute wait.

"Are we sure this is worth it?" I ask.

Rich shrugs. "Alex saw several clear bubbles here and at the Perisphere. Not today. On the date toward the end of May. But maybe someone on Team Viper is just really into dioramas?"

Futurama turns out to be more elaborate than the model in the Perisphere, but it's still another vision of the city of the 1960s. And, much like the rest of the Fair, the exhibit is an ode to the automobile, with an elaborate highway system twisting and winding through the miniature skyscrapers, but at least the tiny cars don't spew toxic smoke. The whole thing is kind of hypnotic, though, so I lean back into the cushioned seat and listen to the music as we slowly spin toward the exit. It would be nice to just stay here for a few more revolutions, given that my sleep last night was far from peaceful. Rich doesn't look like he slept well, either.

The closer we get to the end, the larger the buildings grow. And then we're outside, looking at real versions of the view we saw in the diorama. A smiling girl hands both of us a small blue-and-white button. Richard flips his over and cracks up. I glance down to read the words—*I HAVE SEEN THE FUTURE*—and then I'm laughing, too. The girl looks at us like we're crazy as we leave, but it's been a while since we've shared a laugh. It feels good.

We try to get some stable points on the ramp down, just as we had with the Perisphere. But none of them are really good shots of the Fair as a whole. Rich says we need something higher and starts scanning the skyline. The tallest structure aside from the Trylon stands outside the Soviet Pavilion, where a massive statue of a man stands at the apex of a tall column. He holds a red star high above his head. That's not something we can go to the top of, however, any more than the Trylon. After a moment, I spot the flag at the top of something that looks, from this distance, a bit like a giant flower shedding its petals.

"The Parachute Jump," Rich says. "That should work."

As we get closer, we see that it's not simply the Parachute Jump, but the *Life Savers* Parachute Jump, with dozens of giant lights fashioned to look like Life Savers candies attached to the tower.

That's another difference between this fair and the Expo. There were a few buildings sponsored by businesses back in 1893, but it's become the norm now. Almost every exhibit that isn't attached to a country or a state has a commercial sponsor. General Motors' Futurama, Macy's Toyland, the Beech-Nut circus, the Westinghouse

Time Capsule, and so on, with most of the buildings seeming to be little more than a commercial. This place feels more like one of those shopping malls that start popping up in a few decades than a real World's Fair.

Of course, it's also entirely possible that I'm just in a rotten mood and not in the state of mind to enjoy it. Most of my time at the 1893 Expo was with Saul. We usually spent part of the day posing as a tourist couple taking in the sights, and then we'd head off on our own for a few hours to do individual research before meeting back up at the end of the day.

"You okay?" Richard asks.

"Yes." I nod toward the long queue of people at the ticket booth. "I just don't want to stand in that line."

"Easy fix for that."

We duck between two buildings in the nearby Cuban Village and scroll back to find a time when the line is minimal so that we can simply buy a ticket and get on board. It's just after dusk when we emerge, and I guess most people are off getting dinner. Richard whispers something to the man running the ride and slips him some cash. The guy gives him a smile and a thumbs-up, then gives me a leering wink as we climb into one of the two-person chutes.

"What was that about?" I ask, as we begin our ascent.

"I asked him to leave us at the top for a few minutes. I noticed that they were dropping people almost as soon as their chutes reached the top, and I'm not sure we'll be able to get the observation points set that quickly. A stable point set when we're in motion would result in a weird view for whoever scans it later."

Well, that explains the guy's wink. He's assuming Rich has very different reasons for wanting to keep me at the top. As we rise, the Fair below us grows smaller until it's much like the diorama we saw in the Perisphere.

"Have you been on this type of ride before?" I ask.

"No."

"I suspect I'm going to prefer the Ferris wheel," I say, watching as one of the other parachutes reaches the top and then drops abruptly to the ground. "The wheel is a pretty smooth ride, aside from that little dip your stomach takes when you reach the top and head downward. This seems a bit jerky. Are you nervous?"

"No. Are you?"

"A little."

"I'm surprised," he says. "You seem to like taking chances."

I can tell from his tone that we're no longer talking about amusement-park rides. "Just spit it out, Rich. Whatever the hell is eating you, just tell me."

"Well, first, you agree to the buddy system, and then you pop out a half hour later. And yes, I know that Madi did, too. I knocked. No answer. No one in either bed."

"That's really not any of your business," I say as the chute comes to a stop at the top of the tower.

"Normally, I'd say you were right. Despite thirteen years of friendship, that side of your life is usually none of my business. Right now, however, we're a team. And . . . ah, fuck it. That's not the reason I was coming to talk to you last night. The *team* decided on the buddy system, and the *team* decided that we would wait until after this was all over to give you information that I wanted to give you now. And I agreed to that, but then I'm lying there in bed, and it occurs to me that he lied to you. Saul lied to you about Coughlin."

"You can't know that." I pull out my key to set the observation point, then tuck it back into my blouse. "You haven't even spoken to him."

"I don't have to speak to him. He told you that he was preempting one of their moves with Coughlin. But he couldn't have preempted anything. He found out about the timeline shift when we did, when everything around us changed. And we know that converting

Coughlin wasn't one of their moves. So I don't know why he lied, but he lied. I knew you were going to jump out on your own, because you said, 'Fine, then.' And you gave the same little smile you always give when you agree to something you have no intention of doing."

"So you broke into my bedroom last night to let me know that I have a *tell*?"

"No. I opened the unlocked door, after knocking, because I think Saul is dangerous. And I was worried about you. The fact that Madi wasn't there was actually fortunate, because I was able to get proof. And also unfortunate, because after viewing that proof, even Clio's little sleeping pill wasn't enough to give me a decent night's sleep."

"Madi hadn't even met Saul until this morning. What kind of *proof* could she have?"

"Your diary. An entry you make a few months from now. Or at least that you made in the other timeline." His left hand is gripping the metal bar on the side so tightly that it looks like his knuckles might cut through his skin. "Your cheek was swollen," he says. "Split from where he'd hit you. There was a red mark around your throat where he'd ripped off your necklace. You said you were going to CHRONOS med. That you were going to talk to Angelo about it. And that you'd sent me a message to let me know what was going on."

"I don't believe you!" The words come out automatically, even though my mind is torn. The truth is I don't *want* to believe him, but I know deep down that the possibility is there.

"Katherine, I have never lied to you."

"Bullshit. You lie to me every day."

I can't meet his eyes, so I just stare down at the blanket of neon below us. Why doesn't the guy flip the switch already? How much money did Richard give him to keep us up here?

And, more to the point, why the hell did I call Rich a liar? My relationship with Saul is almost certainly over. Do I really want to alienate my best friend, too? I know that Saul is lying to me about being faithful. I know that he has a hair-trigger temper, and he's gripped my arm hard enough to leave a bruise on more than one occasion.

Rich doesn't respond for a few seconds, and then he says, "Are we really going to do this now? With everything else going on?"

At that instant, the parachute drops, and my stomach along with it. We plunge, the lights of the midway blurring before us, and then jerk to a sudden stop at the bottom. As soon as they unbuckle the restraint, I stumble from the platform.

"Sorry, buddy," I hear the guy say as I push my way through the small crowd at the exit. "Looks like that didn't go so well."

Richard calls out my name, but my sights are set on the alleyway where we blinked forward earlier. He catches up to me before I get there, though, both because his legs are longer and because women's shoes truly suck.

"Katherine, we have to talk this out. We can either do it here, where no one knows us, or back at the apartment, where we'll have a much more curious audience. I've got a little over half an hour before I'm supposed to meet Tyson at Café Society. Let's just go somewhere and talk. Please?"

I stop, partly because I know he's right and partly because tears are now clouding my eyes to the point where I can't see. He leads me toward a bar called Sloppy Joe's in the Cuban Village. It's crowded, but he does his trick with the folded bills again, and a small table near the back magically becomes available.

The waitress takes our drink order. Both of us stare down at the table for a bit, and then Rich says, "You may not believe this, but I really hoped that they were wrong about Saul."

"They who?"

"Madi told Tyson about the video in your diary when she told him about the Cyrists. They think you know more than you're letting on about Saul's involvement in that, by the way. But to the main point, I hoped they were wrong because I didn't want you to have to go through this. I don't like Saul. I've never liked Saul. I don't trust him one bit. And yes, I always hoped you'd decide he wasn't what you wanted. But . . . I didn't want it to be like this. And especially not when you and I both need to be focused on something else."

The waitress slides two rum and Cokes in front of us. I take a long sip, trying to decide how much I want to tell him right now. He's right; this probably isn't the time for all of this. "Where did you find my diary?"

He colors slightly. "In Madi's bag. I sort of . . . um . . . borrowed it. But I put it back before either of you returned last night."

"You could be right," I tell him. "Saul could be lying. But right now, it sort of feels like everyone is lying to me, so . . ."

"I meant what I said, Katherine. I have never lied to you. There have been things that I held back, yes. Things that others told me in confidence that I couldn't share. And sure, I didn't tell you the full truth about . . . my feelings. But did you actually want me to be honest about that when you were with Saul?"

I consider it for a moment, and then shake my head. I'm not even certain that I want him to be honest right now. But I can tell from his expression that shoving everything back inside isn't going to be an option for Rich. I made the mistake of tugging a brick out of the wall, and everything is about to come crashing down.

"Do you remember the first day of training? You came into class in this red sweater with black trim. About halfway through that first day, they told us we'd all be wearing CHRONOS scrubs from now on. You raised your hand and said, 'Can we at least accessorize?' Everyone in the class laughed."

"Including you," I say, because yes, I remember that day very clearly. Those scrubs were ugly. They still are, but at least we get some options now.

"Yes," he admits. "Including me. But then you turned around with one eyebrow arched and asked if we all really wanted to be exactly like everyone else. I didn't give a single fuck about having color options for scrubs—in fact, I kind of liked the idea of not having to make that decision. But you marched over that afternoon in the courtyard and told a group of us that you'd posted a petition requesting some, as you put it, 'very reasonable choices in regard to our uniforms,' and said you'd appreciate our feedback. You knew exactly who you were and what you wanted at age ten. And . . . that was it for me. I was gone."

I smile and shake my head. "You were *also* ten."

He takes a swig from his drink and continues holding it against his right palm, so the burn from the doorknob must still be bothering him. "Why is it everyone seems to think they know more about what I felt back then than I do?"

"That's not what I meant . . ."

"I'm pretty sure that's *exactly* what you meant. It doesn't matter, though. I know what I felt. I know what I feel now. It has never changed. But . . . you did. After that first jump when they teamed you with Saul, you slowly morphed into someone else. You began to question yourself. At first, it was just when he was around, but then it started bleeding over into your entire life. I wasn't the only one who noticed. Adrienne said he was like some sort of confidence vampire. He just sucked it right out of you. And your mom—"

"Oh, no, no, no." I hold up one hand. "I'm not going to sit here while you lecture me about what my own mother thinks! Believe it or not, I know how she feels about Saul. She's my mother, and she's never going to think that anyone is good enough for her child, but she's actually warmed to him in recent months. And as for Adrienne's analysis . . ." I give a bitter chuckle. "Kind of ironic, don't you think, when she flirts with Saul every chance she gets?"

"You're wrong," Rich says. "It's the other way around. Saul flirts with *her*. Probably because he likes a challenge. Adrienne saw straight through him from the beginning."

It's not the first time someone has told me this. Not just about Adrienne, but about half a dozen other women that seem to cluster around Saul like flies. In the past, I've ignored them, and I can feel myself leaning in that direction even now, my mind starting to make excuses for him. But perhaps Adrienne and the others aren't the ones buzzing around Saul. After last night, I at least need to consider the possibility that he's the one buzzing around *them*.

"So I'm just a shell now?" I say. "Saul-the-Confidence-Vampire sucked my personality away? Why the hell do you bother hanging around, since you believe I'm nothing but a doormat?"

As soon as the words leave my mouth, I want to pull them back. I'm lashing out, and Rich just happens to be the person within my range. What I really want to do is tell him about last night. I'd even toyed with the possibility of doing that, but I want to scan the stable points I set first. I want to know exactly what Saul is up to before I pull in Richard and the others.

"I'm not saying you're a doormat." Rich stares down at the table for a long moment, looking completely miserable, and my guilt ratchets up several notches. When he looks back up, however, his eyes are clear and determined. "I hang around because I love you. Because every day I see flashes of the person you are, the person you *can* be when you step out of Saul's shadow. When you're Katherine, not Kathy."

"Did you ever stop to think that the changes you think you see might be part of being in a relationship? Maybe it's a matter of give-and-take."

"I know I'm looking at it from the outside," he says. "And I'm absolutely one hundred percent biased against Saul. He's an asshole and he doesn't deserve you. But it seems like you give everything and get very little in return. So . . . yeah. If that's normal give-and-take in a relationship, I'm better off on my own. Because I won't let anyone do that to me. And I sure as hell would never do it to you."

There's not much I can say, since I'm mostly in agreement with his points on Saul. My head agrees, but my heart is still fighting reality.

"You need to go," I tell Rich. "You're going to be late meeting Tyson. We can talk more about all of this later, okay? I apologize for lashing out. I'm not feeling a hundred percent, to be honest."

It's true. I'm tired and my head is pounding. But mostly, I want to get back to the apartment before everyone else so that I have time to scan through the stable points I set at Saul's place in Miami.

And I want to see this diary for myself. Madi can't really object if I borrow it. After all, the damn thing is apparently mine.

"You're right," he says, glancing at the time on his key. "And it's okay. We're all on edge. But Katherine . . . I'm not naive enough to think I can spill my guts like this and everything goes back to normal. I realize this is going to make things awkward. Just know that whatever else I may feel for you, I am still your friend. I don't want to lose that."

∞

New York, New York
February 21, 1939

I jump straight to the bedroom and cross over to the small backpack on the floor next to the closet. Madi could pop in any minute, so I have to act quickly.

As soon as the diary is in my hands, I know it's mine. The name and address inside the cover are in my hand, and the diary contains personal entries I remember making, right up until about a week ago.

And then the entries diverge. I scan through quickly, reading about things that haven't happened yet. Things that quite possibly will never happen, and several things I hope to God never happen.

When I reach the video entry Rich mentioned, I understand why he gripped the rail of the parachute basket so tightly. I'd have been furious at anyone who left those marks on someone I cared about, too. Even though Saul can be caustic at times, even though he has a temper, I would never have believed him capable of really hurting me.

But it's hard to argue against the evidence, particularly when it's my own face staring back at me, telling me that Saul did this. That I'm terrified he's going to come back, break down the door, and kill me.

Our lamp, one of the first things we selected for our shared quarters, is shattered. The pearls from my necklace, which belonged to my grandmother, are everywhere—on the floor, the bed, the dresser. And the red line at the base of my neck doesn't look like Saul simply grabbed the necklace and yanked. The line is too red, too swollen. No, it looks more like Saul grabbed the necklace and twisted. The fact that the string was old might have been the only thing that saved my life.

I have to remind myself that this never happened. That it almost certainly won't happen in this exact same way. But it *could*. This is proof positive that it absolutely could happen, and I think the odds are exceptionally good that something very similar *will* happen at some point if I stay with Saul Rand.

There are voices in the living room, and I heave a sigh of relief that Madi decided to use that stable point rather than the local point she set here in the bedroom last night when she jumped forward to see Jack. I'm about to drop the diary back into her bag, but screw that. It's *my* diary. I open it and set a password, then shove it under my pillow. Why the hell didn't she tell me what was in it? She has to have known from the moment she met me. Before she met me, for that matter.

And now I'm flashing back to how vulnerable I felt standing in front of the window in Miami last night. Saul could very easily have grabbed the chain of the CHRONOS key, exactly as he did my pearls, and twisted. The chain that holds my key is sturdy enough that I'm pretty sure it wouldn't have broken. And after I stopped breathing, all he'd have had to do was lift the key over my head, and there would have been no more body. No more me.

There's a tap on the door. Madi peeks in and says she needs to get the stable points from my key to deliver to Jack. I tell her I'll be in the living room in a minute. She gives me a confused look and closes the door.

Yes, I know *why* she didn't tell me. I get it. But it still grates.

I center the CHRONOS medallion in my palm and pull up the stable point at the office of the Shrine of the Lotus Flower, where Madi and I met Saul earlier. After making sure my tiny pen of death is in my pocket, I scroll forward to two a.m., blink in, and tuck my key back into the case. I push open the office door and set a stable point in the hallway. Then I continue to the massive main chapel, set a point at the main entrance and then hurry across the auditorium to set one on the other side.

When I'm about halfway to my destination, a clanking noise comes from behind me. I startle, and whip out the laser pen, only to realize it was just the heat kicking on. Still, I need to hurry. I'm almost certain no one is here, but Coughlin does live on the premises, and there's no guarantee that Saul isn't here tonight staging one of his religious epiphanies to help keep his refrocked priest in the Cyrist fold. More importantly, though, the longer I spend here, the less time I'll have to find out exactly what Saul Rand is up to.

I probably have an hour at most before the others return, and I may need to make at least one jump to get information from Saul. The wisest course would probably be to go to the others and tell them everything. Madi could take these stable points to Jack, and he could examine them at leisure. It's pretty clear, however, that they don't trust me to be objective where Saul is concerned. They don't trust that Saul is working with us, which is entirely fair. They don't trust that he'll keep anything I tell him from Team Viper, and again, that's something I can't guarantee, either. But the crux of the matter is that they don't trust *me* to keep secrets from Saul. That's the whole reason they set up this stupid buddy system.

I need real information, though, not the claptrap Saul fed me when I had Madi in tow this morning. And contrary to what they may think, I'm perfectly capable of keeping secrets, even from Saul. Maybe even especially from Saul.

As soon as I get the last point set, I bundle the new locations into the same folder where I stashed the ones I set at Saul's house in Miami. That way I can keep them separate from the ones I set at the Fair that I'll soon be handing over to Madi. Then I blink back to the bedroom, kick off my shoes, wrap the quilt around me, and get to work.

Surveilling the locations at the house in Miami should be fairly simple. The house seems to be empty much of the time. But I can instantly see that this will not be true for the office where I met Saul this morning. A steady stream of people comes and goes, making it difficult to pinpoint anyone in particular. So I leave that for later and move on to the main temple. After the building opens in April 1939, the temple is occupied for two services a week, plus a choral practice and occasional meetings of middle-aged ladies with pink lotus flowers tattooed on their hands. It's quickly apparent that all I have to do is focus on the person behind the lectern at the front of the temple and scan through quickly. Mostly, it's Charles Coughlin, usually in his white clerical robes. Choir practice is easy to spot. A flash of pink turns out to be Elizabeth Dilling there on one occasion in mid-January 1940. I pause for this one and pan around the auditorium, spotting some of the same faces that were at the National Mothers' Union meeting. The group is considerably larger, however, filling about a third of the auditorium.

Several weeks later, Lindbergh is the speaker. It's daytime, and an unusually sunny day because sunlight dapples the faces of the audience, which is evenly divided between men and women, with quite a few children in the pews as well. As I pan around, I see men in military uniforms lining the sides of the auditorium. Although . . . they're not standard US military uniforms. More like something you'd see at a military academy, and there are three different varieties. One group is pretty easily identifiable as the Bund that Tyson and Madi mentioned last night. A few are wearing black shirts with a skull and crossbones above the breast pocket. The largest group is dressed a bit less formally, in pale, silvery-gray shirts. Most of them sport a large red *L* embossed on the left, but a few have the same shirt with a red *U*. It's not a uniform I'm familiar with, and it's making me crazy that I can't simply ask my data system to pull up the information for me, or send a request for more data through one of my CHRONOS diaries.

It's possible, however, that Clio will know, given that the late 1930s are her home turf. I'd planned to hole up here in the bedroom and not let her know I'd returned. She's bored, and I'm almost certain she'll start a conversation that I don't have time for. But maybe there's another way.

As I expected, Clio is draped over the chair next to the window, scanning through something on her key. She startles when I enter the room.

"Sorry," I say. "I jumped in straight to the bedroom because I've got a killer headache. You wouldn't by any chance have aspirin?"

"I do. A few out-of-timeline options, as well, if you'd prefer." Clio unfolds herself from the chair and heads into the kitchen. "My parents have generally been sticklers about not bringing stuff back from the future, but they made exceptions for things like ibuprofen and immunizations. And I occasionally bring my dad a bag of these orange Doritos chips that he likes."

She hands me two tiny red pills. I wash them down with a glass of water and then ask, "Could you take a quick look at something for me? I've been scanning through one of the stable points, and there's a uniform that I can't place. The one with the letter over their chest."

I'm reluctant to transfer the point to her key, so I grab her hand and place the medallion in her palm. She gives me an odd look, but then glances down at the stable point I have open. After a moment, she laughs. "Wow. That's quite an assortment. Not sure who the pirate-shirt boys are, but you've got the Bund, the Universal Front, and now the Silver Shirts. If you can find Klan regalia, I think that will count as a full house. The *L* is for *Legion*, as in the Silver Legion, but everyone just calls them Silver Shirts. Maybe the *U* is for Universal Front, and they're consolidating their costumes? I am kind of surprised that an egomaniac like Pelley would share the stage with anyone else, though, especially with a bigger name like Lindbergh."

"Who is Pelley?"

"William Dudley Pelley. He ran for president on a third-party ticket last time. Got maybe 1,500 votes. Coughlin didn't support him, but ran his *own* third-party candidate, who fared better, but still got less than two percent of the vote. This Pelley guy is a mystic. Says some angels told him that all Jews are bad. My brother Connor secretly listens to Lindbergh's speeches, and he has lousy taste in politics, but even Connor thinks Pelley is a complete loon. Is this the Madison Square Garden event? Looks a bit small."

"No," I say. "A different rally."

"Who are the folks wearing CHRONOS keys?"

"What?" I say. "I didn't see a key. Are you sure?"

She shrugs. "Not certain. It's on the far side of the hall in the upper level. A distinct blue-green glow, and it looks like more than one to me. Three. Maybe even four. Do you have any other stable points for this event?"

"No," I lie. "I'll ask Madi to jump back with me and set a few more. I'm . . . I really need to stretch out for a bit and let this medicine work."

"Sure. You are looking a little shaky."

My hands are indeed shaking when I get back to the room, but I manage to pull up the second stable point that I set on the opposite side of the chapel, just before I blinked out. When I pan to the section of the auditorium that Clio noted, I can see that she's right about the glow. I wouldn't have spotted it immediately because the three people in the balcony are near a window, and while the glow is a bit more vivid than the sunlight streaming in, it's not enough that I'd have instantly assumed someone was up there with a key.

Three someones, as it turns out. One of them is Esther. The other two are Saul.

The fact that my first reaction is jealousy makes me want to vomit. But my brain is hardwired for this response. It's been my automatic reflex anytime I've seen Saul with Esther for the past few years. Thanks to his diaries, I'm well aware that they have a past.

Then the rational side of my brain kicks in. Esther is welcome to him. In fact, she is *more* than welcome to play whatever games she likes with the doppelgänger twins. Although, in the interest of sisterhood, maybe I should send her a copy of that video. Maybe I should let her know exactly what she's getting herself into.

But this isn't the Esther from CHRONOS, of course. It's the one from Team Viper. I remember that at the same instant Saul's twin turns his head slightly toward her and I see the scar and faint red twinkle of his bionic eye.

PART THREE
ZEITNOT

Zeitnot [from German, "time crisis"]: Having very little time on the clock to complete the remaining moves of a timed game.

∞25∞

MADI
NEW YORK, NEW YORK
FEBRUARY 21, 1939

"There. That's all of them." Katherine pulls her key away from mine. She sounds annoyed, although I'm not sure why. I'd think she was still pissed about our conversation at breakfast, but she was friendly enough when we jumped to the Cyrist temple. Well, except for the two occasions that Saul spoke to me directly. Then she developed dagger eyes.

"You're soaked," she says, glancing down at my dress and then back up at my hair. "Aren't you going to change before you go?"

Soaked might be an overstatement, but I'm definitely several stages beyond damp. May 9th was a dreary, drizzly day in New York City, and the stormy weather made most of the fairgoers grumpy. The three hours that Tyson and I spent at the Fair were miserable to the point that we were tempted to scan forward to find a sunny day to set our assigned stable points. But we were reluctant to do that, since we knew there was activity by Team Viper on that day, and we were hoping to spot some familiar faces. The only time we'd been out of the blowing rain was when we were in the auditorium for the writers' conference. We listened to a few minutes of Thompson's short speech after lunch, in which she sounded the clarion call for the United States to wake up. Hitler would not be content with Poland, she cautioned. An ocean would not protect us if he continued to gain power.

Neither of us saw Einstein. I did, however, spot one of the observers from Team Viper. It was the guy who was seated next to Marcy, the other one who was labeled *ACADEMIC*. He came in from the back of the auditorium, and I'm pretty sure he spotted us. I nudged Tyson, and we moved toward the exit, set the stable point just inside the door, and blinked out. That was our main goal, anyway. Anything important from the speeches would likely be in the paper the next day, and once we had a stable point set, we could blink back to the previous night, when the auditorium was closed, and set a few dozen more. That way, Jack could scan through and see if he was able to find Einstein or the observer. Or the best-case scenario, the observer contacting Einstein.

"Tyson and I got caught in a downpour," I tell her. "I don't really have time to change, though. I still need to get these stable points to Jack so that he can run through them. Would you like to come with me?"

"I'll pass," she says. "Pretty sure you can handle it on your own. I'm going to lie back down. My head is pounding." She turns to Clio, who is browsing stable points in the padded armchair near the window. "Would you let me know when Rich and Tyson get back?"

"Sure," Clio says. When Katherine is gone, she adds in a lower voice, "I'm not buying the headache. Pretty sure the bedroom will be empty in three, two, one."

"Probably," I admit. "Do you want to come with me instead? I mean, I don't think it's especially risky for you to drop by your parents' house."

"I don't know about that," she says with a grim look. "Do you know what's going on with my mom in 1966? I've checked the stable points in the living room, and that place doesn't really look like their house. In fact, it looks like it was unoccupied for quite some time before they came in to set it up for Jack."

"I don't know," I tell her. It's the truth. I don't *know*. All I have are suspicions.

"Here's the thing that's troubling me," Clio says. "I meant what I told all of you earlier about wanting to live a linear life. But I was in a pretty bad place about a year ago . . ." She stops, laughs bitterly, and shakes her head. "About a year ago for me, that is. In 1935. The guy I'd been dating for several years gave me an ultimatum. He wants a wife. A family. And I couldn't even fathom the idea of that kind of commitment when I was at Simon Rand's beck and call for his stupid time-tourist jaunts. Matt knew about Simon, understood what I was doing, but he was tired of constantly worrying about me. And while I was in the middle of what my mom calls a pity party and feeling like I was all alone in the world, I had a morbid thought about the future and wondered how long my parents would be around. How long before I really would be alone in the world, aside from my brothers. So I pulled up the stable point out by the lake and turned it toward the hill on the other side of my parents' house to see when new headstones would appear. There's a little graveyard up there. Have you seen it?"

"Not up close, but yeah, I noticed it when I was looking for Jack that first day. Are they . . . people you knew?"

"Yes. One is for Aunt June. Hers is just a memorial stone. There was no need for a burial. She was out of the timeline, so my dad just clipped the cord holding her CHRONOS key, and she was gone. The second one is the baby my mom had between me and Harry, when I was about five, so I don't really remember her. A little girl they named Deborah, after my mom's mom. We had the advantage of vaccinations for all sorts of childhood diseases, thanks to a little stockpile that my parents built up when they were still able to use the key. But they didn't have a vaccination for the flu in 1918. They knew the flu was coming, of course, and Dad said they holed up, steering clear of pretty much everyone for weeks, to the point that the neighbors came knocking to see if the family was okay. And that's probably how the baby caught the flu. She was only three months old. Dad said that as painful as it was losing her, there was a silver lining, at least for Harry and Connor. Because Mom, Dad, and Aunt June hadn't been entirely sure what would happen when they took her body outside the cabin. Unlike me, that baby was conceived in this timeline—or rather, in that timeline, the one we're trying to restore. So they both thought that she'd have been fine outside of a CHRONOS field. But that's not exactly the kind of thing you can check, you know? And there's a tiny grave beneath that second headstone, because the baby didn't vanish."

There's a long pause, and then I give her a verbal nudge. "What about the third stone?"

"But you see, that's just it. There shouldn't *be* a third stone until 1969. And a fourth in 1980. I stared at it on and off all day, trying to get up the nerve to zoom in. And when I finally did . . ." She holds out her key to transfer the stable point to mine.

After a moment, I look up from the location. "It's blank," I say. "No name. No date. Why?"

She snorts. "Because Kate Dunne isn't stupid. She figured out that a blank stone keeps both of us here. If my name was on it, Dad would assume I blink out to the fairground at some point, for some reason, and no force on earth would keep him in this apartment. And if Dad's name was on it, the same would be true for me. At first, I was thinking there was a good possibility that she's playing both of us and no one is beneath that stone. I mean, this could just be her insurance policy to make sure we both behave. But . . . they left the house in Skaneateles. A place they love. Something made it impossible for one or both of them to stay. It could just be the change of government, but . . ."

"All I know is that your mom was very angry when she arrived to pick Jack up at the bus station. Jack said your brother showed up at the house not long after they got there to take your mom back to

Canada. He got the sense that there had been some major bribes involved for them to come across the border at all. And . . . before I left the station, she waved the picture I gave her the other night in Seneca Falls in my face and said that she wanted that future back. That I had better fix it. And I promised her I would. I told Tyson what she said, and we decided it was too dangerous for you or your dad to be out in the field. And that's why you've been stuck here in the apartment."

We're both quiet for a long time, and then she says, "So you and Tyson decided this . . . when?"

"Last night," I tell her, and I'm about to launch into a defense of that decision and why I didn't tell her. Then I notice the raised eyebrows and slight tilt of her head and realize the point she's trying to make.

Tyson and I made the decision to keep Clio and Kiernan out of the action last night. Katherine and Rich agreed.

But despite our firm decision, one that I can't imagine any of us going back on, there are *still* three stones on that hill.

∞

SKANEATELES, NEW YORK
SEPTEMBER 2, 1966

MEET ME ON THE DOCK.

The note is propped against a pillar candle on the coffee table when I arrive at the stable point. I follow Jack's instructions, and head through the kitchen. The little hypospray injector that I delivered on my last trip, filled with the serum Lorena concocted, sits on the counter next to the toaster. It made me a bit nervous when Tyson handed it to me earlier today, along with a note listing the possible side effects. I'm not afraid that it won't work. As Jack noted, there are worse things in life than being stuck in 1966, assuming we get the timeline fixed.

I'm more worried it will have negative effects, and I'm not sure how I'll explain that to medical personnel. *Oh, yes, Doctor. We just injected a bunch of chemicals into his bloodstream. Would you like a list?*

I step out onto the porch. A warm, late-summer sun greets me, and I now understand Jack's reason for leaving that note. When I last spoke to him—a few minutes ago from my perspective and four days ago from his—I handed over the stable points that Tyson and I set at the World's Fair. My hair was, and is still, hanging in damp clumps around my face, and I'd almost certainly been wearing what my father used to call my sulky face. As I was transferring the locations to Jack's key, I'd indulged in a bit of a rant about the weather and the crowds, noting that I really needed a vacation, and not to the damn World's Fair. Someplace warm, sunny, and secluded. A few days on the beach near Nora's cottage in Bray would be perfect. Then came the inevitable memory that Nora doesn't exist, let alone her cottage, followed by the memory of the graveyard on the hill outside this house. My rant about the weather and vacations felt pointless and petty. So I'd focused again on the business at hand. I asked Jack how long he thought he needed, gave him a quick kiss, and jumped forward four days, per his instructions.

It's not the beach. But the temperature is in the eighties, with a light breeze. The lake sparkles invitingly through the trees, and I spot Jack at the end of the pier, in cutoff jeans. There's a green metal box next to him, tied to one of the wooden posts. A cooler, maybe? His feet are dangling in the water as he scans through stable points on his key.

I try to keep my focus on the lake and Jack. But I can't avoid looking at the grave site on the hill. My eyes go there automatically, whether I want to look or not. The third, inexplicable headstone is still there.

But I can't think about that now. We'll fix it. I promised.

"How did you know it was going to be an absolutely perfect day?" I call out to Jack from the path as I make my way through the trees.

Jack smiles. "I didn't *know*. But I listened to a weather report that morning from a station in Syracuse. He predicted 'warm, sunny weather heading into your Labor Day weekend,'" he says in what I assume is an imitation of the weatherman's voice. "Contrary to the myth, weathermen apparently *did* get it right from time to time, even this far back."

I pull off my shoes and join him. My legs are shorter, so my feet are barely below the surface, but the cool water feels good after hours in uncomfortable shoes. I lean into him, and for several minutes just let the tension drain from my body and enjoy the moment, the view, and the company. The sunshine and the wind in my hair are restorative, and I would love to spend the rest of the day here with him, and then go inside, curl up, and watch the show he mentioned. Or read. Or do nothing at all. A light dinner together. Maybe an early evening swim. I want nothing more than to spend a lazy Friday afternoon in early September with the man I love. But . . . we have a little over a day total, and I only have about fifteen minutes before I'm due back at the apartment.

Jack must sense the moment my mind switches back into work mode, because he reaches into the box next to him, which has a scuffed picture of a penguin on it. I expect him to pull out a drink, but he's holding a folder.

"Unusual filing cabinet you have there," I tell him.

"It was selected because it's mostly waterproof," he says. "Plus, it's too heavy for the wind to blow into the lake. I had to fish a folding chair out of the water yesterday. And since I've spent four days and worn out my vision putting together what's in this file, I'm not taking any chances. Yes, I could do it again, in pretty much the blink of an eye from your perspective, but I'd rather not. The good news is that I'm feeling a bit more optimistic about our odds than I was four days ago."

"That *is* good news. What did you find?"

"The full details are in the file, but the short version is this. I pinpointed the time that a young man wearing a silver shirt, which I'm pretty sure is now connected to Coughlin's group, takes a shot at the Japanese ambassador. I've also narrowed down the time that a gentleman who is not wearing a CHRONOS key leaves a suitcase inside the British Pavilion to around nine p.m. on July 3rd, and a second man, who *is* wearing a key, removes it about five hours later. I'm guessing he's one of their observers. The closet is dark, though, so we don't have much to go on in terms of a description for either of them. I may be able to find one or both of them on the stable points outside the pavilion, but I'm not hopeful. And I have several men who might be Tomonaga at locations around the Fair on September 12th, but the photograph is of him as an older man, so I can't really be sure. But I checked a few of the spots that you said Alex thought he might visit."

I frown on the last one, trying to pin down exactly what he's talking about.

"Or maybe that was in the information you brought back from Tyson and Rich. Anyway, one of the exhibits he mentioned was the Theater of Time and Space."

"I don't remember even seeing that on the map. Did we set a stable point there?"

"Someone did. But if you've got a copy of the 1940 season's map, it wouldn't be on there. The exhibit shut down at the end of 1939. Something called *What Do* opened up in that spot. Anyway, I decided to focus on that . . . and sure enough, we have two twentysomething men, one of whom is reasonably close to the picture Alex has of Tomonaga, coming out of the exhibit around eight fifteen on the evening of September 12th. Which still doesn't tell us *where* they'll be mugged, but it does give someone a starting place."

"That's good, then. We have the Court of Peace bombing and the Japanese ambassador. I can't see how a nuclear physicist being mugged could be coincidental, so that would be our three moves."

Jack shakes his head. "I don't think it's going to be that clear cut, unfortunately. Did you get a good look at the women on Team Viper?"

"Yeah. Briefly on the video before the game started. And I saw one of them, Alisa, at the Beatles concert."

He transfers a stable point to my key—May 9, 1939, at 9:34 a.m. "See if that's her."

"Yeah," I say after a moment. "And the guys with her are observers. I might not have recognized one of them because he's got different facial hair, but the other one was in the auditorium during the writers' conference. He was also seated next to the female observer, Marcy, in the video we saw just before the beginning of the match."

"Marcy is the one Tyson saw them kill, right?"

I nod. "And erase, yeah. I'd probably have known he was an observer anyway. I can see the light of the medallion shining through the weave of the vest."

"Which is why we'd be so much better off if *you* had the time to scan these," he says. "I can see the light on the woman's bracelet, but that's only because it's out in the open. Anyway . . . keep watching. They're going to intercept a familiar face in about twenty seconds."

Alisa is dressed in a slim skirt and jacket, with her hair in a neat bun. She's smoking a cigarette as she paces back and forth in front of a large copper statue of three men in ancient attire carved into the facade just above the main entrance to the building. The sky is overcast, and one of the guys is carrying an umbrella.

Her head jerks up. She looks off to her right and then drops the cigarette and crushes it out with her shoe. An elderly man in a dark suit is coming up the stairs toward her. Unlike most of the men wandering around in the background, he's hatless, and his shaggy head of gray hair is easily identifiable, even at a distance.

Einstein nods to Alisa and her escorts and then continues toward the entrance. Alisa scurries to catch up to him and whispers something in his ear. He looks startled, but he stops and listens as she continues speaking and waves the two observers over. One of them hands her something that looks a bit like a computer tablet. Whatever is on the tablet gets Einstein's attention, because he stares at it for a moment and then motions for them to follow him. He takes a step toward the entrance, and then looks back at the two observers. They seem to make him a bit nervous, because he reverses course, and they follow him around the side of the building.

"What is in that direction?" I ask Jack.

"They stuck the Jewish Palestine Pavilion in a spare corner surrounded by food exhibits," he says. "Mostly because the British government wasn't interested in hosting it, given the political climate in 1939. The Beech-Nut building is that direction, along with the National Biscuit Company Theater, which is showing a Mickey Mouse cartoon. It's *possible* they went into one of those buildings, but I also found an image showing something called Tel Aviv Café, which may be on the other side of the pavilion, as well."

"So . . . he's taking them to lunch?" I ask.

"My best guess is that he wanted to remain in a very open, very public setting," Jack says. "The man was not, after all, known for being stupid. Whatever she showed him got his attention, but he was a well-known German Jewish refugee who hadn't exactly kept his views on Hitler's rise a secret. I just wonder what she said to get his attention so quickly."

"Maybe she told him the truth?" I say. "He's probably one of the few people at the Fair that day who might believe someone who claimed to be a time traveler." I'm joking, sort of. But Jack nods.

"They could have shown him a picture of his older self. That's an era before faking photos was especially easy. And . . . they handed him what was pretty clearly a tablet computer. That alone would have argued the case pretty persuasively."

"Hold on. I'm going to find out where they went."

This stable point, like the vast majority of the ones that Katherine and Richard set, is out in the open, since it's intended mostly for surveillance. I scroll back to a little after one a.m. and scan around the plaza in front of the building, but I don't see anyone.

"What happened to the buddy plan?" Jack asks with a crooked grin.

"That doesn't actually apply to me," I tell him as I set a new stable point on the dock. "Unless you're plotting to form a new global religion and commit genocide?"

"Neither of those things are on my calendar at the moment."

"I'm just going to set a few stable points and come right back here. Anyway, if I don't show up back at the apartment at the appointed time, they'll come looking for me. You can have one of them jump in and tell me I'm making a big mistake." I give him a quick kiss and then blink in.

After taking a moment to orient myself, I head over to the steps where Alisa first encountered Einstein. I set stable points in several locations so that I can find out exactly what they showed the man that convinced him he should at least listen to what they had to say. We could probably come up with something on our own, but this isn't an exam. No reason I shouldn't peek over Einstein's shoulder and steal Team Viper's homework.

Then I go back down the steps and around the corner of the building. Everything is still brightly lit, and there's music off in the distance, so maybe there are still a few postmidnight activities going on in the Amusement Zone. On this side of the fairground, however, there are just a handful of people on the street behind the pavilion. Off to the right, I can see the dome of the Perisphere next to the tall needlelike statue behind it, both bathed in a white glow. Off to the left is a tall, red pillar of light, with the statue of a man holding up a glowing red star on top.

Now that the rain and the crowds are gone, it's actually kind of nice here. Before today, I'd never been to a World's Fair. I'm not even sure if they have them anymore. In fact, I had never been to a physical fair at all. There are VR parlors that do an excellent job of simulating carnival rides without the risk and at a tiny fraction of the cost. Nora told me about going to Disney World once when she was a child, but amusement parks were fading already in the mid-21st century. She said most of the rides had been VR even in her day.

As Jack suspected, there's a café behind the building. The chairs have all been put away for the night, and the lights are out, but large letters spell out *Café Tel Aviv* above the entryway of a curved single-story section jutting out of the back of the pavilion. I set a few quick observation points on the patio area, where several tables are scattered about, but the bulk of the seats are inside. Still, if Einstein's main concern is security, I think he'll take a seat outside, where there are plenty of people passing by.

I lean back against the wall of the main building and scroll forward to 9:48, and after a moment, Einstein, Alisa, and the two men come around the building. She's still talking, and he's nodding, but he looks a little nervous to me. Most of the patio tables are empty, probably due to the drizzly weather. The table Einstein points them toward is near enough to where I'm standing that it looks like I could reach out and touch him, and I have the feeling that Alex would be having a serious fan moment right now. There are only three chairs, so one of the observers goes off in search of a fourth. Einstein takes the seat where his back is to the wall. As Jack said, he is not a stupid man.

Unfortunately, that means I need to set another stable point, though, because despite the close proximity, I want to be able to see over his shoulder. I inch my way over until the angle seems right, set another stable point, and then set a few more just to be sure I have all of the perspectives I need. Then I blink back to Skaneateles to spy on their meeting.

I transfer the new points to Jack's key so that he can view them, too. It's annoying that we can't watch on the same device, because we're always slightly out of sync.

"Too bad we can't just cast it to a wall screen," I say.

"Yeah, I don't think you'd much care for the resolution on the TV in there."

The first stable point on the steps is useless because I appear to have set it a few inches too far to the left. It's completely dark, which leads me to believe that it's probably inside one of the observers. The second point, however, is behind Einstein, and just to his left. The tablet screen is clearly visible now.

"And I guessed right about the photographs," Jack says.

"You did, indeed."

The first image is one we both know well. Einstein with his tongue out, taken on his seventy-second birthday in 1951. The second shows Einstein in a sweater, seated on the steps leading up to the front porch of a light-colored house. One of his legs crossed over the other. There's nothing remarkable at all about the photograph, aside from the fact that he's wearing fuzzy slippers.

"It must be a picture that hasn't been taken yet," I say. "But I'm guessing he already has those slippers."

We move on to the locations I set at the café. The left side of the new stable point is partially blocked by dark blue broadcloth and a few strands of unruly gray hair, but I have a clear view of the tablet he's holding and, luckily, of Alisa, who is directly across the table from him. She talks with her hands, which is a little distracting.

Einstein motions for her to shush as the waitress approaches, and in that moment, I can definitely picture him as a professor. The waitress clearly knows him, and I nearly tell Jack that he must be a regular there, before realizing that even back then most people knew his face.

She jots something down on her order pad and turns to the others, who don't order at first, because she starts to leave. Then Einstein waves her back, and she writes something else down.

As soon as the waitress leaves, Alisa hands him the computer again. The video is already playing. It's a mushroom cloud, followed by images of the destruction of Hiroshima and Nagasaki. Alisa doesn't speak for nearly a minute, allowing the images to do the work for her. And it's clear that they do. Einstein's hands begin to shake, and he steadies them by bracing his wrists against the edge of the table.

"I wish I could read lips," I say.

Jack says that he didn't pick up much, either. "But she definitely says the word *Roosevelt*," he adds, "if you go back a bit."

I do, and he's right. But checking was really just a formality. We both saw the video, and we saw Einstein's reaction. Alisa obviously told him about the letter he'll sign, along with Leo Szilard. She told him that the bombs in the video and all of those deaths were the eventual result of his actions in persuading Roosevelt to push nuclear weapons research.

I don't know if she actually said the words, but her message was simple and clear:

This is your fault.

FROM THE *NEW YORK DAILY INTREPID*

ESPIONAGE RING BROKEN BY DANISH POLICE

(Copenhagen, March 11, 1935) Members of a purported espionage ring were arrested today for allegedly plotting with foreign terrorist groups in Moscow. Police claim that several members, including two with Canadian passports, are of Russian origin.

The spy ring, which includes at least two Americans, Leon Josephson and Adolph Rabinowitz, was in possession of large sums of cash and maintained extensive correspondence, which led authorities to suspect that they were in the employ of a foreign government. Their correspondence revealed, according to Danish police, one plot actively under consideration—the assassination of German chancellor Adolf Hitler.

∞26∞

TYSON
NEW YORK, NEW YORK
DECEMBER 27, 1938

"Still not entirely sure this is going to be worth the time," Rich says as we emerge from the stable point at Washington Square Park. "Especially since it's frickin' cold."

I consider the cold a mixed blessing, since it meant we were able to jump in without startling any couples in the bushes. And while I don't challenge him on the issue, I'm pretty sure Rich thinks this jump is very much worth thirty minutes or so of our time. We were able to sort out which picture was Leon Josephson by using the stable points that I set inside the club. It was indeed the one that resembled his brother, rather than the Hollywood-handsome guy who was apparently someone he worked with in Europe. Historians jumbled up the pictures with a guy who was his handler with the Soviet intelligence agency. And we were able to pinpoint a time that he was at the club. A night when the band was practicing for the opening, which is scheduled for tomorrow night. And not just the band, but also the vocalist.

That alone wouldn't have convinced me, or even Rich, to carve out the time. But watching Leon Josephson through the key couldn't provide us with several crucial bits of information. First, we don't even know if he'll be in the country in September 1939, since he apparently takes on foreign jobs, like attempting to assassinate Hitler, from time to time. We also don't know if the rumors about him being a spy are even true. J. Edgar Hoover wasn't above framing people if he didn't like their politics or their attitude. Or if they just happened to look at him wrong.

"I don't know if it's worth it, either," I tell Rich. "But if it works, we'll have a decent idea whether Leon will agree to a side project that's not handed down through his usual party hierarchy. I just wish I'd remembered to set a stable point *outside* the club, in addition to the two I set inside. Kind of hard to explain how you were upstairs in the toilet of a place that's not even open yet."

As we exit the park, Rich stares across the street at the sidewalk and says, "Ah, damn. Didn't realize this was *that* stable point. You made this jump, right? The one where Rose tells us they're all dead anyway?"

"Yeah."

"I was glad when Rose retired, because every time I saw her at HQ after that, I'd hear those words in my head. Don't know about you, but that jump gave me nightmares for days."

It was weeks in my case, but then Rich probably didn't see the girl moving on the sidewalk. And I don't really see the point in sticking him with that nasty visual, so we continue in silence down Waverly Place toward the club.

There's no doorman at the front tonight, but music is playing. I wonder if it's a recording at first, but then someone misses a note and they roll things back a couple of bars. Rich taps on the door. No one responds, but that's not too surprising, given that they're in the basement and a band is practicing.

He jiggles the knob. It's unlocked, so we step inside and make our way toward the stairs. I move my hand toward the gun inside my jacket, because this kind of entrance makes me nervous.

"I've got this," Rich says, tapping his watch gadget. "If we run into trouble, everybody's going to take a little nap. They won't understand what happened, but that's still a hell of a lot better than you shooting people."

I move my hand back down to my side because he's right. I'm still on edge, though, as we head downstairs. It's almost certainly due to what happened last time I was here, because it's not like we're breaking in. The door was unlocked.

There are several dozen people in the room, some working to get the place ready for the opening, and others apparently just hanging out with the Josephson brothers. From what we observed through the key, the band will continue warming up for about two more minutes, and then Billie Holiday will run through a couple of numbers, including "Strange Fruit." It's not a full dress rehearsal—Barney doesn't cut the lights, and some of the people in the club are still chatting. But Richard seems kind of psyched that he'll be hearing it prior to the official debut.

Our first challenge is going to be getting Leon Josephson away from the cluster of men at one of the tables near the back. And then we'll see if Rich's idea works.

We stop at the bar, where Barney is arranging bottles of liquor on the shelves above the inside counter. Rich raps on the wood railing of the bar, which is polished to a high sheen, and Barney turns, giving him an annoyed look. "Sorry. We're not open yet."

Rich nods. "Yeah. We saw the sign. But a friend told me I might be able to find an attorney here. Guy by the name of Leon Josephson. You know him?"

"Hey, Leon!" Barney calls out. "Good news. Maybe you can skip chasing ambulances tomorrow."

Leon laughs and holds up a hand. "Be with you guys in just a minute."

"You fellows want a drink?" Barney asks. "Like I said, we're not open yet, but I'll still take your money."

Rich buys two beers, which must have just been put into the fridge because they're lukewarm, and we take one of the empty tables.

By the time Leon joins us, Holiday is singing. I'm a little worried that Rich's head isn't going to be in the game, but it's actually not a bad thing, because Leon notices his distraction and says, "She's good, isn't she? I think she's gonna pull in a crowd. How can I help you, gentlemen?"

Rich looks away from the stage and offers his hand, along with our first names. "Don't know if you've heard about this nonsense with the Dies Committee," he says, "but my sister is a clerk with the Federal Theatre Project, and—"

"I thought the committee wrapped that up. They've already accused Euripides and Christopher Marlowe of being Red subversives. Are they looking to incriminate Shakespeare now?"

Rich snorts. "Could be. I definitely wouldn't put it past them. Anyway, they already subpoenaed one of her coworkers, and Betsy's scared half to death that she's next. Wanted to see if I could get a lawyer lined up for her, just in case, while I'm up from DC."

Josephson reaches into his breast pocket and pulls out a card. "Tell her to call me if things develop. Out of curiosity, who gave you my name?"

"My cousin, Carl. He said you helped his friends get hold of some papers a few weeks ago."

When we went over this back in the library, Richard came up with three code names from the writings of Whittaker Chambers, a communist spy who switched sides, and one of the only names in all of this that sounded vaguely familiar to me. Carl was Chambers's code name. I'd asked Rich what he was going to say if Josephson asked for Cousin Carl's last name, but he said that wasn't likely to happen. In fact, giving a last name would be more likely to raise suspicion. And the *papers* comment is a veiled reference to a heist that Leon supposedly pulled off for the *Daily Worker*.

Josephson's eyes flicker in my direction, and I pretend to be watching the band, hoping to hide the fact that I am out of my element. I've been in Klan meetings where every man was armed to the teeth and would have happily shot me if he knew I was a spy, and I didn't break a sweat. But I only know the vague outlines of this history, so I'm keeping my mouth shut.

Rich must be right about the first-names-only thing, because Josephson nods and says, "Carl's a good man. Let me know if there's anything else I can do for you."

"Actually," Rich says, "there *may* be something else. Our mutual friend Ulrich may be sending some people this way in September, if you think you'll be around."

Leon laughs wryly. "Got a little problem with my papers, so I won't be leaving the US anytime soon. Only kind of help I can lend is stateside. Tell them Barney will know how to get in touch."

"Good to know," Rich says. "Keep this on the q.t., though. Ulrich's got a couple of different circles working this thing, and . . . well, you know the drill."

"I do, indeed. Nice making your acquaintance." He takes a few steps toward the bar, then turns back. My first thought is that he's realized something Rich told him didn't jibe, and that must be what Rich is thinking, too, because his hand moves toward the button on his Timex. But Leon just grins and nods toward the stage. "You guys should stick around for the next song. It's a good one."

"Thanks for the tip," Rich says. "We wouldn't miss it."

∞

New York, New York
February 21, 1939

"This would be easier at Madi's library," Clio says as she tapes another piece of paper to the living room wall, making a scratch pad that covers most of the surface. "We could put our options up on the wall screen, and Jarvis could delete them and juggle them around. I bet he could even tally our votes, if you weren't married to the whole secret-ballot concept. He could also look things up for us."

"True," I say. "And that's actually a good idea. Maybe we can set up Madi's assistant to comb the news sources and check off our objectives as they're achieved. But I think we should conserve our energy tonight. We've only got fifteen hours. Make a note of anything we need to check, and Madi can ask when she goes to collect the votes from Jack and the rest of the team."

"Including Thea?" Rich asks.

I exchange a look with Madi. We discussed this before the meeting. One of the reasons we were both inclined to make major decisions here in the apartment was a concern that Thea might be a spy. I'm increasingly convinced that she's an unwitting spy, if so, but I still think we'd be wise to avoid giving her more than the bare-minimum amount of responsibility required by the rules of The Game. Madi agrees. Thea is a wild card. But she's a member of the team, even if it wasn't something we planned. She gets a vote, if only to maintain optics.

"Including Thea," I say. "And speaking of Thea, did you give Madi the tablet?"

"It's on the counter," Rich says as he heads into the kitchen. "I took it out when I gave Clio the tablet with all of the newspaper articles, but then I forgot."

"What is this?" Madi asks when he hands it to her.

"No clue," I say. "Your grandmother just told us that she wrote it all down. And then she complained that you weren't spending any time with her and invited us all down to the basement for a quick skinny-dip."

"Did you take her up on it?" Madi asks with a little grin. "She's in very good shape for her age."

"We did *not*," Richard says. "Where's Katherine?"

"She was lying down," Clio tells him. "I'll tap on the door."

While we wait for Katherine to join us, I pick up a fat red crayon from the table, cross over to the paper "screen," and begin making a chronological list of things that changed significantly in this timeline prior to 1941.

CHANGES

1) Conversion of Father Coughlin/Early America First (Date unknown) X

2) Deaths at Pro-America Rally (2/20/39)

3) Einstein (5/?/1939)

4) Attack on Japanese ambassador (6/2/39) ✔

5) Tomonaga (9/12/1939)

6) Attempted assassination of Lindbergh (2/22/40)

7) Fourth of July Bombing (7/4/40)

Madi sighs. "Pretty sure this is the stage where we should be winnowing the list down. And yet it grows."

"I'm just listing everything," I tell her. "I want to be sure we're examining all of the possibilities before we start planning how to reverse this."

"But if we're going to actually examine *all* of the possibilities," Rich says, "we need to acknowledge that this is a very partial list. How many people had their lives disrupted when they came under suspicion for causing the deaths at the Bund rally? Two people are in jail for that, awaiting trial, but dozens more are being called in front of congressional loyalty committees. And even assuming that the events Team Viper entered all happened at the Fair, it's open for several months after the Independence Day bombing. If we had more time to dig, we'd probably find five or ten more substantive changes at the Fair alone."

Katherine comes in and leans against the doorframe. She looks unusually tired. "You can put an *X* next to number two, as well, and not just because it didn't happen at the Fair. I'd almost guarantee that Saul was at the event."

"He was," Madi says. "Unless it was the other Saul."

"Alex was able to rule that out," I say. "His system didn't pick up any Viper signals in that area during the rally. So it was definitely Saul."

Katherine nods. "Number five can almost certainly be chalked up to his activities, too, although I don't know if they planned it or if it was just a bit of serendipitous mayhem. I was just looking through some stable points I set today when we were at Coughlin's shiny new temple. They held a rally on February 10th, nearly two weeks before the guy shoots Lindbergh. I showed the stable point to Clio earlier today, and she identified another group that they pulled into the fold . . . the Silver Shirts."

"Okay," Madi says, "this is going to sound like a stupid question, but are they called Silver Shirts because—"

"Because they wear silver shirts. With a big red *L* on the chest." Clio, who has been thumbing through the tablet of news articles RJ put together from the earlier timeline, taps something and then holds the image up for us to see. It's gray scale, so the shirts really look more white than silver, but there is indeed a large *L* on one side.

"The guys who targeted Thompson at the Bund rally were wearing those silver shirts," Madi says. "I couldn't see the *L* because they had on some sort of sash, or maybe a gun belt."

"Clio also spotted something that I overlooked," Katherine continues. "I thought it was just some very bright sunlight from the windows, although in retrospect that's a fairly rare commodity for early February in Detroit. But Clio said she thought there were three people seated in the balcony, wearing CHRONOS keys. And she was right. Saul . . . along with two of the Vipers. Esther and the other Saul. The three of them seemed pretty friendly. Which I think we can all agree is a complicating factor."

We're all silent for a minute as that sinks in.

"Why?" Clio asks. "And don't give me that look, Rich. I can see that she's upset, and it's completely understandable given the circumstances, but she knows Saul Rand better than any of us. Out of everyone in this room, she's the one most likely to be able to tell us what makes him tick. And we don't even have a full day, so . . . as much as I'd like to give her some time, we don't have it."

"It's okay," Katherine says flatly. "But you're asking the wrong person. Ask Rich. Ask Tyson. They saw through him. They know him better than I do, apparently, in every way that counts. What I can tell you, however, is the one thing that can send Saul Rand into a rage is for someone to call him crazy. I'd bet serious money that the video in my diary—and yes, I've seen it—shows the aftermath of me doing just that. Losing his mind, his grip on reality, is the one thing

Saul has always feared the most. Or maybe he was lying about that, too. Who the hell knows? I'll give you whatever information I have about him. I'll tell you anything you want to know. But I don't have the answer to *why*."

"Okay," I say. "You're right. I don't think we can get at the broader question, but maybe we can narrow it down. You've watched Saul play The Game many times. Does he usually engineer the details? More specifically, do you think he hired a couple of fascist thugs to target Dorothy Thompson? Did he hire someone to shoot Lindbergh? Or does he just like to set the chaos in motion and then step back to see what happens?"

Katherine considers the question for a moment, then says, "It depends on his goal. If he's trying to prove a particular point, he'll map everything out in minute detail. But sometimes, he just likes to watch things burn. He's willing to suffer a loss. To sacrifice a pawn or even something more valuable. And if he knows he's going to lose, especially to Morgen Campbell, or even if he thinks it's headed toward a draw, he'll make sure to cause as much chaos as possible on his way out. Campbell once said Saul delighted in pissing in the punch bowl, even if it meant that he went thirsty, too. But in some of these cases, I think he probably had to get involved directly."

"Probably not for Dorothy Thompson," Clio says as she types something into the tablet. "In the previous timeline, she waltzed into a Bund rally. She definitely targeted Kuhn and the Bund in her column, so it was risky even then. But once they expanded the guest list, it was an entire shopping list of people and groups she'd either written about in her columns or spoken about in the radio show. Coughlin, William Dudley Pelley and the Silver Shirts, Dilling. Lindbergh, too—she was one of the few who actually came right out and called him a Nazi. If Saul put money and effort into drawing together all of those bad apples? They might not actually kill her, but there would probably be more than a few in the auditorium who would think it might be fun to shake her up a bit. As for the bomb scare? Who knows? I'd heard the name Lawrence Dennis, but that's as far as it goes. And yeah . . ." She squints at the screen. "I've been combing through her articles, and it looks like Thompson took on Lawrence Dennis, too. She called him an appeaser. Get this. 'The Harvard-educated Mr. Dennis, being intellectually integrated, is openly for appeasement with the Nazis, and even occasionally, in his letters, calls a spade a spade. He does not, of course, go further . . .'"

"Whoa," I say. "Let me see that."

She hands me the tablet. The article is from December 1940, but that was in the other timeline, before Dennis was added to a major event like the Bund rally. One veiled reference to race might be a coincidence. If she'd used only the word *integrated* or only *calls a spade a spade*, it probably wouldn't even have caught my attention. But both in the same sentence?

"Thompson knew Lawrence Dennis was mixed race," I say. "Something he took pains to hide in the 1930s, for obvious reasons. She was taunting him in her column. I still don't think that the recorded explosion is the kind of idea he'd come up with. But that's based on a twenty-minute-or-so conversation with the man and a vague knowledge of his personal history. But he may have wanted to scare her."

"Although the same goes for every other group in the auditorium," Richard says. "Sounds like she'd called pretty much everyone out for being a Nazi or, at the very least, Nazi adjacent. So it could have been a group effort. The only question is whether she signaled in advance that she was planning to attend the Bund rally, and we might be able to find that out, but is that the best use of our time when we know that's not one of Team Viper's moves?"

"But it's one of *Saul's* moves," Katherine says. "Three people are dead who shouldn't be. And I don't give a damn whether they're viewed as historically significant or not. We're fixing that." She looks around at the rest of us, and then says, "Right? If we let that stand, we're no better than he is."

"We'll fix it," I tell her. "If it's not unraveled when we make the other changes, we'll fix it. But Richard is right. Since we know it's not one of the moves Team Viper made, it probably shouldn't be our first priority."

"True," Katherine says. "Unfortunately, we have a lot more certainty about which moves they didn't make than which ones they did."

"But we do know one move for certain now," Madi says. "Einstein is definitely a Team Viper move. Alisa and two observers contacted him outside the Jewish Palestine Pavilion on May 9th. They show him videos of Hiroshima and Nagasaki. It hits him pretty hard."

"And he just believed them?" Clio asks. "Without any sort of verification?"

"They had photos of him from the future. I would have gone with something more detailed, but if it was enough for Alisa to catch his attention, I think it will be enough for me to do the same. The only question is what I tell him to convince him to sign the—"

"You don't have to convince him of anything," Katherine says. "Just keep him away from the meeting with Alisa."

"What's to stop them from contacting him later?" Clio says.

Katherine shrugs. "They might. But they'll have entered that date and time into the system as their official move, so it won't matter."

"If this was simply a computer simulation," I say, "you'd be right. But if he doesn't sign that letter, we could win the game and still have a screwed-up timeline. So . . . yeah. Whoever handles this needs to come up with something."

Madi waves her finger. "I'll take this one. I've already watched the stable points, so I have a head start. Maybe I can show him some data from the nuclear exchange with the Western Alliance."

"The . . . what?" Clio says, and then holds up her hands. "Never mind. I'm not sure I want to know."

"Wise choice," Madi says. "And I think it would need to be either me or Katherine dealing with Einstein, anyway, since he's rumored to be a bit of a ladies' man. The two male observers with Alisa made him nervous, and . . . I'm pretty sure he was checking out Alisa's tush as she walked away."

"Something Alisa would have counted on," I say. "So . . . that's one down. We already know that the attack on the Japanese ambassador at the Court of Peace is a match. So that means we have to choose between the July 4th bombing and the mugging of the Japanese physicist."

"We're going to have to prevent both, though," Katherine says. "I mean, if the physicist getting mugged turned out to be a weird coincidence, which I sincerely doubt, we might let it slide. It's just a minor injury with a tiny blurb in one newspaper, right? But we're not going to know one way or another unless someone follows him. The bombing's a different story, though. There were only two people killed in the other timeline because the police got it out of the British Pavilion in time and the damage was contained. And now we've got seventeen killed and dozens injured, so whether it's caused by Team Viper, Saul, or some unholy alliance between the two, we have to correct the course. I think we each pick one event to take the lead on. We can decide if we work individually or team up after we know what exactly we'll be doing. The two most likely to require physical strength are stopping the masked guys attacking the ambassador and the two muggers. Madi can handle Einstein. I'll alert the police to the location of the bomb and let them deal with it as they did last time."

Katherine seems to have taken over as team leader, at least for the moment. Maybe that should bother me, but it really doesn't. Rich opens his mouth to say something, but then quickly closes it and looks over at me. Is he thinking the same thing? Or simply worried about Katherine putting herself in potential danger? We're all going to have to put ourselves at risk. And she and Rich may not have extensive weapons experience, but they have far more research and field experience than I do. One of them probably *should* be leading this show, so I give him a shrug.

He responds with a resigned look and then says to Katherine, "Wouldn't it make more sense to check the stable point that we set in the closet—the one I burned my hand for—and intercept the bomber there, rather than waiting until the bomb is placed in the crowd? It seems like that would be the safer alternative for everyone concerned."

"It would," Katherine says. "I've already checked that stable point for a two-day period prior to the bombing, however, and the briefcase was never placed in that closet. Maybe it's somewhere else in the British Pavilion, but it's not there. The only place where we know it will be is the Court of Peace, which, between the attack on the ambassador and this bombing, sounds like a complete misnomer."

"But . . . the bomb not being there doesn't make sense." Madi pulls out her key and begins scrolling through as she speaks. "Jack said both stable points were kind of dark, so he was going to see if he could get a glimpse of the guy from one of the locations you set outside the building. But he definitely said that a man drops off the case. I don't remember the exact time, but it was around nine on the evening of July 3rd. And then a different guy—possibly one of the observers—takes it out in the wee hours of the morning of . . . July 4th." Madi draws in a sharp breath. "Oh my God."

She stares in stunned silence for a moment, and then holds her key up to transfer the location to mine.

"What is it?" Katherine says.

Madi just shakes her head and holds her key out. Katherine frowns and taps the back of her key to Madi's, then transfers the point to Rich and Clio.

As soon as I open the location, I see why Madi is speechless.

The location isn't dark at all anymore. A single bare bulb illumi-
nates two bodies on the floor in the center of the closet. They aren't
simply dead. Their skin is shriveled and splotched, their flesh wasted
away. *Desiccated* is the word that comes to mind. I've seen similar
images in history class, but not from the 1930s. These look more like
bodies from one of the targeted biological weapons used during the
Genetics War.

There's one big difference, however. I don't recall those bodies
being tied together with red ribbon, like these are, capped with a
giant bow. In the center of the bow is a CHRONOS key, and propped
against the display is a large, handwritten sign:

Morgen 27V, you miserable fuck.

It won't be pawns next time.

This world isn't your playground.

Collect your people, and GET OUT.

I have no clue what the numbers mean, and even though there's
no signature, there's no doubt in my mind who left this horrid package for Team Viper. The sight of the bodies sickens me. I'm pretty
sure this is only going to make our situation worse, and these people
didn't deserve to die like this. Those are my surface emotions. But
what I'm pretty sure is going to cost me sleep tonight is what's lurking deep beneath. Something I don't want to admit and that I'd have
sworn I'd never feel—a tiny, grudging shred of respect for Saul Rand
for sticking it to Morgen Campbell.

FROM THE *NEW YORK DAILY INTREPID*

BRITISH AGENT PLANTED EXPLOSIVE TO FRAME BUNDISTS

(July 18, 1940) William Miller Pell, a British citizen posing as a journalist for the London *Daily Express*, has been charged in the July 4 bombing at the World's Fair, following a massive police roundup of individuals with histories of political agitation. The attack killed eight members of the military and nine civilians and hospitalized thirty-two more. Dozens of other individuals, including journalist Dorothy Thompson and her son, were treated at the scene and released.

Police Commissioner Valentine held a rare press conference, noting that detectives had been convinced from the beginning that the bombing was likely an inside job. The most telling clue was the upholsterer's hair used as padding inside the briefcase that housed the bomb, which was a variety more commonly used in Great Britain than in the United States.

Anonymous calls to the police pointed toward the involvement of the German-American Bund. At the command of Mayor La Guardia, dozens of Bund members and leaders were rounded up, along with members of other fascist groups, including the Universal Front, led by Brother Charles Coughlin, and several communist groups, as well. In addition, detectives questioned all 110 employees of the British Pavilion, including a dozen individuals, all British citizens, who were recent hires. Pell claims to have undertaken this action entirely on his own, out of concern for a brother recently killed at the Battle of Dunkirk. In his remarks, however, Commissioner Valentine suggested that there is evidence of a connection to British intelligence.

In his statement to police, Pell acknowledged that he placed the device on the second floor of the British Pavilion, with a timer set to go off in the early morning hours, when the building would be unoccupied. At some point afterward, Pell alleges that an unknown individual changed the time to five p.m., rather than five a.m., and moved the explosive to the Court of Peace. The goal, according to the accused, was to damage British artifacts housed in the building (many of which are actually replicas, not originals) in the hope of pinning the crime on the Bund and fanning anti-Nazi sentiment that might push the nation toward entering the war against Germany.

∞27∞

KATHERINE
NEW YORK, NEW YORK
JULY 3, 1940

The apartment is eerily quiet for a small space with six people. It almost feels like exam week when we were in training. Well, except for the risk of failure. There's a very real chance that we'll fail, and no one ever failed exams at CHRONOS. We were created to be good at the job, so flunking out wasn't something that happened. Studying for exams was less a matter of fearing that we'd score poorly, and more a matter of wanting to come out on top. Every chair in the commons area would be occupied by students poring over the *Log of Stable Points*, reading from their tablets, or taking notes. Each focused, each very much in his or her own world.

We're all in our own worlds this morning, too, working on our separate pieces of the puzzle, now that we've divided up the tasks. Madi is digging through everything she can find dealing with Einstein and putting together an argument for why he must follow through on signing the letter Szilard sends to Roosevelt. Tyson and Rich have just returned from a trip to set a few other stable points that they'll need in order to intercept Tomonaga and disrupt the attack against the ambassador. Rich seemed unusually psyched when they got back, possibly because he never really expected arcane knowledge from one of his musical-history projects to be of much use. Their two quick jumps answered the key question hanging over us. The bombing in the Court of Peace wasn't Team Viper. We were fairly certain of that after seeing the observers' bodies last night, but Tomonaga and his friend were grabbed by the communist Rich suspected and two other guys. One of them was the Saul from their side, wearing an eye patch to hide his prosthetic eye. Apparently, he looked a bit too much like a pirate for comfort, and both of their intended victims seem to have had some martial arts training. Tomonaga, the physicist, clearly thought they were being robbed. He retaliated by jabbing his straightened hand into Other-Saul's solar plexus.

Tyson is focusing on the attack on the Japanese ambassador, but he also plans to stop in and disable the recording of the explosion at Madison Square Garden. Clio is watching the stable points that all of us will be using, since she'll act as the liaison point for all members of the team, both here and in 2136. When we all complete our assignments and meet up in 2136, Thea will enter one of the moves into the system, and Clio will enter the rest. That way, we'll have the all-members-must-play element covered.

Sorting all of that out took over half of the six hours that we've been at it. Then we decided on our disguises, because we can no longer assume that Team Viper will abide by their agreement to target only observers, and we don't know what else Saul might be doing. He could have already taken out one of their actual players, so a bit of precaution is in order. I hate wigs with a passion, but I'll be wearing a dark wig, along with a maternity dress and a strap-on baby bump. On the plus side, I'll be wearing rather sensible shoes, and I'm actually impressed with the pockets, which have openings that allow me to hide things inside the pregnancy pillow and still access them easily—like the laser device and one of the CHRONOS-field extenders that Tyson brought back for all of us from 2136 as a bit of insurance against someone snatching our keys. We wouldn't be able to jump without a key, but at least it would keep us from instantly blinking out of existence.

With the various details nailed down, we're now in final-check mode, watching the stable points where we'll be jumping in to make sure we're ready. The goal is to make all of our moves in rapid succession within a single hour and meet back at the library, but we're leaving an extra hour on the clock as a margin for error.

All five of us were up and working even before the wake-up time we agreed upon. Looking around the room, it's clear that I'm not the only one who slept poorly. I lay awake for well over an hour, staring at the ceiling. Each time I tried to close my eyes, I saw the mummified bodies, wrapped up like a sick Christmas gift. Or worse still, I saw Saul's face. Felt his hands touching me. The only way I managed to get any sleep was by swiping another of Clio's magic pills from the cabinet. One might not wipe you out the next morning, but it turns out that two will leave you feeling a bit zapped. Or maybe that's just the aftereffect of discovering that the man you planned to spend your life with is, in fact, a psychopath who has killed not just the two men he left in the closet, but dozens more, according to Madi and Clio, by poisoning a village well.

The fact that the rest of us are so quiet is probably why the steady tap-tap of Kiernan Dunne's foot against the leg of the coffee table is so unnerving. He clearly doesn't like the idea of being restricted to the apartment any more than his daughter does. For the first few minutes after his arrival about an hour ago, he argued that him being at the Fair as extra boots on the ground in case he was needed would be worth a small bit of risk. His protests were fairly feeble, however, and I think they were mostly for show. Clio said she made it clear when she telephoned him that she's fairly certain in this version of reality, as things stand right now, one of them doesn't make it. Kiernan can't see the stable points anymore, but she told him about the extra gravestone in their family cemetery, crossing her fingers that he'd decide to stay home. I don't think she really ever believed that was a possibility, however.

Now he's slumped at the end of the couch across from Clio's chair, coffee in hand, foot tapping.

"Dad, just go back to Skaneateles," Clio says. "I told you before you left that you'd be cooped up here with nothing to do."

"You did. But your mum and I didn't want you here alone. And there may be *something* I can do. Plus . . ." He waves a hand toward the coffee table, which is laden with three trays of cookies, brownies, and some sort of nut roll. "I had to make the care-package delivery. Even your brothers were saying she made too much."

"We're glad you're here, Mr. Dunne," Tyson says, taking a brownie from the tray. "It goes without saying that we wouldn't have stood the slightest chance without everything your family did to prepare the way. And these brownies are really good."

Kate Dunne is apparently a nervous baker. And this is Kate Dunne *before* she knows that something happens to someone in her family. Something that it's entirely possible will still happen, despite our decision to place them under house arrest, since there are apparently still three graves on that hill in Skaneateles.

It's irrational, but I'm very angry at CHRONOS today. Not just for the audacity of thinking something like this could never happen. I'll admit that I shared that belief. We aren't supposed to change the timeline, and there are extraction teams and other groups to correct things, if you screw up too badly. It's more anger that they didn't prepare us for the possibility—no matter how slight they may have imagined it to be—that something of this sort *might* happen. Maybe if we'd had that kind of training, we'd have a better idea of what to do right now. Rich says that we're overthinking this. That you can't see timeline changes until you embark on the *specific* action that changes them. I hope that's true, because I've spent the past half hour combing through the various stable points at the Fair. All of the things we need to reverse still happen, right on schedule, despite the fact that we have decided they must be prevented. Is it because we are not yet certain *exactly* how we will prevent them? Because we haven't taken a first decisive step in that direction? Or is it because we *fail* to prevent them?

In the case of the Court of Peace bombing, we've even taken a concrete move in the direction of prevention. This morning, Richard telephoned the police from a pay phone, noting that there is a bomb on the fairgrounds and even giving them our best bet for exactly where it is located and what time it will go off. The police dispatcher sounded bored, and Clio said we'd only need to comb through the past few years of New York City newspapers to understand why. Bomb threats were commonplace in the 1930s, and there was a general sense that the ones who telephoned to tell you they'd planted an explosive were almost always the ones who hadn't actually done it.

They did send some detectives out to poke around, however. One of them found a small suitcase in the bushes. The detectives took it out to the same spot where they'd taken the bomb before. In our own timeline, that resulted in two deaths and injured others severely enough to require hospitalization. I watched through the stable point, however, and this time, there was no explosion. When the experts eventually opened the case, a single red balloon floated up into the sky.

Ten minutes later, at five p.m., the actual bomb went off in the park. And despite careful surveillance of stable points, we still have no clue who dropped it off, when they did it, or exactly where it's located. And that's why I've been cycling through these locations for the past few hours. I've seen no CHRONOS keys. No faces that look familiar. Also, not that many hiding places, aside from the shrubbed area where they found the decoy explosive.

I've been in one position for so long that my back aches. On the plus side, maybe it will make my pregnancy disguise more effective. I stretch and then go to the kitchen in search of caffeine.

When I turn back with my coffee cup filled, I see Kiernan standing in the doorway. He's probably in his late forties, and still a very handsome man. That's especially true when he smiles, and he's smiling now.

"The first time I saw you, you were about the same age you are now, and I was eight. The *last* time I saw you, you were in your seventies, and Clio's mum was nineteen. We never imagined you'd actually get to see Clio, let alone get to see her when you were damn near the same age. Time travel is a kick in the head."

I return his smile, because in a few short sentences, the man has given me more information than anyone in the house. "So Clio is my granddaughter?"

He frowns, shakes his head, and takes a few steps back into the living room. "Damn it, Clio. You told me the woman knew her history. Or . . . future history, I guess."

"No," Clio says from her armchair. "What I said was that she knew about her relationship to *Madi*. Cat's out of the bag now, I guess." Clio leans forward so that I can see her face through the door. "There's a reality in which you are my great-grandmother. But given what you now know about my great-grandfather, I sincerely hope you won't repeat that mistake. I'd be entirely okay with that decision, since this medallion is my jewelry for life, either way."

I sink down into one of the kitchen chairs. Kiernan does the same.

"Sorry about that," he says.

"I already suspected something of the sort. She looks quite a bit like Saul's mother. Nicer, though, thank God. And your daughter doesn't seem to have inherited any of her great-grandfather's homicidal tendencies."

"That's true now, perhaps. You didn't see her as a teenager when she was pissed at one of her brothers." He stares down at the tiles on the floor for a moment, then looks back up at me. "Clio told me about the two bodies in the British Pavilion. Based on her description, they match the ones that Kate—the *other* Kate—and I saw in a small village in 1911 Georgia."

"How many were there?"

"Forty-seven, by most accounts. One said forty-eight, but they may have been basing that on the total number of people in the group, and there was one survivor who chose not to stick around for the inevitable questions. I guess you'd call the place a religious commune, but not one of the crazy variety. Quite a few kids in the mix, many of them orphans. The neighboring towns had another name for the village, but the people there called it God's Hollow. The people there mostly kept to themselves, so no one realized anything was off until they didn't come into town for their groceries a few weeks in a row. And the real pisser is that we couldn't risk stopping Saul on his test run, because we needed to make sure we stopped his grand finale. So, those deaths weigh heavy on me. Not the kind of thing I ever wanted Clio drawn into, but those CHRONOS keys are cursed, and like she said, the medallion is her companion for life."

He's quiet for a moment, and then says, "Listen, I know none of this is easy for you to hear, and I'm not trying to make things harder with everything you've got on your mind right now. But I didn't want you to head out with even the slightest thought that this might be a onetime act of violence by a man who's justifiably angry at these off-world bastards. If he's helping our side, he's doing it to further his own personal goals. And he'll stab every single one of us in the back, including you, if we give him a chance."

"Yes. I *know*. The shriveled bodies at the stable point kind of tipped me off to that." There's a sarcastic tone to my voice that I really didn't intend. I do think he's trying to be helpful. Maybe he even has fond feelings for the person I might have become in some other reality.

"I'm certain that you know *here*," he says, tapping his temple. "But in my experience, it's the heart that tends to lag behind. Just . . . be careful if you cross his path."

I pull out my personal death ray. "Killed a man in Memphis with this a few days ago. If necessary, I'll do it again."

Kiernan shakes his head, laughing softly, but his dark eyes are sad when he looks back at me. "Your head seems willing. Let's just hope that's what guides your hand."

Back in the living room, the others are now discussing style points. I've been exempted from that, since there are dozens of lives on the line if that bomb goes off in the Court of Peace. If I can find a way to do something that will increase our total without risking those lives, I'll do it, but I don't plan to expend many brain cells on that.

"I'm just not sure what else we can do," Madi says. "We're going to be working backward, like they did, so we'll get the chronological points and bonus. We'll correct all of their moves *at* the World's Fair, so it will be within the range to get full geographic points, plus the bonus. If we do all of that, we should get at least most of the style points they earned, right?"

"Maybe?" Rich says. "But we're not sure how they got some of their other points. I'm just thinking that they barely got any of the probability points. And we didn't do well on the initial predictions. We could recoup some of those points if we can think of quirky ways to achieve our objectives."

Kiernan resumes his spot on the couch, and we listen as Rich and Tyson debate an idea Rich came up with for accruing style points.

"I think we could get the costume," Rich says. "There's a stable point only a few yards away from the restroom at Toyland, which is where the actor changes out of his street clothes on July 3rd, 1940.

The only catch is that I really don't have the build for it. You're closer, Tyson."

"Not by much," Tyson says. "If any kids see me, their faith in Superman will be shattered. And can I just add this—the fact that we're even semiseriously debating me dressing up as a comic-book character tells me that whoever invented this stupid game should be shot."

"Drawn and quartered," Clio suggests.

Madi shakes her head. "I vote battered and deep fried. I'm feeling vindictive."

"Are you the one in charge?" Kiernan asks Tyson. "Because I'd like to make just one little suggestion." There's something about Kiernan's clipped tone that tells me that this isn't a *little suggestion* at all.

"Dad . . ." There's a note of caution in Clio's voice, so apparently she picked up on the same thing I did.

Tyson nods. "Officially, I'm the team leader. But I call a vote for any major decisions. And sure. Anything you want to add would be appreciated."

"Your *game* was thrown out the window when Saul Rand left his grotesque little fuck-you present for Morgen Campbell. If this Team Viper ever intended to abide by the rules of The Game and the decisions of the computer judge they set up, you can be sure they won't be following those rules now. Your only way to fix this, God help us, is to follow Saul's lead. To hell with the style points, to hell with *winning* the game. Just fix the bloody timeline. All of it or as much as you reasonably can. Because unless you can find a way to block them, to slam the door in their faces, they're going to be back. Saul just guaranteed that. The game is over. We're at war."

He's right. I was thinking something similar a few minutes ago, although I hadn't really followed it to its logical conclusion. Looking around the room, I can tell I'm not the only one whose thoughts have ambled at least partway down that path.

"It's a fair point," Tyson says. "We've been so focused on the game that we haven't really dealt with the fact that Saul didn't simply move the goalposts last night. He blew them the hell up. We could just dispense with any added complications. I mean, what are the odds that their cameras will even pick up the fact that I'm in a costume, or that we trick one of the Silver Shirts into stopping the guy aiming at the ambassador, and so on. We could say we did, and they'd likely have a hard time proving otherwise." He pulls out his key to check something. "And yeah. Style points are the least of our problems. The utility closet in the British Pavilion is once again empty."

"How did they get the bodies out of . . ." Madi begins, and then shakes her head. "Never mind. That's the easy part. How Saul got them into the place is a bit of a mystery, but all Team Viper had to do to get the bodies *out* was pull their keys."

"Or more likely just that one key in the center of that bow," I say. "Which probably means Saul pocketed the spare."

"Hold on," Madi says. She scrolls through her key. After a moment, she nods. "One of the two men was with Alisa when she met Einstein. I'm guessing she now has some screwy memories, because he's no longer in the picture when I look back at the stable point."

"Good to know," I say. "Unfortunately, however, we've been working on a game plan—or battle plan, if you prefer—where we take these moves in reverse order. With just under six hours to go on the timer, do we really want to toss all of that away?"

Tyson sighs. "And that's also a fair point."

"How about we still enter the moves?" Rich says. "It costs us almost nothing to do that. And we continue with the order we have set up, because that's what we're prepared for. But aside from that, Kiernan's right. This isn't a game. It never really has been."

Tyson calls for a quick vote. In apparent deference to Clio's earlier comment, he doesn't insist on a secret ballot this time. The decision is unanimous, including Kiernan, although judging from his expression he seems to be a bit skeptical of leadership by show of hands.

"Okay," Tyson says. "Who wants to go forward and explain all of this to the crew in 2136?"

"I'll go," Madi says. "I can stop by and tell Jack, too, since it's on my way. We need to let them know about Saul's . . ." She's clearly having trouble finding words for his action, then shakes it off. "We also need to impress upon Thea the importance of listening to Alex and the others and entering her move carefully. And she'll probably take direction better from me. I'm thinking I'll ask her to enter the move dealing with Einstein. I don't know that she'd necessarily focus more when doing something specifically for me, but it can't hurt."

"Shouldn't we wait until we have their votes to make a decision?" Clio asks.

"I guess we could take their vote as a formality, but I don't think they'll argue the point, and even if all of them did, there are six of us and five of them, so . . ."

"What, you're not holding out for a unanimous decision? No caucusing? No consensus building?" Kiernan asks. Clio gives him another stern look and he chuckles. "Just saying it seems a bit undemocratic to me."

∞

NEW YORK, NEW YORK
JULY 4, 1940

I blink in at one of the hidden stable points that Richard and I set in the gardens behind the British Pavilion just after two p.m., taking a few minutes to stop and examine several varieties of roses as I amble toward the gate. In the distance, a band is playing what I'm pretty sure is a John Philip Sousa march.

Most of my travel today will be on foot. Aside from the wig and the weird sensation of having a small mountain of stomach, the pregnancy costume is one of the more comfortable options I've worn for fieldwork. My initial plan is to walk around the edges of the Court of Peace and see if I can get a better sense for where the bomb might be hidden.

Clio will, in fact, be doing more actual time travel than any of us, since she's the liaison between 1940 and 2136. Her job is to watch the stable points at the Court of Peace and the Flushing Gate, which is where the bomb was taken to try and disable it in the other timeline.

Because we're fairly certain that today's bombing is not one of Team Viper's official moves, Rich and Tyson have already jumped to the Amusement Zone on the evening of September 12, 1939. They will intercept Tomonaga and his friend inside the Theater of Time and Space and divert them away from the location where they would be mugged, either by persuasion or force. Hopefully, they'll also be able to convince them to ignore anyone who contacts them with nuclear information. Rich and Tyson will then go back to June 2, 1939, and foil the attempt against the Japanese ambassador.

Madi will then proceed with our last official move by waylaying Einstein at the train station and explaining why he should go ahead with an action that will result in the US using nuclear weapons. Once that move is in the system, the timeline will, hopefully, flip. It's entirely possible that it will flip after one of our other moves. At that point, assuming the deaths at the Bund rally still happen, Tyson will go back to prevent the fake explosion that causes them and also the attack on Lindbergh the following year.

Assuming everything goes according to plan, we'll still have to deal with the mess Saul has made. And worry about when Team Viper will hit next, because after Saul's stupid decision to murder two observers, there's no way they'll take their win (or, if we're lucky, loss) and move on to the next universe. They'll be looking for revenge.

I turn onto the avenue that curves around the fountains, and make my way at a leisurely pace through the foreign-government exhibits, keeping an eye out for police among the hundreds of people lining the sidewalks, since I will probably need to alert them to the presence of a bomb in the next few minutes. Two officers are standing outside the Netherlands Pavilion, talking to a third officer behind the wheel of the only convertible police car I've ever seen, with the Trylon and Perisphere logo on the side. Maybe the vehicle was in the parade that ended about an hour ago.

I continue on toward the Court of Peace. Unlike the garden area I just left, this place is mostly concrete. There are bushes lining the fence that separates the wide walkway from the massive oval Lagoon of Nations, presumably to keep fairgoers from diving into the fountains. The Court of Peace itself, however, is relatively barren of anything aside from folding chairs, most of them occupied by people listening to the military band, which has now shifted to "God Bless America."

The suitcase that we pointed the police toward earlier was in one of the few clusters of greenery large enough to hide it, along the southern edge of the court. My best guess, based on viewing the stable points and the blast radius, is that a second case is hidden farther into the bushes. As I draw closer, however, I see that my perspective was limited. The greenery surrounding the trees that dot the perimeter of the court is sparser than it appeared at a distance. That's probably why the police had no trouble finding the decoy case. It would have been clearly visible from the sidewalk.

A second suitcase bomb would also be visible, and I don't see anything large enough to do the kind of damage I saw through the key. Given that the purpose of this area is to accommodate large numbers of people for everything from presidential speeches to equestrian events, it's an open space. Looking out at the veritable ocean of chairs, I say a prayer that the bomb isn't tucked beneath one of them. That would be unlikely for a bomb from this era, as it would be too large, but now that Saul is involved, who's to say what we're dealing with? It could be something made centuries from now. The only things dotting the concrete slab, other than chairs and people, are speakers mounted on tall poles, a few pedestrian benches, and the occasional light post.

And . . . trash cans. Three of them within the blast zone. There are still two hours until the thing goes off, so I make a quick tour of those three bins. Nothing in the first one. There appears to be nothing in the second, either. But then I see it. Beneath the wadded newspaper is a large, circular hatbox. Not the flimsy cardboard type, but the old-fashioned kind that women used for foreign travel and definitely not the sort of thing that would be casually discarded.

I turn back toward the Netherlands building to fetch the police. Two young men in silver shirts with the Universal Front logo on the left side each grab one of my arms. I cry out, yelling for someone to call the police. Several people jump up from the crowd and move toward me, but they step back when they see three officers who are, in fact, heading straight toward us at a rapid clip.

Morgen Campbell, the younger, who is clearly not used to running, brings up the rear. "That's her," he says, panting. "I saw her put a round . . . suitcase . . . thing in that trash can after the parade, when everyone was finding a seat. I thought it looked suspicious. I asked her what she was doing, and she told me I'd better get out of her way or she'd blow me clear to hell."

He leans forward and puts both hands on his knees as if he's catching his breath, but it's mostly just a cover so that he can give me a sly smile.

"There *is* a hatbox in the bin," I say through gritted teeth. "But I didn't put it there. I thought I heard a noise when I walked past. So I checked. It's very faint. I didn't want to touch it, so I was going to find someone to come investigate."

"I don't hear anything coming from the trash, ma'am," the older cop says. "In fact, I can barely hear you over the band."

"She's lying," Morgen says. "And she might even have an explosive in whatever that is she's got strapped beneath that dress. I can look at the way she walks and tell you that she's not pregnant. My mother's an ob-gyn, and—"

"An oh-bee . . . what?" the second officer asks.

"A lady-parts doctor," Morgen says. "That's what we call them in Virginia."

"Where you want us to take her?" the Silver Shirt on my right asks, squeezing my arm a bit tighter.

"*You* ain't takin' her anywhere, son," the first officer says. "We've got it from here. I thought you tin-soldier Nazis were protesting the Fair."

Silver Shirt #2 exchanges a look with his counterpart, then says, "Well, if we let her go, you gotta grab her arms, then. She's dangerous."

That cracks two of the officers up. The other one is too busy looking into the trash to pay attention. "Take both of them to the station so we can sort this out. Get Alice to search her. I don't know what the hell either of them is talking about. There's nothing in this trash can except hamburger wrappers and several months' worth of chewed bubble gum stuck to the side."

Morgen takes a couple of steps back toward the sidewalk. He's looking straight at me when he blinks out. The Silver Shirts both see him, and the taller one says, "Where did he go?" They're well trained, though, because neither of them lets go of my arms.

"Hey, the kid's got a point. Where *did* he go?" one of the junior cops asks. Several people in the audience who were watching seem to be wondering the same thing.

The older cop scans the crowd, then looks back at me. "Looks like your friend is a regular Houdini, ma'am. He got lucky. You . . . not so much. We're gettin' a bit tired of the bomb-threat games, though, so you're gonna need to answer a few questions. Come on."

I'm escorted back to the convertible police car in front of the Netherlands Pavilion. They don't cuff me but keep an eye on me as I'm ushered into the back seat along with the senior officer.

"Your friend back there is faster than he looks," the officer says.

"He's not my friend," I say with a tight smile and stare out at the fairgrounds. Personally, I'm much more concerned about where the bomb went than about Morgen. And I've got too much to do to waste time on this detour.

Clio is monitoring all of our stable points, so hopefully she'll pass the word along that I've run into difficulty. One option would be to pull out the CHRONOS key and try my praying-to-St.-Eligius routine, but disappearing right in front of three policemen and dozens of people lining the streets—in broad daylight, no less—goes against everything I've been taught. It might also convince the cop next to me, who seems like the suspicious type, to put the cuffs on me. And so I bide my time as we inch our way across the fairgrounds to the World's Fair Police Station just beyond the main gates. If I play it cool, maybe I'll still have my hands free so that I can blink out quickly when they turn me over to a policewoman to be searched.

In the end, however, none of that is necessary. When we arrive at the station, Saul is waiting at the counter. "Oh my God, Kathy! There you are. I've been looking everywhere."

The woman behind the desk gives me a smile that is sympathetic, but still somewhat wary. "Mrs. Rand, you've given your husband here quite the scare." She looks over at the older cop and discreetly taps her temple while pretending to smooth her hair. *Great.* Saul has told her that I'm insane. And, unfortunately, what I'm about to say next will probably reinforce that.

"Go ahead and toss me in jail," I tell her. "I'm not leaving with him."

Saul sighs. "Will you at least *talk* to me, love? Over there on the bench, where all of the officers can see, but we'll have some privacy. No one wants to put you in jail. And I'm certainly not going to hurt you. I would *never* hurt you." He crouches down so that his eyes are level with mine as he speaks, and I can tell that he intends those last words not simply for show, but as a plea. I reach up for the chain inside the bodice of my dress and tug it out.

He sighs again with an extra touch of drama. "Yes, dear. You can hold your mother's locket while we talk. But you don't need magic tokens to keep you and . . . the baby . . . safe from me."

Saul pauses when he mentions the baby, staring down at my abdomen with a look of deep sorrow. And I know instantly what he told them. Losing the baby unhinged me. Did he simply say that I've taken to faking the pregnancy? Or did he add that I keep thinking I hear the baby for added pathos?

The whole act is smarmy, obnoxious, and overplayed, but apparently, I'm the only one who notices. So I nod and follow him to the bench.

"Where the hell have you been?" he asks under his breath. "By my calculations, you only have a few hours left. We don't have time for silly games."

"No kidding," I hiss. "What happened to the bomb?"

"I took care of it."

"What does that mean?"

"I blinked back to two a.m., extracted it from the damn trash can, and returned it to where it was in the previous timeline. You know . . . the one we're trying to get *back* to? And I could have told you that if you'd met me as agreed. I'm going to take a wild guess and say that you and the others found the message I left for Morgen, and you don't approve of me breaking the rules. But, in case you've forgotten, Kathy, I'm the expert at Temporal Dilemma. And this isn't a game for *us*. This is a goddamn war."

The words are so close to what Kiernan Dunne said back at the apartment that they take me off guard. And thinking of Kiernan pulls up the memory of his face as he told me about Saul's supposed test run at God's Hollow. *Supposed?* Damn it, I'm doing exactly what Kiernan warned me against. I need to keep emotions out of the equation when it comes to Saul, and I'm sitting here, letting him talk to me. Letting him try to justify the murder of the two observers. That thought must wipe the angry look from my face, but Saul misreads my revulsion as something else.

"Yes! It's war. There are casualties in war. I'm trying to minimize those casualties. I don't know about the rest of you, but I don't play by Morgen Campbell's rules. I had to send him a strong message. Shock value. And I needed something that would get your attention, too, when you didn't show up as promised. So . . . since you saw what I left for Team Viper, did you at least pass the message along to Max's physicist friend?"

That comment baffles me. "Yes. He knows you killed their observers. But why does it matter whether he knows?"

Saul rolls his eyes. "No. The *message*. 27V. I don't know what it means, but I've had several . . . conversations with two of his jumpers who thought I was working for them. Their Esther said something about a drink they have in 27V. And I don't think she was talking about a bar. You said he's trying to find a way to block their signal or whatever, but he's not sure which universe they're coming from, remember? It might not be of any use at all. I doubt the realities are conveniently labeled. But maybe it will narrow down something." He glances over at the policewoman and smiles. "Can we just go now? Tell the nice lady you're sorry and that you've been really mixed up since the accident. That's all you need to say, and I promise you they'll let you walk out of here with me."

He's right. Of course. There are tears in the policewoman's eyes, and she tells me to take care and that I'm lucky to have such a kind and devoted husband. The one male officer behind the desk gives me an uncomfortable smile and quickly turns back to his paperwork. Saul takes my arm, and it requires all of my self-control not to run when his fingers brush against the bare skin of my elbow.

As soon as we round the corner of the building, I tell him I need to go. "The clue in your note. I don't think Max's friend got it. Plus, I need to let them know that the bomb is taken care of."

"Okay," he says. "But will you promise to meet me in Miami later so that I can explain everything? I'm trying to buy us some time. Until we're at the point where we can block them, we need to let them know that this world is not safe for their games. Our timeline does not belong to them."

"But what's to stop them from jumping back further, Saul? From sending dozens of people into our history and completely destroying us? You seem to think you can reason with Morgen—"

"No," he says. "You're missing the entire point. What's the fun of playing time chess in a world where there are no constants? Any move they make, I will top it. If we make the field unplayable and risky, if we take the *fun* out of their game, they'll go away."

"Except the playing field is our history, Saul. The risk isn't just to them."

"Oh, come on, Kathy! Do you really think we couldn't do better? No matter what the CHRONOS manual says, history isn't sacred, and it sure as hell isn't spotless. You know that. Race continues to divide people for centuries. How long did it take for women to get real equality? Look around at these cars. These people are killing the planet and don't know it . . . But even once they do know it, they won't stop. People make shit decisions as a group unless they are led with a strong hand. And we could do that through the Cyrists. I've already laid the groundwork."

He's making arguments that he knows will appeal to me. Equality. Protecting the environment. Arguments that I'm not even entirely sure he believes. I close my eyes for a long moment, and when I open them, I paste on a smile. "Maybe you're right. We didn't break the timeline. And there's no rule that says we can't make a better version as we right this wrong. I'm going to help them finish out the game. See if we can get the timeline to flip. But . . . we don't need to go back to CHRONOS after that, assuming it even exists. I'll meet you at your place in Miami, and we can figure out our next steps."

He smiles back. "That sounds like an excellent plan." Then he tips my face up to kiss me.

I slip my hand into my pocket and close it around the laser pen inside the pillow. Flicking the safety off, I pull it out into my pocket, and point it toward Saul's chest. An insane man with a deeply flawed moral code is dangerous enough. That same man with a time-travel device in his hands could be unstoppable.

My brain tells my finger to click the damn button.

But my brain is apparently not in control.

FROM THE *NEW YORK DAILY INTREPID*

Security Officer Killed in Attack on Japanese Ambassador

(June 3, 1939) A security officer was killed at the World's Fair yesterday while in pursuit of masked gunmen who fired on Japanese Ambassador Kensuke Horinouchi.

Just prior to the attack, Horinouchi watched as the Torch of Friendship was lit by a flame that Miss Japan, Akiko Tsukimoto, transported from the Grand Shrine of Izumo across the Pacific Ocean and then from California to New York, taking great care that it was not extinguished.

Ambassador Horinouchi stated, "The Japanese people symbolize their ardent hope that the glorious tradition of peace and amity between America and Japan will remain as bright and eternal as the temple fire at

Izumo." Moments later, the ceremony ended as 150 doves were released celebrating the enduring peace between our nations.

As the sound of wings filled the air, a shot rang out. Grover Whalen, head of the New York World's Fair Committee, was injured slightly when he dove forward to shield the ambassador. Two guards hired by the Fair Committee pursued the shooter, who fled toward the Flushing Gate. Shots were fired, and one of the guards was killed.

Ambassador Horinouchi was unharmed aside from a mildly singed arm when the Torch of Friendship toppled, catching the bunting surrounding the podium on fire. Luckily, the torch was not extinguished.

Police are questioning several groups across the political spectrum, including Brother Charles Coughlin's Universal Front, which was holding a protest outside the gates shortly before the attack, and members of the Communist Party of America, who protested the event due to Japan's ongoing war with China.

∞28∞

TYSON
NEW YORK, NEW YORK
SEPTEMBER 12, 1939

It's not even close to the lamest virtual reality I've experienced, but for this era, the Theater of Time and Space is impressive. Not the building itself. It's barely finished and seems more like a warehouse than a theater. The seating leaves a lot to be desired, too, since we're packed into every available space on the bleachers. But the curved screens are a huge innovation. They cover the entirety of the back wall and about one-third of the walls on the right and left. While the popping-flashbulb effect when you go to what I guess is supposed to be hyperspeed is kind of cheesy, combined with the music and the camera angles, it works. They've done a decent job of blocking the light from the Amusement Zone outside, and once the film starts, it does kind of feel like you're flying through space, if you can avoid looking around you.

Of course, Richard and I can't avoid looking around us. We're keeping an eye on the two Japanese men one row down and just to our left. They speak quietly several times as the show begins, but it's mostly in Japanese and probably about the exhibit, since they're pointing at the screen.

When the show ends, Tomonaga and his friend exit on the left. Rich and I follow. If we can intercept them inside the building, we stand less chance of being spotted by Team Viper and Leon Josephson, who are only a few buildings away.

"Mr. Tomonaga? Shin'ichirō Tomonaga?"

The taller of the two men turns and nods his head. Richard flips open the badge that RJ printed. "Agent Mulder, and this is my partner, Agent Scully." I pull out my badge as well. Personally, I would have gone with names that weren't quite so odd, but that's what the badge says, so we're kind of stuck. RJ's handiwork seems to be decent, though. We waved it at the ticket taker when we came in, told him that we were going to be questioning two individuals—two nonviolent individuals—and asked whether there was a back door we could use if necessary. He'd happily shown us the exit at the rear of the building.

"FBI?" the friend says, looking confused.

"Federal Bureau of Investigation. Kind of like the police. We've had a report of some suspicious activity . . ."

Both men look a bit confused.

"We have done something wrong?" Tomonaga asks.

"No, no," I say. "It's just that we received a report that an agent of the Russian government may be targeting you with some disinformation."

They both nod. The second guy says, "We have documents," and reaches into his breast pocket.

"That's okay," Richard says. "We don't need them."

The men seem confused, and I think we may be tapping the limits of their English skills. I bring out the tablet, open the translation tool, and Rich proceeds to explain we have information that an agent of the Soviet Union is planning to contact Tomonaga, posing as an American citizen, to give him false information that the United States is currently testing atomic weapons.

As we feared, the two men seem more interested in the tablet than in what we're trying to tell them, especially once it translates Rich's speech into Japanese.

Tomonaga says something in his language, which the tablet translates as "But why do they come to me? I am not a person who does weapons. And why tell Japan at all?"

"Maybe they assume that you will understand the atomic component and know who should be contacted," Richard says. "We think their goal is for your government to waste resources on research that Professor Heisenberg, with whom I believe you studied recently, considers impractical. President Roosevelt believes that Japan is currently a valuable counterbalance against the USSR and instructed Director Hoover to send us here to caution you. The spy will most likely claim to be a friend of Japan, and he will be accompanied by a man wearing an eye patch."

"Ah, *aipatchi*," Tomonaga says. The men look at each other and nod. "We see him at dinner."

"How did you discover the plan of this spy?" the other man asks. He seems a bit more wary than Tomonaga.

I reach forward and tap the edge of the tablet. "This also functions as a code breaker. Neat little gadget." I can tell that they definitely agree on that point.

Richard pauses for a moment, and then adds, "The US government is planning to have these on military ships and planes by the end of 1941. Personally, I can't see why it would take that long, but hey, I'd work slow, too, if I was stationed somewhere I could go to Waikiki Beach during the off-hours, you know?"

The translator does its thing, and then the other two men smile and nod.

"How does it work?" Tomonaga asks.

That's a question neither of us is really equipped to field, so I just smile and shake my head. "I'm not a scientist. To me, it's magic, just like that television thing they're debuting over at the main fair-grounds. Listen, they may be planning to make their move when you leave here. We'd be happy to escort you out the back and to the subway station if you'd like."

Tomonaga says they would appreciate that, and we make our way to the rear exit of the theater, where a door opens onto a grassy area behind this strip of buildings. The entrance to the Independent Subway station is visible as soon as we step out the door. Less than five minutes later, the two men are on the train, with no sign of a single member of Team Viper.

"That felt . . . too easy," I tell Rich as we look for an unobtrusive place to blink out.

"I knew you were going to say that. You're such a pessimist. How about we take the easy win and move on? Because you know our luck isn't going to hold."

"And you say *I'm* the pessimist?"

∞

NEW YORK, NEW YORK
JUNE 2, 1939

Our luck does, however, seem to be holding. When we arrive at our stable point near the Fountain Lake gate at 1:20 p.m. on June 2nd, we find the usual cluster of Universal Front thugs protesting as they have been most days since the Fair opened in May. If security chases them away from one gate, they just head to the next, and they've been such a steady presence that the police aren't paying much attention to them unless they get rowdy and start actually harassing the paying guests.

Richard and I step out from behind the ticket booth and wait for a stream of schoolkids headed toward the buses in the parking lot to pass. When we reach the UF protestors, I flash the badge. "FBI. Gonna have to ask you to move along. You can come back and tell everyone about the awful international menace tomorrow, but we've had a report that someone from UF is planning to get up to more than their usual low-level bullshit today. We've notified the police on the fairgrounds, so if any of you are planning something, this ain't the day to do it, boys."

Most of them disperse, grumbling. I've watched them through the key on several occasions when the World's Fair Police have tried to urge them along, and there's usually a bit more pushback. They seem more inclined to listen when you're holding an FBI badge.

The young man who is planning to enter the Fair and take the shot at the ambassador is one of the last to leave. As he walks off toward the parking lot, I see his hand move toward his jacket.

"Stop!" I whip my pistol out of the shoulder holster. "Hands behind your head. Right now."

I give the gun to Rich and tell him to cover me. He gives me a look of horror. "Now I'm wishing I'd kept the Timex," he whispers.

"Wouldn't matter. Too many people around to use it." He takes my gun and I cross over to the UF guy. "Keep your hands up. Just so you know, your boss was paying two other people, in case you chickened out. They both folded like paper airplanes when we took them in for questioning this morning, so unless you want to be the only one in prison, you might want to think about doing the same."

"Piss off," he says as I take his gun.

Rich snorts. "Tough guy now, but a few weeks in the pen usually fixes that."

We've drawn attention from the security guard outside the ticket booth. "I already called the WFP," he yells, keeping his distance. "They're on their way."

Rich shouts back that we're FBI.

"Really? No one mentioned that we had federal agents on the premises today."

"Someone reported a threat against the Japanese ambassador," Rich says.

"Yeah," I say. "We're going to have to hand him over to you, though, because we've got somewhere else to be."

"Me?" The guard looks stunned. "I'm not regular police. I'm just in a uniform to keep kids from comin' through without a ticket. No handcuffs. No weapon."

"Easy fix for that." I hand him the guy's gun. "I think you'll find that this was stolen. Tell the WFP we'll be back before nightfall, if they can hold him until then."

Rich shoots me a questioning look. Which is fair. I have no idea if the gun is stolen, just as I have no idea if there were other people tasked with shooting the ambassador if this one failed to follow through. It's a bluff, but it's the one thing that came to mind that might get them to hold the man for a bit. By the time they realize we're not coming back, Ambassador Horinouchi will no longer be on the fairgrounds.

We leave the guard in charge, then hurry toward the gate and duck behind a bank of cypress trees. By prior agreement, I open the stable point at the Court of Peace and Rich pulls up the location in the library in 2136. I scan through the Japan Day ceremony. No shooting. Grover Whalen, head of the World's Fair Committee, doesn't get to play hero by shielding the ambassador. The Flame of Friendship or whatever it's called is never in danger, and the ambassador is ushered from the stage and over to his waiting car at the end of the event.

Rich confirms this based on the message on the library wall screen. "Two check marks now, but no time shift. I was really hoping this would flip the timeline," he says. "That maybe Einstein was just icing on the cake."

"Would have been nice," I say. "Are you going to the apartment now or straight to the library?"

"Library. I want to make sure we've actually reversed these two events, and for that, I'm going to need a public data system. I'd also like to make sure that Thea enters the moves correctly. Are you going to wait until Madi is done or head straight to Madison Square Garden?"

I pull up the stable point on the ground floor of the arena. The same scene unfolds, exactly as before. I *could* wait and see if Madi's move undoes these deaths, but it seems far more likely that this is something Saul screwed up. Might as well get a head start on our next hopeless task.

And this is personal for me. I see too many parallels between my own experience at CHRONOS and the path Dennis has followed. I want him to make the right choice and refuse to be part of the bomb hoax.

"Do you want me to come with you?" Rich asks, but I can tell he knows the answer.

"Thanks, but I'll meet you there shortly. First, I need to go play Ghost of Christmas Future."

FROM THE *NEW YORK DAILY INTREPID*

CITIZEN EINSTEIN

(June 22, 1940) World-renowned scientist Dr. Albert Einstein passed the test for US citizenship today "with flying colors." He was tested along with his daughter, Margot, his secretary, Helen Dukas, and twenty other prospective citizens.

For years, Einstein and Hitler have represented two sides of the German spirit. Hitler embodies brute force and domination, while Einstein has come to symbolize intellect and the curiosity that pushes mankind toward great scientific achievement. In his rise to power, Hitler drove out men like Einstein and his fellow refugee Thomas Mann. It is a testament to our principles of freedom, democracy, and equality that these great men should not merely seek shelter on our shores but choose to become part of the great American experiment.

∞29∞

"You look good as a redhead," Clio says, tugging the wig into place.

The color is really more of a strawberry blonde, and not dramatically different from my own shade, but with subtle waves and tucked rolls that scream 1940s.

"We really should have done your hair into a tighter knot," she says as she adjusts the hairline.

That gives me a shudder. I already feel like my chin is stretched clear to my cheekbones. Aside from a cheap costume wig I wore one year at Halloween, I've never actually worn one of these torture devices. I'd prefer not to wear one now, but I doubt we can count on Team Viper to abide by the agreement not to target the four of us after Saul's grisly little stunt. Tyson and Rich have an advantage in that they're both relatively average build and height in an era where the vast majority of men wear some variant of the standard uniform—dark suit and hat. All they had to do was dress as usual and blend in with the crowd. And apparently, it worked . . . at least for their first objective. When we scanned the stable point where Tomonaga and his friend were attacked, they never arrive. Leon Josephson, Other-Saul, and the third man just stand there, looking bored as they watch the people on the midway for two Japanese tourists. Next, we checked the wall screen in 2136, and it now reads:

✔ *Tomonaga mugging averted*

Clio says she'd feel better if we had some word about the July 4th bombing, but Katherine has only been gone for a short time.

My scalp wasn't itchy at all until it was encased in the wig. I grab one of the hairpins from the dresser and try to scratch, but it's a lost cause. Hopefully, I'll get used to it. "I'll be so glad when this is over, and I can just go back to adding my normal streak of blue down one side and be done with it."

I can see Clio's face in the mirror. Her lip pulls down slightly on one side when I mention the accent streak, and I have to laugh. She's curiously old fashioned in some ways, which shouldn't surprise me at all, given that she was born in 1913. But it still catches me off guard every now and then. "There," she says. "You're all set. You just need to get your coquettish side going. Think Marilyn . . . Monroe." She flinches slightly when she says the name. "And you probably have no idea who she is."

"I have a vague mental image of a woman in a white dress. And I know she was married to the guy who wrote *Death of a Salesman*. Arthur—"

"Miller. Yes."

"Plus, you mentioned her before. You said Simon was obsessed with her. Speaking of Simon, have you told your father that he's gone yet?"

Clio shakes her head. "I need to. But I haven't really had a moment alone with him, and . . . it's not the thing I'd want to tell him in a room full of people. I should probably tell him here, though, rather than at home. He's going to have the same wildly mixed feelings that I did, and he'll have a harder time than I did admitting that the news makes him a bit sad, too. I doubt he'd admit it at all in front of Mom. We didn't even tell her I was babysitting Simon, because just thinking about the guy could give her the shakes. Aunt June said she had a touch of PTSD, which wasn't even a thing back when I was born or now, and it's not like she could go talk things out with a therapist anyway. Simon never hurt her physically, but keeping someone prisoner for six months or so is bound to leave them with some damage. If she'd known he was doing something similar with me . . ."

Clio shakes it off. "We need to get you on your way to the Fair so you can charm the good professor. I'll meet you in 2136, and we'll both feel that nasty stomach lurch from the time shift, but this time we'll be happy to feel it because it will mean that this is *over*. You can do this, okay?"

Her chipper tone seems very much out of place. I'm pretty sure she knows even if we do feel the time shift, it won't *really* be over. Team Viper will still be here. Until we find a way to block them, they'll just go break something else, and I doubt they'll give us much time to regroup before striking. Plus, Saul will still be a rogue element, and the new timeline probably won't be exactly like the one we know. No point in reminding her of that, though. Instead, I just note that she's in a very optimistic mood.

Clio responds with a shaky grin. "Mostly because I'm scared. Aunt June always said the best way of dealing with fear was through positive affirmations. Which I think is something she got from the Cyrists, but . . . not all of their ideas are bad. So . . . this is me, positively affirming. But I do think you can fix this. Really."

"Thanks." I smile, but the pep talk that Jack gave me a few hours ago did a lot more to calm my nerves. I dropped in to update him and get his vote on how to proceed. Given that we were all in accord, not just in New York 1939, but also in Bethesda 2136, his one vote was indeed a technicality. But it was still important to get that vote, despite Kiernan's skepticism. Jack had simply taken one look at my face, correctly gauged my level of trepidation, and scooped me into his arms.

"Whatever happens today," he told me, "we will wake up tomorrow and do whatever we can do to *fix* this world. Even if that timer ends and the game is over with no time shift, we will keep working every day to make whatever situation we land in a better one. Even if I'm stuck here in 1966. In the end, that's all we can do. It's all anyone can do."

It's not a short and catchy positive affirmation like Clio's *you can do this*, but it calmed my nerves. It reminded me that even if *perfect* is unattainable, *better* is always possible.

I pull out the key and check the stable point in Bethesda again. The wall screen now displays three check marks.

✔ *Court of Peace bombing prevented*

✔ *Tomonaga mugging averted*

✔ *No attack on ambassador*

"Guess you're up next," Clio says with a worried smile.

The living room is now empty aside from Kiernan. "You look like that lead singer of the Andrews Sisters," he says. "Although, I doubt she'd be wearing a man's watch."

I was a bit hesitant to trade weapons with Richard. He wasn't too keen on it himself. Both Katherine and Tyson pointed out that he'd be more likely to need something with actual firepower, though. Of the four assignments, mine is the only one that relies solely on persuasion. Which is part of the reason that I'm nervous.

"This is completely out of my comfort zone," I say, tugging down the sleeve of my sweater to cover the watch. "I'm not a very good actor."

"It's not really acting, though," Clio says. "I mean, you're a time traveler telling him the truth."

"*Parts* of the truth. I'm glossing over some pretty important stuff."

"True," Kiernan says. "But it's for the greater good."

"Can we really say that for certain, though? I mean, in terms of lives lost? It just seems murky to me. I know that far more people died when we dropped the bombs on Japan than in the nuclear exchange between the US and the Western Alliance, but then there are the theories saying the overall loss of life would have been greater if the US *hadn't* ended the war that way. Maybe the Anomalies Machine could do that sort of calculus, but there are so many variables . . ."

"You're comparing the wrong thing," Kiernan says. "This isn't just about whether, or when, the US uses that god-awful weapon. It's about whether we enter the war *at all.* Focus on the issue that hits home for Einstein. How many more people would have died in the Holocaust if Hitler had won? *That* is the argument that will sway him. That's what got the man to sign the letter in the first place. He probably had a better idea than most how dangerous nuclear weapons could be, and he knew there was only a possibility that Hitler was on his way to getting them. Einstein believed a world with those weapons would be better than a world where Hitler went unchecked. Show him the photos that were taken when Allied troops liberated the concentration camps. Tell him Hitler takes the rest of Europe if the US doesn't enter the war. If you give him that information—all of which is true, I might add—I'm pretty sure that when Szilard shows up at his door later this summer, he'll agree to sign that letter."

∞

New York, New York
May 9, 1939

The Independent World's Fair Line was built for the New York World's Fair and then promptly disassembled when the Fair closed in the fall of 1940. It wasn't the only subway line serving the fairgrounds, but according to the information in my file, it handled around seven million overflow riders in the 1939 season alone.

It feels like there are roughly that many in the terminal this morning, and finding a moment when I could speak with Einstein alone isn't easy, partly because he's traveling with Thomas Mann. The one time they separate is when Einstein makes a quick trip to the restroom before they head out of the station and onto the fairgrounds. And so I wait just outside the restroom door. I watched this stable point numerous times this morning to get the sequence right. There is a tiny window of opportunity, barely even a second, where I should be able to grab his arm and get his attention before he steps back into the throng of people heading off for a day at the Fair.

I center the CHRONOS key in my palm and wait.

The man with the straw hat exits the men's room. Next, is the woman with a baby carriage, who pushes past him on the right, and then two young boys hurry out toward their mother, who is waiting at the end of the corridor. While I could tell through the key that they were excited about something, without the audio, I'd just assumed they were eager to get to the Amusement Zone. But they're telling their mother that they saw Albert Einstein at the urinal.

She laughs, shaking her head. "You saw an old man with wild hair, that's all. Let's go." The kids are still arguing with her as they head off.

My focus is on them for a second too long, and I very nearly miss my chance. I have to take a few steps forward and call out his name as I tap his shoulder. "Professor Einstein?"

He turns back with the patient smile of a man who is accustomed to and perhaps a bit weary of his fame.

"I will be back in exactly thirty-four seconds," I tell him. "You need to move to the side, though."

He frowns, and I'm sure he's thinking he will no longer *be* here in thirty-four seconds. Then I blink out, just before a cluster of three teens leaves the men's room and he has to press against the wall to let them pass. He's still against the wall when I pop back in, but he's definitely staring at the stable point.

"How did you do that? What is that device?" His accent is heavy, but much easier to understand in person than it was in the videos I watched this morning.

I explain that I traveled thirty-four seconds into the future, then wait for a group of women to pass by. One of them turns back, clearly trying to figure out whether the old man is who she thinks he is.

"I'm from the year 2136," I say as I pull the tablet out of my handbag. The two images that Alisa used are already on the screen. "These are pictures that will be taken of you in the future. I desperately need to talk to you, but—" Another man exits the restroom, nearly bumping into Einstein, whose eyes are now pinned on the tablet I'm holding.

"But we cannot talk here," he says, moving toward the terminal. "You're right. There's a café over at the Jewish—"

"No! You can't go there today. We need to get you back on the train. Tell Dr. Mann that you're ill. Or some other excuse that he'll believe. You could be in danger, but that's only part of what's at stake. Please . . ."

He looks at the tablet again, then back at the medallion. "Okay. Wait here."

I step back against the wall, and Einstein pushes through the crowd toward a tall, thin man standing next to a lamppost. He has salt-and-pepper hair and wears a light-gray suit. The man looks toward me for a moment after Einstein speaks to him, and his lips flatten in disapproval. But he nods, patting his friend on the back, and heads toward the exit.

Einstein shuffles back toward me, then nods in the direction of the turnstiles. We drop two nickels into the slot, which is apparently double the usual fare to help cover the expense of building a temporary subway line to support the Fair. A train is pulling away just as we enter the platform, so we find a spot on a nearby bench.

"This is a marvelous little machine," he says, examining the tablet. "Is it only for the photographs?"

I shake my head and tap a link to the video of him speaking on opening day at the Fair a few days back.

"Ah, yes. Opening day was very bad. It was so rainy, and they lost power right in the middle of our demonstration. Margot was disappointed."

"That's your stepdaughter, right?"

"Yes. She gave me the slippers in your photograph. For my birthday, a few months ago, but I'm quite certain I have not yet worn them outside the house. And why am I sticking out my tongue in the other picture?"

"Because it was your birthday and you were tired of photographers asking you to smile. That image is in the apartment of my friend who is a temporal physicist."

"Is he the one who developed your time-travel pendant?"

I nod. "Along with a geneticist. The medallion is keyed to my DNA."

He frowns. "DNA?"

"Di . . . something nucleic acid. My genetic code. Maybe that's not a thing yet? Anyway, only a few people can use them. Otherwise, you'd have many more situations like the one we're facing now."

The roar of the station gradually subsides to a between-trains lull, as I proceed to make my case. In the end, I tell him pretty much everything, although I couch it in vague terms, without dates and details. Maybe it's because I've seen his face so many times, or because I know of his later work against nuclear weapons, but I trust him to make the right decision.

One train arrives, unloading a stream of passengers who flow past us toward the exit. I offer to ride with him, but he says he can wait for the next train, which I'm pretty sure means I haven't yet convinced him. He's still weighing the option to ignore my warning and head off to listen to his friend's speech.

"There are other time travelers," I tell him, "who may try to contact you. They will make this out to be a simple case of good versus evil, but the truth is far more complex. And they have ulterior motives. They want to ensure not only that we avoid war with Japan, but that we do not engage in the war against Hitler."

I pull up the images from the concentration camps that Kiernan suggested, knowing that they are as manipulative as the mushroom clouds Alisa used. "If we do not enter the war in Europe, Hitler will win. And this country will morph into one run by people in league with the Bund. It will fracture . . . and the weapon I showed you will be used against our own citizens. In the timeline I know, Hitler murdered over six million people, most of them Jews. In the path we're currently on, he will kill millions more. So it's not nearly as simple as—"

Someone behind us cries out, "He's got a gun!" Without thinking, I pull Einstein off the bench and onto the station floor. I reach into my pocket for my weapon, and then remember that Rich has it.

Shots ring out as I'm fumbling with the knob on the Timex. Looking through the slats of the bench, I see a tall man in a police uniform, holding a gun and approaching the body of Morgen Campbell. Junior, I guess, although I'm not sure if that's the correct nomenclature for a clone. A pool of blood begins to spread from beneath his head.

I don't realize that the cop is Saul until he flips the body over, grabs Campbell's medallion, and yanks it over the man's head. The body vanishes, and a woman cowering against the wall passes out, sliding to the floor.

Saul looks at me, crouched behind the bench with Einstein, and gives me a little salute. Then he blinks out himself as dozens of people watch. Someone screams. The crowd begins rushing for the exit, and I wonder how this will be explained away by the police. By the papers.

"Which of those two men is on your side?" Einstein asks, staring at the spot where Saul vanished.

"Neither of them," I answer, glad that I don't have to lie. "As I said, the situation is far from simple. But you only need to focus on one thing. One decision. The remaining chaos is for the rest of us to resolve. And we will."

I help him back onto the bench as we hear the rumble of the next train approaching the station. Einstein is silent until the train pulls to a stop in front of us. Then, he squeezes my arm. "I wish you luck, young lady. And wisdom. I think you will need both."

He heads toward the open door of the train. I hesitate for a moment, hoping, praying for the gut punch to the stomach that will tell me I've succeeded. But all I see is the retreating back of an old man. I get up and hurry toward the train. There has to be something more I can say, something that will convince him.

Through the window, I see Einstein take a seat. He stares out at me, looking in that moment far older than his sixty years. I break into a run, but the door closes before I reach it, and I watch the train until it is only a tiny speck.

I pull out the key. I'll go back and see where the best spot is to intercept myself. Try other tactics, other arguments. Yes, I'll have a double memory, but it will buy me a second chance.

And then I remember. *I'm in 1939.* There's no way to tell whether the time shift occurred until I'm past the point when it happened. I sink back onto the bench, breathing a sigh of relief.

A hand clasps my shoulder, and I look up to see someone in a police uniform. For a moment, I think it's Saul, but this guy is shorter, with a round face. "Are you okay, miss? I think we've got a gas leak or somethin'. People are spreadin' some crazy stories as they leave this part of the station."

"I'm fine," I say. "I'm just . . . I need to get to the ladies' room."

Before he can stop me, I bolt toward the corridor with the restrooms, fling open the door, and find an open stall so that I can jump out. I pull out the key, intending to go straight to Bethesda 2136. They'll have more complete information on exactly what has changed, and the time shift that's going to hit me once I'm past the dateline will be less of a jolt that far into the future.

I pull up the stable point in the library and see Jarvis's updated list on the wall screen:

✔ *Court of Peace bombing prevented*

✔ *Tomonaga mugging prevented*

✔ *Attack on ambassador prevented*

✔ *Manhattan Project begins on schedule*

✔ *December 7—Japan bombs Pearl Harbor*

✔ *December 8—US declares war*

TIMELINE RESTORED!!

My breath whooshes out in relief at those last words, even though I suspect they don't convey the full picture. I'm curious to get the details, but more than anything else, I want a moment to enjoy the good news. I want to share it with Jack. So I stare at the list for a few seconds longer, but stop short of jumping in. Instead, I move on to the next stable point, 170 years and 350 miles away.

FROM *THE BOOK OF CYRUS* (NEW ENGLISH VERSION, 3RD ED) CHAPTER 7:20–21

[20]Charity to the weak is a tainted gift that poisons the soul of the giver and the receiver. [21]What do you owe your brother? Your best effort for yourself and nothing more.

∞30∞

KATHERINE
BETHESDA, MARYLAND
NOVEMBER 20, 2136

I see the list as I open the library stable point, but it takes a second for the full import of the words to hit me. My flash of nausea and disorientation confirms the last bit—the timeline has definitely flipped. What surprises me most is the first bullet point on the list. Yes, Saul told me he'd prevented the bombing, and yes, I'd hoped he was telling the truth. That he wasn't so far gone that he would allow innocent people to be killed. But I was mentally preparing to head right back to 1939 and try again, because some part of me wasn't convinced.

Of course, the fact that Saul told the truth about this doesn't change anything. I still should have taken the shot. True, I have no idea what would have happened to me if I'd pushed that button. I think there's a decent chance that either the dress I'm wearing, the pregnancy pillow, or both are flammable.

And if I do as I promised and meet Saul in Miami, I can try again. But will my head be in control even then? I don't know for certain, and my stomach sinks at the thought of being put to the test and failing yet again.

I turn away from the wall screen, expecting to see Alex inside his nest of displays. But he's not there. His displays aren't even on. In fact, the library appears to be empty. The SimMaster countdown is still projected above the machine, however. One hour, twelve minutes, and two seconds. I half expected it to say *GAME OVER*, but I guess they haven't entered our moves yet. Barring some sort of emergency, we agreed earlier that Clio and Thea should hold off until we're all here, so that Tyson, Rich, and Madi can give full details about each of the three official moves.

As I step forward, the room flickers. An aftereffect of the time shift, perhaps? But that doesn't seem to fit. My nausea has dissipated already, and otherwise I'm feeling fine. And the timer now reads one hour, thirteen minutes, and nine seconds. It's not moving backward, though. It's like it simply skipped back a minute or so.

I take another tentative step forward, and the entire room ripples. The countdown is gone. Shards of mirror and wood are everywhere, and black chunks of something that looks like the housing of the SimMaster are ground into the carpet. One of Alex's computers has been moved to the small table just to my right. The library I thought I saw when I jumped in wasn't real at all. It was projected onto Alex's computer displays.

"So glad you could join us," Esther says. "It's Kathy, right?"

"Katherine, actually." I turn toward her voice and see that the library isn't deserted after all. In fact, it's unusually crowded.

Two of the Vipers are in the room, along with their lone remaining observer, who is standing near the door to the hallway. The observer doesn't appear to be armed, but Other-Saul is pointing an ostentatious rifle of some sort in the general direction of the sofa. Esther motions me toward the office chairs with a little gun that looks a bit like the one Madi carries. Or rather, the one she usually carries. Rich has it today, or at least he *had* it, which makes me wonder if the one Esther is holding isn't actually Madi's gun.

Alex and Rich are seated in two of the five office chairs, which are now pulled up near the couch along the back wall. Thea, RJ, Lorena, and the baby are on the couch. Luckily, the baby is asleep against her father's shoulder. A tiny version of the field-extender bracelets that Alex has been working on is now on her upper arm, and I see a familiar amber glow shining through the sleeves of RJ's sweater. I doubt that Yun Hee would recognize the threat of being held at gunpoint at her age, but she'd probably pick up on the tension in the room.

A lot of that tension is emanating from Thea. Her eyes are locked on Other-Saul, and she keeps repeating something under her breath, almost like an incantation.

Esther motions again with the gun and then goes over to discuss something with Other-Saul. I sit down next to Rich and squeeze his arm. "What the hell is going on?" I whisper.

"They're saying Saul killed Morgen. The clone version. Plus the two observers we already knew about. And since he's our ... colleague, they're assuming we okayed those executions. Once everyone is here, we'll be facing an audience tribunal. At least, I assume they're still waiting for everyone to get here. There's been some disagreement about that. Esther said they could stretch it out over two episodes. I was really hoping you'd see that something was off with the stable point before jumping in."

"Not until I jumped in, and then . . ." I shrug. "I should have jumped back out, but I took that extra step and . . ."

"Wish I had kept the Timex."

"Wouldn't work here anyway," I tell him. "The entire house is under a temporal field in our frequency."

"God. I hadn't even thought about that."

"What happened to the game console?" I ask.

"We were scattered around the room to begin with," Lorena says. "I guess they thought it was enough just to guard the door. Esther knocked down the tent of mirrors that Alex had put up to block the game console from recording us nonstop. Thea was nearby, and while they were moving Alex's system to set up the decoy displays . . ."

"I smashed it," Thea says with a proud lift of her chin. "Crushed it under my heel and stopped that nasty countdown. Their game is evil. Plus, I don't like spy cameras. The Templars put them in our dorms after one of the Sisters sneaked out. I consider them rude. Where is Madi?"

Alisa pops in at that moment, carrying another game console. She waves it toward the couch. "See? Easily replaced, you crazy old bitch." Thea responds with a happy smile, as Alisa heads back over to the desk, stepping gingerly around the splinters of glass and wood. And then Thea goes back to her muttering. I only pick up a few words: "Not him, that's not him."

"Nerd boy," Alisa says. "Get over here and hook this up."

Alex sighs, but there's clearly no way he can refuse. I need to get Saul's message to him, but his chair is at the far end of the couch, and there's really not much I could say to cloak something like *27V* in normal conversation. "He's going to need my help syncing it up," I say.

Alex opens his mouth, and I'm pretty sure he's about to say he can handle it. He probably can, to be honest, now that he's seen what I did earlier this week. But RJ apparently clues in that I need an excuse to speak with him, because he taps his cousin's leg sharply with his foot. Alex looks down at his leg, then over at me, and says, "Oh. Yeah."

"Their system is pretty archaic," I tell Alisa. "It took about an hour last time, but I remember most of what I did. Shouldn't take long."

Esther scowls in our direction, and I'm almost certain she suspects I have ulterior motives. And apparently, I'm right, because she motions for me to follow Alex, and then she follows me. She parks her behind on the desk next to me and proceeds to watch my every move.

I keep flashing back to seeing her up in the balcony of the new Cyrist temple, seated between the two Sauls. Was that a trap she and her Viper colleague were trying to set for Saul? Or are they working *with* Saul, and this is just an elaborate ruse on their part? And this message I'm about to pass to Alex, assuming I can even find a way to pass it to him, is probably useless. It's not like he can type it into the system and some wormhole will come along and suck them back into their universe. Worse yet, it could very easily be false information, given that it's coming from Saul. After everything he's done in the past few days, trusting that he is actually trying to help us is crazy. But right now, our choices seem a bit limited.

For several minutes, Alex and I work together on syncing up the systems, taking our time. I even say aloud that we should take it slowly, or else we'll have to rip everything out again like we did last time. Which never actually happened, of course, but I'm hoping that Esther will grow bored and wander off. The Esther from our timeline definitely would. Saul once said he thought she lacked patience for The Game because her design team customized her to fit their notions of what was needed in ancient Akan society, in much the same fashion that Tate Poulsen's team fashioned him to fit in with Vikings.

Eventually, Esther's attention *is* pulled away. I have a hard time seeing this as a good thing, however, since the distraction is Tyson jumping into the stable point near the wall screen. That leaves only Madi and Clio outside the trap. And Saul.

I'm determined not to waste the opportunity, no matter how it was gained. Leaning forward, I whisper, "They're from World 27V. Two. Seven. Vee."

He doesn't respond, probably because Esther is back on her perch. But his eyes clearly telegraph the question, *Are you sure?*

I nod, even though I'm very much the opposite of *sure*.

My decision to trust Saul is a gamble, but it's not entirely a shot in the dark. Saul is insane. I have no doubt on that front. In fact, I suspect that he would sacrifice everyone in this room, including me, for this future he intends to craft based on his *Book of Cyrus*. All of which means he was never the person I believed him to be. Our entire relationship was built upon deception, although if I'm being honest, a good deal of it was *self*-deception on my part.

But beneath all of those layers of lies, there is still one thing I know. One thing of which I am certain. Whether Saul truly believes this is a war or simply some variant of his beloved Game, he sees this as a battle—perhaps the ultimate battle—between him and Campbell. And as long as Saul Rand has breath in his body, he will be doing everything he can to ensure that Morgen Campbell doesn't win.

FROM *THE BOOK OF CYRUS* (NEW ENGLISH VERSION, 3RD ED) CHAPTER 7:13–14

[13]The faithful have no need of those who are blind to The Way. You owe them no obligation of brotherhood. [14]The moral objective of any life is its own existence, for its own sake. Each soul is an end unto itself.

∞31∞

TYSON
NEW YORK, NEW YORK
FEBRUARY 20, 1939

There's something eerie about an empty auditorium, and that's even more true for one as massive as Madison Square Garden. I've been here twice before, but it was always teeming with people. Now it's practically deserted, and you can almost hear echoes from the crowds that came before. Aside from the man down on the ground floor, sweeping the aisles clear of debris from whatever event happened here last, I'm fairly certain that there are only two people in this building—myself and Lawrence Dennis.

I'm not sure who put the phonograph into this closet. I suppose I could scroll back on the key and find out, but it's really only a question of whether it was a member of Team Viper, an observer, or someone they hired or convinced to support their cause. I suppose it could even be Lawrence Dennis at some earlier point in time. The only difference that makes is in terms of style points, however, and Kiernan is right on that count. The game is over, and the war is on.

I press my back against the wall and wait in the shadows just outside the balcony storage closet. A computer tablet is clutched in my hands, and I've queued up the slideshow of information I asked RJ to put together from the protected archives. My first choice is to convince Lawrence Dennis that he should leave tonight and walk out on his new alliance with the Cyrists and the Bund, but I suspect that won't happen. He doesn't strike me as easily persuadable. If persuasion fails, however, the wax cylinder that contains the recording of the explosion will be blinking out with me.

When Lawrence Dennis steps out of the closet, I step out of the shadows. The light is still dim, but at least he'll realize someone is here before I speak.

Or not. He turns toward the stairwell without even looking my way. "Excuse me. Mr. Dennis?"

He jumps back, bumping his shoulder on the wall, his expression the very image of someone caught red-handed. "Who the hell are you?"

"Tyson Reyes," I say. "You answered a rather impertinent question that I asked at a book signing a few years back. It's a question that would actually fit the current situation quite well. Except . . . I know why you're here. I've come to tell you the consequences—both immediate and long term—of your actions tonight. Three people will die at the Bund rally because of what you just did. A woman and two little girls will be crushed in that stairwell when the crowd panics. This time next year, they'll hold a memorial for them here, and an angry man will severely injure Charles Lindbergh and then shoot himself to protest the wrongful prosecution of his friends for the deaths at the Bund rally. Lindbergh will drop out of his Senate race to ensure the safety of his wife and kids, and he won't enter politics again."

I'm being selective with my information here. Lindbergh never enters politics after World War II in our timeline, either. But I'm not looking to give the man a full history lesson. I'm trying to make him do the right thing, and I'm willing to use half truths to get there.

"How would you know the consequences of anything . . . short or long term? I don't know what you've been told, but there's nothing the slightest bit dangerous in that room."

"It's the reaction to the sound that will be dangerous. People will push toward the exit because they believe there's a bomb. And then a man will stop dead in his tracks at the base of the stairs because he sees someone with a gun. Someone who is out to kill . . . or more likely, in my opinion, simply scare, a journalist that everyone on the roster of speakers at tonight's event has fallen afoul of at one time or another, since she has a low tolerance for fascism. As for how I know all of this . . ." I place my CHRONOS key in the palm of my hand and jump forward thirty seconds.

As I expected, he doesn't look entirely surprised. He saw me blink out after his book signing. The only change is that this time I blink back in.

Remembering his demand to hold the key when we were in the alley behind Café Society, I tuck the medallion back inside my shirt. "That was a very short time jump," I say. "I can go much farther, however. The last time you saw me use this device, after your book signing, I was heading back to the twenty-fourth century. I know what this country will be like in 1960. You'll know that, as well . . ." I stop, trying to remember when he dies in this timeline. "At least, I'm pretty sure you will. You do in my timeline. It's really not much like the exhibits at the World's Fair, although they've gotten the number of cars about right. You won't make it to 1990, or 2060, or other times I've seen, but you will see some measure of progress before you die. Capitalism adapts and survives for a time, waxing and waning until it eventually becomes irrelevant, although that's long after you're gone. Fascism has its occasional heyday, too, and the nationalism you keep pushing tends all too often to be white nationalism. Eventually, racism morphs into something less toxic, but it never entirely vanishes, because it's an unfortunate element of human nature that some people tend to revert to when things are rough. In my time, though, people like you and me? We're the norm."

"How long did you practice that pretty speech, Future Boy?" Dennis asks. "I'm guessing you've been running it around in your head all day, trying to figure out what you could say that might convince me."

He's right, of course, but I'm not going to give him the satisfaction of admitting it.

"Let me ask you this, though," he continues. "What's in it for you? Why do you give a damn one way or the other whether that woman and her daughters die? Is one of the little girls your great-great-grandmother, and you're traveling back in time to save her? Doesn't make sense to me, because if you're really from the future, we're all dead to you anyway."

"It really *doesn't* matter to me," I say. "I'm going to prevent their deaths either way. But the deaths of those two little girls will haunt you. And you'll always have this niggling doubt as to whether you were at fault for Lindbergh's injury and the fallout that follows from it. I'm just giving you the chance to have a hand in fixing it. Bring me the cylinder from the phonograph. I don't know if you have any role in the attack on Dorothy Thompson, but you'll probably sleep better over the years if you stop it. She has a son. And seriously . . . Coughlin and the Cyrists? You called Coughlin a hypocrite back in 1936. He hasn't changed one bit. Have you?"

I hold his gaze for several seconds. There's a good deal of skepticism in his eyes, along with some low-level anger, and a glint of devious curiosity.

"I *could* bring you the recording," he says eventually. "Or I could just take that device from you and see all these things you've been talking about for myself."

"You could try. But I'm younger, in better shape, and armed. You wouldn't win, and even if you did, it's keyed to my genetic signature. Mr. Dennis, my only reason for coming here is to give you a chance to change something you're going to regret. Otherwise, you're going to feel a twinge of guilt every time you look at your own two daughters."

I don't know if that's true. It's entirely possible that Lawrence Dennis is, at his core, the kind of jerk that he likes to project. He might be the kind of man who would simply view those two little girls as collateral damage. But I still can't help but wonder how much he was shaped by his determination to pass as white in a society that would have never listened to him if they'd known the truth about his race. That's what pushes me to extend the benefit of the doubt, whether or not he deserves it.

After a long moment, he takes several steps back into the storeroom and removes the wax cylinder with the recording of the explosion. When he comes back into the seating area, he hands it to me.

"I have now done my part to keep the two little girls and their mother safe," he says. "I'm not in charge of the deal with the Thompson woman. That's Pelley's bunch of soldier boys. But I do think she needs something to shake her up a bit. As for Coughlin, I was right. He *is* a hypocrite. That hasn't changed. But I've spoken with the actual *leader* of the Cyrists, and I think his movement has potential. We need a civic religion to tie us together in a common cause. In fact, I'm considering reentering the ministry."

"This leader of the Cyrists you've spoken with is a murderer," I say. "Just in case you want to factor that into your career plans."

I think I see a tiny flicker of doubt, but then Dennis shrugs. "Caesar. Nero. Hitler. Alexander the Great. Stalin. Roosevelt." He nods down at the massive painting at the front of the auditorium. "Even Washington himself, if you take the British point of view. Every political leader throughout history has been called a murderer. Why should this Cyrus fellow be any different?"

"Well, for one thing, he's supposed to be a *religious* leader, not a political leader."

Dennis considers it for a moment, then shakes his head. "Not much difference, as I see it. Thanks for the glimpse into my hopefully *slightly* less guilt-ridden future. As for the rest, I make my own decisions. Chances are, I'll live to regret most of them. Chances are, so will you."

Dennis nods and backs off toward the staircase. His last point is one that I can't really argue with, so I just let him go.

I don't entirely trust him not to pop back up and try to take the key, however, so I quickly pull up the library stable point in Bethesda 2136. It shows the same checklist as before, but with several new additions:

✔ *Three Bund deaths & Lindbergh attempt prevented*

✔ *Court of Peace bombing prevented*

✔ *Tomonaga mugging prevented*

✔ *Attack on ambassador prevented*

✔ *Manhattan Project begins on schedule*

✔ *December 7—Japan bombs Pearl Harbor*

✔ *December 8—US declares war*

TIMELINE RESTORED!!

I can't help but grin, even though I'm guessing that conclusion at the end is a generalization. It's hard for me to see how Saul's actions promoting the Cyrists could have no impact on the timeline, and as Alex pointed out earlier, we still have to find a way to block Team

Viper. Given Saul's stunt with their observers, I wouldn't be surprised if they're already planning their next moves.

But it's progress. I'll take it. And as I blink in, I send up a silent prayer that we'll have at least a short time to enjoy it before hell breaks loose again.

FROM *THE BOOK OF CYRUS* (NEW ENGLISH VERSION, 3RD ED) CHAPTER 7:15-16

[15]If evil is done unto you, the fault lies within your own weakness. The strong cannot be victims. [16]Those too weak to demand their blessings do not deserve them. A plentiful store awaits all who follow The Way.

∞32∞

Madi
Skaneateles, New York
September 3, 1966

When I pull up the stable point for noon on September 3rd, which is the time Jack and I agreed upon last night, I find a note propped up on the coffee table. I expect to see the same words as last time, telling me to meet him at the dock. But instead, it reads:

> *Library stable point is a trap.*
>
> *Bombing wasn't prevented.*
>
> *Happened at British Pavilion instead.*
>
> *Clio went back to fix it. I have to do what I can.*
>
> *I love you. ~ Jack*

The note and the fact that Jack isn't there don't make any sense for a moment, but then I remember the hypospray. I scroll backward slowly . . . trying not to worry. He can't have been erased. If he had been, the note wouldn't be there. Or would it? Clio said something about this house being under a CHRONOS field at one point, so . . .

And then I see him at 11:47. He enters the room from the staircase that leads up to the bedrooms and goes into the kitchen. A few seconds later, he comes back into the living room and places the note on the coffee table. Just as I'm about to blink in, I spot Lorena's hypospray in his hand. I don't know whether he's used it yet, but if he has, I'm fairly certain he's going to hit me with a bunch of reasons why he should handle this emergency with Clio, whatever it is, even though we have no idea whether that injection will allow him to make multiple jumps or even how long it's likely to last. I'll feel much better about that conversation if the hypospray is in my hand, rather than his. So I scroll back two minutes and jump in.

The time shift hits me hard before I can brace for it. I stumble backward onto the couch, pulling in deep breaths to calm the tempest raging in my stomach. As I look around the room, I'm torn between relief that we managed to flip the timeline and the realization that some things are still very broken. This is not the living room I saw in Kate and Kiernan Dunne's family photos. It remains barren, aside from a coffee mug on the end table next to a notebook flipped open to a page filled with Jack's handwriting. No family pictures on the walls. No artwork, no knickknacks, none of the many little things that make a house a home.

Despite the nausea and dizziness, I force myself up and stumble into the kitchen. The hypospray is next to the toaster, exactly as before. I slip it into my pocket and then head back into the living room to collapse on the couch. I hear Jack's footsteps on the stairs a few moments later.

"Madi?" he says. "Oh, thank God. Clio said you jumped straight home."

"Guess I did, in a sense. I wanted to be with you when I found out whether it worked."

He wraps me in a tight hug and then quickly steps away. "Clio showed up here about twenty minutes ago to tell me we should not jump to the library, because there was something off about the stable point. She thought you were already there, because she scanned through this location and never saw you jump in."

I shake my head. "That doesn't make sense . . . oh. Maybe it does. I was planning to jump to Bethesda. Told her that was the plan. Even opened the stable point, fully intending to jump in. But at the last second, I changed my mind. What's wrong with the stable point?"

"She said it's a trap. The note about the bombing being averted is highly misleading, for one thing. While the bomb didn't go off in the Court of Peace, it exploded in the location where it was originally placed—inside the closet at the British Pavilion. Killed nearly twice as many people, because the top floor collapsed. She jumped back and called in a bomb threat, but the police made it clear that they'd had quite enough bogus bomb threats for one day."

"They ignored it?"

"Yeah. To be fair, they'd already checked that utility closet after the first call. The one that the bomber or whoever placed before any of the time-travel insanity began. And then they get a second call to find the suitcase with a damn balloon, and apparently there was someone else who claimed there was a bomb in a trash can at the Court of Peace. So it's not too surprising that they were skeptical."

"Please tell me Clio isn't planning to try and remove it herself."

"She is. Or she did. I checked the July 5th paper on the microfilm. Seven people injured, but no mention of any deaths. They do mention the possibility that a woman was the bomber, but she got away."

I center the key in my palm, but he shakes his head. "You need to wait, though. There's more. Pull up the stable point in the library."

"Which one?" He gives me a confused look, and I say, "There's one next to Grandpa James's desk and—"

"The one you transferred to everyone else. Over near the wall screen."

I open the location and see the display from earlier, with a new addition at the top.

✔ *Three Bund deaths & Lindbergh attempt prevented*

"The timeline-restored part seems true," I say. "I felt the shift as soon as I arrived. I'm still feeling it, to be honest."

"Yes. Just . . . pan around to Alex's cave."

The first thing I notice is that Alex isn't there, which is a rare sight. His displays aren't even on, and he never turns those off. No one is in the library at all. The only display is the one for the SimMaster, off to the left, which is currently counting down from one hour, twelve minutes, and six seconds. That seems a bit off to me. According to the timer on my key, it's just over one hour and five minutes.

And then it says one hour, thirteen minutes, and twenty-two seconds.

"It's a loop," Jack says. "Clio noticed it. Someone appears to have hacked the stable point. And if you simply looked at the wall screen, or even if you'd only been in the library a few times . . . you might not realize anything had changed. And speaking of . . ." His brow creases and he looks vaguely ill. "Something changed here. Because I have a memory of going straight to the kitchen. I wrote you a note . . ."

"Yes. I saw it. You were planning to try Lorena's serum, even though you swore you wouldn't do it when you were alone."

As I speak, I pull up the second location at the library. Unlike the room depicted in the stable point next to the wall screen, the room I'm seeing now isn't empty at all. Alex's display cave is still missing, and he's not at his desk. He's in one of five office chairs lined up by the sofa, along with Tyson, Katherine, and Rich. Thea, RJ, Lorena, and Yun Hee are on the couch.

When I pan to the right, I see why. The three surviving Vipers are also in the room, along with their lone remaining observer. Esther and Other-Saul are armed. The observer seems to be monitoring stable points on a CHRONOS key. And the SimMaster countdown is no longer working. There's something on the display, but I can't see it from this angle.

I hold out my key to transfer the location to Jack. "Clio's not the only one in trouble."

He takes a look and curses softly. "How the hell did—"

The telephone rings, startling both of us. We follow the sound into the kitchen.

"Have you been answering it?" I ask, staring at the phone as it rings again.

"This is the first time it's rung."

I pause with one hand above the receiver, and then pick it up. "Dunne residence," I say.

"Like hell it is." The elderly voice on the other end has a faint Irish lilt, and a pronounced slur. It's Kiernan, but either he's been drinking, or he's had a stroke. "No one named Dunne has lived in that house since July 1940. We'd have sold the cursed place if not for the fact that putting your friend up for the past few weeks might be our only shot at getting Clio back."

"What happened to Clio? I'm going back to fix it, and we'll scroll through the stable points to fill in the blanks if we need to, but any details you can give me will save time."

I hold the phone between us so that Jack and I both can hear. Kiernan's voice is a bit less harsh when he continues. "Cliona was watching through the key like she told you she would. Watching the list on your wall screen. She sees all those check marks, and she's pretty excited, thinking it worked. Then she sees Katherine jump in and realizes there's something odd going on with the stable point.

That it seemed to sort of ripple, and then Katherine vanished. She thought maybe Katherine just jumped back out for some reason, but then she scrolls forward, and the same thing happens with Tyson. And something is off with the countdown. So she starts to get a little panicked, and I'll admit I was feeling the same. Anyway, she jumps forward to the next day to grab the newspaper, and we learn the bomb didn't go off in the Court of Peace. It went off inside the British Pavilion, from that very same closet where Saul left the bodies for Team Viper to find. Clio and I both try calling it into the police, but that's like the third, or maybe fourth time someone has dialed in to say there's a bomb at the Fair, and the police are to the point of thinking it's all a big series of hoaxes. And they know for a fact there's no bomb in there, because they checked the damn room, you know? The bomb squad had already checked it, and they didn't find a bloody thing, and there were police crawlin' all over the place, so they can't imagine how someone could have sneaked anything in without them seeing. They'd even closed off that part of the building."

He takes a deep, shuddering breath, and when he continues, his voice is faint and tired, and I realize with a jolt that he would be over eighty now. "Anyway, she could see the damn thing in the closet through the stable point. It's dark in there, but some guy with a key, quite possibly Saul, drops it off maybe four minutes before it explodes. So there's not a very big window between the time it's dropped off and the blast. And she knows . . . we *both* know . . . from the paper and from what she can see through the stable point outside that half the top floor collapses about ten seconds after five o'clock. They don't make World's Fair buildings to withstand an explosion, or much of anything, really, because they know they'll be torn down when the Fair closes. She told me she was going to Skaneateles. Hoping that she'd find you there, because she knew the other three were in the library. Said she'd come back to the apartment if she didn't find you, but I knew. I knew from the way she hugged me goodbye. And then

I get the phone call from Connor maybe twenty minutes later. Said Clio showed up in the living room, bleeding badly."

He's rambling, not really making much sense to me. Jack seems confused, too.

"So, you think she carried the bomb to the same location as before?" Jack asks. "I just read the article from the next day's paper on the bombing. It said that the explosion happened near the fence around the fairgrounds, same as in the original timeline. A few bystanders did say they saw a woman running out of the building carrying something. That she might be the bomber. But they claimed she got away."

"Most of them probably thought she did," Kiernan says. "And if anyone saw her, do you really think they'd mention a girl torn to bits who vanished right in front of their eyes? Or that the papers would report that? Not exactly the sort of thing you write up in your article if you want to keep your job, now, is it? Connor and Harry both said they didn't know how in hell Clio managed to even use the key in that condition. She died in Kate's arms there in the living room. So, yeah. That grave up on the hill, that's hers. We buried her with the key, though. So she's dead but not erased. And I've been waiting twenty-six years to tell you that you could still fix this."

There's more than a bit of judgment in his tone, and I want to object that there was never a time when we *didn't* fix it. But there must have been, because here we are in 1966 with Clio dead for the past twenty-six years. The one thing I do know is that whatever happened, it wasn't by choice. I made a promise. And if something happened so that I couldn't keep my promise, I sure as hell wouldn't have vanished without trying to change it or even explaining it to her family. I don't think Tyson would. Even though I don't know Katherine and Richard as well, I don't believe they would, either. And Jack was about to inject himself with this serum without anyone here to oversee the possible complications to try and save her, so I know damn well that he wouldn't have.

"If Clio doesn't make it in this timeline, Kiernan, it's because we didn't make it, either. Clio was right about the situation at the library in 2136. Team Viper set a trap, and they have the others hostage. Not just the three you met, but five more, including a ten-month-old baby and my grandmother Thea. They're alive, but I don't know for how long. We already know that Esther and their version of Saul are a bit trigger happy. And yes, Clio did come here looking for me. I guess she assumed I went straight to the library, as well. I told her I'd meet her there, but I decided to stop here first and let Jack know. Now that I know when she was here, however, I'll go back and intercept her. And we'll fix this."

There's a pause, and then Kiernan says, "There are hunting rifles in the garage if you need them. Ammo, too."

"Can you tell me why she physically carried the bomb out?" I ask. "Is there a limit on how much weight you can carry with you? I don't even know how much a bomb like that weighs."

"I don't know," Kiernan says. "I never jumped with anything heavier than a large suitcase. I'm pretty sure Simon or Prudence brought back some computer equipment for Saul at one point, but they likely did it piecemeal. It's possible she didn't think about blinking out with the thing, but . . . I don't think so. She'd used the key a lot. Too damn much. Kate might know. Connor said she went to the fairground. Set stable points, nearly drove herself crazy watching them. Tried her best to use the key so she could save her."

The fact that he's reporting this as something his son told him rather than as something he observed or something Kate said is telling.

"Okay," I say. "I'll see what I can figure out from watching the stable point."

"This is gonna sound harsh," Kiernan says, "but I have to say it anyway. It's not enough to just save her. If Clio thinks she was saved at the expense of a bunch of other people, whether it's the people in the British Pavilion or all of you, she won't be able to live with herself. That's not who she was. So you have to fix it all. Or as much as you can. And I'm not saying this just for her sake, but for you and your friends as well, since you didn't strike me as callous people. I've spent most of my life haunted by nightmares about those folks at God's Hollow, the kids I couldn't manage to save. If you can avoid that sort of regret, you'll be better for it in the long run."

"That's the plan, sir," Jack says. "I've got close friends at Madi's place. And we both made a promise to your wife."

Jack and I go back into the living room and spend the next few minutes scanning through the stable points around the British Pavilion and the back fence. We get three glimpses of Clio. One is in the utility closet, and it answers the question of why she didn't use the key. The bomb is in a large, circular box. If it ever had a handle, it doesn't anymore. She spends nearly a minute trying to work out a way to hold the box and still have two hands free to pull up the stable point and blink out. Finally, she grabs the box, shoves the door open, and runs.

"She panicked," Jack says. "She should have jumped back. Gotten some rope, or . . . something."

He's right, but when you're faced with a ticking bomb, only a few minutes on the clock, and dozens of lives on the line, panicking is a pretty natural response.

Our second glimpse is outside the British Pavilion. I spot her white dress with the tiny red flowers that look like polka dots from a distance. There are tourists everywhere. She turns back for a split second, and I can tell she realizes she's made a mistake, and she's probably thinking the very things that Jack just said. Then a group of people walks between her and the stable point, and she's gone by the time they pass.

The final image is at the clearing near the fence, and it's more of a blur than anything else. She's walking rapidly, very nearly running, toward a clear patch of land off to the left of the gate, where the bomb-disposal unit took the device in the previous timeline. Then she stops, places the bomb on the grass, and runs. The device goes off almost instantly, but we can't see her clearly with the debris in the air. Shrapnel, I guess, and padding of some sort. By the time it clears, we can't see her at all.

"Look at the time," Jack says.

I do. It's 4:59:20. "Do you think Clio had the time of the explosion wrong?"

"Maybe. Or maybe it exploded early because she was running with it. Either way," Jack says, "you'll have less than four minutes."

We could pull up one additional location. The one here in the living room, the one that I first thought of as clearly a daughter's stable point. If we scrolled back to July 4, 1940, at 5:01 p.m., we could see the aftermath. But there's no point. Because I'm going to fix this.

"Let's find some rope," I say. "Maybe in the garage, with the guns that Kiernan mentioned."

The garage is detached from the main house. We go out through the back door. I take a deep breath of pine-scented air as we cross the lawn. The guns are mounted on the back wall. Jack cleans and loads two rifles, and searches for rope to make a handle. While he's busy with that, I scan through the various stable points in Bethesda, and we try to formulate a plan. The observer they have posted at the library door is clearly doing the exact same thing I'm doing with his key. I'm guessing they've assigned him to monitor observation points set around the house, so we're going to need to be stealthy. I have a stable point in the kitchen, one in the backyard, one in my bedroom, and three or four in the living room and library. I also have one in the basement, which I set just after the others moved in, during a brief period when I was doing my best to avoid bumping into Jack and spending quite a bit of time in the pool doing stress-relief laps.

"Of all the locations in the house," I say, "the basement seems the most likely spot they might have missed. From the upstairs landing, it just looks like a basement, especially if the sliding stone cover is in place."

"Which it may not be," Jack says, "given that Thea is inviting everyone down for communal nude bathing. But yeah, I'd say it's our best bet."

We head back across the yard, with both guns and a length of rope. I keep my eyes on the ground, determined not to look at the graves on the hill, and this time, I succeed. Once we're in the kitchen, Jack holds out his hand. I'm not sure why, but then he glances over at the toaster, and I remember the hypospray in my pocket. I pull it out and he rolls up his sleeve.

"Did you read the info Lorena sent with this?"

He nods. "I'm fully aware of all the possible side effects. I may lose my lunch, or breakfast in this case. Might also be a bit punchy from the adrenaline."

"Pretty sure there were a few other things mentioned," I say with a wry twist of my mouth. "She said to give it a few minutes before you try to make the jump. And if it doesn't work—"

"Wait another ten minutes and use it again to inject the second dose. Yes."

I hesitate as I hold the injector to his bicep. Jack rolls his eyes and takes it from me, then pushes the little button on the end. We both hold our breath for a moment, because several of the more severe side effects she mentioned were the type that would kick in quickly—respiratory distress, heart arrhythmia, tremors.

"Are you okay?" I ask.

He nods. "A bit of a head rush, but yeah."

I set a time on my stable point in the basement and press the back of my key to Jack's to transfer the location. "I will meet you there. I'm not sure how much good that gun will do me, since I don't know how to use it, but bring both of them with you. I'd rather not travel with a bomb *and* a gun, and there's not much room in that storage area."

"Especially not once both you and Clio are in there."

"Except that's not going to happen. She and Kiernan will have a double memory to contend with—come to think of it, you will, too—but she's not leaving that apartment until I've disposed of the bomb. As soon as I'm done, I'll meet you at the stable point by the pool." I hold his gaze for a long moment, because I know exactly what he's thinking. "Jack, you've got *one* jump, if we're lucky. Disposing of this bomb is a one-person job. Your help will be needed much more in Bethesda. And if, for some reason, I don't make it, there are eight people in that house you need to find a way to save."

He sighs and pulls me close. "You're right. I know you're right. It's just . . ." I feel him tensing up. "We don't even know if the serum will work anyway. You may end up doing it all on your own."

"Stop it. No pessimism allowed. I'll dispose of the bomb. The serum *will* work. And then we're kicking those assholes out of our house and out of our timeline."

∞

New York, New York
July 4, 1940

I arrive in the living room of the apartment in Manhattan at 1:53 p.m. on July 4th, just as Clio slams the phone down onto the receiver. Kiernan is just behind her. They both turn toward me, and I tell Kiernan, "You can try calling. That's what you did last time, but they didn't listen to you, either. They've had quite a few calls about bombs today, and they're in boy-who-cried-wolf mode right now. You're both going to have some double memories, but it's better than the alternative."

Clio casts a wary eye at the rope in my hand. "What's that for?"

"It's for tying you to a chair if you don't stay put," I tell her. "I've got this. Kiernan . . . I just spoke to you in 1966. That grave belonged to Clio, and it will continue to belong to her if you can't keep her here with you. So wrap her in a bedsheet or whatever you have to do."

I pull up the location at the British Pavilion, a bit past 4:56 p.m., which is about ten seconds after the man who I'm fairly certain is Saul drops off the bomb.

"The library stable point is a trap!" Clio says.

I give her a smile. "Yes. That was a very good catch. Thanks for the warning. But I've got this. Really."

And with that, I blink into the storage closet, not at all sure that I have this.

A large round box sits in the middle of the small space. I take one end of the rope and attempt to feed it through the loop on the right side of the box. The rope is too thick, however. I try shoving it through, to no avail, then I quickly begin fraying the rope into smaller cables. When I get enough unwound, I try to loop one end through the hole. It's still too thick.

"Fuck, fuck, fuck." Even as the words leave my mouth, I want to yank them back. There could be a guard out there. I twist the cord back and forth a few times and manage to thread what feels very much like the eye of a needle. With a sigh of relief, I tie off the end and move on to the left side. The weave is a bit more stubborn here, and sweat is now pouring down my arms, making the rope slippery, but I finally manage that side, too.

By the time I get the box ready to travel, I've eaten two and a half minutes from the clock.

I bend down and loop my arms through the rope. I'm about to open the stable point near the fence, but I can't bring myself to do it. There are no guarantees about casualties if I'm a few seconds off in either direction. People will almost certainly die, but they will also almost certainly not be the two bomb-squad detectives who die in our timeline. There's no reason to add any more deaths to the tally. There's no time god demanding a sacrifice.

So I lock in the first outdoor stable point that I see. It's the one Clio transferred to show me that there was no name on the gravestone. There's a certain poetic logic to leaving the bomb there. I won't risk doing it when Jack is in the house, because if I fail, he shouldn't have to witness that. So I roll the date back to a random day, October 16, 1957.

In that last moment, I wonder what kind of delay there is when you travel through time? Will this bomb explode en route? And if it does, what would that mean?

Too late for second-guessing, though. I blink.

I land in the same crouched position in which I began, my arms still looped through the rope holding the bomb. Leaning forward, I rest the bomb on the ground, then quickly pull my arms away. Unsure whether to trust my shaking hands to pull up a stable point, I take off running. About a quarter of the way down the hill, I lose my balance. And that's probably what saves me. As I hit the ground, I hear a loud whoosh and boom. I keep to the ground, rolling the rest of the way down the rocky hill until I smack into a pine tree near the base. About a foot above my head, three carpenter nails are sticking out of the tree. Several more are scattered around me. As I look back up the hill, I see a cloud of smoke and dust. The box is gone.

And so is the third gravestone.

∞

BETHESDA, MARYLAND
NOVEMBER 20, 2136

The familiar smell of salt water hits my nose before my eyes open. My body relaxes instinctively, and promptly tenses back up as I scan the basement. Jack isn't here. That can only mean the serum didn't work, and I'm going to be on my own, unless I go back and ask for Clio's help. I'm reluctant to do that, however, given that she's probably working through a rather strong double memory at the moment—one where she was mortally wounded and one where she wasn't. The plus side is that her double memory won't last long at all, while the same can't be said for the rest of the Dunne family. In the diaries, both Katherine and Kate said that their extended double memories faded over time, to the point where they were more like a book they'd read or a movie they'd watched. I hope that's true, because otherwise, they'll have several decades of disjointed memories.

I start to pull up the library on the CHRONOS key, but then I remember that I'm now in the same house and have a better option. "Jarvis, show the library on the wall screen. Volume to two."

"Yes, mistress. Did you know that there are uninvited guests in the house?"

"I *do* know that," I say, taking a few steps toward the wall so that I can hear better. "I'm working on a plan for kicking them out. Can you tell me where they're located?"

"In the library. And one was in the bathroom inside suite three briefly, but not any longer."

"Is that first or second floor?"

"Second," he says.

The scene in the library hasn't changed much since I last checked, aside from the fact that Katherine and Alex are again in the office chairs near the sofa, rather than crouched in front of Alex's desk.

Everyone is against the back wall, either on the couch or in the chairs. Yun Hee is awake and cranky. Thea's hand keeps fidgeting inside the pocket of her dress, like she's rubbing at a worry stone. She's saying something, too, although no one is looking at her, so maybe it's under her breath. Probably one of her positive affirmations. Or maybe she's cursing the lot of them. In which case, kudos to Thea.

The countdown is visible again, and I realize with a start that it now reads 00:01:07. Which is wrong. I look down at my key. We should still have a little over twenty-seven minutes. Not that it matters, of course. If Team Viper is holding an entire household hostage, we've moved well beyond the realm of style points and advance predictions or whatever they were called. This is, as Kiernan noted, war.

A hand falls on my shoulder, and I very nearly scream.

I turn, one finger on the Timex, ready to fight. But it's Jack. The two rifles and his backpack are slung over his shoulder. He gives me a sheepish smile. "Sorry! And, yes. I was waiting to see you jump in before I committed to coming here rather than to 1940. And I'd like to think I'd have followed through on my promise rather than trying to save you if you hadn't made it, but . . . I'm glad I don't have to find out."

I hug him tightly, grinning as tears of relief fill my eyes. "The serum worked! You're home."

"It was a close call," he says. "It took the full dose. And I knew you'd succeeded with the bomb because the house . . . I was still there by myself, but it was clear that they'd simply vacated the premises for a bit in order to accommodate me. There are pictures on the walls now, and it looks like a home. And . . . just two gravestones on the hill."

Jack looks toward the wall screen. The red timer has now disappeared, and a holoscreen display hovers above the game console with a different timer, currently at twenty-seven seconds, beneath the *TD*

Off-World logo, which is slowly spinning. "I hadn't thought about the fact that we can utilize Jarvis for this. I wonder . . ."

The logo stops spinning when the timer hits zero, and Morgen Campbell comes into view. He doesn't look quite as gleeful as he did last time, and the reason why becomes clear as the face of Morgen Jr. appears on the screen behind him. "They know he's dead," I tell Jack. I'm not sure why that surprises me. According to the rules, it was clear that their side of the game, and possibly ours when we were at the Fair, was being recorded for the benefit of the studio audience.

Saul's face is on the screen now. Not their Saul, with his scar and weird eye, but our own in-timeline version. He's in the police uniform I last saw him wearing, standing over the body of Morgen Jr. Then there's another image beside that of the storage closet, not with the bomb as I saw it a few minutes ago, but with the two desiccated bodies. A large stamp with the words *WANTED FOR MURDER* is now superimposed over Saul's image.

"It's a trial." I'm about to add that it's Saul's trial, and at least somewhat justified, but then more pictures pop onto the screen. Me. Clio. Jack. And then the image of the others seated against the wall in the library.

"Jarvis," Jack says, "can you cut power to the library without disrupting the protective field around the house?"

"No. The enclosed bookcases in the library are wired directly into the grid, but the amplification device that extends the field to the house and yard is not."

I look back at the screen. I'm certain that Lorena, RJ, and the baby are wearing the field-extender devices that Alex designed. I can't see Alex's hands, but he had one of the bracelets on last time I saw him. He said that the bracelets amplified any CHRONOS field within a hundred meters. Thea, Tyson, and the others are all under a CHRONOS key.

"They'll be okay," I tell Jack. "The bracelets will extend the field around the books to protect them."

"You're sure?"

I give him a helpless shrug. "That's what Alex told me."

"Okay, then," Jack says. "If anyone would know, it's Alex. Jarvis, on my command, shut down power to the library. Everything not on the main grid."

"Don't turn yourself off, Jarvis. Otherwise, you're not going to be much help."

"Yes, mistress. Should I switch to one of the backup generators?"

"No," Jack says. "And immediately after you cut power, announce over the house intercom that there was a surge. That you have attempted to restore power to the room, but it will require a manual override at the terminal in . . ." Jack looks at me.

"Um . . . something on the ground floor where we don't have to go through any of the main rooms to get there. The laundry room?"

"But there is no power terminal in the laundry room," Jarvis says.

"We know that," Jack says. "And so do you. But they don't. Can you repeat those words back?"

"Yes, Master Jack." There's a brief pause and then Jarvis says, "A power surge has disabled the outlets in this room. My attempts to reset them have failed. A manual override is required at the power terminal in the laundry room."

"Perfect," I say. "Welcome to the team, Jarvis. I like our odds a lot better with three."

"But they're even better with four," says a voice from behind us.

I want the voice to be Clio's. But it's much too deep.

Jack's hand goes up to the rifle. Saul, however, already has his gun out—a small silver pistol that I suspect is an energy weapon of some sort, since there's a red light blinking on one side of the barrel.

"Who is this?" Saul asks. "Tell him I'm on your side. Morgen's carbon copy would have blown you to kingdom come if I hadn't taken him out of the equation. He might even have killed Einstein for good measure."

"How did you get in this house?" I ask. "Who gave you this stable point?"

"No one *gave* me your stable point," Saul says. "I came in the old-fashioned way . . . through the servants' entrance."

"We don't have a servants' . . ." I trail off, realizing that he means the side exit used by the pool service that handled regular maintenance during the years the house was unoccupied.

"That door seems to be the only one our friends from Team Viper didn't know about and therefore aren't monitoring with stable points of their own. Furthermore, the only reason you have this house is the goodwill of Cyrist International, which owes me a certain debt of gratitude for elevating them above a navel-gazing cult hanging out in the swamps of Florida. They provided me with the code, so I didn't even have to break your door. Are you happy?"

I'm not at all happy, actually. I don't trust him in the slightest. But it seems like a bad idea to mention this when his gun is out, so I just give him a curt nod.

"Very well, then," he says. "Could we go? Assuming you want to save Katherine and the others from Campbell's little tribunal?" Saul nods toward the screen, where the camera is focused on the baby, who is currently seated in Lorena's lap. There's a meter at the top of the screen, and the needle is hovering between *Guilty* on the left and *Innocent* on the right. It flickers near the middle for a bit and then flips toward *Innocent*.

"No shit," Jack says as he backs toward the staircase. "She's a baby, for God's sake."

We hurry up the stairs and take a right into the hallway, which sits just below the library. Sounds of background music and applause drift down to our level. Ahead on the left is the laundry room. The linen closet is just beyond that. I open the door to the closet. There's only room for two, thankfully. Saul hides behind the laundry room door.

"Jarvis," I say softly. "Cut power as we discussed and make the announcement."

"Yes, mistress."

I expect a snide remark from Saul or at least a chuckle, but he doesn't seem to find Jarvis's mode of address unusual. "Why aren't you armed?" he hisses.

"I've never fired anything that large."

Saul rolls his eyes. "Give me the other rifle," he says as Jarvis is announcing the outage and the need for someone to do a manual override. As soon as Saul has the rifle, he hands me the little silver gun. "It's very simple to operate. Point and pull the trigger."

"Does it stun or kill?" I ask.

"It *kills*," he says, looking at me as if I've asked an exceptionally dumb question. "So don't go waving it around. And once we have a hostage, get ready to storm the library."

I'm not sure why he assumes we'll have a hostage. I think it's equally likely that they'll just send one of our people down, given that they have everyone else as leverage. But at least that will give us one additional person on this side of the door.

We can't pull up the wall screen here, so I open the library stable point and watch the discussion in pantomime. The display above the SimMaster has vanished. The Anomalies Machine is also quiet. I haven't really looked at it yet. I'm sure there are some differences between this timeline and the last, but maybe they're minor enough that the machine has already ground through them.

After about a minute of arguing and attempts to plug the system into a different outlet, Esther finally grabs Katherine's arm and yanks her up out of the chair.

I lean back against Jack, trying not to think of all the ways this could go horribly, horribly wrong as we wait.

FROM *THE VERSES OF PRUDENCE*

For if the Scourge shall rise, the Sisters shall
restore.
He who slaughtered Gizmo and would have
slaughtered more
Will not set Earth's future and will not shape
our path.
Take as our solemn vow, he'll face the Sisters'
wrath.

∞33∞

The *TD Off-World* intro music is appallingly cheerful until the very end, when a discordant note reverberates just as the words *Justice for Team Viper* are stamped on the screen in red block letters. As the logo fades away, Campbell appears on a dais very much like his throne in Redwing Hall at the Objectivist Club. Unlike last time, his expression is far from genial.

"I'm Morgen Campbell, your host for *TD Off-World*," he says in somber tones. "Tonight's episode—and quite possibly our next one as well—is a departure from our usual proceedings. For the past three sessions, you've watched as our team was subjected to bloodthirsty, illegal actions by Team Hyena, which seems incapable of following the rules. We made some concessions for the fact that they are new to our variant of The Game, but still they insisted on not only removing our observers from the contest but doing so in the most gruesome way possible."

The screen behind him now displays the bodies of the two observers Saul killed. "Our observers know there is risk involved," Campbell says, "but the rewards are substantial enough to make it worthwhile. The jackpot this season topped all previous records. However, the fact that Team Hyena refused to put their observers in the field meant that they offered up no hostages, limiting our ability to retaliate within the rules of The Game. Again, we were tolerant, willing to let the match play to its inevitable conclusion. Even if they won, we had the advantage in style points." His mouth tightens. "And then they went too far."

Now the screen shows what looks like a subway terminal. Morgen the Younger is pointing a weapon toward a bench where a redheaded woman is talking to an elderly man. I realize that it's Einstein before I recognize Madi in her costume. Morgen raises his weapon toward them, and Madi executes an impressive tackle, pulling Einstein off the bench and onto the platform. I expect to see Morgen advance on them and fire again, but then he crumples to the floor. A police officer moves in quickly, reaches down, and yanks Morgen's key. When the officer looks up, I see that it's Saul.

The audience gasps as Morgen's body vanishes and the image freezes on Saul's face.

"This is the man who should be before the tribunal today," Morgen the Elder says. "He was not a member of Team Hyena, and yet he operated as one. I make a solemn promise to you that he will eventually be brought to justice, as will the three other individuals not currently in our custody. For now, however, I ask you to serve as jury for his accomplices on Team Hyena."

There's a slight whirring sound from the SimMaster as the camera zooms in first on Lorena, then on Yun Hee. "Are you crazy?" RJ yells. "She's an infant."

"How could a baby be guilty of anything?" I say.

Morgen sighs dramatically. "A valid point, I suppose. What say you, jury members? Is the child innocent, or shall the sins of the parents be visited upon her?"

The needle on the meter flirts with *Guilty* briefly, then settles on *Innocent*.

"And what of the child's parents? They played only supporting roles in the murders of our team. Are we a merciful people?"

Two meters pop onto the images of Lorena and RJ. The needles hesitate longer in the red zones than with Yun Hee, but eventually they tip over to *Innocent*, as well.

Now the camera settles on Alex, who glares at the screen defiantly. "And now we come to the—" Both the audio and video go out midsentence.

"What happened?" Alisa says.

As if on cue, the virtual assistant comes on over the intercom. "Apologies for the interruption. A surge has disabled the power in this room. My attempts to reset have failed. A manual override is required at the power terminal in the laundry room."

"Morgen is going to eviscerate us. Do you have any idea how many people are watching? You!" Alisa points at Alex. "Find an outlet that works."

Alex heads over to the computer area and crawls around under the tables, testing the outlets. Finally, he says, "Jarvis, are there any functional outlets in here?"

"No. As I said previously, a surge has disabled the power in this room. My attempts to reset have failed. A manual override is required at the power terminal in the laundry room."

"Someone go reset the damn thing," Other-Saul says. "Take one of them with you."

Esther glares at him but grabs me by the arm and drags me toward the door.

"Why me?" I ask as we enter the hallway. "I don't live here. I'm not even sure where the laundry room is."

"Better figure it out fast," she says. "Your jury is going to be a lot less merciful if they're kept waiting."

"Jarvis," I say. "Where is the laundry room?"

The virtual assistant says that it's on the main floor and directs us to take a right and then another right at the bottom of the stairs. We follow the directions and step inside the laundry. I look around for a power terminal, unsure what that even is or what it would look like in this era. I'm about to ask Jarvis when I hear a loud thwack and a moan from Esther. She whirls around and fires the little gun, leaving a hole in the wall about six inches from Saul's knees as she slumps to the ground.

"Grab her weapon, carry this, and follow me." He tosses me the rifle. There's a tiny smear of blood on the stock. "She looks as strong as her counterpart back at CHRONOS, which means I'm going to need both hands to subdue her if she comes to." He leans outside the door and says, "I need my gun back. Do you have rope? Or sturdy tape? Personally, I'd prefer to wrap them up with the red ribbon I used on their observers, but I'm all out."

I'm about to ask who he's talking to, but then I hear Madi's voice. "Duct tape. Should be on the shelves to your right."

She steps inside the laundry room and begins scanning the shelves. Jack is right behind her. At least, I'm pretty sure it's Jack. He's about the same height and build as the guy I saw running through the lobby with her in Memphis.

"Okay," Saul says. "Once we're in the library, I'll handle my ugly twin." He nods to Jack. "You're on Alisa. If things go well, the door may take out their observer, but if not, Katherine and Madi are on him." He looks at me. "Has your physicist friend isolated their signal yet?"

"I don't know," I say. "I gave him the information, and bought him as much time as we could under the guise of setting up the new console, but . . ."

Saul smiles grimly. "Well, if he hasn't, this is likely to be a very *temporary* eviction." He looks down at the time on his key again and then hoists Esther over one shoulder. "We need to go *now*."

"Can you jump in carrying her?"

"No," Saul tells me. "That's *why* I gave you the gun, so you could cover me. Let's go!"

"Do you want an audio diversion?" Madi asks. She's now holding a thick roll of gray tape, and I hand her the weapon Esther was carrying.

"Yes!" Saul is already headed down the hallway as he speaks, moving at a fast clip.

Madi and Jack follow. "Jarvis," Madi says, "announce on the main intercom that you're working on restoring power, then blast my swim mix into the library at maximum volume."

"Yes, mistress."

"The timeline *did* change, right?" I ask when I catch up with Madi. Loud, pounding music fills the house, and she has to raise her voice to respond.

"It flipped." She glances pointedly at Saul, now at the base of the curved staircase, and leans toward me. "But the July 4th bomb went off *inside* the British Pavilion. Clio tried to change it. I had better luck, fortunately. Saul may be helping us now, but . . ."

"I know. We can't trust him."

Saul is already halfway up the stairs, with Jack close behind. Clearly, they're opting for speed over stealth, and if not for the pounding music—and now, the crying baby—I'm pretty sure everyone in the library would hear us coming. Saul pauses when he reaches the top and is about to kick the library door, but Jack motions for him to stand back. It's the sort of thing Saul would usually contest, because with the exception of Tate Poulsen, he's never willing to admit that anyone is stronger. Maybe the fact that he's carrying a woman who is at least two-thirds his own size allows his ego to stand down.

Jack levels a sidekick at the door. Judging from the thud and the resistance on the other side, it does hit the observer. Jack kicks the door again, and Saul steps forward with Esther's body as a shield in front of him, pointing the pistol at Other-Saul. I aim the rifle to the left just as Clio blinks in on the far side of the library. Saul jerks his weapon toward her.

"She's with us!" I yell over the noise, as Madi tells Jarvis to cut the music.

Other-Saul takes advantage of the diversion to lunge forward. Saul fires his weapon, and his slightly altered twin drops to the ground, cursing and clutching his calf. "That's for assuming you could touch me the other day, you arrogant fuck," Saul hisses. Then he adds in a louder voice, "Someone take his gun."

Tyson is already there by the time Saul gets the words out. He takes the weapon, points it at Other-Saul, and tells him to empty out his pockets. Which is a good thing, because there's another small weapon like the one Esther was carrying in his front pocket.

Saul drops Esther, who is beginning to stir, onto the carpet and says, "Alisa, we can give you a going-away present, too, if you'd like, or you can be a good girl and come sit over here with Ess so we can wrap you up to send back to your papa. Your call."

Alisa glares at him but does as she's told. I grab her wrists and start to bind them behind her back, and then realize they need to be in front. Lorena and the baby have left the room, which was a smart call on Lorena's part. Thea is pacing back and forth in front of the couch, still mumbling to herself, and Alex is already at the computer, typing frantically. Everyone else is focused on the four remaining members of Team Viper. Within a minute or so, they're arranged in a circle in the middle of the library, backs to each other, hands and feet bound.

Saul glances at the time and mutters a curse. "Start the simulation again."

Alex tells Jarvis to resume power to the SimMaster. It takes about thirty seconds for the system to come online, and then we hear the rustle of audience noise. As soon as Morgen's face comes into view,

Saul says, "Do you want your people back, Campbell? Just to be clear, your younger spare-parts factory was killed because he was breaking the rules. He was about to shoot an active member of Team . . . What are we called again?"

"Hyena," I say. He rolls his eyes, and I add, "We didn't choose the name."

"An active member of Team Hyena," Saul says. "We didn't target players until you did. And I'm sure you have at least one more clone in reserve, so don't act like a grieving father." There's a sharp intake of breath from the audience, followed by loud booing. Did they not know he had a clone?

Morgen's expression is apoplectic. When he doesn't respond, Saul says, "Fine. If you don't want them back there in *27V*, I'd be happy to dispose of them here."

Campbell's eyes narrow when he mentions the number, and then he says, "Send them home."

"We will be blocking further incursions from your corner of the multiverse," Saul tells him. "So this is the last I'll be seeing you. You lost, old man. As usual."

The transmission ends before Saul finishes the sentence, and he turns to our prisoners. "You heard the man. Go home to Daddy."

All four struggle to get their keys situated. It takes Esther three tries, probably due to the head injury. She's starting to look a little panicked, and with good reason, given that Saul is pointing his weapon at her, very obviously impatient.

"I'm trying!" she says. "Tell that old woman to stop pacing back and forth. It's hard to focus on the display with her in my field of vision."

Thea, who has indeed been pacing back and forth near Alex, stops. But she seems unable to relax, and her hand continues clutching at the object in her pocket. She looks like she's ready to bolt, and Saul takes a few steps in her direction.

Esther is apparently telling the truth about the movement being distracting, because she manages to blink out on the next try. As soon as she vanishes, Saul snakes out an arm and pulls Thea to his chest, pressing his weapon into her side. "I'm going to take my leave now. I would have let you folks muddle through this on your own, but I just couldn't stomach the idea of Campbell and his minions screwing up *my* timeline and getting away scot-free."

It hits me then that this isn't just Madi's grandmother that he's threatening. In some sense, Thea is my daughter. Saul's daughter, too. She's five decades older than I am, and several clones away from a child that I might have carried, but she is my flesh and blood.

"Let her go," I say.

"Sorry, but no. She was actually quite useful in making sure we had this base of operations, so I'd *prefer* not to hurt her, but I obviously will if I have to. I just need to get somewhere I can blink out without weapons in my face."

"But I'm coming with you, Saul! You don't need a hostage."

He cocks his head to the side. "You were *never* going to meet me in Miami, love. I could tell you were lying at the Fair. I'm not going back there anyway. I have other plans. Rich, I'm sure you'll take good care of our girl here, and equally sure you'll never satisfy her. And that reminds me. I have a little parting gift for you, Kathy."

Saul reaches into his pocket and pulls out a small vial of viscous fluid, which he places on the shelf near the door. "Just in case you decide you want to go through with this whole Mother-of-Prudence gig. Although . . ." His eyes drop down to my abdomen and he grins. "The die may already be cast, thanks to our reunion the other night."

∞34∞

MADI
BETHESDA, MARYLAND
NOVEMBER 20, 2136

Saul tells us to give him to the count of one hundred. Thea doesn't look frightened as he drags her through the door with him. In fact, there's a tiny smile on her face, which has me wondering whether this was part of the plan. Saul said she'd been useful. Was this all arranged in advance?

No. I don't believe that. And either way, we have to stop him.

I take out my CHRONOS key and pull up the stable point downstairs in the living room. Panning left, I see Saul and Thea on the landing. It looks for a moment as if he's going to pull out the key right there in the hallway, but he apparently decides to get a bit farther from the library and nudges Thea to head downstairs. I keep scrolling forward until I see him stop at the bottom of the stairs and lower the weapon in order to use his key.

I debate watching a bit longer, but I know I'm going in, and I know from experience how confusing it is to do what you've already watched yourself do through the key. It's not as bad as a double memory or spinning off a splinter, but there's still a bit of a feedback loop. So I stop and catch Tyson's eye. "Downstairs stable point. The one I transferred to your key in Memphis. One minute back."

He gives me a quick nod. I squeeze Jack's hand, then I set the location, roll back one minute, and jump. When I land in the living room, I hear Esther upstairs telling Saul that she's trying to blink out, but Thea's pacing is distracting her.

I move out of the stable point. Tyson arrives. Clio is right behind him. Rich and Katherine pop in a few seconds later. I'm glad to see the others, but I'm not entirely sure whether Katherine is going to be an asset or a liability. Would she actually be able to kill Saul?

"Jack tried to come," Clio whispers. "I think he's out of jump juice."

I nod. "I'm taking the spot behind the couch. Find a place to take cover. I scanned forward, and Saul will lower the weapon when he pulls up the stable point, just after they reach the bottom of the stairs at 9:42:09. That's when we make our move."

Tyson says, "Anyone who gets a clear shot that doesn't endanger Thea, take it."

Katherine and Rich head for the kitchen. Clio and Tyson hurry toward the hallway to the left of the library staircase. I duck behind the sofa, which I selected because I know Saul's back will be to me at least briefly from this vantage point, and then I check the time. Twenty-three seconds. I clutch the gun and take deep breaths until I hear the door opening at the top of the stairs.

The door closes. There's the brief pause that I saw through the key, and then footsteps on the stairs. "I meant what I said," Saul tells Thea. "I'm not planning to hurt you unless you fight me."

"Why would I fight you?" Thea asks as they continue down the steps. She sounds calm. In fact, her tone reminds me of a few days back, when she said she was going upstairs to the attic to meditate.

I watch through the key as Saul relaxes his hold on Thea at 21:42:08. She takes a few steps away as he pulls out his CHRONOS key. One second later, I rise from behind the couch, and the others step out as well, weapons drawn. But Saul is already crumpling to the ground.

Thea stands a few feet away from him. Her hand is in her pocket, or rather in what used to be a pocket. Now it's just a frame of melted fibers that surrounds her hand, which is wrapped around her bronze cuff with the glowing amber stone. I don't see a weapon, though. Did she drop it?

"That was for Gizmo," Thea says. "For Gizmo and for the Sisters."

I have no idea what she's talking about. Judging from the expressions on the others' faces, I'm not the only one. Thea marches forward, grabbing for the key in Saul's hand.

Katherine yells out, "No!"

Before I realize why, Saul raises his weapon and fires. The beam catches Thea in the stomach. She stumbles back, and I catch her just before she falls.

Katherine gets to Saul first and stomps his wrist to the floor. He looks up and smiles at her. "'Twas on a May Day of the far . . . old year . . ."

His eyes close and his body goes still. The room is now silent, aside from Thea's labored breaths.

Clio reaches down for his key, but Katherine pushes her hand away. "Wait."

She gives Katherine a look that clearly conveys disgust.

"I'm not acting out of sentimentality," Katherine says. "Just wait!"

Beyond Katherine, I see Jack coming down the stairs. And then I realize why Katherine wanted to wait. There's no wrist under her foot now. No gun. No hand. No Saul.

"How did you know?" Clio asks as she stares at the empty spot on the carpet.

"Mostly a hunch," Katherine says. "He kept looking at the time. Plus, he has a penchant for spinning off splinters. And Saul loves himself far too much to be so cavalier with his own safety. If we'd pulled his key, we wouldn't have known for sure. Is Thea . . ."

She turns toward me and realizes there's no need to finish the question. My grandmother is still alive, but it's clear that she won't be for long.

"I'm sorry," Katherine tells her. "I tried to warn you. Why did you—"

"It's okay." Thea reaches out with her free hand and gives Katherine's arm a feeble squeeze. "It's in the diary I sent to Madi. Help her find your daughters. Let them know that he's . . . gone. And if there's no CHRONOS," she adds, looking up at me, "maybe he'll be gone for good this time."

I exchange a look with Katherine. Thea must have missed the fact that the Saul she shot was a splinter. And even though I have every intention of fixing this, I don't have the heart to tell her in her current condition.

"You're going to be okay," I say. "I'm going to go back and fix this."

"I knew you'd say that," Thea says, smiling. "But no, sweetie. This was my path. All . . . part of . . . the plan."

It's the same maddeningly calm tone she was using earlier, even though her breath is ragged. Even though her blood is pooling on the wood beneath my knees.

"No," I tell her. "This isn't your decision."

Katherine gets to her feet. "I'm going to grab some cushions from the couch. If we prop her up, maybe it will be easier for her to breathe."

Jack helps me lift Thea, and we wedge the pillows beneath her. Her eyes are closed, but she's still breathing.

"Set a stable point from where you were standing," I tell the others. "And at various locations around the room. Find a vantage point where we can stop Saul from firing. Or a moment when we can shoot

him before Thea gets the chance. We'll have double memories, but
. . ."

They all nod and spread out around the room. I take a few steps
toward the couch to set a stable point at the spot where I was crouched
just before Thea took the shot, and I set another from a few feet away.

When I look back at Thea, she's still breathing. Her eyes are half-
open, watching me, and her hand is clutched tightly around the brass
cuff. I wonder again if she dropped the weapon she used or if the
thing is more lethal than it looks. She gives me a sad smile as she
uncurls the fingers holding the bracelet. It rolls out of her hand and
onto the floor. By the time it comes to a stop about six inches away,
all that remains of Thea Randall is a slight indentation in the cushion.

∞Epilogue∞

Tyson
Bethesda, Maryland
November 22, 2136

Katherine and Rich slide over to make room for me at the octagonal kitchen nook, but it's crowded already, with Lorena, RJ, and the baby's chair taking up about half the space. I smile and shake my head, carrying my plate of turkey and stuffing out to the patio, where Madi, Jack, Alex, and Clio are sitting. I take the spot across from Clio, and for a few minutes, we eat our simple Thanksgiving meal in silence, looking out at the backyard and enjoying a warm autumn afternoon.

Alex finishes the last of his food and starts to get up. Madi tugs on his arm. "Stay," she says, and when he reluctantly sits back down, she tops off his barely touched glass of wine. "All the wormholes and twisty, tangled timelines will still be waiting for you. You need to relax. It's a beautiful Thanksgiving Day, and we have a lot to be thankful for."

She's right on both counts.

Our losses could have been so much worse. This timeline could be far worse as well. The air is clear. The grass is green. There are several large trees, and Madi says the place looks exactly as it did in our timeline, as best she can tell. This house once again belongs to Madi, willed to her by her grandmother. The only difference is that the title was in Thea's name, not Nora's, and cosigned by a group called Sisters, Inc.

All told, the Anomalies Machine only registered a few thousand differences between this timeline and our original version, and most are minor. The western states are no longer a separate entity, there was no nuclear exchange on this continent, and the government is currently engaged in only a few middling international crises. Jack's family is alive and well, and he seems relieved to learn that some leader in Akana is no longer threatening to annihilate her neighbors, at least for the time being. She's apparently found religion, and reporters noted the presence of a lotus-flower tattoo on her hand when she was last sighted.

There is one rather massive change, however, at least from our perspective, and it's the reason Katherine, Rich, and I are still here. We've tried to blink home on several occasions. The local points we set while working on the report for Angelo and the point Richard says he set in Sutter's office at the Objectivist Club are all inactive. A location that I set—the one outside the library that stands where CHRONOS HQ is in our time—is still active, but only until 2160. In fact, none of our stable points work after that year. This is the one thing that suggests to us that there is a CHRONOS, or some variant thereof, in the future. In our timeline, 2160 was the cutoff date beyond which no time travel was allowed.

But Rich, Katherine, and I have all made jumps to times and places where we traveled for training or with other historians, hunting for a familiar face. I looked for Glen, the mentor with whom I studied the Klan, at the trailer we shared in Polk County, North Carolina, on and off between 1964 and 1966. The trailer is there, but a family is renting it. At first, I thought maybe it was because Glen wasn't training me, and therefore he picked some other place to live. But he's not studying the Klan in that area at all. I set local points inside the community center where most Klan gatherings are held. Glen never shows up.

Rich and Katherine report the same thing. No CHRONOS historians. No CHRONOS keys.

Madi is also right that Alex needs to relax, but I get why he can't. He's fairly confident that he's blocked the signal for any hitchhikers from 27V. But there's no guarantee that he'll be able to keep them out. Even more troubling, however, are the red dots that keep popping up on his displays. The first was in 1780, which didn't seem to surprise Katherine at all. She said the last words Saul's splinter uttered were from a poem about an event predicted by Jemima Wilkinson, a quirky minister in 1780. Only now, instead of fading into obscurity, Jemima was burned at the stake, along with quite a few of her followers. A hundred years after the witch frenzy ended in the United States, a second wave started.

Earlier this morning, Alex told us a second cluster of red dots had begun popping up, this time in Salzburg, Austria, during the panic over the Zauberjackl in the late 1600s. I'd never even heard the name, but Katherine went pale and left the library.

Saul is taunting us. Taunting Katherine, mostly. And I suspect that soon these changes will flip the timeline again. He didn't like Campbell screwing with our history, but he seems more than willing to mess it up himself.

Madi lifts her glass. "To Thea. She would have preferred that we toast her with champagne, which she always called *bubbles*, but this pinot blanc is the closest thing I had."

We join the toast, and I can tell Madi is fighting back tears.

"I should have told her. Maybe she wouldn't have been so keen to make some grand gesture if . . ." She takes a deep breath and closes her eyes. "Nope. Not going to go there. We've hashed through all of this over and over."

We have indeed hashed through all of it. Madi blamed herself. Then Alex blamed himself for simply telling Jarvis to turn on the simulation, rather than restoring all power to the room. That led to Jack and Madi telling Alex that he really couldn't have known the specific command that Jarvis was given. Jarvis chimed in at that point to apologize for taking the command too literally. I wouldn't have thought it was even possible to guilt a virtual assistant from this era.

"I'm not going to spoil the day," Madi says. "We will simply honor her memory and give thanks for her sacrifice. Even if . . ." She cuts herself off again, blinking back tears. "I'll go get dessert."

The pumpkin pie she brings out clearly pushed the limits of Madi's food unit, but the whipped cream is good. We talk a bit as we eat, but mostly we sit in companionable silence as the sun sets behind the willow tree.

When Alex, Jack, and Madi head inside, I'm about to follow, but Clio asks me to wait. "I have a stable point to share with you." She holds up her key and taps the back against mine. "I wasn't sure of the exact time. Or even if that was the right drugstore. But then I saw the dress you mentioned, and . . ."

Antoinette Robinson is leaning against the wall, her orange dress vivid against the dusty bricks. Laughing with the other girls as they look at something in the magazine with the Ronettes on the cover. Passing a smoke back and forth. Waiting for the friend to pick them up and take them to the Beatles concert where John Lennon will *not* be murdered prematurely. We checked.

I stare at the stable point for a long time, and then look up at Clio. "Thank you. I was going to go back and check the phone book like I did last time. But this is so much better."

She shrugs, looking a bit uncomfortable. "I was just doing a little stalking of this house near Chicago, with a white picket fence and a happily married ex-boyfriend with too many kids and . . ."

I pour the last bit of wine into our two glasses. "Any reason why you're torturing yourself like that?"

"The same reason that you do. Because while I can't have, and might not even want that life, I still want to know that *he* has it. We need some sort of objective test, right? Something other than wars, and systems of government, and all of the big-picture things the Anomalies Machine measures. Because the small, fragile things matter, too. Otherwise, how will we know whether any given frog-tongue universe is worth keeping?"

It's a conversation that very few people would understand. I like that.

I tap the edge of my glass against hers. "To frog-tongue universes."

"Well, maybe not all of them," she says.

"Fine. To *our* frog-tongue universe."

She smiles. "Yes. I can definitely drink to that."

∞Acknowledgments∞

I began writing this book in 2019, having no idea how strange the next year would be. As I finish the last stage of edits, it feels as if our time train has veered seriously off course. I've gotten many emails and messages on social media pointing out parallels to my books and asking if I could send someone back to fix 2020. If any of you happen to have the CHRONOS gene, please let me know. The keys I have are 3-D printed replicas, but after the year we've had we're due at least one miracle, right?

In this era of alternative facts, it's more important than ever to take a few minutes to sort out fact from fiction, especially in a book where some of the characters are historical figures. I've retained as much as possible of their actual words and opinions suggested in interviews and biographies. While I've taken a few liberties in furtherance of the plot, this is generally in sections after the timeline was altered.

Excerpts from the *New York Daily Intrepid*, a fictional newspaper, appear between chapters. These are all based to varying degrees on articles from the time period, although they diverge a bit from actual history once alterations to the timeline begin.

Verses from *The Book of Cyrus* are sprinkled throughout the manuscript. This is obviously a work of fiction, but Saul Rand stole liberally from the Bible and other religious texts, so if you had flash-backs to your religious-education classes while reading, that's why.

For those who have not read the first CHRONOS books, some background on the Cyrists may be helpful. The Koreshan Unity, a group that Saul co-opted to form his religion, was an actual religious community founded in Chicago in the early 1890s by Cyrus Reed Teed. They relocated to Estero, Florida, a few years later and were active into the 1960s. The group believed that Earth is a hollow sphere, that God was both male and female, and that celibacy would result in eternal life. When Cyrus Teed died, his followers placed him in a bathtub and waited for him to awaken, agreeing to bury him only when the county health inspector insisted. Cyrus was his given first name, but he believed that he was the reincarnation of the biblical King Cyrus, who was hailed as a messiah. (Any of you interested in an eerie modern parallel should google "King Cyrus coin.")

Laura Houghtaling Ingalls was an acclaimed pilot and Nazi informant. She dropped antiwar leaflets over the White House in 1938, in addition to numerous other activities with isolationist women's organizations. Five years earlier, she went missing for a day, prompting some concern for her safety. Her quote about landing so that she could practice using her six-shooter is from her comments to journalists upon landing a day late in Miami. Elizabeth Dilling was also active in the isolationist movement and a vocal supporter of Father Coughlin, although she did not work directly with him.

Most information about Father Charles Coughlin, one of the most famous radio evangelists of all time, is historical. He was indeed on Hitler's payroll, and his weekly sermons were aimed at Americans who were generally willing to embrace fascism and anti-Semitism if there was a chance it would help to ward off communism. In his publications, Coughlin, who often lifted lines verbatim from published speeches by German Minister of Propaganda Joseph Goebbels, remained a Catholic priest in Detroit for several decades after his radio empire crumbled. His organization, the Christian Front, did not become an official ally of the German-American Bund, but they shared goals and members with the Bund and other American Nazi groups.

Both Dorothy Thompson articles are paraphrased from her weekly columns, as are her comments about other figures such as Lawrence Dennis, Charles Coughlin, and Charles Lindbergh. While hers is far from a household name today, she was widely considered to be one of the two most powerful women in prewar America, second only to Eleanor Roosevelt. Thompson was married to author Sinclair Lewis who wrote the book *It Can't Happen Here*, a fictional depiction of a United States in the grasp of a uniquely American variant of fascism. She was the first American journalist Hitler evicted from Germany, and she did attend the 1939 Bund Pro-America Rally at Madison Square Garden, where she was ejected for laughing at the Nazis.

No one was killed at the 1939 Bund Pro-America Rally, but several bomb threats were noted in newspaper accounts. Aside from Saul's additions to the speaking roster, the descriptions of the event closely track the historical record and were based in part on an excellent Oscar-nominated short documentary, *A Night at the Garden*.

Charles Lindbergh was not shot at a Bund event and, like Coughlin, never officially joined forces with the organization. Lindbergh and some other members of America First did, however, express sympathy for the Nazi cause prior to Pearl Harbor.

While Lawrence Dennis's story may seem a bit implausible, it is historically accurate. As a child evangelist, he toured churches in the US and Europe, billed as Lonnie Dennis, the "Inspired Child." He cut ties with his African American family as a teen, attended Exeter and Harvard as Lawrence Dennis, and would eventually become a leading writer in fascist circles. The only references to his career that are fictional are those specifically noted in the story as being changes to the timeline.

Events at the 1939–1940 World's Fair adhere closely to the historical record, aside from those noted explicitly as alterations to the timeline. Descriptions of the exhibits are taken from articles and films about the Fair. Albert Einstein and Franklin Roosevelt both spoke on opening day. Einstein was active in promoting the Jewish Palestine Pavilion. A terrorist bombing did occur on July 4, 1940, at the British Pavilion. Two police officers were killed, and while the case was never solved, there is some suspicion that it was the work of British intelligence agents, hoping to stir up sympathy and tip the needle of public opinion toward the US joining the war.

The super-many-time theory is based on a real theory by Japanese physicist Shin'ichirō Tomonaga. He was studying with Werner Heisenberg and had to leave Germany abruptly when World War II began. On his way back to Japan, he took a day to visit the World's Fair . . . and I think it would have been hard for him to resist stopping by an exhibit called the Theater of Time and Space.

The sections about Café Society are mostly historical, although I have no indication that Lawrence Dennis ever visited. Barney Josephson may or may not have known, but it's fairly certain that his brother tapped friends in the Communist Party for the loan to start the business. Leon Josephson was arrested in Europe as part of a plot to kill Hitler. Billie Holiday was the first vocalist at the club and gained considerable recognition after performing the anti-lynching song, "Strange Fruit." Tallulah Bankhead was performing *The Little Foxes* in New York during the time that Tyson visited the club. She was every bit as over-the-top as I've portrayed her here, despite the fact that her father was a member of Congress. Bankhead was fairly open about her sexuality, especially her numerous affairs with both men and women, including a brief fling with Billie Holiday.

This is just an overview, and I'm probably forgetting something. If you have a question about some aspect of the history, feel free to give me a shout on social media.

And now, on to the acknowledgments. First, a huge tip of the hat to my publishing team at 47North, including Adrienne Procaccini who helped get the series off to a fabulous start. Mike Corley's covers are always eye-catching, and I'm grateful to Kate Rudd and Eric G. Dove for bringing my characters to life in the audio version. Thanks to Tegan Tegani for helping me unravel time threads in the developmental edit, and to the dedicated group of copyeditors and proofreaders (especially Katherine and Patty Ann) who patched up my assorted gaffes.

My friends on Facebook and Twitter helped keep me relatively sane during the truly crazy period in which this book was written. Special thanks to my CHRONOS Repo Agents and beta readers for their feedback and support: Cale Madewell, Chris Fried, Karen Stansbury, Ian Walniuk, Mary Freeman, Meg A. Watt, Alexa Huggins, Alexis Young, Allie B. Holycross, Amelia Elisa Diaz, Angela Careful, Angela Fossett, Ann Davis, Antigone Trowbridge, Becca Levite, Billy Thomas, Brandi Faith, Chantelle Michelle Kieser, Chaz Martin, Chelsea Hawk, Cheyenne Chambers, Chris Fried, Chris Schraff Morton, Christina Kmetz, Claudia Gonzaga-Jauregui, Cody Jones, Dan Wilson, Dawn Lovelly, Devi Reynolds, Donna Harrison Green, Dori Gray, Emiliy Marino, Erin Flynn, Fred Douglis, Hailey Mulconrey Theile, Heather Jones, Hope Bates, Jen Gonzales, Jen Wesner, Jennifer Kile, Jenny Griffin, Jenny Lawrence, Jenny MacRunnel, Jessica Wolfsohn, John Scafidi, Karen Benson, Katie Lynn Stripling, Kristin Ashenfelter, Kristin Rydstedt, Kyla Michelle Lacey Waits, Laura-Dawn Francesca MacGregor-Portlock, Lindsay Nichole Leckner, Margarida Azevedo Veloz, Mark Chappell, Meg Griffin, Mikka McClain, Nguyen Quynh Trang, Nooce Miller, Pham Hai Yen, Roseann Calabritto, Sarada Spivey, Sarah Ann Diaz, Sarah

Kate Fisher, Shari Hearn, Shell Bryce, Sigrun Murr, Stefanie Diegel, Stephanie Kmetz, Stephanie Johns-Bragg, Summer Nettleman, Susan Helliesen, Tina Kennedy, Tracy Denison Johnson, Trisha Davis Perry, Valerie Arlene Alcaraz, and the person—or more likely, persons—I've forgotten.

As always, a special thanks to my family—immediate, extended, and chosen. Extra-special thanks to the four guys in my household, including the furry guy, Griffin. In a year where we've had more together time than ever, I'm grateful beyond measure that I not only love but also *enjoy* the company of all the people with whom I'm lucky to share a home.

Last but not least, thanks to my readers for traveling with me through time. I'm crossing my fingers that this will be a year in which we all move forward.

∞About the Author∞

RYSA WALKER is the bestselling author of The Delphi Trilogy (*The Delphi Effect*, *The Delphi Resistance*, and *The Delphi Revolution*); the CHRONOS Files series (*Timebound*, winner of the grand prize in the 2013 Amazon Breakthrough Novel Awards; *Time's Echo*; *Time's Edge*; *Time's Mirror*; *Time's Divide*; and *Simon Says: Tips for the Intrepid Time Traveler*); and *Now, Then, and Everywhen* in the CHRONOS Origins series. Her career had its beginnings in a childhood on a cattle ranch, where she read every book she could find, watched *Star Trek* and *The Twilight Zone*, and let her imagination soar into the future and to distant worlds. Her diverse path has spanned roles such as lifeguard, waitress, actress, digital developer, and professor. Through it all, she has pursued her passion for writing the sorts of stories she imagined in her youth. She lives in North Carolina with her husband, her two youngest sons, and a hyperactive golden retriever. Discover more about Rysa and her work at www.rysa.com.

Photo © 2014 Jeff Kolbfleisch